CAVALCADE

Also by Walter Satterthwait

Mystery Novels
Cocaine Blues
The Aegean Affair
Wall of Glass
Miss Lizzie
At Ease with the Dead
Wilde West
A Flower in the Desert
The Hanged Man
Escapade*
Accustomed to the Dark
Masquerade*
Scherenschnitte

*The Pinkerton Series

Short Story Collections
The Gold of Mayani
The Mankiller of Poojegai and Other Mysteries (due in 2005)

CAVALCADE

Walter Satterthwait

THOMAS DUNNE BOOKS   ST. MARTIN'S MINOTAUR ♏ NEW YORK

THOMAS DUNNE BOOKS.
An imprint of St. Martin's Press.

www.minotaurbooks.com

ISBN 0-312-33974-7
EAN 978-0312-33974-6

First Edition: February 2005

10 9 8 7 6 5 4 3 2 1

For Sarah C.,
who won't be helping with this one

Acknowledgments

Thanks once again to my wife, Caroline Gordon, for putting up with me while I put another one of these things together.

A couple of people have read portions of the manuscript as it was being written and offered valuable suggestions. Thanks to Tilo Eckardt and Eva-Marie von Hippel for their efforts. Any errors, mistakes, or outright lies that remain are entirely my responsibility.

For answering endless questions about Germany and the German language, I thank Wolfgang Mueller.

I thank Michael Shackleford and Les Peters for information about pre-War German vehicles, and Leslie Graham for information about German POW camps in England.

Following is a partial list of the books from which I stole information. I'm particularly indebted to the books by Ernst Jünger, Ron Rosenbaum, and Klaus Theweleit.

Baedeker's *Guide to Northern Germany (1925)*
Baedeker's *Guide to Southern Germany (1929)*
Baedeker's *Guide to Berlin (1912)*
Allan Bullock, *Hitler: A Study in Tyranny*
Michael Burleigh, *The Third Reich: A New History*
Norman Cameron and R. H. Stevens (translators),
Hitler's Table Talk, 1941–1944
Houston Stewart Chamberlain,
The Foundations of the Nineteenth Century

John Cornwell, *Hitler's Pope*

Tom Dalzell, *Flappers 2 Rappers: American Youth Slang*

John Dornberg, *Munich 1923*

Roger Eatwell, *Fascism: A History*

Otto Friedrich, *Before the Deluge*

Felix Gilbert with David Clay Large, *The End of the European Era, 1890 to the Present*

Arthur de Gobineau, *The Inequality of Races*

Mel Gordon, *Erik Jan Hanussen: Hitler's Jewish Clairvoyant* and *Voluptuous Panic: The Erotic World of Weimar Germany*

Robert W. Gutman, *Richard Wagner: The Man, His Mind, and His Music*

Ernst Hanfstaengl, *Unheard Witness* (also called *Hitler: The Missing Years*)

Ernest Hemingway, *By-line: Ernest Hemingway* (William White, editor)

Adolf Hitler, *Mein Kampf*

Claudia Jansen-Fleig, *Das Hotel Adlon*

Ernst Jünger, *The Storm of Steel*

John Keegan, *The Face of Battle*

Ian Kershaw, *Hitler, 1889–1936, Hubris*

Harry Kessler, *Berlin in Lights: The Diaries of Count Harry Kessler (1918–1937)*

David Clay Large, *Where Ghosts Walked: Munich's Road to the Third Reich*

Stan Lauryssens, *The Man Who Invented the Third Reich*

Lothar Machtan, *The Hidden Hitler*

Ben Macintyre, *Forgotten Fatherland: The Search for Elizabeth Nietzsche*

Thomas Mann, *Diaries, 1918–1939*

Field-Marshal Bernard Montgomery, *A History of Warfare*

Alexandra Richie, *Faust's Metropolis: A History of Berlin*

Ron Rosenbaum, *Explaining Hitler*

William L. Shirer, *Inside the Third Reich*

Klaus Theweleit, *Male Fantasies*
Gottfried Wagner, *Twilight of the Wagners*
Robert G. L. Waite, *Hitler: The Psychopathic God*
and *Vanguard of Nazism*

And now at our first glance of horror we had a feeling that is difficult to describe. Seeing and recognizing are matters, really, of habit. In the case of something quite unknown the eye alone can make nothing of it. So it was that we had to stare again and again at the things that we had never seen before, without being able to give them any meaning. It was too entirely unfamiliar.

—Ernst Jünger, *The Storm of Steel*, 1920

FRANKFURT

Frankfurt Hauptbahnhof
Monday
May 14th, 1923

Dear Evangeline,

I have only a few moments—the train is already on the platform, the big Teutonic locomotive is snorting and snuffling, the passengers are scurrying along the walkway, mothers towing their children, husbands towing their wives. As I sit on this uncomfortable wooden bench, feverishly scribbling, Mr Beaumont paces alongside the line of passenger cars. Occasionally he glances over at me. Probably he is snorting and snuffling himself, and probably he would relish a spot of towing. From time to time, in a kind of ponderous masculine mime, he stops and pulls his watch from his pocket and glares down at it.

I told you in my last letter that we've been assigned to investigate an assassination attempt. This is still true, but we'll be going not to Munich, as I'd told you, but to Berlin. We didn't learn about this change in plan until this afternoon, when Mr Caudwell—I believe I've mentioned him—suddenly materialized at our hotel.

Mr Caudwell told us that Mr Adolf Hitler, the party leader, had—

Oh dear! I must go. I'll post this now and write more on the train. We have a brief stopover at Nürnberg. I'll try to send a full account from there.

All my love,
Jane

CHAPTER ONE

I WAS LYING on the sofa, reading the Baedeker guide to southern Germany. It was a fine book, but it didn't have much of a plot. I had just gotten to the part about bicycling in Bavaria, and what a swell thing that was, when someone knocked at the door.

I put the book on the coffee table, swung my legs off the sofa, walked to the door, and pulled it open.

Peter Caudwell from the London office stood out there in the hallway. In his forties, he was short and overweight. He wore a black raincoat over a two-piece black suit that had probably fit him better when he bought it. He held a black homburg in his right hand and a rolled umbrella in his left. Next to him stood a bellboy who was dressed like a French general on parade and who looked old enough to be Caudwell's father, or maybe his grandfather. On either side of the bellboy, a leather suitcase was standing upright atop the runner of carpet.

Caudwell said to me, "I'm know I'm late. It couldn't be helped."

Caudwell didn't believe in apologies.

Reaching into his pants pocket, he turned to the bellboy. "*Danke,*" he said, and pulled a German mark note from the pocket. One thousand marks. At the current exchange rate, it was worth about two cents. The bellboy looked down at it, looked up, and nodded. He'd been doing this kind of work for a while, and you couldn't tell from his face whether he was delighted or homicidal. "*Besten dank, der Herr,*" he said, and then turned and walked away.

Caudwell didn't believe in shaking hands either. It wasn't my job to change his mind about that, so I grabbed one of the bags, lifted it, lugged it over to the side of the big leather sofa, and plopped it down.

Behind me, Caudwell had carried in the other suitcase and shut the door. "Well, well," he said, glancing around the room. "The Germans have done you proud."

It was a suite, acres of dark wood paneling and heavy padded furniture here in the large sitting room. Everything that could be polished, the metal and glass and woodwork, had been polished, vigorously, and it all glistened under the electric lights like a politician's grin.

The electric lights were on, even though it was just past noon and the curtains were open, because the weather outside was gray and rainy. It had been gray and rainy since Jane Turner and I arrived in Frankfurt, two days ago.

"I've always wondered what the suites at the Carlton were like," he said, and put the second suitcase down next to the first. He set his hat on top of it and leaned the umbrella against its side.

"Where are you staying?" I asked him.

"A dreary little *pension* on Beethoven-Strasse. Floral wallpaper and the stink of cabbage." He took off the raincoat. "Any trouble on the trip?" he asked me, his glance sliding around the room.

"At the border, but not for long."

"Goodness, is that a bar?" He turned to me. "Do you mind? I've picked up a bit of a chill this morning."

"Go ahead."

He tossed the raincoat to the arm of the sofa, waddled over to the bar, lifted a bottle of cognac, uncorked it.

"Did you bring the money?" I asked him.

He turned slightly and smiled bleakly at me. "Straight to the point, eh, Beaumont?"

"Miss Turner and I are supposed to catch the Munich train tonight."

He had turned his back to me and now he was splashing cognac into one of the balloon glasses. He must've picked up a very large chill. "Actually," he said, "as it happens, you and Miss Turner won't be catching the Munich train tonight."

He turned to me and smiled the smile of someone who's just scored a small but significant point.

"And why is that?" I asked him.

"Because you'll be catching the Berlin train." Holding the balloon glass, he walked across the carpet.

"And why is that?" I asked him.

He sat down on the sofa. I heard the sound of a small sigh, coming either from Caudwell or from the sofa's thick cushion. He held up the balloon glass, stared into it for a moment, then brought it to his nose and sniffed at it delicately. The cognac probably smelled all right, because he took a big healthy slug of it. He cocked his round head and he smiled. "Why don't we wait for Miss Turner?" he said. "I stopped at the desk and had them send a note up to her room. She should be joining us in a moment. How is she doing, by the way?"

I sat down in one of the armchairs. "She's fine."

This time the sigh definitely came from Caudwell. "I meant, of course, how is she doing as an operative?" He said it slowly and patiently so I could understand it. He was a very patient man.

Caudwell was Administration, not Operations. He had no direct authority over me and no real right to ask the question. But I answered it anyway: "She's doing fine."

He nodded and then pursed his lips. "The two of you had a bit of bother in France, I gather."

"A bit," I said. "But everything worked out all right."

"Cooper wanted me to tell you that the client is satisfied."

"Good."

He sniffed again at the brandy. Looking at me over the rim of the glass, he said, "So just who *did* kill Richard Forsythe?"

"You'll have to ask Cooper."

Caudwell waved the balloon glass lightly. "One is curious. The decadent young publisher. The bodies in the locked room."

"Sure," I said. "One can ask Cooper."

He smiled his bleak smile again. "No need to be argumentative, Beaumont. I was merely passing the time."

"Fine. But you know I can't talk about the operation."

He nodded. "Your dedication to duty is admirable."

There was nothing to say to that, which is what I said.

Someone knocked at the door.

"Ah," said Caudwell. "That'll be Miss Turner."

He was probably grateful for the interruption. I know that I was. I got up, crossed the room, and opened the door.

She was wearing the outfit she'd bought yesterday, a navy blue dress that buttoned up the front, and a pale blue cardigan sweater, unbuttoned. Behind her rimless spectacles, her large eyes were very blue. Today she was wearing her thick brown hair pulled back behind her slender neck.

"Come on in," I told her.

Caudwell might not have believed in shaking hands with me, but he did believe in shaking hands with Miss Turner. As she entered the room, he beamed up at her. "Miss Turner! So good to see you again!" He set his glass down on a side table, got up from the sofa, and then strode across the carpet, his plump hands out.

"Mr. Caudwell," said Miss Turner.

He took her hand between both of his. "You're looking very well, I must say."

Miss Turner smiled. "Thank you."

"And Beaumont here tells me that you did a simply smashing job in France."

She glanced at me briefly. "Mr. Beaumont exaggerates."

He was still holding her hand. "Not at all, not at all. I'm sure you did splendidly. Come along, my dear. You and Beaumont sit down and I'll explain what's going on."

He led her over to the sofa, where he finally let her go. I noticed that when Caudwell turned to sit, Miss Turner put the flat of her hand lightly, quickly, against her dress, as though smoothing the fabric. She was much too polite to let anyone see her wipe it dry. She was English.

I returned to my armchair.

"Now," said Caudwell, addressing himself to Miss Turner and sounding like a professor about to begin a speech, "you know something, of course, about the attempted assassination of this party leader."

Miss Turner nodded.

Caudwell looked at me.

I nodded. "We got the telegram from Cooper," I said.

He turned back to Miss Turner. "This happened on the eighth of this month. Last Tuesday. The party in question is the German National Socialist Workers' Party. The leader is a fellow named Hitler. Adolf Hitler. Do you know anything about German politics, Miss Turner?"

"Nothing at all, I'm afraid."

He smiled. "Well, of course not. Why should you, really?" He lifted his brandy, took a sip. "What about you, Beaumont?"

"No."

He nodded, as though this was about what he'd expected from me. "Right," he said, and turned back to Miss Turner. "Until fairly recently, the Nazi Party, as it's called, was virtually unknown. But ever since this Hitler fellow took over, things have changed. He's a demon speaker, evidently. And a demon organizer. He's brought in hordes of new members, and the party's going great guns now. In Munich, in particular, the Nazis have become a genuine alternative."

He looked over at me to see if I was still following.

"A genuine alternative to what?" I asked him.

"The Bolsheviks, for one. The Social Democrats, the chappies who run the Weimar Republic, for another. Quite a few Bavarians feel that the government in Berlin has no business representing them. Bavarians have never had a fondness for Prussians, and they have even less fondness for Socialists."

I nodded.

"Right," he said. He sipped at the brandy. "Well. A week ago, while our friend Hitler was on a visit to Berlin, someone took a shot at him."

"Where in Berlin?" I asked.

"The Tiergarten. A large park in the center of the city."

"Rifle or handgun?"

"A rifle. From a distance of about one hundred yards, we've been told. The bullet missed him by only an inch or two."

"What was Hitler doing in the park?"

"He was meeting with someone." He held up a plump red hand. "Don't ask me who, because we don't know." He frowned, probably because he didn't like to admit that there was anything he didn't know. "Someone in the government, that's all we've been told."

"Who else knew he'd be there?"

"Yes, that's the obvious question, isn't it? Apparently, at his end, Hitler's end, merely a handful of people knew about the Berlin trip. Most of them are party members in Munich. You'll have to interview them all."

"Then why are we going to Berlin?"

"The police investigation in Berlin is being handled by a Sergeant Biberkopf. The party doesn't trust him. Well, to be honest, they don't trust anyone in the Berlin police department. Most of the police, they assume, are Marxists or Marxist sympathizers. They may well be right. And that's why they've called in the Pinkertons. They felt that we, as a private enquiry agency, would conduct a more thorough investigation."

I liked that *we.*

Caudwell took another sip of brandy. Looking over at Miss Turner, he said, "Our best information on Biberkopf, from reliable sources, is that he's a good police officer. But, probably because of that mysterious 'government someone,' he's had to conduct his investigation with enormous discretion. And nearly all the people he needs to question are in Munich, and few of them seem anxious to help him."

I said, "So we go to Berlin, check out the scene of the crime, hook up with Biberkopf. And then we go to Munich and talk to the party people."

"In a nutshell, yes. You'll be met in Berlin tomorrow, at the station, by a fellow named Hanfstaengl. Ernst Hanfstaengl. Quite a pleasant sort, I've been told. An art dealer. He'll get you started."

"We'll need the money," I said.

"*Yes,* Beaumont," he said patiently, "I know." He reached into his right-hand coat pocket, pulled out a small cardboard box, set it on the coffee table. "Ammunition for your Colt .32. You haven't lost the gun, have you?"

"The pistol," I said. "No."

He reached into his left-hand coat pocket, pulled out a small pistol. "Another Colt. For Miss Turner." He offered her the weapon.

I was curious to see how she'd react to it. I knew that she'd taken a weapons course in London—all the London operatives were required to take it—but I'd never seen her handle a pistol.

She must have gotten an A in the course. She took the weapon nonchalantly, as though it were a cup of tea. She thumbed the magazine release, caught the empty magazine in her left hand, and then used the same hand to snick back the slide. She looked into the breech, making sure there was no cartridge in there.

"Cooper thinks we'll need the Colts?" I asked Caudwell.

"The opposition has already used a rifle. He wants to be on the safe side."

Miss Turner slipped the magazine back into the Colt, pulled back the slide, released it, flipped the safety on, and then lay the pistol on the coffee table.

Caudwell reached into his inside jacket pocket and took out a large leather wallet. He plucked some tickets from the wallet and slapped them onto the table. "Tickets for the night train to Berlin, separate compartments. First-class."

"Very swank," I said.

"It wasn't my idea." That didn't surprise me. "The party people insisted," he said, "and they're the ones paying for it."

He pulled out a thick stack of currency. "And now we have the money."

He counted it aloud out onto the table. It was in twenty-dollar bills and it came to five hundred American dollars. A lot of money, even in the United States. In Germany right now, it was a fortune.

He took one last item out of the wallet. "The receipt," he said. "I'll need you to sign it."

I got up, crossed the room, picked up the receipt.

He opened his jacket, pulled out a pen, held it up to me. I took it, signed the receipt, and handed it back to Caudwell, along with the pen.

"Right," said Caudwell. He reached into the other side of his coat, pulled out two British passports, tossed them onto the table.

"Just in case," he said. "They're in the name MacNeil, Joseph and Charlotte. The visas say you arrived in Germany from Rotterdam two days ago, in Bentheim. They should pass a casual examination. We'd rather you not use them, however, unless they become absolutely necessary."

"Not much point in using them otherwise, is there?"

He looked at me and smiled bleakly. "There's one thing more."

I waited. I could be patient too.

Caudwell said, "Cooper would like you—both of you—to learn as much as you can about this chap Hitler."

"Learn what?"

"Whatever you can. What sort of man is he. What is it he wants, for himself and for Germany."

"Who wants to know?"

"I told you. Cooper does."

"When Cooper wants to know something, it's usually because someone else wants to know something."

"I don't think you need worry about that."

"I'm not worried. I'm curious."

Another bleak smile. "If you just do your job, everyone will be happy."

"That's my goal in life," I said. "To make everyone happy."

Caudwell sighed again. Patiently.

I wasn't getting any closer to my goal, it looked like.

The night train to Berlin
Monday
May 14th

Guten Tag, Evangeline!

This is really quite lovely. I have a first-class compartment all to myself, complete with a darling little wooden writing table that will cleverly fold away when the porter arrives to unlatch the bed.

On my left is the window, closed now against the endless rain. Out there is the darkness, the sprawl of German countryside whizzing by in the night. But here inside the car, within the protective yellow nimbus of my wonderful writing lamp, I feel almost preternaturally snug. Whenever I peek at my reflection in the window, invariably I discover that I am wearing the smile of a Cheshire Cat.

In an hour or so I'll be joining Mr Beaumont for supper in the dining car. There's something incredibly romantic about eating food from a thick china plate set upon a thick linen tablecloth, being lulled all the while by the steady, reassuring rhythm of the wheels against the tracks. I am confident that this is true even when the food is German.

Perhaps the meal and the rhythm of the wheels will arouse in Mr Beaumont some incredibly romantic response. But I have grave doubts about this. He has so far evinced not the slightest interest in romance, nor in me. This afternoon, when he was bustling me through the shops of the Kaiser-Strasse, he was utterly indifferent to each and every article of clothing I considered.

I did buy some lovely things, Evy. The prices were extraordinary. A black cloche hat—my first cloche—for a few pence. A gorgeous black silk shawl, beautifully fringed, for about two shillings.

I also bought, for less than a pound, a terribly shocking black silk cocktail dress with an offset hem that falls to just beneath my knees and a draped décolletage that falls—well, it falls in a terribly shocking way, I promise you.

Not that Mr Beaumont was shocked by it. I had just put on the dress this afternoon, in the shop, and I was eyeing myself critically (as always) in the mirror—wondering (as always) whether a bosom like mine might become fashionable at some point within its own lifetime—when Mr Beaumont galloped in from the street and immediately tugged his watch from his pocket. The man is insanely fond of that watch.

When I asked him what he thought about the dress, he looked me up and down with quick indifference, like a passerby appraising some new lamppost on a familiar street corner, and he said, 'Very nice.'

Very nice. He used exactly the same phrase to describe the cloche and the shawl, and the black pumps and the sensible walking shoes and the raglan overcoat.

Oh well. I shall probably never wear the dress. It's not my sort of thing at all, really. I bought it only because it was absurdly inexpensive; and because I harboured some foolish notion that with this new investigation about to begin, with a new chapter of my life (it may be) about to open, I could change not only my wardrobe, but also, perhaps, myself.

Change myself just a teensy bit, anyway. From Aging Spinster into Seductive Vamp.

It was quite silly of me, really.

But it *is* a lovely dress.

Now, as to Mr Hitler—

No, no. Before I tell you about Mr Hitler, I really *must* tell you about the remarkable experience I had yesterday. After wandering around the Old Town, between the Zeil and the river, admiring Goethe's house and the Dom from beneath my umbrella, I took a tram to Sachsenhausen and the Städel Art Institute. There are two galleries at the Institute and I hadn't time enough to see them both, so I chose the new one. I'd read in Mr Beaumont's Baedeker guidebook that it possessed some good Impressionist art.

And indeed it did. There was a van Gogh I quite liked (a portrait of Dr. Gachet), a Monet, a Manet, a dreamy Millet, and a pair of gorgeous Renoirs, each bathed in that wonderful shimmering, sensual light of his.

Afterward, I strolled up the stairs to look at paintings by some German artists. I didn't think much of them, really, until I came to one called *Die Sünde, The Sin.* A naked woman, in a three-quarter view, is staring out at the observer, her long brown hair tumbling down to her hips. A large, darkly mottled snake is curled along her shoulders, its huge dark head resting just above her right breast, its big yellow eyes peering out from the canvas, its wide mouth parted to show its fangs. The woman, presumably, is Eve; and she has, presumably, just eaten the apple. From her expression, she has enjoyed it immensely.

I'm not terribly fond of symbolist paintings, but for some reason I found this one immediately arresting. It was only after staring at the woman's face for a while that I realized—with a start—exactly what that reason was. If the artist (a Franz von Stuck) had painted a pair of spectacles on the woman, she could have been my twin. Her face, Evy, was my face. The features were in shadow, and one couldn't absolutely determine the colour of the woman's eyes. But their shape was the shape of mine. The eyebrows, the cheekbones, the mouth: all were identical to my own.

It was so strange, Evy—to look into a painting that had been painted over thirty years ago, painted before I was ever on this earth, and to find myself looking out from it. I—

.   .   .

THE PORTER HAS just knocked at the door. It is suppertime. I'm off now. I'll write more later.

DINNER IS FINISHED. The only red wine was a warm *Blauer Spätburgunder,* thin and watery. The elk stew was clotted with fat. And Mr Beaumont is a vile, disgusting pig.

I can't—never mind.

Love,
Jane

BERLIN

⟡

CHAPTER TWO

⟡

THE SUITCASES THAT Caudwell brought to the hotel held clothes that were supposed to replace the clothes that Miss Turner and I had left behind in France. But none of the new clothes fit Miss Turner, so we had to go shopping before we caught the Berlin train. The train left at six. At noon the next day, we pulled into Berlin.

As we came from the walkway into the station, people jostling us on either side, I saw a man standing up ahead, holding up a white cardboard sign that read "Mr. Beaumont." Even without the sign, he would have been hard to miss. He was at least six foot five, and he had slicked-back black hair, a large knobby nose, and a jaw the size of Rhode Island. His expensive gray suit, elegantly chalk-striped, had been cut to flatter his massive torso, but you can do only so much with fabric, even when you've got a lot of it.

The crowd was making a wide sweep around either side of him. After passing him, some of the people looked back, their foreheads furrowed in disbelief.

"There," I told Miss Turner, and nodded toward the man.

"Oh my goodness," she said.

The man's bushy eyebrows were raised expectantly and his glance was sliding from left to right and back again. As we came nearer, the glance locked on us. The eyebrows rose higher.

I held out my hand. "Phil Beaumont."

"Hey!" he said, and the face lit up. "Fabulous!" He tucked the cardboard under his left arm and reached for my hand with his right. "Great to meet you!"

My hand isn't small, but it disappeared inside his.

"Ernst Hanfstaengl," he said as he pumped my arm. "But call me Putzi, yes? Everybody does." He had only a faint German accent.

"This is Jane Turner," I said.

He dropped my hand, which had gone slightly numb, and he took Miss Turner's. "*Entzückt!*" he said. He held the hand horizontally, as though he were going to kiss it, but instead he made a formal German bow over it, lowering his heavy shoulders and smacking his big heels together, *clunk*.

Grinning hugely, he spoke to her in German. She spoke back in the same language.

Releasing her, he clapped his hands together. I could feel the breeze from where I stood. "Fabulous!" he said to me. "She speaks it perfectly!" He turned back to her, his big face bright with happiness. "They told me you spoke German, but I had no idea how well!"

"It's been a while," she said. "I'm out of practice, really."

"Oh, that's hooey!" he said. "It's perfect! Absolutely the bee's knees! Where'd you learn it?"

"My mother was part German."

He clapped his hands again. "And so you're part German yourself! Fabulous!"

Grinning, he looked back and forth between Miss Turner and me. "Shall we go? We'll get a porter to help with your bags. There's a cab waiting. I've reserved rooms for you at the Adlon."

Miss Turner said, "Would it be possible for me to drop this in a postbox?" She held up a small envelope. I've never met anyone who sent as many letters as Miss Turner.

"Absolutely," said Hanfstaengl.

IN THE TAXICAB, things were a bit cramped with three people in the backseat, especially when one of them was only a little smaller than a polar bear.

While we rode to the hotel, Hanfstaengl told us a little about himself and the famous people he'd managed to meet. Before he graduated from

Harvard in 1909, he'd met T. S. Eliot and John Reed—"a Communist, you know, but a really great fella." When he ran the family art business on Fifth Avenue in New York, he'd met Henry Ford, Caruso, and Toscanini.

He was as eager as a Boy Scout, peppering his monologue with American slang, grinning his big grin, bobbing his big head, waving his big hands. I don't think he was trying to impress us by dropping all those names. I think he was genuinely pleased as punch that fate had brought all those people into his life.

"And Charlie Chaplin too! The Little Tramp, yes? He came to the gallery all the time. He was a pip! A really great fella!"

Hanfstaengl looked out the cab's window and the animation drained from his face. We were passing through a wide formal park, the grass looking gray now in the rain, the trees looking black and sodden. "Ah," he said sadly. "The Tiergarten. This is where it happened."

He looked at me, his face grave. "It was a terrible thing. You know of the"—he glanced at the driver—"incident?"

"A little. We'll need a lot more information before we start. For one thing, we'd like to see where it happened, exactly."

"Yes, of course. We'll go there after lunch." He shook his head. "A terrible thing. Had it succeeded, it would have been a tragedy for all of Germany."

Suddenly he smiled. "But it failed, yes? And before we speak of it, we must eat!"

HANFSTAENGL SAID THAT he'd wait in the bar. Miss Turner and I took the elevator up to the seventh floor, along with two bellboys, one for each of us. The bellboys and the elevator operator were dressed up like the staff officers of some wealthy mythical kingdom. The Germans like their uniforms.

"He's quite enthusiastic, isn't he?" Miss Turner said to me as the elevator operator unfolded the interior brass doors. "Mr. Hanfstaengl."

"Yeah," I said. "He's a pip."

She smiled. "What *is* a pip?"

"A really great fella."

She smiled. "Do you think he really knows all those people? Charlie Chaplin? Theodore Roosevelt?"

"Probably. If he'd made up the stories, he wouldn't get such a big kick out of them."

She canted her head. "Yes, that's true, isn't it? The people who lie always make a great pretense of not being impressed by the lies themselves."

"You'd make a good Pinkerton," I told her.

She moved her shoulders slightly and let out a small sigh. "I certainly hope so."

"You'll do fine."

Our rooms were adjoining. Mine was only slightly smaller than the suite at the Carlton in Frankfurt, and that had been only slightly smaller than a river barge. There was a huge double bed with a carved wooden headboard, an end table that held an elaborate French telephone, a pair of mahogany wardrobes, two or three dressers, and a big cabinet. There was no sit-down bar, but someone had stocked the cabinet with French red wine, German brandy, Scotch whiskey, and even a bottle of American bourbon. I walked into the bathroom and admired the marble sinks, the huge marble tub, the white marble floors. I undressed and took a fast bath. After drying myself off with a towel the size of a beach blanket, I got into some clean clothes, loaded the Colt, put it into my suit coat pocket, and went back downstairs.

The American-style bar was long and narrow, with a barrel-vaulted roof of ornately carved wood. There were seven or eight round tables, each topped with a circular slab of gleaming white marble, and each surrounded by dark, comfortable-looking leather chairs.

Hanfstaengl was standing at the bar counter, saying something loudly in German to the bartender. Two men in business suits were sitting a couple of stools away. As I approached him across the parquet floor, Hanfstaengl threw back his big head, let out another booming laugh, and slapped his hand against the dark wood bar. The bartender laughed too, but without much conviction. He cast a glance at the bartop, where Hanfstaengl had slapped the wood, as though eyeing it for dents.

Hanfstaengl lifted his beer glass, which held about a gallon of the stuff, and turned to me. "Ah, there you are, Mr. Beaumont."

"Phil," I said.

"Phil. And as I said, you must call me Putzi."

"If you say so."

He laughed. "You know what it means, yes? It means something like 'Little One.'"

"The same as someone calling you Tiny."

Another laugh. "Exactly! Right on the nose! Now, what would you like to drink?" He raised the beer glass. "A beer? It's not as good as Munich beer, of course, but it's drinkable."

"A glass of water would be fine, thanks."

He said something to the bartender, took a sip of beer, set down the glass, then turned back to me. "Tell me something, yes? If I may ask a personal question?"

"Depends on the question."

"Not *too* personal, I hope."

"Go ahead," I said.

"Did you participate in the Great War?"

"Yeah. I participated. You?"

The bartender put a glass filled with ice in front of me and poured mineral water into it from a small bottle. Hanfstaengl waited until the man moved down the bar before answering me. "No, alas," he said. "When the hostilities began, I was still in New York. The authorities nearly threw me in the slammer. I had friends who helped prevent my internment, but even so, I wasn't allowed to return to Germany until after the War. I regret it deeply."

"Don't."

He frowned. "Excuse me?"

"There's not much to regret about missing a war."

"Oh, but Phil, I disagree." His big face was serious. "Surely it is one of the high points of a man's life? The camaraderie, the intensity of feeling—the terror, yes, but also the exultation. Surely the experience is unforgettable?"

"Yeah. That's the problem."

"Yes, but—"

"Putzi," I said.

He looked at me for a moment, and then he nodded. "You'd prefer not to discuss it, yes?"

"Yes."

"As you wish, of course." He took a sip of beer. "But I brought it up for a reason, you see."

"What's that?"

He frowned. "This is a delicate thing. But I really must discuss it with you. There are some people in the party who are . . . concerned about you and Miss Turner."

"Concerned," I said.

"You're an American. Miss Turner is English. Some of the members are worried that the two of you may still harbor some antagonism toward us, toward the Germans. Toward the krauts, yes? The heinies. The Wicked Hun." He smiled sadly. "I heard all those when I was in New York. I knew women, society women, who actually stopped walking their dachshunds because they were afraid to be seen with a German breed."

Miss Turner and I had discussed the War last night, and I told Hanfstaengl now the same thing that I'd told her then. "The war's been over for years."

"Yes, of course, but old attitudes die hard."

"If the party people are so worried, why'd they hire the Pinkertons? There must be private detective agencies here in Germany."

"Hiring the Pinkertons was Herr Hitler's idea. He knows their reputation and he has complete faith in them. And in you and Miss Turner too, of course. He's an extraordinary man, Phil, with an extraordinary breadth of understanding. I honestly believe that he'll be the savior of Germany."

"If Hitler's not worried—"

"Not all the party members possess such an understanding." He smiled sadly. "Some of them, I'm afraid, harbor antagonisms of their own."

"I can't do anything about that."

"No, but if I could offer them some reassurances . . . ?"

"What kind of reassurances?"

"First, that you understand how absolutely serious this investigation is. For many of us today, Herr Hitler is the most important man in Germany. As I said earlier, his death would be a tragedy for us and for the German people. Whoever is responsible for this must be brought to justice."

"Well, Putzi, I'll do my best."

"Can you give me your word, Phil?"

"My word on what?"

"That you'll conduct an objective and thorough investigation."

"I always do."

"And that you will keep confidential whatever you learn."

"All Pinkerton investigations are confidential."

He beamed at me and held out that big hand. "Fabulous!"

I gave him my own hand and let him pump it for a while.

"Thank you, Phil! I'm delighted that—" He looked beyond me, past my shoulder. "Ah, Miss Turner!"

The night train to Berlin
Tuesday morning
May 15th

Evy—Ignore my last letter! Or ignore at least the passage in which I accuse Mr Beaumont of being a pig. Mr Beaumont is *not* a pig. I'll explain when I can. I'll post this when we arrive in Berlin.

Love,
Jane

CHAPTER THREE

"I RECOMMEND," SAID Putzi Hanfstaengl to me over his menu, "today's special. The *Pfälzer* pig stomach, yes? A fabulous provincial dish. Stomach stuffed with pork, onions, and potatoes, and then steamed gently for several hours."

"Maybe some other time," I said.

We were in the restaurant toward the rear of the hotel, the larger of the two restaurants in the building, according to Putzi. The room was nearly a hundred feet long and thirty feet wide, and the walls were festooned with marble pilasters and marble medallions. The place was packed with well-fed Germans and well-fed foreigners and the soft buzz of complacent conversation. The waiters moved around so smoothly on the thick wall-to-wall carpeting that they could have been wearing roller skates.

"Then perhaps the *Finkenwerder* plaice," suggested Putzi. "This time of year, the fish are fabulous—small and sweet, very tasty. Absolutely the cat's pajamas. They're sautéed in a little butter and bacon fat, and then bits of fried bacon are sprinkled on top."

"Is there any beef?" I asked him.

He glanced down at the menu. "Sauerbraten. And an entrecôte."

"The entrecôte will be fine. Rare. And could I get potatoes and a salad?"

"How would you prefer the potatoes? Boiled and buttered? Or as a *Kartoffelpuffer,* a pancake?"

"Fried."

He nodded. "*Bratkartoffeln.* And you, Miss Turner?"

"The plaice, I think," she told him. "And the white asparagus, with hollandaise."

He nodded again. "And I'll have the *Pfälzer Saumagen.*"

The waiter came and took our order. Putzi ordered another beer for himself. Miss Turner ordered a glass of Riesling. I ordered another glass of water.

As the waiter left, I said to Putzi, "We'll need a list of all the people who knew that Hitler would be coming to Berlin."

"Absolutely. I have it with me." He reached into the inside pocket of his suit coat and came out with a small folded sheet of paper. He handed it to me.

I opened it. The names were hand-printed, neatly and in alphabetical order:

Captain Hermann Goering

Ernst Hanfstaengl

Rudolf Hess

Emil Maurice

Frederich Nordstrum

Captain Ernst Roehm

Alfred Rosenberg

Gunnar Sontag

"All of these people," said Putzi, "were sworn to secrecy."

I handed the paper to Miss Turner. "How many of them came to Berlin with Hitler?"

"Myself and Emil Maurice, Herr Hitler's chauffeur. And Gunnar Sontag. He's an aide to Herr Hess."

"And who is Hess?"

"Herr Hitler's private secretary."

"Who are the other people?"

"Captain Goering is the head of the party's athletic section. Frederich Nordstrum is his aide. Alfred Rosenberg is our press secretary."

"And Captain Roehm?"

"Our liaison with the army."

"Okay. The attack took place on Tuesday, is that right?"

"Tuesday the eighth, yes. At approximately five fifteen in the afternoon."

"And when had the meeting been arranged?"

"On the previous Friday."

"So, as of Friday, all these people knew about the meeting."

"Yes."

"When did you leave Munich?"

"At around noon on Sunday."

"Did you stop anywhere on your way to Berlin?"

"In Bayreuth, that night. It's a small town about a hundred miles from Munich."

"You stayed in a hotel?"

"Yes. That is, we did, Emil and Gunnar and I. Herr Hitler stayed with the Wagner family. Cosima Wagner, the wife of the composer, and her son, Siegfried."

"We'll need to talk to them."

"Whatever for?"

"We need to talk to anyone who could've known about Hitler's meeting in Berlin."

"But, Phil—"

"Sorry, Putzi. We'll need to talk to them."

He nodded. "Very well. We can stop in Bayreuth on the way to Munich."

"Fine. When did you and the others leave Bayreuth?"

"Early Monday morning. We picked up Herr Hitler at approximately seven thirty."

"And when did you arrive in Berlin?"

"That evening. Around eight."

"Stops along the way?"

"For food and for gasoline."

"Where did you stay in Berlin?"

"The Kaiserhof. A very nice hotel."

"And what did you do when you arrived that night?"

"We had a late meal, and then went to bed."

"None of you went out?"

"So far as I know. We were all quite tired. I know that I went to bed immediately after dinner."

"Hitler went to the Tiergarten on Tuesday."

"Yes."

"When did you go back to Munich?"

"We left Wednesday morning. Emil drove straight through. We arrived on Thursday morning."

I nodded toward the sheet of paper. Miss Turner had placed it on the table. "How many of those people have friends or relatives in Berlin?" I asked him.

"I couldn't say."

"Can you find out?"

"I can telephone Hess. He'll know. Oh, wait. Gunnar does—he has a girlfriend here. An English girl, yes?" He smiled at Miss Turner, another English girl, and then turned back to me. "I don't know her name, but Maurice was teasing him about her. Gunnar is very stuck on her, it seems."

"We'll need the name."

"Hess will know."

"And all these people will be in Munich when we get there?"

"Actually," he said, "Roehm is in Berlin at the moment. Do you wish to speak with him?"

"Yes."

"I'll arrange it, if I can."

"And we need to talk to whoever was meeting Hitler in the park."

Putzi pursed his lips. "It was a confidential meeting."

"We still need to talk to him."

"I can assure you, Phil, that this person had nothing to do with the assassination attempt. It would be virtually impossible for him to be involved."

"Maybe so. But he could've mentioned the meeting to someone else."

Putzi took a deep breath, let it out slowly. He nodded. "Very well. I'll ask Hess to ask Herr Hitler. Without Herr Hitler's permission, of course, I can't reveal the name."

"Fine. And you can tell Mr. Hess that if we don't get the name, there's no point in our staying in Germany."

Putzi looked puzzled. "What do you mean?"

"I mean that without the name, Miss Turner and I will be heading back to England."

His big face sagged, as though I'd just ripped away his baseball glove and told him he couldn't play in the big game. "You would abandon the investigation, Phil?"

"Putzi, if we can't do our job the right way, we won't do it at all."

He looked from me to Miss Turner and then back to me. He took another deep breath. "Very well," he said sadly. "I'll tell Hess."

PUTZI CHEERED UP when the meal arrived. I had a feeling that he always cheered up when the meal arrived.

The plates were piled high with food. My entrecôte was as wide as an automobile tire and almost as tender.

After ordering another beer, Putzi told us about the first time he'd seen Hitler give a speech.

"He looked like nothing special. Like a waiter in a railway station restaurant, yes? But when he got onto the stage and started talking, he was amazing! At the beginning, he spoke softly—so softly you had to strain to hear him. People were leaning forward on their chairs."

He glanced at Miss Turner, to make sure she was following, or maybe to make sure she was still there. "And then slowly, once he had the audience with him, he began to speak more loudly, with more passion. He criticized the nationalists. He criticized the Socialists. He criticized the Kaiser and then the Weimar republicans who had surrendered Germany to the Allies. He tore into the Marxists. He tore into the war profiteers. He was fabulous! He was a ball of fire!"

Putzi took a sip of beer. "By the time he was done, the people were screaming and stomping their feet. It was an amazing performance. But it was *more* than a performance. Herr Hitler is the real McCoy, Phil. He *identifies* with the German people, with German history and tradition. He identifies *totally*. When he speaks, it's as though he *is* Germany."

He looked back and forth between Miss Turner and me. "So many Germans, today they are without hope, without faith. We lost many of our finest young men in the War. We lost nearly as many with the Spanish influenza, just after the War. And with the Versailles Treaty, we lost the peace. And now, of course, the inflation rate is absolutely insane. The life savings of entire families have been wiped out. People are starving. Children steal food from garbage cans. Here in Berlin, good women have been reduced to prostitution." He shook his big head. "It is not a happy time."

Another sip of beer. "For the German people, Herr Hitler represents the possibility of change, the possibility of hope. When they hear him speak, they believe once again that Germany will survive. That *they* will survive. Their hearts are lifted. They love him, believe me. They adore him."

Miss Turner said, "One of them doesn't adore him, it would seem."

Putzi had returned to the pig stomach, and he was busy with his knife and fork. He looked over at her. "Pardon me?"

I said, "Whoever took a shot at him."

"Yes," he said. Still holding the cutlery, he nodded. "Yes. I feel sure it was the Bolsheviks. The Reds. Herr Hitler is a terrible threat to them, yes? Every day, more and more workers join the Nazi Party."

"If it was the Bolsheviks," I said, "how'd they know that Hitler would be in Berlin?"

He nodded his big head again. He put the knife and fork down on the plate, as though he'd lost his appetite. "Yes," he said sadly. "It seems that someone in the party must be a traitor." He turned to Miss Turner. "Someone on that list."

THE RAIN WAS still falling when we got outside, but it had softened to nearly a mist. We picked up a cab across the street from the hotel, and it took us into the Tiergarten through a huge stone gateway, four or five stories tall, that looked as if it had been snatched up from ancient Greece and dropped there.

"The Brandenburg Gate," said Putzi. "And over there, over on the right, yes? That's the Reichstag, the seat of the German parliament. It was built in 1894."

The Tiergarten was a big park, hundreds of damp dark trees on either side of us, stretches of damp dark grass that seemed to go on for miles. We came to a huge circular plaza with a towering fountain in its center, roads shooting out from the fountain in every direction.

"The Grosser Stern," said Putzi. "Constructed in 1904."

The taxi looped around the circle and we took a narrow road to the southwest.

"Fasanerie Allee," said Putzi. "We'll be stopping soon."

The cab pulled over to the right. I got out and offered Miss Turner my hand. She took it and stepped out onto the sidewalk and opened her umbrella. Putzi paid the driver a couple of hundred thousand marks.

Each of us holding an umbrella, Miss Turner carrying her purse tucked under her arm, we walked along the path. The sky was the color of lead. The mist chilled the air.

"This leads," said Putzi, "to the Zoological Garden. One of the finest in the world. There are over thirteen thousand different animals, many of them not available in any other zoo."

That may have been true, but there weren't many pedestrians going to, or coming from, the zoo. A pair of elderly women in tattered raincoats, handkerchiefs hooded over their heads. An old man in a ragged black coat, muttering to himself as he shuffled along. A trio of young boys in sailor suits, big black bows flopping at their necks, all three huddled beneath a large umbrella held by the boy in the center. They eyed us as we passed, smiling widely and nudging each other.

"Trick boys," said Putzi, and frowned. "Homosexual prostitutes. There are thousands of them in the city."

We walked by a wooden bench that held a large, bulky bundle of newspaper, soaking wet. A pair of feet, shod in cheap leather shoes, stuck out from one end of the bundle.

I looked at Putzi.

He sadly shook his head. "This is not a happy time."

We came to a narrow stone bridge. Putzi stopped walking, and so did Miss Turner and I.

"This is the Lichtenstein Bridge," Putzi said. He nodded to the black water that moved sluggishly beneath it. "And that's the Landwehr Canal. It was here, in January of 1919, that Rosa Luxemburg was shot. Her body was tossed into the canal. It wasn't found for four months."

"Who was Rosa Luxemburg?" I asked him.

"One of the leaders of the Spartacists, the Bolsheviks who tried to take over the government. Those were difficult times, Phil. Tempers were running high. For a while it seemed that the Reds would control all of Germany. For a while, they did control Berlin."

"Who shot her?" Miss Turner asked.

"A *Freikorps* lieutenant, a man named Vogel."

"*Freikorps*?" I said.

"After the Versailles Treaty, the German army was forced to break up. The *Freikorps* were groups of soldiers who banded together to protect Germany from the Communists."

"What happened to Lieutenant Vogel?" Miss Turner asked.

"He was convicted, but he escaped to Holland."

"So what are we doing here, Putzi?" I asked him.

He looked surprised. "But, Phil. I thought you understood. It was from here, from this bridge, that the sniper fired at Herr Hitler."

CHAPTER FOUR

A s we stood there on the narrow stone bridge under that grim leaden sky, the mist that swirled around us began to thicken into a drizzle again. Raindrops pattered at my umbrella and dimpled the flat black surface of the canal.

"The shot was fired from here," I said, "and that's why you think the Bolsheviks were responsible?"

"That's not the only reason, of course," said Putzi. "The Reds would like nothing better than to see Herr Hitler dead. There are hundreds of death squads roaming the countryside, Phil, all of them under orders from Moscow. The Reds are still very strong here, yes? And by using this bridge, they'd be making a statement."

"What kind of statement?"

"That they were avenging the death of Rosa Luxemburg."

"Uh-huh. And where was Hitler when this happened?"

He nodded his big head toward the west. "Over there. That little island."

I looked off, through the black, dripping trees. Just beyond a thin strip of water flowing north from the canal lay a slightly humped patch of land that held more trees.

From beneath her umbrella, Miss Turner said, "How do you know that the rifle was fired from here?"

Putzi looked at her as though he'd forgotten she was there. Maybe he had. "Because the weapon was found here," he said. He leaned his hip against the stonework and pointed down toward the water. "There. On that ledge."

"Not in the water?" she asked him. It was a good question.

"No doubt he intended to throw it in the water," Putzi said. He turned to me. "But he was clearly in a hurry, and it got caught on that ledge. There wasn't time for him to run down there and correct the mistake."

"What kind of rifle was it?" I asked.

"Some sort of infantry Mauser."

Miss Turner said, "You said that the shot was fired at about five fifteen?"

Once again he seemed surprised that she'd be asking a question. Women probably didn't ask Putzi too many questions. "Yes, that's right."

"But surely," she said, "there were people wandering about? Witnesses?"

"It was a day like today," Putzi said. "Very rainy. And even colder than it is now."

"You were here," I said to Putzi, "when it happened?"

"Yes, of course," he said. "I was with Herr Hitler on the island."

"All right," I said. "Let's take a look at this island. Miss Turner, could you wait here on the bridge?"

She smiled. "I'm to be the sniper."

"Right."

I FOLLOWED PUTZI along a footpath through the trees. Water was plopping heavily from the leaves.

"The Seuer See," Putzi told me, and nodded toward a small gray lake that nearly surrounded the island. On the far side of the lake there were more black trees. Beyond them, I could see traffic moving along the road.

It wasn't really an island, I discovered—it was connected to the rest of the Tiergarten by a narrow ribbon of land. We crossed this and followed the path to a small clearing in the center.

Putzi stopped, looked around, nodded. "Herr Hitler was standing here."

"How many people were with you?"

"Two other men. I'm sorry, Phil, but until I get permission, I can't tell you their names."

I nodded. "And you're standing right where Hitler was standing?"

Beneath the umbrella, his big head swiveled back and forth. He took a step to the right, then a step backward. "Here," he said. "Yes."

"And where were you?"

"Back there. Beneath that tree, with one of the other men."

"The fourth man was standing with Hitler?"

"Yes." He moved to the right. "About here."

I walked over, stood beside Putzi, looked back at the bridge where Miss Turner stood. I couldn't see her. On the Tiergarten side of the Seuer See, the thick branch of a large elm tree, heavy with leaves, slumped down toward the water and blocked my line of sight.

I moved to the right, until I could see Miss Turner. I waved. She waved back. I signaled for her to move to her left along the bridge, toward the Zoological Garden. She did. At the south end of the bridge, she stopped.

I walked back to Putzi and turned to look at her. A small, dark figure in the rain, she stood to the right edge of the elm's branch, just barely visible.

I said, "Looks like a pretty tough shot to me, Putzi."

He was frowning. "But someone took the shot, Phil. Remember, this is still springtime, and the shot was fired a week ago. There were fewer leaves on the trees then, yes?"

"But just as many branches. And the branches could deflect a shot. A sniper would worry about that."

"But the shot was taken. We all heard it, coming from that direction." He inclined his umbrella toward Miss Turner.

"When you heard it," I said, "did you turn toward the bridge?"

"Yes. I turned—" He stopped, thought a minute. He nodded. "Yes, I turned in that general direction. To my right."

"General direction. Not exactly toward the bridge."

"But *generally* toward the bridge." He raised his eyebrows. "Ah! Now I see!"

"What?"

"The sniper fired more from that direction." He pointed to the right of Miss Turner. "And then he must have run across the bridge, throwing in the rifle as he went."

"Maybe. But if he wanted to get rid of the rifle, he would've thrown it into the water as soon as he came to the bridge. Why did it land on the ledge on the *far* side?"

"He was excited, he used too much strength."

I nodded.

"That's what *must* have happened, Phil. The police were here almost immediately, and they found the rifle only a few minutes later. I heard them talking. It had just been fired."

"I was told that the bullet missed Hitler by only a few inches. Is that right?"

"Yes. Only an inch or two to the right, and he would have been killed. I thank God, every day, that the bullet missed him."

"The police have the slug? And the rifle?"

"Yes. I've made an appointment for you tomorrow, at nine o'clock, with Sergeant Biberkopf. He's the officer handling the investigation."

"Fine. Thanks."

"Have we finished here, then, Phil?" He glanced around. "I once enjoyed the Tiergarten. As a child, whenever I came to Berlin with my family, I spent many happy hours here. But now it gives me the willies."

"Yeah," I said. "We're done for now."

He smiled happily. "Then I suggest that I take you and Miss Turner for a drink. There's a wonderful beer hall nearby, the Bauer. A beer would really hit the spot, eh?"

"Let's do it another time, Putzi. Miss Turner and I need to write up our reports."

His face deflated. "Well. All right. If you insist." He smiled again. "But *I* insist upon taking the two of you to dinner tonight. And there's someone you must meet."

"Who?"

He smiled slyly. "That will be my little surprise, yes? But I assure you, Phil, you won't regret it."

"Fine. And you'll call Hess? We need that name. The man who was with Hitler."

He nodded, but without much enthusiasm. "Yes, yes, of course. May I ask you a question?"

"Sure."

"About Miss Turner?"

"What about her?"

"She said that her mother was German. Do you know if she has any relatives still living here?"

"Not as far as I know. Why?"

"It's strange. She reminds me of someone. But I can't think who."

WE TOOK ANOTHER taxi back to the Adlon, where Putzi dropped us off, promising to pick us up again at seven that evening. The two of us went back into the bar and sat down at one of the small tables. She ordered a cup of tea and I ordered a coffee.

As the waiter walked away, his white jacket crackling with starch, I asked her, "So what do you think?"

"About the assassination attempt?" she said.

"Yeah."

Behind her spectacles, her blue eyes narrowed. "By asking me the question, aren't you suggesting that you have certain reservations about it?"

I smiled. "Could be."

She nodded. "Mr. Hanfstaengl was standing where Herr Hitler was standing when it happened?"

"Yeah."

"How large a rifle was it, the one the police found? How long?"

"Putzi said a Mauser. A good-sized rifle. Over four feet long."

"I know that Mr. Hanfstaengl said there weren't any witnesses. But could a sniper, someone carrying a rifle that large, could he know for certain that a witness wouldn't just happen along while he was going about his business?"

"No," I said. "What else?"

"There's a tree between the bridge and the island, so presumably he didn't actually fire from the bridge. Do we know whether in fact he fired from anywhere *near* the bridge?"

"Putzi said he heard the sound of the shot, and that it came from somewhere to his right. To the south."

"From the grounds of the Zoological Garden."

"Right."

"But then why would the sniper run *toward* the bridge? Wouldn't he be more likely to run in the other direction? Through the Garden, *away* from the bridge?"

"Maybe."

"But if he did run toward the bridge, and he wanted to conceal that rifle, how is it that he didn't manage to throw it in the water?"

"According to Putzi, the man was in a hurry. He missed the canal."

"It's rather a large canal to miss, isn't it? And wouldn't he have been extremely anxious *not* to miss it? Lying on the ledge like that, the rifle must've been discovered by the police almost at once."

"In a couple of minutes, Putzi said."

The waiter returned. He set down the coffee and tea and then marched off to sprinkle some more starch on his jacket.

I poured some coffee. "So where do we stand?" I asked her.

She smiled. "Is this a test, Mr. Beaumont? Is there a prize if I win?"

"I'll pick up the tab for the tea."

She laughed. She had a good laugh.

She looked down as she stirred a spoonful of sugar into her tea. She looked up. "Well, as I see it, there are several possibilities."

"And they are?"

"For one, the assassination attempt might've been a hoax, one perpetrated either by Mr. Hitler or by the man he met on the island. Perhaps no shot was ever actually fired."

"I don't think Putzi's lying. And the police came. A shot was fired."

"Then perhaps it was never intended to hit anyone."

"Perhaps," I said.

"But to what end? And all the secrecy that everyone's maintaining—wouldn't this suggest that it wasn't a hoax?"

"Maybe."

She frowned. "Why do you suppose they're all maintaining the secrecy? I should think that the people in the party would use the assassination attempt to create sympathy for Mr. Hitler and themselves."

"It's probably got something to do with the other man. The one Hitler was meeting. Several possibilities, you said."

She sipped at her tea. "Well, one thing does occur to me."

I tasted my coffee. For a couple of hundred thousand marks, I had expected something that didn't taste like dishwater. I was disappointed. "What?" I said.

"That the rifle was put on the ledge *before* the shot was fired. It was a red herring. And another rifle was used to fire the shot."

I nodded. "I'll pay for the tea."

"And there's another possibility too, isn't there?"

"Which?"

"That the shot wasn't meant for Mr. Hitler. That it was meant for the other man."

I smiled. "I'll also buy the dinner tonight."

As it turned out, I didn't buy the dinner. The dinner was bought by the most famous psychic in Germany.

Hotel Adlon
Berlin
Tuesday
May 15th

Dear Evangeline,

This will be a short missive, I'm afraid, quickly scrawled and abruptly ended. In an hour or so, Mr Beaumont and I will be going off to supper with a gigantic German teddy bear of a man named— I am not inventing this—Putzi Hanfstaengl.

It's still raining here. I begin to believe that it always rains in Germany.

But I want to tell you about Mr Beaumont's swinehood, or rather his lack of it.

As you'll remember (I hope) we were sitting, he and I, in the dining car. The china plates and the silverware and the linen were all wonderful; but the elk stew, as I said, was a catastrophe. The service, however, was perfect, and the lighting was cosy and romantic.

Mr Beaumont is not, at the best of times, the most forthcoming of conversationalists. He seems to feel that a simple 'Yeah' or 'No' will suffice as an answer to any question. And so I was rather taken aback by his answer when I asked him, 'Is this your first trip to Germany?'

He said, 'Yeah.' The standard response. And then he added, almost casually, 'Thank God.'

I frowned. 'What do you mean?'

'I saw enough Germans in the War,' he said.

'But Mr Beaumont,' I said, 'isn't that a somewhat . . . narrow-minded attitude?'

He smiled faintly. It was one of those rankling smiles which suggest that the person smiling knows infinitely more about something—about everything, perhaps—than the person being smiled upon. 'You think so?' he said.

'I'm sure,' I said, 'that the War must have been terrible for you. But it was terrible for the British too, you know. Nearly a million men killed. A million and a half men gassed or wounded. And surely it was terrible for the Germans as well?'

He sipped at his wine. 'I wouldn't know.'

'Not all the Germans fought in the War. Not all of them wanted a war.'

'Maybe. I never met any of those Germans.'

'That doesn't mean that they don't exist. Certainly there were militaristic Germans—jingoists, warmongers—and I'm sure there still are. But there were, and are, hundreds of thousands of decent, cultured Germans. Germany has always had a remarkable cultural tradition.'

'No kidding,' he said flatly.

'Beethoven? Bach? Goethe?'

'I never met any of them, either.'

I smiled. He was being, I thought, deliberately obtuse.

'Come now, Mr Beaumont,' I said. 'You can't tell me that anything you saw in the War would prevent you from looking objectively at the Germans of today.'

It was, of course, in retrospect, a terribly stupid thing to say. God knows what monstrous things he saw in the War. In fact, as soon as the words tumbled from my mouth, I realized how asinine they were. But, still, his reaction stunned me.

His face, Evy, went suddenly cold. For a moment he stared at me, a silent, stony stare. Then he said, 'Miss Turner, forgive me, but you are full of shit.'

It was like a sudden slap in the face. And I knew that the skin along my cheeks was just as red and tight as if he had, in fact, just smacked them.

But I was very calm. I took my napkin from my lap, placed it calmly beside my plate, stood up, turned, marched down the corridor between the tables, marched out of the dining car, marched across the passage separating that car from our sleeping car, marched to my compartment, unlocked it, and marched in, calmly shutting the door behind me. The porter had prepared the bed. I calmly sat down on the edge of it. Then I calmly cried my heart out, for hours.

I knew, of course, that I should be obliged to resign from the Agency. There was simply no way that I could continue to work with Mr Beaumont, not after what he'd said, and simply no way, without appearing a hysterical wretch, to explain to Mr Cooper why I could not.

But now we come—very quickly, for I must run—to the sequel:

I scribbled those last few frenzied lines to you (the elk stew, Mr Beaumont's swinehood), sealed the letter in an envelope, and stamped it. When the train reached Nürnberg, where some more passenger cars would be added, I dashed from the car and thrust the envelope into a postbox. I dashed back. As I came toward the compartment, I saw that Mr Beaumont was standing there in the passageway, his shoulder against the partition wall, his hands folded across his chest, his head bowed.

I turned, trying to retreat before he saw me, but I heard him call out: 'Miss Turner?'

I stopped and I stood there, not looking back at him. My breath was coming very quickly. I could sense him moving up behind me. Over the sound of my panting, I heard him sigh.

For a moment he said nothing. Then he said, 'I'm very sorry.'

It was one of those moments in which all of one's emotions have accumulated, trembling, behind a membrane so thin and taut that it might at any moment rupture. I couldn't turn to look at him—had I done so, the membrane would have burst.

'I had no right to say that,' he said. 'I . . . Look. I'm really very sorry. You're right. The War's been over for years. It's probably time for me get used to that idea.'

Reluctantly, I turned to face him.

And just then the train moved, shifting with an abrupt lurch, and I was thrown back against Mr Beaumont's chest, which was being thrown in the same direction, and at the same velocity, along with the remainder of Mr Beaumont, including his feet, and so for several seconds we were dancing in frantic reverse down the passage.

Finally he caught himself, and then he caught me.

'Are you all right?' he said. He had his hands on my shoulders. He's quite strong.

'Yes, yes, I'm fine.'

An awkward moment of slapstick had punctured the membrane, draining away the emotions it held in check. They had been replaced, in an instant, by simple British embarrassment. There are advantages, you know, to being British.

'I'm fine,' I said again, and, as his hands released me, I turned to face him. 'And it was quite asinine of me to say what I did. It was unforgivable, but I hope you can forgive me.'

For a moment he simply looked at me. He does have very attractive eyes. And then he smiled. 'Why don't we just call it even?'

'All right,' I said. 'Yes. Thank you.'

He nodded. 'Thank *you,* Miss Turner. I'll see you in the morning.'

'Good night, Mr Beaumont.'

And so to bed, each of us to our own separate compartment.

Miss Turner. He called me 'Jane' once, in France—did I tell you?

I see that this has not, after all, been so short a missive. But now, Evy, I must run.

All my love,
Jane

CHAPTER FIVE

◈

AT SEVEN O'CLOCK that evening, we were waiting for Putzi under the awning outside the Adlon, on the Pariser Platz. Miss Turner had mailed another letter. I was beginning to wonder if she were secretly an author, sending out installments of some serial novel.

I'd left my Colt in the suitcase that Caudwell had brought me in Frankfurt. I didn't think I'd be needing it at dinner.

It was still raining, a slow, steady drizzle. In the yellow glow of the streetlights it glittered like beads of molten sliver. The Unter den Linden was filling up with big, expensive cars, the bright reflection of their lights streaming across the slick black asphalt. Horns honked. Engines rumbled.

The sidewalks were filling up with pedestrians and umbrellas. There were more young boys in sailor suits, giggling to themselves or staring out at the passersby with knowing eyes. There were strutting young men in stylish suits who weren't young men at all, but young women with closely cropped hair. There were other young girls who were dressed like very high priced young girls. There were tall, arrogant women in long leather jackets and brightly colored leather boots. There were plump, red-faced middle-aged men, prosperous shoppers in a mammoth department store, thoughtfully appraising the merchandise that passed them by.

And mixed in with the hustlers and the hustled were the beggars, an army of them, outnumbering the rest. Old men and young men with missing limbs. Old women in widow's black. Children in rags. A thin, young mother with her thin, young daughter. More children in rags.

Outside the Adlon, there were two doormen dressed like Romanian generals who kept shooing along the beggars. But the generals ignored the rest of the crowd, just as the rest of the crowd ignored the beggars. Quite a few people, male and female and various combinations of each, wandered into the lobby of the hotel and headed for the bar, to begin their negotiations. The smell of perfume and aftershave, most of it cheap, some of it expensive, mingled in the damp, heavy air with the smell of automobile exhaust.

Miss Turner adjusted her spectacles and said to me, "It's rather like the end of the world, isn't it?"

"How so?"

"All this poverty, all those beggars, and yet no one seems to care."

"They probably can't afford to. Tomorrow it could be them."

"All the more reason, I should think, for them to be concerned."

"If they were, they wouldn't be able to enjoy tonight."

She was about to say something when a horn honked nearby.

A taxicab had pulled up in front of the hotel. The back window was rolled down and somehow Putzi had managed to get his big head and his big shoulder through the opening. The taxi looked as if it were giving birth. "Phil!" he called out, blinking against the rain. "Miss Turner!"

I held the umbrella over Miss Turner as we ran through the shower to the cab. The door swung open and Putzi moved to the far side, so he was taking up only half the seat. I waited for Miss Turner to climb in, then I furled the umbrella, climbed in myself, and tugged the door shut. I held the umbrella upright between my knees. It was warm in the car, and damp, and both Miss Turner and I unbuttoned our raincoats.

"Hello, hello!" said Putzi. There was a large book on his lap, beneath his homburg hat. "Miss Turner, you look lovely tonight."

"Thank you," she said. On her head was a black cloche hat. Her brown hair was tied in a tight, low swirl at the back. Under her coat she was wearing one of the dresses she'd bought in Frankfurt, a high-waisted, gray silk number that reached down to midcalf. She had good midcalves.

Putzi leaned around her to speak to me. "Phil, I talked to Hess and he spoke with"—he glanced at the back of the driver's head—"our friend. Everything is absolutely hunky-dory, I'm pleased to say. I can give you that name. The man in the Tiergarten."

"Who was it?"

Another glance at the driver. "Later, yes? And Hess gave me some more information. First, the telephone number of Gunnar's English girlfriend. Her name is Nancy Greene. I telephoned—it's a boardinghouse in Charlottenburg—but she wasn't there. The landlady said that the girl would be at the Black Cat tonight. She works there."

"What's the Black Cat?"

"A cabaret. We can go after dinner, if you like."

"Fine."

"Hess also told me that Frederich Nordstrum has a sister here in Berlin. Greta."

"Nordstrum is one of the people on the list."

"Yes. Goering's assistant, as I told you. I'm afraid that the sister will be more difficult to interview than Miss Greene. She has no telephone. On my way here, I stopped at the registry in the Central Police Station on Alexanderplatz, and I tried to find her address. But she's not registered as living in Berlin."

"She's using another name," I said.

"She must be. She is, I'm sorry to say, a prostitute." As we passed beneath another streetlamp, I saw him glance quickly, apologetically, at Miss Turner. "As I told you, Phil, these are unhappy times, and many a good woman has been forced to sell herself simply to remain alive."

"There's no way to locate her?"

"One, perhaps. She apparently has some connection to the Institute of Sexology."

"The Institute of Sexology?"

"So it's called. It's run by a psychoanalyst named Magnus Hirschfeld. He's a maniac, Phil. A madman. Somehow he's managed to parlay his own obsession with sex into this institute, and into a small fortune for himself."

"The sister works for him?"

"On an occasional basis, Nordstrum says."

"Where's the Institute?"

"On Beethoven Strasse. In the Tiergarten, near the Spree."

"Do you have a description of the woman?"

"Yes." He reached into his coat pocket and pulled out a slip of paper. As we passed through the light of another streetlight, he read out, "She's twenty-three years old and her hair is blonde. She weighs fifty-nine kilos and she's one meter eighty centimeters tall."

He handed me the paper.

"Fifty-nine kilos would be how many pounds?" I asked him.

Miss Turner said, "One hundred and thirty. Her height would be just under six feet. Quite tall."

"Thanks," I told her. I took my wallet from my coat and slipped the paper inside it. I turned to Putzi. "We'll check on her tomorrow. What about Roehm? Is he still in Berlin?"

"Yes, but I haven't been able to reach him. I left a message. He should telephone me tonight, at the restaurant."

"Fine."

"And I learned something else, also." We passed under a streetlamp, and in its light I could see that Putzi was smiling.

"What's that?" I asked him.

"Miss Turner," he said, turning to her, "this afternoon I asked Phil if you had relatives still living in Germany."

"I don't," she said. "My mother's family all moved to England."

"That may be, but as I told Phil, you reminded me of someone. This evening, while I was dressing, it came to me. It isn't a person you resemble, Miss Turner. It's a painting. Do you know of an artist named Franz von Stuck?"

She thought for a moment. "I don't believe so."

"Ah, but it appears that he knew of you. And more than thirty years ago." He tapped the book on his lap. "This is one of the books published by my father. Reproductions of works by Bavarian artists." He hooked his homburg over his big knee and opened the book. "You see?" he said cheerfully. "*Die Sünde.* The Sin. The resemblance is extraordinary."

For a moment we flashed through the light of another streetlamp, and I saw the painting. It was of a woman, mostly naked, with a snake as thick as a fire hose draped around her neck. Then the taxi moved out of the light and we were in darkness again.

"I'm sorry," said Miss Turner. "I'm afraid I don't see the resemblance."
She sounded genuinely apologetic.

"It's the light," said Putzi. "Wait until we get to the restaurant. But I
assure you, the resemblance is there. Herr Hitler will go nuts!"

"Nuts?" I said.

"Stuck is absolutely his favorite painter in the whole entire world, and
this painting, *Die Sünde,* The Sin, it is absolutely his favorite painting. He
has stood for hours, *hours,* peering into the eyes of the woman on the canvas. He will go nuts when he sees you, Miss Turner."

WE ATE AT a place called the Haus Vaterland on Potsdamer Platz. It took
up a whole block and it was actually five different restaurants. We didn't
see them all, but according to Putzi, there was an authentic Bavarian
beer hall, an authentic Viennese café, an authentic Rhineland wine ter-
race, an authentic Spanish inn complete with authentic Spanish gypsy
women, and an authentic Wild West bar. Putzi thought I'd feel more at
home in the authentic Wild West bar. He explained to Miss Turner, re-
gretfully, that there was no authentic English pub. She took the news
well.

The three of us checked our coats and then walked through a gigantic
batwing door into a saloon so big that if it had existed in Dodge City,
there wouldn't have been any room in the town for cattle or much of anything else.

The tin ceiling was high and supported twenty or thirty electric crystal
chandeliers. The bar was at least a hundred feet long, and most of the
stools were occupied. Behind the bar were an equally long mirror and several million liquor bottles, and bartenders who wore leather vests and
white twenty-gallon hats. The waiters wore the same vests and hats. They
also wore embroidered leather chaps over their dungarees, and they carried their order books in oversize leather holsters.

Scattered around the enormous room were maybe fifty or sixty brightly
painted cigar-store Indians, standing at rigid attention. The red-flocked

walls were decorated with the heads of dead animals, deer and elk and even a buffalo or two, all of them staring out through the cigarette smoke at the crowd, probably in disbelief. On the stage at the north end of the room, a band was playing. The musicians were all wearing old-time two-piece suits and canary yellow vests. The singer was a thick-bodied blonde woman in a low-cut red taffeta gown. She was singing "Home on the Range" in German. Never was heard a discouraging word.

The maître d', sporting a fringed buckskin jacket and a coonskin cap, led us through the thickets of customers to an empty table.

"It's amazing, yes?" said Putzi, who was carrying his book under his big arm. "Just like a real saloon in the Wild West."

"Yeah," I said. "Exactly."

As soon as we were seated, Putzi opened the book and placed it, with a flourish, in front of Miss Turner. "You see, Miss Turner?" he said. "It's extraordinary, the resemblance."

She looked down at the painting. She adjusted her spectacles. After a moment she said thoughtfully, "Well, I suppose there *is* a certain small resemblance. Around the jawline, perhaps."

"Bushwa!" said Putzi. "The woman could be your sister." He lifted the book, swung it around to me, slapped it onto the table. "What do you think, Phil?"

In the bright light of the chandeliers, I could see that the woman did, in fact, look a lot like Miss Turner. But Miss Turner didn't seem happy with the resemblance, so I said, "A bit, maybe."

"Identical," said Putzi, and he leaned over and took back the book. He turned it around, admired the painting for a moment, then grinned and said, "Herr Hitler will go nuts."

A waiter arrived, looking a bit unsteady on his cowboy boots, and handed out menus.

"Would you like a drink?" Putzi asked me. "They have special Wild West American cocktails."

"Like what?"

He glanced down at the drinks menu, studied it. "For example, the

Old Shatterhand. The name is from a character in the books of Karl May. Have you read any of these?"

"No."

"They're wonderful! Absolutely the bee's knees! Filled with fabulous Wild West action. Herr Hitler loves them."

"What's in the Old Shatterhand?"

He looked down at the menu again. "Absinthe, orange juice, crème de menthe, bitters, and American bourbon. Genuine American bourbon, it says."

"Could I get a glass of genuine American bourbon? Straight up? With a glass of water on the side?"

"Of course. Miss Turner?"

She looked up from the drinks menu. "I'll have the Natty Bumppo," she said.

"And what's in that?" I asked her.

"Chartreuse, absinthe, and pineapple juice." She smiled. "I feel like living dangerously."

"And going blind."

She laughed. "I doubt I'll finish it. I haven't much of a head for alcohol."

"And I," said Putzi, "will have a beer." He looked up and spoke with the waiter, who nodded and then strutted off, wobbling a bit on his boots.

Putzi was examining the dinner menu. "Phil, would you like another steak?"

"No thanks. Is there any fish?"

He studied the menu. "Santa Fe halibut. San Antonio mountain trout."

I smiled. "From the San Antonio mountains?"

"From a lake to the south of Berlin."

"The trout'll be fine, thanks."

He nodded. "Miss Turner?"

"I think just the mixed salad. I'm not terribly hungry."

"The mixed salad," he said. "And I'll have the Wild Bill Hickock pork stew."

"So who was it, Putzi?" I said. "Who was Hitler meeting in the Tier-garten?"

He glanced quickly around the room, to make sure no spies were lurking nearby. He leaned slightly toward me. "It was General Hans von Seeckt, Phil. The head of the German army."

CHAPTER SIX

And who was the other man?"

"His aide, Colonel von Hippel."

"Why was Hitler meeting von Seeckt?"

Putzi glanced around the room again. He looked at me. "First, I must give you some important historical background."

"Fine."

His voice low, he said, "On the first of May, a few weeks ago—May Day, yes?—the Bolsheviks held a big parade in Munich. This was an outrageous act, because in a very real way it was a celebration of the time in 1919 when the Reds took power in Munich."

"I thought Berlin was where they took power."

"No, no. Not only in Berlin, but also in many other German cities. Remember, Phil, in 1919 the Bolshevik Revolution in Russia was a recent phenomenon. Reds all over Europe were attempting to duplicate the Bolsheviks' success."

"Right. So on May Day . . ."

"On May Day, yes, Herr Hitler realized that the anti-Bolshevik forces must assemble for a show of strength, a kind of antidemonstration. A number of patriotic groups, under Herr Hitler's leadership, gathered at the Oberweisenfield, north of Munich. While they were staging their military maneuvers—"

"Military maneuvers?"

"Practicing. In case the Reds attacked, yes? As I told you, these are difficult times. The Reds are—"

His mouth snapped shut as the waiter arrived with the drinks. Putzi thanked him and gave him our food order. Afterward, the waiter wobbled off, the heels of his cowboy boots clomping against the floor.

Putzi took a swig of beer. Miss Turner tasted her Natty Bumppo.

"How is it?" I asked her.

"Not as strong as I expected." She smiled. "I suspect that's a good thing."

I tasted my bourbon. It tasted like genuine American bourbon with a lot of genuine German water added.

Putzi said, "The Reds are armed, Phil, and they're dangerous. Their defeat in 1919 has only made them more determined."

"Right. So what happened while the patriotic groups were staging their maneuvers?"

"They were surrounded by the Bavarian State Police and the Munich garrison of the Reichswehr—the German army. Although the leaders of the police and the army are naturally sympathetic to Herr Hitler, they wanted to avoid a confrontation with the Reds. And so Herr Hitler's forces were made to surrender their weapons. It was quite a blow to him, to his prestige, yes?"

"Right."

"He decided then, he told me later, that the time for simple demonstrations was over. The government itself, the traitors in Weimar, must be removed from power. It was time, he felt, for a march on Berlin. You know of Mussolini's march on Rome? Last year?"

"Yeah."

"Patriots marching toward the capital to save their country. After the Oberweisenfield, Herr Hitler wanted to do the same thing here. He spoke with General Otto von Lossow, the head of the Munich army garrison, and he proposed the idea—groups of loyal *Freikorps* soldiers marching to Berlin, gathering more strength as they went along, yes? Like every good German, von Lossow is unhappy with the Weimar government, and he was prepared to keep the Munich garrison in its barracks. But only if he received assurances that the army in Berlin, under General von Seeckt, would not attack the marchers. It was to get these assurances that Herr Hitler met in the Tiergarten with von Seeckt."

I nodded. "There hasn't been any march on Berlin, so I'm guessing he didn't get the assurances."

"Alas, no."

"Is it because of the general that everyone's keeping his mouth shut about the meeting? About the assassination attempt?"

"Yes. Von Seeckt insisted upon it. And it works out well for us too, for the party."

"If people found out about the meeting, they'd figure out what Hitler was trying to do. And you don't want that."

"No."

"The people on that list. Did any of them know that Hitler was planning to meet the general?"

"They all knew."

"And who arranged the meeting with von Seeckt?"

"I did. I know him through some friends."

"Did you tell anyone else about the meeting?"

"No one. Not even my wife. And the general gave me his word as a German officer that he would tell no one but Colonel von Hippel. The general is a man of the utmost honor. And so, naturally, is Colonel von Hippel. They would have told no one, Phil."

"Maybe so, but we've still got to talk to them."

He nodded. "I told Hess you would say so. I'll contact the general tomorrow."

Miss Turner said to Putzi, "This General von Lossow . . ."

Putzi turned to her, looking a bit surprised again. "Yes?"

"Is he the same man who ordered the army to take away the weapons on May Day?"

"Yes, but he had no choice at the time."

She took a sip of her Natty Bumppo. "But if he was worried that the Socialists would clash with Herr Hitler's people on May Day, why wasn't he worried that they'd clash with anyone who marched to Berlin? Why wasn't Herr Hitler worried?"

He smiled. It was the kind of smile that doting fathers smiled when their bright young daughters were talking nonsense. "A march is something totally different from a demonstration, Miss Turner. As I said, the number of marchers would increase along the route. Most good German citizens are opposed to the Weimar regime. We would be joined by townspeople, farmers, peasants, patriots from all walks of life. The Reds would have no way to stop us."

"You said they have rifles. Couldn't they—"

Just then, maybe because we were discussing the Reds again, the waiter returned with our food. Putzi held up a cautioning hand to Miss Turner. The waiter set the plates down on the table and then wobbled off. Sooner or later he might get the hang of those cowboy boots, but it probably wasn't going to happen tonight.

"You said they had rifles," repeated Miss Turner. "What's to stop them from attacking the marchers?"

"We have rifles too," said Putzi, and smiled his fatherly smile. "On a march like that, we would outnumber them by a hundred to one. To attack us would be suicide. Herr Hitler has carefully considered all this, of course."

"I'm sure," said Miss Turner, and she said it the way bright young daughters do when their doting fathers were talking nonsense.

Putzi didn't seem to notice. "But enough politics for now, eh?" he said. "Now we eat and we discuss more pleasant matters. Tell me please, Miss Turner, how is it that you became an agent for the Pinkerton detectives?"

As I ate my fish, which had the consistency of sawdust but almost none of its flavor, Miss Turner told him about her involvement in a Pinkerton operation in England, at a manor house in Devon called Maplewhite. She told him that I'd been working as a bodyguard for Harry Houdini, the American magician. At the time, she said, she'd been only a bystander, but she'd been able to assist me "in a small way," and after the operation had ended, I had suggested she join the Agency.

She relayed the things that had happened at Maplewhite in a matter-of-fact voice, polite if a bit distant, and I got the feeling that she'd made some decisions about Putzi, about who he was, and that these probably weren't the kind of decisions that Putzi would want to hear.

"Fascinating!" said Putzi. "And have you had many other exciting adventures since you became a female sleuth?"

She smiled, glancing at me briefly from behind her spectacles. "A few," she said. "But I'm not allowed to discuss them, I'm afraid."

"Of course not! Mum's the word, eh?" He turned back to me, as though he had gotten all the Miss Turner information he needed, and said, "Phil, did I tell you that I once met William Pinkerton?"

I looked at Miss Turner and saw that she was rolling her eyes in mock exasperation. Or maybe it was real exasperation.

I noticed too that her glass was empty.

"No, Putzi," I said, "you didn't."

"A really great fella. In New York, this was, at the Rockefellers. He told me some absolutely amazing stories." Suddenly he looked up from the table and his big eyebrows climbed up his forehead. "Ah, Erik. I'm so pleased you could join us." He stood up, slowly unfolding his bulk, and he held out his big hand.

The dreamboat who took it was nearly as tall as Putzi, about six foot three, with broad shoulders beautifully encased in a black silk dinner jacket. The perfect knot of his white silk bow tie was tucked perfectly between the crisply folded wings of his white silk dress shirt. His hair was thick and black, flowing in small, even waves back over his ears. His clean-shaven face was square, his strong jaw was cleft, his nose was sharp and even. His large eyes, beneath the double slash of dark eyebrows, were as black as his dinner jacket. Under his left arm, he held a bottle of Dom Pérignon champagne.

"I hope," he said, "that I am not interrupting your dinner?" His voice was a baritone, rich and theatrical.

"No, no," said Putzi. "We're finished. Erik, permit me to introduce Mr. Phil Beaumont of the Pinkerton Detective Agency. Phil is from the United States. Phil, this is Erik von Dinesen." He said the name as though it belonged to one of those really great fellas I'd probably heard about.

I stood up and von Dinesen took my hand.

"A pleasure," he said. For a moment, as he smiled, he narrowed his eyes in such a way that they seemed to be looking into the depths of my mind.

It's a stage magician's trick. A few years ago, Harry Houdini had explained it to me: *You look into their eyes, and you make yourself focus beyond the eyes themselves. It causes people to become uneasy, you see. It causes them to believe that you can somehow see past the masks of their face. It works, of course, only when the people are quite stupid or quite ignorant.*

I wondered who Erik von Dinesen was, and why he wanted me to think he was seeing past the mask of my face.

CHAPTER SEVEN

AND THIS," SAID Putzi, "is Miss Jane Turner, also a Pinkerton agent. Miss Turner is from England."

Smiling up at him from the table, Miss Turner held out her hand. Von Dinesen took the hand, bowed deeply over it, and brushed his lips against it. Still holding her hand, he began to rise, but stopped just as his head came level with Miss Turner's. "A great pleasure," he said, looking into her eyes. From where I stood, I couldn't tell whether he did his squinting trick again, but Miss Turner blinked. Von Dinesen stood, releasing her hand.

Putzi said, "Sit, Erik, sit!"

Von Dinesen lowered himself to the extra seat beside Miss Turner, moving with the easy physicality of an athlete or an actor. Putzi and I sat down.

"I brought this along," said von Dinesen, setting the champagne on the table, "because I know that the champagne here is unbearable." He turned to Miss Turner. "And I did want to toast your arrival in Berlin." His English was as good as Putzi's, but more formal.

"Ice!" cried Putzi. "We must have ice and glasses!" He waved to one of the passing cowboys. When the cowboy reached the table, he looked around and spotted von Dinesen, and suddenly he started grinning and bobbing his big white hat and coughing up some rapid-fire, enthusiastic German.

Von Dinesen nodded, smiling, and lightly held up his hand, like a traffic cop who wanted to stop the traffic but didn't feel that any real urgency was involved.

Putzi gave the excited cowboy some quick instructions in German, and the cowboy bobbed his hat some more and picked up the bottle and scurried off.

Von Dinesen reached into the inside pocket of his dinner jacket. "Before I forget," he said, "the maître d' gave me this. There was a telephone call from Captain Roehm." He handed Putzi a folded scrap of paper.

Putzi took the paper, opened it, read the message. He looked at me. "Captain Roehm will meet with us at the Mikado at nine o'clock." He turned to von Dinesen and his face lit up with a great smile. "Once again you amaze me, Erik. The message is signed only 'R.' And yet you knew it was from Captain Roehm."

Across the table, von Dinesen smiled a small, mysterious smile.

Putzi turned back to me. "Erik is the most famous psychic in Berlin— in the entire country. His stage presentation is legendary. Listen to this, Phil—just last year, in the middle of his performance, he suddenly pointed to a man in the audience, a complete stranger, and told him that his factory was on fire *at that very minute!* The man was wise enough to heed Erik's warning. He ran from the theater to his factory, several blocks away, and he discovered that Erik was absolutely right. He rang for the fire department, and they came lickety-split, thank God. They saved the factory from ruin. An amazing story, yes? It was written up in all the newspapers."

Von Dinesen moved his shoulders in a faint shrug. "It is a gift," he said.

Putzi told me, "Before he came to Berlin, Erik helped the police of Hamburg with many of their investigations. He's brought hundreds of dangerous scoundrels to justice. Herr Hitler himself believes that Erik is one of the greatest men in all of Germany."

"Yeah?" I said. I was beginning to see where this was heading.

"Erik knows all about the—" Putzi glanced around the room again, then lowered his voice "—the incident in the Tiergarten. He has been kind enough to offer his help."

"No kidding," I said.

Von Dinesen smiled. "I see that you are skeptical about these matters, Mr. Beaumont."

"Maybe a tiny bit."

He squinted again, peering into my mind once more, and then he nodded. "Did you develop the skepticism in New York City as a young man, growing up with your brother Thomas? Or did you develop it when you worked as a professional boxer? Or was it afterward, during the War? You fought at Château-Thierry, did you not?"

"Yeah," I said.

Putzi clapped his big hands with delight. "Hah! You see, Phil! I told you!"

I said to von Dinesen, "But by time I got to Château-Thierry, I was already fairly skeptical."

Von Dinesen smiled his mysterious smile.

Those particular facts were available in only one place—in my file at the Pinkerton office in London. I wondered how the contents of the file had made their way to von Dinesen.

The name that came to mind was Peter Caudwell. He had access to all the personnel files, and he was the only person from the Agency who'd been in Germany recently. But I couldn't think of a single reason why he'd help out von Dinesen, or anyone else, by supplying the information.

Von Dinesen looked at Miss Turner, his handsome eyebrows lightly arched. "And what of you, Miss Turner? Are you a skeptic as well?"

"I—"

Just then the second cowboy returned, pushing a cart. The bottle of champagne was resting inside a sweating silver bucket, and around the bucket stood four flat-bowled champagne glasses sparkling like rhinestones beneath the electric lights.

The cowboy quickly set out the glasses and began fiddling with the foil at top of the bottle.

"Miss Turner?" said von Dinesen. "You were saying?"

She smiled. "I try," she said, "to keep an open mind."

"Yes. I suspect that the good Miss Applewhite, back in Torquay, would be very proud of you."

I had no idea who Miss Applewhite was, but Miss Turner clearly had.

She laughed aloud. "That's wonderful!" she said. She turned to me, her face flushed with pleasure. "Miss Applewhite was headmistress at the school I attended. In Torquay."

Von Dinesen smiled again, mysteriously.

With a loud pop, the cork exploded from the bottle of champagne. Quickly, the cowboy lifted the bottle, wrapped a white napkin around its base, and moved the bottle toward von Dinesen. Von Dinesen waved his hand softly and said something in German. The cowboy did a military about-face, brought the bottle to Miss Turner, bowed once, and then carefully filled her glass. He went around the table and filled each of the glasses with similar care, slipped the bottle back into the bucket, and said something else to von Dinesen.

"*Danke,*" said von Dinesen. He reached into his pocket and pulled out a twenty-thousand-mark note. He folded it lengthwise and handed it to the cowboy, who grinned and bobbed his hat some more, then hiked up his leather belt and swaggered off.

Von Dinesen raised his glass. So did the rest of us. Von Dinesen looked from me to Miss Turner. "I hope that the two of you discover, here in Germany, that which you most wish to discover," he told her.

We drank.

As we set down the glasses, I said, "And what have *you* discovered so far, Mr. von Dinesen?"

"Please." He smiled. "Call me Erik. You mean relative to the assassination attempt in the Tiergarten?"

I saw Putzi glance around the room, as though he expected people to leap to their feet at the word *assassination.* No one did.

"Yeah," I said.

"Nothing. In order for my gift to operate properly, you see, I must come into close physical contact with the person or the object in question. I've asked Sergeant Biberkopf, the police officer responsible for the investigation, if I might examine the weapon found at the park. He has refused, so far. Perhaps you would be able to persuade him to cooperate?"

"I'll be seeing him tomorrow. I'll bring it up."

Von Dinesen nodded. "Thank you. I can ask for no more."

"In the meantime," I said, "do you have any theories?"

"I try not to theorize," he said. "Creating a theory could bias my results."

"Right."

"Erik," said Putzi, "are you performing in Munich at the moment?" He took a gulp of champagne.

"No," said von Dinesen. "At the moment, I am on hiatus. I felt that I needed some time for myself."

Putzi put his glass down quickly, as though he'd just remembered something. "Oh! You must see this!"

The book of reproductions had been lying on the table, between Putzi's plate and mine. He grabbed it now and flipped it open. I glanced at Miss Turner and saw that her face was flushed again, but probably not with pleasure. "Look, look!" said Putzi. "Isn't this woman a double for Miss Turner?" He reversed the open book and held it across the table to von Dinesen.

Von Dinesen took it in both hands, looked down at it, his face without expression.

Miss Turner lowered her eyes and took a sip of champagne.

"Not at all," said von Dinesen lightly, and handed the book back to Putzi. "Miss Turner is infinitely more attractive."

Her face pink again, Miss Turner smiled. "You do exaggerate, Mr. von Dinesen."

He smiled at her. "Indeed, I do not. And, please, you must call me Erik."

I reached into my pocket and pulled out my watch. Nearly nine. I said to Putzi, "If we're going to meet with Roehm, we should probably go now."

Miss Turner turned to me. "But what about the cabaret? And that woman, Nancy something?"

"Nancy Greene," said Putzi. He looked at me. "Perhaps you could speak with her tomorrow?"

"Or," said Miss Turner to me, "you and Mr. Hanfstaengl could speak with Mr. Roehm, while I go to the cabaret and speak with Miss Greene."

"Miss Turner," said Putzi uneasily, "I must tell you, the cabarets of Berlin are not safe places for a woman to venture into unaccompanied. In these troubled times—"

"But Miss Turner will not be unaccompanied," said von Dinesen. He looked at her. "If, that is, she will permit me the honor of acting as her escort?"

Miss Turner smiled, then turned to me, her blue eyes wide. "If that's all right with Mr. Beaumont?"

"Splendid!" said Putzi. "A absolutely nifty solution, eh, Phil?"

"Nifty," I said.

"I assure you," von Dinesen told me, "that Miss Turner will be in good hands."

I wondered if that was a double entendre.

"And it *will* save us time," Miss Turner pointed out. "If I interview Miss Greene tonight, we'll be able to do more tomorrow." She took another sip of her champagne. Her glass was nearly empty.

"Come on, Phil," said Putzi, and slapped me heartily on the back. "Miss Turner will be perfectly safe with Erik. And, really, she should live a little while she's here in Berlin. She should have some *fun*!"

I looked at Miss Turner. "Okay. But we'll be having breakfast tomorrow morning at seven thirty. We're supposed to see Sergeant Biberkopf at nine."

"I'll be back at the hotel before midnight," she said.

Von Dinesen said, "I shall of course make certain that Miss Turner comes on time."

I looked at him, wondering once again if he was deliberately choosing words that had two meanings, one of them sexual. His handsome face was open and guileless.

"At midnight," said Miss Turner, and smiled at me. "Rather like Cinderella."

I noticed that behind her spectacles her blue eyes were shinier than usual. She'd had one stiff drink and nearly a full glass of champagne, and she'd eaten only a small salad.

But she was a trained operative, and a grown woman, and there really wasn't anything I could say.

But, as it turned out, Miss Turner wasn't the person I should've been worried about.

CHAPTER EIGHT

T HE RAIN HAD turned to mist again by the time Putzi and I grabbed a cab. With only two of us inside the vehicle, there was almost room for us both.

As he settled back against his three-quarters of the seat, Putzi put his hat on his lap, onto the book of reproductions, and said, "About Captain Roehm, Phil. I must tell you a thing or two."

"Some important historical background." I was holding my umbrella, once again, upright between my knees.

"In a manner of speaking," said Putzi, "yes."

"Go ahead."

"You must know, first, that the captain was absolutely a brave soldier during the War, totally respected by the troops he led. After the War, he helped save Munich from the Reds. And right now he is extremely valuable to the party. He has Herr Hitler's total trust."

"I get the feeling that there's a 'but' coming up pretty soon."

"Excuse me?"

"He's wonderful, he's a real prince, *but* . . ."

"Ah, yes. Yes. Well, there is one small thing that perhaps you should know about Captain Roehm."

"What's that?"

"Yes. Well. He's something of a homosexual, you see."

"Uh-huh."

Against the light from the buildings we passed, a silhouetted Putzi cocked his head. "This doesn't bother you?"

"Not unless he's supposed to be my date."

He laughed, his big hearty laugh, but one that lasted for maybe a bit longer than necessary.

"No, no," he said, "not at all. But, Phil, you should know about the Mikado, the bar where we'll be meeting Captain Roehm. It's a well-known gathering place for homosexuals. They congregate there, yes? And sometimes, well, sometimes they dress in . . . an unusual manner."

"In drag?" I said.

"In what?"

"In drag. Men dressing up as women."

"Yes, that's what I meant, but 'in drag'? Where does it come from, this phrase?"

I shrugged. "Maybe from the way a long dress tends to drag across the floor. Especially if you're not used to wearing it."

"Amazing." In the half-darkness of the cab, I could see him shake his head. "I try to keep up with all the latest slang, you know, but it changes so quickly."

"You do a fine job, Putzi."

"Well, yes, I like to think so. But it's difficult." He looked out the window. *"In drag,"* he said, as though he were committing the words to memory. Probably he was.

THE BAR WAS on Puttkamer Strasse, which according to Putzi was a few blocks east of the Anhalter train station. It was at No. 15, its entrance a simple wooden door beneath a slightly battered-looking Japanese lantern of steel and frosted glass. There were no windows, and only a small sign in black, oriental-looking, metal letters attached to the brick wall: MIKADO.

Putzi had the driver turn left onto Wilhelmstrasse and stop opposite the mouth of a narrow alleyway. "Best not to go in through the front door," he told me.

"Why's that?" I asked him.

"Security reasons," he said, sounding very serious. I think he was talking about his own security—he was worried that someone who knew him might see him enter the building.

We left the cab and crossed the street and walked down the dark, narrow alley, around the empty beer bottles, the scraps of newspaper, the shreds of tattered cardboard, a flattened leather shoe with no laces and no sole. We came to another wooden door, this one lit by a single overhead bulb that jutted out from the brickwork. Beside the door was a mechanical bellpull. Putzi pulled it.

After a moment, the door was opened by a man who could have been a professional wrestler, except that most professional wrestlers don't wear low-cut red dresses and red patent leather pumps. The dress was a bit loose in the chest and a bit tight across the stomach, where a certain amount of beer had settled as sediment over the years. He'd shaved his lumpy pectorals and his beefy arms, and probably he'd shaved his face before he'd troweled on his powder and mascara and lipstick. But his beard was growing back. Washed in the glare of the overhead bulb, his heavy jaw looked like something you could sharpen your cutlery on.

He wore a nice wig, though—a neatly trimmed pageboy with glossy black Theda Bara bangs.

Putzi said something in German, and the man in the red dress answered him in a gravelly voice, then stood aside for us to enter. He said something else to Putzi as he pulled the door shut. Putzi turned to me, the book of reproductions under his left arm, the homburg in his right hand. "This way, Phil."

I followed him down a corridor piled high on each side with liquor and beer crates, and then out into a large, square, dimly lit room. From a pedestal in its center, a traffic light blinked off and on, flashing a bizarre red light over the dozen or so tables. Most of the tables were occupied. There were booths along the walls, and dark cavelike alcoves, the arches at their entrances draped with hanging beads and paper Japanese lanterns.

Another man who could have been a professional wrestler, this one wearing a floral dress and a hennaed wig, was sitting at an upright piano in the corner, banging out a tango. On the small dance floor in front of him, two couples in evening dress were sliding back and forth, dipping and swooping.

As we crossed the floor toward an alcove beside the bar, I got a closer look at the people at the tables. Some of the women were beautiful in their stylish gowns, and some of them might even have been women. Some of the men were handsome, but a few of these, beneath the dinner jackets they wore, were also wearing breasts. Without a scorecard, it was hard to tell which players were playing which position.

Putzi walked to one of the alcoves. He pushed aside the hanging beads, ducked his big head, and led me under the arch.

The air in there was thick with some floral cologne. Sitting at opposite sides of a small table, in the flickering yellow light of a Japanese lantern set against the wall, were two men. One of them was young and lean, with a pale, thin, earnest face, like a monk's. He wore a gray business suit, a white shirt, a black tie.

The other man was shorter and older. His hair was cut so close to his scalp that I couldn't tell what color it was. His pale face was round. On both his cheeks were deep puckered scars, from a knife, or maybe a saber. Another scar dented his bulbous nose, and beneath the nose was an undersized brown mustache that resembled the bristles of a toothbrush, a bit like Charlie Chaplin's mustache. But his eyes weren't like Chaplin's. Looking out at me from between plump creases of flesh, they were small and dark and empty. They had seen just about everything and they hadn't liked any of it much.

Circling his broad neck, above the tight white collar that dug into his flesh, there were more plump creases. His black business suit was inexpensive, and he'd obviously bought it when he'd carried around a bit less meat than he carried now. It was tight against his shoulders and torso, like a sausage casing, and he sat upright within it, his back rigid.

"Captain Roehm," said Putzi to me, then turned to the short man. "Herr Phil Beaumont."

The two men stood up, and the shorter man held out his hand. He clicked his heels together and briskly nodded. *"Guten Abend."* His fingers were stubby and strong. As I shook the hand, I got a stronger whiff of the cologne.

He nodded to the other, younger man and said, *"Leutnant* Felix Kalter. "

The lieutenant offered his hand and I shook it. He didn't smile either. Roehm said something to Putzi, and Putzi turned to me and said, "Sit, please."

I sat down, next to Kalter, and rested my umbrella against the wall of the alcove. Putzi sat down beside Roehm, putting the book and his hat upon the table.

Roehm's small brown eyes were watching me. He smiled a small, prim smile and said something.

Putzi translated, "Captain Roehm would like to know how you're enjoying the Mikado."

"It's swell," I said.

Putzi translated this, or something like it. Roehm smiled briefly, primly, and spoke again.

"He wonders," said Putzi, "if you've ever been in a bar like it before."

"Not this week."

Putzi translated.

Roehm smiled that smile. Each time, the smile lasted exactly the same length of time, which wasn't very long, and it had exactly the same intensity, which wasn't very intense. I got the feeling that he allowed himself to be amused only up to a certain, clearly defined point. Which wasn't very amused.

Roehm said something. Hesitantly, Putzi said something back. In a flat voice, Roehm snapped some German at him.

Nodding, Putzi turned to me. "The captain," said Putzi, "wants to know if you fought in the War. I told him that you prefer not to discuss it."

"Tell him I said yes."

Putzi did, and Roehm asked me, through Putzi, "What rank?"

"Private when I went in."

"And when you came out?"

"Sergeant."

Roehm's left eyebrow rose. "A battlefield promotion?"

"They were short of sergeants at the time."

Another prim smile. And then he nodded. He had decided, I think, that I was okay. I had been in the army. Even if it was the American army.

"So," he said, and ran the palm of his hand back over his bristly scalp, "you have questions. Ask them."

Just then a woman, or someone who looked a lot like a woman, poked her slim, bare shoulder beneath the alcove archway. She wore a short, high-waisted silk dress and she was carrying a drinks tray. Behind her the bizarre traffic light flashed, giving her slender body a red aura that winked on and off. She said something in German.

Putzi asked me, "Phil, would you like a drink? A schnapps? Maybe a beer?"

"No thanks. We're not going to be here that long."

Putzi frowned sadly. Probably he'd been hoping for that beer. He spoke to the woman and she swung back through the archway.

I turned back to Roehm. "Who would want to assassinate Adolf Hitler?"

"Every piece of Communist scum in Germany."

I asked Putzi, "He said 'scum'?"

I wouldn't have thought that someone of Putzi's size would be capable of sheepishness, but there was a definite sheepishness about him now. "Well, no, Phil," he said. "Actually he didn't. What he said was something stronger."

"Putzi, do me a favor. Don't edit. Just tell me what he says, exactly. And tell him what *I* say, exactly. Word for word."

He nodded. Sheepishly. "All right, Phil, yes, of course."

"What did he say?"

"Yes. He said, 'Every piece of Communist shit in Germany.'"

Both Roehm and Kalter were watching us as we talked, Roehm with blank indifference, Kalter with intelligent eyes that darted back and forth between us, which suggested to me that he was following the conversation. Which suggested, in turn, that Roehm had brought him along because he didn't trust Putzi's translating skills. Or didn't trust Putzi. Or didn't trust anyone, except possibly Kalter.

"Why would the Communists want to kill Hitler?" I asked Roehm.

Through Putzi, Roehm said, "Because they are terrified of him. They know that they, and the Jews, and the traitors in Weimar, all of them, all the filth and the muck, will all be swept away when Herr Hitler comes to power."

Roehm leaned forward. "Listen to me. You were in the army, so perhaps you can understand. You fought in the trenches?"

"Some. Not much."

"I fought in them for years. And there are German soldiers alive today who fought in them for longer than I did. For three years, for four years. You know that the line, the Western Front, it shifted back and forth in France?"

"Yeah."

"Sometimes, when we dug new trenches, we found the rotting corpses of men who had died in some earlier campaign. Months before, a year before. German, French, English. Sometimes our shovels would catch on something, and we discovered that it was a skull, or a pelvis, or an arm."

I nodded.

"Do you know," he said, "what I hated most about them, about the trenches?"

"No."

"Not the filth. Not the smell of shit or the smell of decay. Not the rats." He smiled and held out his left hand. With his right forefinger he pointed to yet another scar, a small half-moon-shaped cicatrix on his left thumb. "A rat did that. While I slept." He lowered his hands to the table. "But it wasn't the rats I hated most. Nor the lice. Nor the flies in the summer, so thick you couldn't breathe. No, what I hated most was the water."

In front of him was a glass of clear liquid, probably water. He picked it up and stared into it. "From September until May the trenches would fill with water. We had pumps, and sometimes they worked. Sometimes they didn't."

He set the glass back down and looked at me. "The water was as cold as death, and it seeped into everything. Your bedding, your food, your clothes. Your boots. Sometimes, when you took off your boots and your socks, the skin of your feet would come off as well, like rotten cloth."

I nodded.

"But I can tell you now," he said, "that if Adolf Hitler ordered me back into those flooded trenches, I would go back into them in an instant. That is how I feel about Adolf Hitler. I believe that he will one day become the savior of the German race."

"And if Hitler asked you to kill?"

"Of course." He smiled. "You are not the only investigator working on this matter, you know. I have people of my own looking into the assassination attempt. Good people. Loyal Germans."

As opposed to detectives from the United States.

Roehm leaned forward again. "If I learn the name of the stinking piece of shit who fired that rifle, he will never take another breath of German air."

I nodded. "Have these people of yours come up with anything?"

He sat back against his chair. He shook his head. "Nothing useful."

Obviously they hadn't learned who had fired the rifle, or I wouldn't be here.

I said, "You knew that Hitler was coming to Berlin."

"Yes."

"You knew who he was meeting here."

"Yes."

"And you knew why."

"Yes."

"And why was that?"

Roehm turned to Putzi, asked him something. Putzi responded. Roehm turned back to me. "Hanfstaengl tells me you know. He came here to meet with General von Seeckt. To arrange for the army's noninvolvement when we began a people's march on Berlin."

"Did you tell any of this to anyone?"

"No." He canted his round head toward Kalter. "Not even the lieutenant. He is my aide, and I trust him implicitly, but I kept the visit a secret even from him. I was under orders." He smiled. "As I am now. At the moment I am under orders to cooperate with you."

"Whose orders?"

"Herr Hitler's."

I nodded. "Is there anyone you suspect? Anyone in your party who might have helped plan this thing?"

Roehm smiled. "If I suspected such a person, he would no longer be in the party. He would no longer be on the face of the earth."

"All right, Captain. Thank you for your time."

I got out of the chair and snagged my umbrella. Putzi stood and gathered together his hat and the book of reproductions. Roehm and Kalter remained seated. I nodded to each of them and turned to leave.

"Herr Beaumont," said Roehm.

I looked back.

He spoke some German, his small eyes steady.

I looked at Putzi.

"If you find the man," he said, "Captain Roehm will want his name."

"Didn't you tell me it was Hitler who decided to hire the Pinkertons?"

"Yes."

"Right. If I find the man, I'll give the name to Hitler."

Putzi turned to Roehm and translated that.

Roehm never looked at Putzi. He kept his eyes on me. Even after Putzi finished, he kept his eyes on me. Finally, he nodded.

Lieutenant Kalter's pale slender left hand was resting on the table, palm down. As I turned to go, I saw Roehm move his arm and settle his stubby fingers over the hand. Kalter turned to him, a smile forming on his lips. Roehm was still watching me, and he was smiling now too, that small prim smile of his.

AS WE CAME back into the alley from the back door, Putzi put on his hat and said, "And what did you think of Captain Roehm?"

We started up the alley toward Wilhelmstrasse.

"I thought he was swell," I said.

"You mustn't take him lightly, Phil. He's an important man."

"Uh-huh."

"You know, when he says 'the Jews,' what he means are the Jews who acted as war profiteers."

"Right."

"There were many people—not all of them Jews, of course—who

made huge profits during the war, at the expense of the German people."

"Doesn't look like Roehm was one of them."

"As I told you, he was wounded three times." He shook his head. "It must be terrible for him, to be homosexual and look like that."

"Probably be terrible to be heterosexual and look like that."

Putzi smiled. "Yes. Yes, of course."

"Putzi," I said. "I need a favor."

"Of course, Phil. What is it?"

I didn't get to tell him, not then, because when I looked up at the mouth of the alley, I saw that it was blocked. Against the dispersed light of the streetlamps on Wilhelmstrasse stood the silhouettes of four men. They were big and they were wearing dungarees and what looked like peacoats. They were all carrying long, wooden truncheons in their right hands, held down at their legs. They started walking toward us.

I remembered that my pistol was in my suitcase, back at the Adlon.

Putzi had seen the men too. He stopped walking. I put my hand against his arm. "Back to the bar," I said.

We turned. In time to see, stepping from the back door of the bar, two more men, dressed like the first four in peacoats and dungarees. Maybe they all belonged to the same club.

I glanced back at the other four. They weren't in any hurry, but they were still coming.

I turned to the two who'd just come from the bar. As they moved toward us, they both opened their coats and pulled truncheons from beneath them. The man on the left, a big man with tufts of blond hair poking out from beneath a black watch cap, raised his truncheon and smacked it down against his open palm. I could hear the sound of it from thirty feet away.

He knew that I could hear it. He grinned, and then he smacked the truncheon against his hand again.

Hotel Adlon
Berlin
Tuesday night
May 15th

Dear Evy,

I'm terribly tiddly, I'm afraid.

Well, after oceans and oceans of Dom Pérignon, I expect that I have a right to be terribly tipsy. Actually, I have more than a right. I have a duty. I have a moral obligation.

Goodness. I'm writing gibberish. I really should just peel off my lovely new dress and collapse into bed.

But speaking of peeling off dresses, I spent most of the evening watching a woman named Celly de Rheidt do exactly that. She was the star performer in something called 'The Dance of Beauty' at the Black Cat Cabaret. She and her troupe of women dancers performed a series of what purported to be aesthetical *Ausdruckstanze* ('expression dances', in case you've forgotten the German that Mrs Applewhite tried to drum into you). All of these aesthetical dances began with Miss de Rheidt and her troupe wearing very little clothing; and all of them ended with Miss de Rheidt and her troupe wearing no clothing at all.

The last dance of the evening was an adaptation of Calderón's *The Nun*. It's rather a loose adaptation, for it ended with the persecuted young nun stripping off her habit and begging for divine intervention from a statue of the Virgin Mary, who promptly stepped down from her pedestal, into the spotlight, and began to fondle her naked breasts. The young nun's naked breasts, I mean.

Oh dear. I'd best finish this before it becomes even more addled. I'll write again in the morning.

But I must tell you one thing—I've met the most remarkable

man. His name is Erik von Dinesen and he's a psychic. He knew things about me that he couldn't possibly have known without possessing some sort of 'sixth sense'. It was really quite extraordinary. *He* was really quite extraordinary.

And he was also—not that this is in any way relevant, of course—fabulously good-looking.

All my love,
Jane

CHAPTER NINE

I THOUGHT ABOUT making a run for it. Maybe, on my own, I could have gotten past the two men by the door. With some swerving, some dodging, and a little luck, I might have made it. But I wasn't sure that Putzi would.

I stepped away from him, to give myself room to operate, and I swung sideways to cover both approaching groups of men. I knew that I wouldn't be operating for very long—it wouldn't take six men with truncheons very long to bring me down.

Briefly, I wondered who they were and where they'd picked us up. But I knew that it didn't really matter. They were here now.

It would have been nice if my umbrella concealed some sort of secret weapon. It didn't.

But it was a sturdy umbrella, with a solid metal shaft. Sturdy enough to parry a truncheon—for a while, anyway. And the point was sharp enough to take out an eye or rupture a larynx. I was in the mood for rupturing a larynx.

I looked over at Putzi, across the alleyway. Like me, he was standing sideways to both groups of men. His legs were braced and his head was moving back and forth as he watched them come closer. If he was frightened, he didn't show it. He held his book up at waist level, his hands at either end of the lower part of the cover.

I was going to stab at them with an umbrella, and Putzi was going to smack at them with a book of art reproductions. The Charge of the Light Brigade.

Just then, behind the pair of men who'd emerged from the bar, the door opened away from the brick wall and Captain Roehm, short and squat and plump, stepped out into the alley. His round, shaved scalp was shiny in the light of the overhead bulb.

"*Halt!*" he growled.

Things happened fairly quickly. The two men closest to Roehm spun around and raised their truncheons and charged at him. Roehm's hand darted inside his suit coat and came out holding a Luger automatic. He fired it three times. The shots were explosively loud in the enclosed space of the alley.

One of the men, the big blond, doubled over and went cartwheeling, his shoulder smashing into the pavement, his watch cap flying off to the side. His legs swung through the air and crashed to the ground, nearly hitting Roehm. Roehm stepped casually away from them. The second man had lurched at the third shot, as though hit, and now he veered around Roehm and ran toward the other end of the alley. Roehm raised the pistol, took careful aim, and then lowered it without firing. The sound of running footsteps faded.

I looked back. The four men behind us were running too, and they were already back at Wilhelmstrasse.

When I turned back to Roehm, he was squatting down beside the blond man, feeling at his throat with his left hand. He still had the Luger in his right.

I looked at Putzi. "You okay?"

For a moment his face looked empty, but then he nodded and blinked and said, "Yes, yes. Absolutely fine."

I walked down the alley toward Roehm. Putzi followed me.

Roehm unbuttoned the man's coat, flipped it open to reveal a worn and baggy gray sweater, smeared with red along the stomach.

"He's dead?" I asked Roehm.

He ignored me, sliding his left hand into the coat's interior pocket.

I looked at Putzi. "Ask him."

He said something. Roehm answered.

"He says that the man's back-alley days are over," Putzi told me.

Roehm had found a wallet. He set the Luger on the dead man's chest and rifled through the wallet. He pulled out an identification card. "*Ah,*" he said. Holding the card in his left hand, he picked up the Luger with his right hand and stood up. He might have been overweight, but he moved from a squat to a standing position without a grunt.

Smiling his prim smile, he handed me the card.

I looked at it in the light from the overhead bulb. There was a photograph on it, but I couldn't read the writing. It was Russian.

Roehm looked down at the body and spat out some German.

"A filthy Red," Putzi translated.

The back door to the bar swung open. Roehm whipped around, bringing up the Luger.

It was Lieutenant Kalter and the big man in the red dress, who was holding a shotgun like someone who'd held a shotgun before. The double barrels rose toward Roehm.

Roehm put up his left hand and slipped the Luger back inside his coat. He and Kalter began talking earnestly to the man in the red dress.

I asked Putzi, "Can you read Russian?"

"A little," he said. "Better than I can speak it."

I handed him the card. I noticed that his hand was shaking. I noticed that mine was too. Fear had pumped both of us full of adrenaline, and it was still throbbing in our veins.

"It's a seaman's card," he said. "Issued to a Pyotr Semnovitch." He looked at me. "Pyotr is the Russian equivalent of Peter."

"Yeah." I looked down at the body. The man seemed smaller now, shrunken within his clothes, diminished by death.

I sighed. I'd seen enough of death and its diminishment in the War to last me for a long time.

Probably Roehm had saved my life, and Putzi's. Almost certainly he'd saved us from a brutal beating.

And yet a part of me couldn't stop thinking that a wooden truncheon didn't stand much of a chance against a nine-millimeter bullet.

I was being finicky. I hadn't liked Roehm. I hadn't liked his threats and his prim little smile. And I hadn't liked the way he had set the Luger on the dead man's chest, as though it were a convenient shelf, while he went through the man's wallet.

But the fact was that Putzi and I were still upright. Without Roehm and his pistol, we might not have been.

Roehm was handing over some folded banknotes to the man in the red dress. The man was nodding, the glossy black wings of his wig swaying slightly.

Roehm approached me. Behind him, the man in the red dress chatted with Lieutenant Kalter—about the weather, maybe. Now that he'd been paid off, the man acted as though nothing unusual had happened out in that alleyway tonight. And maybe it hadn't.

Roehm said something to me.

Putzi translated: "He says he saw those two leaving after we did and wondered what they were up to."

Roehm said something else.

Putzi said, "You and I should leave now, Phil, in case the police come."

I took the seaman's card from Putzi and offered it to Roehm.

He held up his hand, smiled the prim smile, and said, *"Nein."* He added something more.

"He wants you to keep it," said Putzi. "As a memento."

I tucked the card into the pocket of my raincoat.

"We should leave, Phil," said Putzi.

"Thank Captain Roehm for me," I said.

He did, and Roehm, still smiling, nodded his head and clicked together the heels of his shoes. Looking up, he said something more.

"Come along, Phil," said Putzi. "We can catch a taxi on Wilhelmstrasse."

I turned and we started back.

"What was the last thing he said?" I asked Putzi.

"The captain? He said, 'Anytime.' "

"Jesus," I said. "I hope not."

As PUTZI HAD said we would, we picked up a cab on Wilhelmstrasse.

Inside the darkness of the car, with the book and his homburg on his lap, Putzi sat silently for a while. Then he said, "You were going to ask me a favor, Phil." His voice was listless. "Before . . . before all that happened."

"Yeah. Roehm said that he's got people asking about the assassination attempt. See if you can get your friend Hess to pull them off. For a while, at least. The cops are asking questions, Miss Turner and I are asking questions, and now Roehm's people are asking questions."

"Too many cooks spoil the broth." His voice was still flat, drained of emotion. He was staring straight ahead.

"Yeah," I said.

He shook his head. "Captain Roehm is headstrong—as you saw. I'm not certain that Hess will be able to persuade him to stand aside."

"See if Hess can persuade Hitler to persuade him. I can't work this case if I keep bumping into other people."

"Yes." He was still staring straight ahead, and his voice was still empty. "Captain Roehm will listen to Herr Hitler."

I said, "You looked good in there, Putzi. You looked like you were going to demolish someone with that book of yours."

"Well, I had no choice, of course." He took in a deep breath, let it slowly out. He turned to me. "But to be honest with you, Phil, I was terrified. Those men gave me the heebie-jeebies."

"But you stood your ground, Putzi."

"I had no choice."

"Sure you did. You had a lot of choices."

"Running away? Begging for my life?"

"There were choices. You didn't take them."

He looked off, frowning. After a moment he said, "No, I didn't, did I?" He sounded mildly surprised.

"You did great."

A moment of silence, then he said, "Thank you, Phil. Thank you for saying so. But if Captain Roehm hadn't shown up, I fear that I wouldn't have done very well at all."

"Well, he did, and you did, and it's over now."

"Yes. Thank God. But now do you see why we must fight against these

Reds? Right here in the capital, nearly at the center of Berlin, they attack us! Where do they get such gall?"

"I'm more interested in where they got the information."

"Which information?"

"Who we were. Where we were. Putzi, who knows about me and Miss Turner?"

He thought about that for a moment. "Well, I should say, substantially the same people who knew about Herr Hitler's visit. The people on that list I gave to you."

"And they all knew we'd be staying at the Adlon?"

"Yes." He took another deep breath. "And so we are back to the list. Someone on the list must be a traitor."

"It's looking that way."

"Phil!" he said suddenly, his voice strained.

"What?"

"Miss Turner! Do you think she's in danger?"

I'd been wondering that. I said, "I hope not, Putzi."

BUT AT ELEVEN thirty, when we got back to the Adlon and checked at the desk, we learned that Miss Turner had returned safely, only a few minutes before.

I told Putzi that we wouldn't be needing him tomorrow morning, when Miss Turner and I would be talking to Sergeant Biberkopf. If Biberkopf didn't speak English, Miss Turner could translate.

"Yes, of course, Phil." He seemed disappointed.

I smiled. "Get some rest, Putzi. We'll meet you for lunch."

"Ah." The idea of lunch cheered him up. "Then may I suggest the Romanische Café? It's just opposite the Memorial Church. Any taxicab driver will know it."

is. Briefly: he's a psychic, a professional mind reader, one with a genuine gift, I believe, who's also tall and dark and Heathcliffian. Last night he volunteered to be my escort while I went off to a cabaret in search of an Englishwoman named Nancy Greene.

While we were in the taxi, and later, at the cabaret, he explained something of what's been happening in Germany since the War.

It's dreadful, Evy, this inflation. A simple loaf of bread costs what amounts, for most people, to a fortune. Families have been ruined, the parents compelled to sell everything they own in order to obtain food, and then compelled to beg on the streets, or to steal, or to sell drugs. The children, male and female both, are often compelled to sell themselves.

At this point Erik and I were in the Black Cat Cabaret, sitting alone at a small table near the stage.

'Here in Berlin,' he said, 'there is no form of sexual appetite, no matter how outré, that cannot be satisfied. There are areas of the city that specialize in old women, in pregnant women, in mother and daughter "teams". I do not exaggerate, Jane. There are areas, even, that specialize in deformed women—in cripples, hunchbacks, and amputees.'

Now, you may wonder whether this conversation wasn't perhaps a tad too explicit, in light of our having been introduced to each other, Erik and I, only an hour or so before.

All I can say, Evy, is that in Berlin, where a smilingly perverse sexuality shimmers like a grey mist over everything, the conversation seemed a perfectly normal one between two sophisticated adults. That one of the adults, behind her sophisticated mask, wore on her hidden face a pair of widened eyes and a startled mouth, should be irrelevant.

What disturbed me most, I confess, was the notion of children working as prostitutes. What will happen to these boys and girls when their most valuable asset, their youth, has been ground away? What is happening to them *now,* behind their seductive smiles and their shuttered eyes?

Hotel Adlon
Berlin
Wednesday morning
May 16th

Dear Evy,

I know that I wrote you a short letter last night, but this morning I simply cannot find it. What I think must have happened is that, last night, before I went to bed, I toddled out of the room and down the hall and slipped the letter into the brass mail chute that runs alongside the lift.

It's rather curious about that mail chute—I've walked directly past it on three or four occasions, but I never actually *saw* the thing until last night, when I was quite tiddly with champagne. Isn't it extraordinary how sometimes you can't see a thing that's right before your eyes?

I should tell you, Evy, that it's not only my perspective on mail chutes that has altered. I've been terribly naive, really so naive that I feel criminally stupid. Ever since I arrived in Germany I've been prattling on, in my featherbrained way, about the cost of things, how wonderfully inexpensive they all were. My cloche, my shoes, my Vamp-in-Training cocktail dress. I never once stopped to think that the same inflation which provided me these bargains would be having exactly the opposite effect on the people who, unlike myself and Mr Beaumont, have no access to American dollars or British pounds: the people who live here, the people who've watched helplessly as their life savings diminished, dwindled, and finally disappeared.

It was Erik, last night, who was explicit about the problems caused by the inflation.

Oh dear. Unless I did mail that letter, you won't know who Erik

I didn't mean to depress you. But in fact I find the situation terribly depressing.

I feel that Erik does as well. Behind *his* sophisticated mask there is, I suspect, a face taut with anger. I got a glimpse of it in the taxi when we returned to the Adlon last night. I had asked him whether there was any hope for Germany, for Berlin, for the children.

He looked at me. As the taxi drove past a streetlamp, the light slipped across his features, quickly, like the caress of an uncertain hand, afraid to linger. He has black hair and very dark brown eyes, 'Yes,' he said. 'I believe there is. Sometimes when I sleep I see a vision.'

'A vision?'

'Yes. Always the same.' He put his neck against the seat, his head slightly upraised, as though he were gazing up through the roof of the taxi. His profile was sharp against the lights of the street. 'I see a conflagration,' he said. As the light slipped over his face again, I saw that his eyes were closed.

'It burns throughout all of Germany. In the cities, I see proud buildings topple into ruin, great monuments collapse into choking dust. In the countryside, I see flames roaring through the farms, the fields, the forests. Black clouds billow up everywhere, thick and oily, to a sky strangled with smoke.'

His voice is a dense, rich baritone, Evy, and sometimes when he speaks I can actually feel its suave rumble along my spine.

'I don't quite understand,' I said, 'how such a vision could provide you with hope.'

Laughing, he turned toward me. I couldn't see his eyes just then, in the shifting shadows of the taxi's interior, but I could hear the smile in his voice. 'But my dear Jane,' he said. 'The vision is a dream, only. And, like all dreams, it is symbolic. What it represents is the drastic change that must come over this country, that *will* come over the country. You know the story in the Bible, of Jesus entering the Temple and sweeping away the money changers?'

'Yes,' I said.

'This,' he said, 'is exactly what Germany needs at the moment. Someone, some leader, who will come in and sweep away the avarice, the corruption, the despair that infect us today, like a rot. Someone who will sweep away the profiteers, the exploiters, the swindlers, the thieves.'

'But isn't it true,' I said, 'that things didn't go terribly well for Jesus after he swept away the money changers?'

He laughed again. 'Indeed. We Germans will need a leader who can plan beyond the temple.'

'And you believe that Herr Hitler is that leader?'

'Perhaps,' he said. We passed through the light of another streetlamp, and I saw that he was smiling. 'We shall see,' he said.

As I said, Evy, he's an extraordinary man. I do not entirely understand him. Perhaps I'll learn more tonight. He has asked me to dinner, and I've accepted. Subject, of course, to the demands of the case, and of Mr Beaumont.

With whom I shall now be having breakfast.

All my love,
Jane

CHAPTER TEN

"DID YOU SLEEP well?" I asked Miss Turner.

"I did, thank you. Very well."

We were in the other restaurant at the Adlon, the smaller one, at the southwest corner of the building, adjacent to the huge lobby. Miss Turner had just joined me. I had been early; she was a few minutes late. This morning she wore a fitted gray cotton jacket over a gray skirt, a white cotton blouse, and a black silk tie. Her silk stockings were white and her shoes were sensible. It was a very businesslike outfit, but only if you ignored what was inside it, the way I did.

Today, for the first time since we'd arrived in Germany, there was no rain. Outside the nearest window, sunlight washed across the Pariser Platz and down the massive flank of the Brandenburg Gate. The people in the streets, on the sidewalks, moved with a lightness they hadn't shown before.

"Do you want some coffee?" I asked her.

"I've already had some tea, thanks, in my room. I arranged for it last night." She smiled. "But I could manage to eat something." Adjusting her spectacles, she peered at my plate. "Ham and eggs?"

"Yeah."

"That sounds lovely."

I signaled for the waiter, and, when he arrived, Miss Turner gave him her order.

"So," I said as the waiter walked away, "how did it go last night?"

She shook her head. Her hair was loose this morning and it trembled at her shoulders. "Miss Greene never came to the cabaret."

"She works there, I thought."

"Yes, but according to the manager, she's not a terribly reliable employee."

"What does she do?"

"She sells cigarettes and works as barmaid while the other barmaid is eating supper. Sometimes she takes a part in the chorus."

"The chorus of what?"

"Oh," she said, waving her hand lightly, dismissively, "they have a sort of silly song and dance program."

"It doesn't sound like a job the manager would have a hard time filling. Why does he keep her on?"

"He's fond of her, I think. He calls her a 'scatterbrained Englishwoman,' but he says it with a smile."

"Putzi gave me her address and telephone number. We'll talk to her this afternoon."

She cocked her head. "Wouldn't it be better if we divided the responsibilities again? You and Mr. Hanfstaengl could speak with Miss Greene, while I speak with Dr. Hirschfeld at his Institute, to see if he can direct me toward Greta Nordstrum."

"The sister of Goering's aide." I'd forgotten about her. "The prostitute."

"Yes."

"That's the Institute of Sexology you're talking about," I said.

"Yes." She smiled. "Are you afraid that I shan't be able to conduct myself properly in an Institute of Sexology?"

"You'd probably do fine."

"So you agree?"

"I'm not sure."

"And why not?" she said.

I told her what had happened last night in the alley behind the Mikado. I edited it a bit, but not much. She had a right to know.

She listened without asking any questions. When I was finished, she said, "But you're all right? They didn't actually hurt you? Or Mr. Hanfstaengl?"

"They didn't get a chance. Like I said, Roehm showed up."

"Luckily for you. They could have killed you both."

"I don't think they wanted to do that. One guy with a gun could've killed us. I think they just wanted to rough us up a bit."

"But why? Who were they?"

I reached into the side pocket of my coat, pulled out the ID card that Roehm had given me. I handed it to her. "This belonged to the man Roehm shot."

She took it, frowned down at it. "It's in Russian."

"Yeah," I said. "It's a seaman's card."

"They were Communists? Bolsheviks?"

"Roehm thinks so."

She handed it back to me. "But how did they know you were there, at the Mikado?"

"Seems to me," I said, "there are three possibilities. One—Roehm told someone, and that person told someone else. Two—your friend von Dinesen told someone—"

"Why on earth should *he* tell anyone?"

"I didn't say he did. I said it was a possibility."

"He couldn't have done. He was with me the entire time."

"He's the one who gave Roehm's message to Putzi. He knew that Roehm would be waiting for us at the Mikado. He could've passed that information on to someone at the Wild West Bar."

"And why should he do that?"

"Like I said, I don't know that he did. I'm only saying that he could have."

She waved her hand again, quickly. "All right, yes. He *could* have. What's the third possibility?"

"They picked us up here, at the hotel, and they followed us."

She frowned. "There was someone following us last night?"

"It's one of the possibilities."

"And which possibility do you think the most likely?"

"I don't know. But from now on we start watching our backs. We take two or three cabs, switch from one to another, whenever we go anywhere. And I'm not sure that you should be going off on your own."

She sat back in her chair. "If I were a man, would you say the same thing?"

"I don't know," I said.

She stared at me, waiting for more.

"Probably not," I admitted.

Her eyes narrowed. "You didn't bring your pistol to the restaurant last night, you said."

"No." I smiled at her. "Right. You brought yours, didn't you?"

"Yes."

"A good thing for von Dinesen that he didn't get out of line."

She looked at me for a moment, and then she frowned. "Why do you dislike him so much?"

I was surprised. I thought we'd finished with von Dinesen. "I don't dislike him."

"But you don't trust him."

"No."

"You don't believe he's a psychic."

"I don't believe anyone is a psychic."

"How did he know so much about you? He knew about your brother; he knew about your war service. How did he know so much about me?"

"There are two possibilities."

"And they are?"

"One—he can read minds."

She shook her head impatiently. "You don't believe that."

"Two—he somehow got access to our personnel files in London."

"How on earth could he do that?"

"Maybe he got them from Caudwell."

"Caudwell? Why should Caudwell give him our personnel files?"

"Maybe he didn't give them to von Dinesen. Maybe he gave them to someone else, and that person gave them to von Dinesen."

"But why should Caudwell give *anyone* our personnel files?"

"I don't know."

"And if he had, why should von Dinesen reveal what he knew about us?"

"Putzi was hinting that von Dinesen should help us with the case. Maybe von Dinesen thought that if he looked like a genuine psychic, we'd want him on the team."

"And why should he *want* to be 'on the team'?"

"I don't know. To keep an eye on us, maybe."

"Well, if you don't know—"

"But I'm going to find out."

She sat back, crossed her arms beneath her breasts, and looked at me, up and down, as though measuring me for a suit. "What about—"

The waiter arrived and placed in front of her a plate of ham and eggs and a glass of orange juice. She thanked him. She kept her arms folded beneath her chest. As the waiter left, she said, "He's invited me to dinner tonight."

"Von Dinesen."

"Yes."

"And you accepted."

"Tentatively, yes. I asked him to telephone the front desk at seven. But I expect you'll think it's a terrible idea."

"I think it's fine idea. Maybe you'll be able to find out what he's up to."

She was picking up her glass. She set it down and put her hands flat on the tablecloth. She nodded, her lips pursed. "Well, yes. Obviously he's up to something, isn't he, or he wouldn't be asking me to dinner."

"That's not what I meant."

She looked abruptly down at her plate, and her hair swept along the sides of her face.

"Miss Turner," I said.

She looked up at me, her mouth tightly downturned.

"That's not what I meant," I said. "If von Dinesen did get information from our personnel files—and I'm sorry, but I think that's the only way he could've gotten it—then I'd like to know how he did it."

"Oh yes, if he's a fraud, I'm sure he'll be happy to tell me all about that."

"No, but maybe you can learn something."

"So you want me to go to dinner with him and act like . . ." She searched for the word. It couldn't have been a pleasant word, because her face was screwed up with distaste.

"A Pinkerton operative?" I said.

She looked at me for a moment, and then she looked away. She took a long, deep breath. She looked down at her plate and took another long, deep breath. When she looked back up at me again, there was a small wry smile on her lips.

"Sometimes," she said, "I can be a frightful idiot."

"I doubt it."

"That *is* what we're supposed to be doing here, isn't it?"

"Being frightful idiots?"

"No." She smiled. "Being a frightful idiot is merely one of my hobbies. Being Pinkerton operatives, I meant."

"Yeah."

Sitting back, she adjusted her spectacles and looked through them at me. "Doesn't it ever . . . well, doesn't it ever disturb you?"

"What?"

"The, um . . ."

"Deceit?"

She nodded.

"In this case," I said, "there's no deceit involved. He knows you're a Pinkerton."

"Yes, but don't you ever wish you could be with someone and not be . . . observing him? Observing him as a Pinkerton, I mean. Judging him."

"Sure. But when I'm on a job, I don't have any choice."

"Yes, but doesn't all that . . . wariness . . . doesn't it ever, well, make you feel somewhat depressed?"

"Somewhat," I said. "Sometimes."

"And what do you do?"

"I wait until the case is over, and then I take a vacation."

"A holiday, yes." She smiled. "I think that when we're finished with all this, I'd like to take a holiday."

"You're due for one. We'll see if we can arrange it. In the meantime, you've got other things to deal with."

"Sergeant Biberkopf, you mean."

"I meant your ham and eggs."

CHAPTER ELEVEN

PINKERTONS, HAH?" SAID Sergeant Biberkopf, grinning. "I thought they wore big white hats and carried big six-shooters." He raised his hand at arm's length and pointed his finger at me as though it were a six-shooter. "Bang bang," he said, his thumb waggling.

"Bang," I said.

He laughed, his big shoulders bouncing up and down. Somewhere in his thirties, he was as tall as I was but he was broader across the chest and stomach. His round face was red and fleshy, and his blond hair, so pale it looked white, was cut close to his skull. He wore a black woolen suit vest over a white shirt. His black tie was loosened at his open collar, and his sleeves were rolled back along beefy pink arms. He wasn't fat, really, but he looked like a man who wouldn't say no to a beer, under any circumstances. He was so jolly that I wondered if he hadn't said yes to one about ten minutes ago.

He turned to Miss Turner. "Do you ever wear a big white hat, fräulein?"

"Only at the beach," she said, and smiled.

"Or carry a six-shooter?"

"Almost never."

He laughed again, slapping his hand against the desk. "Almost never," he said. He liked that.

We were in the Criminal Police Division of the cavernous Central Police Station on Alexanderplatz. If the people at the nearby desks hadn't been talking German, it could have been a police station in any large city in the United States. It had the same low, utilitarian, claustrophobic ceilings. It had the same feel of slow, steady, unending toil. In the air it had the same stale smells of sweat and fear, and of the cheap cologne that was supposed to cover them up, but didn't.

Before we left the Adlon, I had sent a telegram in standard office code to Cooper in London. I had thought about putting through an international telephone call, but they usually took forever to set up.

Then, with Miss Turner using my Baedeker to navigate, the two of us had taken a taxi from the hotel, around the Reichstag and the Tiergarten, and across the river to the Lehrter train station. After fighting our way through the crowd at the main entrance, we slipped out a side entrance, grabbed another cab, and took it here. So far as I could tell, no one had followed us.

"About the case, Sergeant," I said.

He lifted a green folder from the side of his desk and slapped it down in front of him. He opened it. "This is the famous top-secret case, *ja?*" He picked up the sheets of paper inside. There weren't many of them. "Someone shoots someone with a rifle in the middle of the Tiergarten. In the middle of Berlin, *ja?* A big thing, this would be, normally. A lot of people running around, asking questions. Interrogations, *ja?* Investigations, *ja?* Newspaper stories, *ja?* But, no. I do one interview with this little . . ." He turned to Miss Turner. "You know *Schweinehund?*"

"Swine dog," she said. "A pig. A rotter."

"A rotter, *ja.* My English is terrible."

"It's very good," said Miss Turner. "Where did you learn it?"

"Some in secondary school. But my graduate work, you know, that I did that in Handforth, in Cheshire."

She seemed surprised. "Handforth? There's a university in Handforth?"

He smiled. "Your colleague there, he knows Handforth. I see it in his face."

He was good. I hadn't known that my face had changed. "It was a prison camp," I told Miss Turner. "For German prisoners of war."

"*Ja, ja,*" he said happily. "The Tommies get me at Verdun. The guards in Handforth, they are all English. My favorite is Alf, from Liverpool. We talk. He gives me books. You ever go to Liverpool, fräulein?"

"No. I'm very sorry that you had to—"

"Oh no no," he said, and grinned. "I am lucky. Some of the others in the company, some of my friends, not so lucky. Verdun is bad, very bad, but the camp is not so bad. And my English, it gets improved."

"It's really quite good," said Miss Turner.

He nodded, beaming. "Thank you."

I said, "Which rotter were you talking about, Sergeant?"

"*Ja,*" he said, "back to business. Good, good." He nodded, delighted to get back to business. "I'm talking about this little Hitler *Wiesel* from Munich. You say *weasel, ja?* And you know who the little weasel is meeting with, in the middle of the Tiergarten, in the middle of Berlin?"

"General von Seeckt," I said.

"Aha!" he said. "They like you, hah? The Nazis? They give you the general's top-secret name. Very good! Excellent!"

"They want me to investigate the sniping," I said. "They had to give me the name."

"Or course, of course. They hire the famous Pinkertons to do the job, naturally they give them the name. Me, I get the name because the copper on the spot, he thinks that maybe I should have it. He lets the general walk away before I come there, naturally, but he gives me the name."

"You talked to the general?"

"The general? Of course, of course! We have a wonderful talk, me and the general. Right in his own office. He wants to cooperate with the Berlin police authorities, naturally." He held up another sheet of paper. "You see? He cooperates for over fifteen minutes. A very generous man." He looked down at the paper, began to read from it. "Did he know who fired the shot? *Nein.* Did he have any idea who fired the shot? *Nein.* Did he have anything to add? *Nein.*" He looked at us, beaming. "It was a *wonderful* talk!"

"Did he say why he was meeting Hitler?"

"It was a big important matter of state, he said. Well, naturally I understand how a big important general like him, he can't talk about a big important matter of state with a little copper like me." Grinning again, he leaned toward me. "But everyone knows how the little weasel, he wants to make a putsch against the government. Like that fat Italian, the journalist in Rome. Mussolini. You know Mussolini?"

"Not personally."

"Not personally!" Laughing, he smacked the desk again. My wit amazed him. "Very good. And so, *ja,* everyone knows why the little weasel is there, to ask General von Seeckt if he can make a putsch. *Please, Papa, can I make a putsch?*" His jolly shoulders bounced.

"How does everyone know that?" I asked him. "About a putsch?"

"This is all they talk about in Munich. They don't like Weimar down there, none of them, so they want to make a putsch."

"You said you interviewed Hitler?"

"*Ja,* of course. I talked to the little weasel in his hotel. He had a theory." He leaned forward. "You want to hear it?"

"Very much."

"His theory, see, is the Reds are out to get him."

"Isn't that possible?"

"For sure it's possible. Here in Germany, we got lots of Reds killing people. Between 1919 and 1922, we got Reds, the left-wing bastards—" He turned to Miss Turner. "Sorry, fräulein. This is how I express myself, *ja?*"

She smiled. "I've heard the word before."

He turned back to me. "We got the Reds killing sixty, seventy people, maybe. But you want to hear an interesting thing?"

"What's that?" I said.

"Same time, between 1919 and 1922, we got the other side, the right-wing bastards, we got them killing over three hundred people. Two years ago they get Erzberger, a big important Catholic. Last year they get Walther Rathenau, a big important government person. The foreign minister. Shoot him right in the street." Smiling again, he shrugged. "Of course, *he* was only a Yid, so who cares, hah?"

Miss Turner said, "But it *could* have been the Communists who tried to kill Hitler."

"Oh, *ja,* sure." He grinned.

I said, "We have a list of the people who—"

"The famous list! I got it too! See?" He held up a slip of paper. "A *wonderful* list. Some of the people I talk to, here in Berlin. Hanfstaengl, Maurice, Sontag. This is afterward, at their hotel. They don't know nothing, naturally. And the other people we got on it, see, they're all in Munich. I send them messages, letters, I say, 'Please, sir, I want to talk to you about this happening in the Tiergarten, this happening with the rifle and Herr Hitler, could you please contact me?' And you know what I got from them?"

"Nothing?"

"Exactly right! Nothing. So I go to my superior, I say, 'Listen, what about I go down to Munich and talk to these other people? A friendly talk, a friendly conversation, just to get some answers to some little questions I got.' He says to me, he says, 'Forget it, Biberkopf. The army, they want us out of it,' he says. So what can I do?"

"Nothing."

He laughed. "Exactly!"

Miss Turner said, "What about the rifle?"

"Oh, *ja, ja.* We got a nice rifle, a very nice Mauser rifle, from the Tiergarten. We find it by the side of the canal, very lucky for us. You know about the Landwehr Canal?" he asked her.

"We've seen it," she said.

"Did you recover the slug?" I asked him.

He frowned. "The what?"

Miss Turner said, *"Die Kugel."*

"Ah, the bullet. *Ja, ja,* we got a nice bullet also. But, see, it gets damaged. It hits the ground, it goes *splat,* it gets damaged, it's no good for us."

"You can't match it to the rifle," I said.

"Exactly correct!" He grinned as though nothing could have made him happier. "We can't match it to the rifle no way."

"But the slug," I said, "the bullet, definitely came from a Mauser."

"Oh, *ja,* from a Mauser, definitely."

"The rifle you found was a standard infantry Mauser?"

"Ja, ja. Standard Mauser. Model 1898." He was still smiling, but I thought that his eyes had narrowed slightly.

"Isn't there a shorter version of the rifle? A carbine?"

The eyes widened in surprise. "A shorter version?" He smiled widely. "Well, naturally, you Pinkerton people, you know more about rifles than we do, hah?"

I turned to Miss Turner. "What's the German word for *shit*?"

Before she could say anything, Sergeant Biberkopf gave me the answer himself: *"Scheisse."* He grinned. *"Shit,* this was one of Alf's favorite words. This is shit, that is shit. Everything is shit. Sometimes, you know, on some days, I totally agree with him." He laughed.

"Okay, Sergeant," I said. "Can we stop all the shit?"

CHAPTER TWELVE

B IBERKOPF LAUGHED AGAIN. "What shit are we stopping?"

"Sergeant, I can understand why you're frustrated. You're a police-man and everyone, including your superior, is making it impossible for you to do your job."

He was still smiling. "*Ja?* And?"

"And I think you should start wondering how all of us can help each other."

"We can help each other, you think?" he said.

"Miss Turner and I are going to Munich. We'll be talking to the people on that list."

"*Ja?*"

"When I'm done, I'll send you a copy of the report."

He nodded. "That's good. That's a good thing. So maybe you get to be lucky, and maybe you get to know who pulled the famous trigger. And so you tell your friends the Nazis, and the next day we find another dead body in the Landwehr Canal. *Ja,* that's excellent. That's top-notch. Now, because I got your report, I know why the dead body is dead." He grinned happily.

"If I find out who pulled the trigger, I can wait for a while before telling the people in the party."

"*Ja?* Wait until when, exactly?"

"Until I tell you."

He nodded. "This is an idea the Nazis will love."

"The Nazis won't know about it."

He grinned. "So. You want to . . ." He turned to Miss Turner. *"Betrü-gen?"*

"Betray," she said. "Cheat."

"You want to cheat the Nazis." He shook his head. "Not so clever, I think. They won't like this." He winked at me. "But maybe you want to cheat me too, hah? Maybe just a little bit?"

"It wouldn't make sense for a Pinkerton to cheat a policeman. We operate all over the world, and we need local cooperation. A policeman in Spain tells a policeman in France that we lied to him, and it gets harder for us to operate."

He nodded again and sat back and put his hefty arms along the arms of the chair. "*Ja. Ja,* okay. Maybe this is true. So let's hear it. I know how you help me—you give me your famous report. Let's hear how I help you, exactly."

"The Mauser you found. Had it been fired?"

"Oh, *ja,* definitely."

"But probably not at Hitler."

He grinned. "You know what we think? We think the man who shoots at Hitler, the sniper, he gets someone else to fire that rifle, someplace safe, and take it to the canal later. When the sniper is ready, some person, maybe two persons, they carry the Mauser inside a rug, maybe, and they let it fall down to the canal. To the side there, so we can find it, *ja?* This they do when no one's looking. We think the man who shoots, he's on the other side of the canal. He hides in the trees near the Zoological Garden. And you know what he uses, we think?"

"A Mauser carbine."

"Exactly, *ja*! The famous Mauser carbine."

"You never found the weapon. He hid it under his coat and walked away while everyone was busy with the other rifle."

"A good plan, hah?"

"Not bad," I said. "He didn't care whether you could match the bullet to the rifle. By then he was long gone."

"Exactly right."

"But why did he fire only once?"

Biberkopf shrugged his big shoulders. "He's afraid, maybe. If he stays too long, then maybe he gets caught."

I nodded. "If it happened the way you say, we're talking about at least two men."

"Oh, *ja.*" He grinned. "Two or three."

"Do you know a man named von Dinesen?" I asked him. "Erik von Dinesen?"

"*Ja,* for sure, the famous magician. You know him?"

"We've met him," I said.

"So maybe you know he wants to hold the famous rifle in his famous magical hands. He does some hocus-pocus, some abracadabra, and he tells us who fired it."

"But it's not the right rifle."

"It's not the right rifle, correct. One of my superiors, he tells me maybe it's good if von Dinesen does his hocus-pocus. Maybe we learn the name of the people who help the sniper. He believes this hocus-pocus shit." He shrugged. "Maybe I let him do it." He grinned. "A good idea, you think?"

"Swell."

He grinned. "*Ja, ja.* Maybe he comes up with something."

"I heard that he helped the police in Hamburg."

"Hamburg, *ja.* The police in Hamburg, they need all the help they can get."

Miss Turner said, "What if he tells you that this rifle wasn't the rifle used by the sniper?"

"Then," he said, and smiled, "I take a look at where Herr von Dinesen is, the day of the famous attack."

She nodded, her lips pursed together.

"You're sure," I said, "that Hitler was the target?"

"Oh, *ja,* totally. They shoot General von Seeckt, they get everyone in the army and everyone in the *Freikorps*—you know the *Freikorps*?"

"Yeah."

"They get everyone in Germany—everyone with a gun, *ja*?—looking for Reds to kill. They get a civil war. But they shoot the little weasel instead, then maybe some Nazis down in Munich get angry. Not so big a thing, hah? Outside of Munich, outside of Bavaria, the little weasel is a nobody."

"You think it was the Reds," I said.

"Maybe the Reds, sure." Smiling, he shrugged again. "Or maybe some right-wing bastard who wants to make us think it was the Reds." He turned to Miss Turner. "Sorry, fräulein."

She smiled.

"If it was the Reds," I asked him, "how'd they find out that Hitler would be in the Tiergarten?"

"We got no idea at all." He grinned. "It's a good thing we got you helping us out, hah?"

"And if it was the Reds, you've got no idea which of them might have been involved."

"Totally none," he said cheerfully. He clasped his hands together on the desk and leaned toward me. "So when you are going to Munich?"

"In a day or two."

He grinned again. "Just so you know something. Munich is crazy, okay? Most of the right-wing bastards, they're in Munich. You know Captain Ehrhardt?"

"No."

"A captain in the navy. After the war, he makes up a *Freikorps* group, the Ehrhardt Brigade. Excellent soldiers. Very tough. And very patriotic, of course, *ja*? For a while he goes all around the country with his men, killing Reds. Killing Reds is a very patriotic thing. In 1918, they're in Kiel, killing Reds. In 1919, they're in Munich, killing more Reds. Now he is back in Munich. He has a top-secret group, the Organization Consul. You know what they do?"

"Kill Reds?"

He laughed. "Exactly! And not Reds only. They kill everybody they don't like. They got *Mordkommando,* death squads, called *Feme*."

"The Munich police can't stop them?"

He leaned forward, grinning. "The Munich police? Listen to this, this is good, this is a true story. Someone comes to Pohner, he's the Munich chief of police then, and he says to him, 'Chief Pohner, is it true we got political assassins in Munich?' And Pohner, he says, '*Ja,* but not enough of them.'" Laughing, Biberkopf slapped his hand against the desk.

Miss Turner said, "Sergeant, what's the connection between the Nazi Party and Mr. Ehrhardt's group?"

Another big shrug. "They're all right-wing bastards. The weasel, probably he doesn't like Ehrhardt, probably he thinks Ehrhardt got too much power in Munich. The weasel, he likes to be in charge. But they all want the same thing. Kill all the Reds. Get rid of Weimar. Get rid of the Jews."

She frowned. "Why the Jews?"

He grinned. "The Jews, they want to take over the world. You didn't know that? It's all in print, in the famous book about the Elders of Zion. *The Protocols.*"

"I've read about that book," said Miss Turner. "It's a forgery."

"Sure it's a forgery," he said happily. "The Russian secret police, they make it up years ago. But who cares? It says what they want. The Nazis. Ehrhardt and his friends."

"How important, Sergeant," said Miss Turner, "is Mr. Hitler in Munich?"

"He's the big important head of the Nazi Party, and the Nazi Party is the big important right-wing party in Bavaria. Most of the *Freikorps* people, they are in the party now."

"Mightn't he have rivals, then? Mightn't there be people on the right who resent his importance?"

He grinned. "Sure. And like I say before, maybe one of them makes a plan to shoot him in the Tiergarten. And have everyone think it's the Reds, hah?" He nodded. "But I hope, fräulein, for you and Herr Beaumont, that it don't happen this way."

"Why?"

"You're in Munich in a few days, *ja?* If the Reds do this thing, this sniping, you got no problem in Munich. Why is that?" He grinned. "Because the Reds in Munich, they're mostly dead now, *ja?* But if it's right-wing bastard, you got a lot of choices. You got a lot of right-wing bastards in Munich. And if it's a right-wing bastard, he's not very happy about you and your questions, you understand?"

CHAPTER THIRTEEN

"Y OU NEVER TOLD him about the attack on you and Mr. Hanfstaengl last night," said Miss Turner.

"I didn't want to confuse him," I said.

It was nearly eleven o'clock and already we'd taken two taxicabs since we'd left the Alexanderplatz police station, switching from one to another at the Central Post Office. At the moment we were on König Strasse, a busy street lined with elm trees. The sun was shining and the sky was so blue that it was almost impossible to believe that it had ever been anything else. Almost.

After all the rain, the bright green of the trees seemed festive and buoyant. But the buildings beyond the trees weren't especially festive— like the post office, they were heavy and squat, all of them built of dark brick or dark stone, elaborate hulking municipal buildings that had been put up to show the municipality how important and somber it was. They looked like wedding cakes made of lead.

"Confuse him in what way?" she said.

I glanced at the cabdriver. Maybe I was getting as nervous about cabdrivers as Putzi. But the man was behind a sheet of glass—even if he spoke English, he couldn't have heard us.

"Confuse his loyalties," I said. "Someone got killed at the Mikado last night. If Biberkopf knew that I was involved, he'd have to do something about it."

"But you told him you'd cooperate with him."

"I can't cooperate with him if I'm in jail."

"It wasn't you who shot the man."

"He doesn't know that."

She nodded. "All right. But why didn't you tell him about Nancy Greene and Greta Nordstrum?"

"Because I want to talk to them before he does."

"You don't trust him?"

"I trust him to be a good cop."

"How so?"

"Biberkopf's stuck," I said. "He knows that he can't get anything out of those people in Munich. He knows that we might get something, and he wants whatever we can give him. But he's a cop, and as far as he's concerned, we're just civilians. So he doesn't want to give us anything back. All we really got from him today was the fact that the rifle they found, the Mauser, probably wasn't the rifle that fired the shot."

"Not only that. He did tell us that more than one person might have been involved in the shooting. And he did give us quite a lot of background information."

I nodded. "That's all useful, maybe. But in exchange, he got me to agree that we'd give him whatever we learned from the people in Munich. And, more important, that we'd give him the name of the sniper, if we find it, before we give it to the Nazi Party."

"You were serious about giving him the name?"

"Yeah. Roehm told me last night that when he gets the name of the sniper, the sniper is dead. I told him that I'd give the name to Hitler. But there's a good chance that giving it to Hitler is basically the same thing as giving it to Roehm. I'd rather cheat a little and give the name to Biberkopf first. That way, there's at least a possibility the guy will get a fair trial."

"So you wanted, all along, to make that agreement with Biberkopf. To promise him the name."

"Not all along. Only since I talked to Roehm."

She smiled. "Isn't that a tad Machiavellian? Letting the sergeant believe that he's persuaded you to do something, when in fact you'd already decided to do it?"

"I like to think of it as diplomatic."

Canting her head slightly, she said, "But it was, in fact, the party who hired us. Sergeant Biberkopf is right. You'll be betraying them."

"I'm exercising my judgment, the way I'm supposed to."

She smiled again. "Well, I think that your judgment, in this instance, is admirable."

I shook my head. "Common sense. I told Biberkopf the truth. If the cops, anywhere in the world, think that we'll hand over someone for execution, they're not going to give us much help with anything."

"But if you're willing to give the sergeant that name, why aren't you willing to give him the names of the women?"

"If he talks to them before we do, and either one of them has anything useful, he's probably not going to give it to us. And he may decide to put them out of the way, somewhere we can't get to them."

She nodded, smiling once more. "So it's really a sort of game, isn't it? Neither one of you is actually cooperating with the other, in the truest sense of the word."

"In the truest sense of the word," I said, "no."

AFTER WE PASSED through the Tiergarten again, Charlottenburger Chaussee became Berliner Strasse, and that soon became Bismarck Strasse. The address Putzi had given me for Nancy Greene's boardinghouse was a stately brick building that had obviously once been a single residence. It was set back on a narrow swatch of green lawn on a small side street off Bismarck Strasse. A couple of tall old oak trees draped their shade over the roof and across the grass.

Miss Turner and I walked up the flagstone walkway and up the steps. I tugged at the bellpull. I didn't hear the bell ring, but after a moment the door was opened by a short middle-aged man in a fastidious gray three-piece suit. *"Bitte?"* he said. He had a smooth round face and pale blue eyes and he wore an expensive gray wig. You could tell it was expensive because you kept glancing at it until you realized why. A cheap wig took only one glance to spot.

Miss Turner began to speak in German, but he interrupted her. He said, "You're English!" From his accent, he was obviously English himself. "How nice!" He looked back and forth between us. "But if you're looking for a room, I'm afraid that Frau Schroeder is quite full up just now."

I said, "We're looking for Miss Greene."

"Ah." He smiled. It was a small smile, as fastidious as his suit. "Sometimes it seems that all of Berlin is looking for Miss Greene."

"Has someone been asking about her?" I asked him. "Recently?"

"Oh no," he said. "I simply meant that Miss Greene is a very popular young girl." He smiled again. "Not that her popularity, or lack of it, is any business of mine, of course."

"Is she in?" I said.

"Well, now I *am* going to disappoint you," he said, "because I know for a fact that she isn't. Frau Schroeder was telling me just this morning that she hadn't seen Miss Greene for two whole days. Miss Greene is apparently off on . . . an adventure again. Frau Schroeder's a bit scandalized by this, of course, or so pretends." Smiling, he leaned slightly forward, conspiratorial. "Secretly, I think, she takes a certain amount of pleasure in Miss Greene's adventures." He stood back, smiling. "Of course, Miss Greene's adventures aren't really any business of mine, are they?"

"Is Frau Schroeder in?"

"Ah, well. Once again, I'm the bearer of bad news. Frau Schroeder has gone to the market. She's only just left, not ten minutes ago, so I expect she won't be back for another hour."

I pulled out my pocket watch. Eleven twenty. We were supposed to meet Putzi at twelve.

"Can I help you with anything?" he asked me.

"Do you know where Miss Greene might be?"

"I'm afraid not. I scarcely know the girl."

I put away the watch and reached into my suit coat for my wallet. I took out a business card that had only my name on it, and a London address. "My name is Beaumont," I told the man. "Phil Beaumont. Could you give this to Frau Schroeder, Mr. . . . ?"

"Norris," he said, taking the card, "Arthur Norris. Very pleased to meet you." He turned to Miss Turner, his eyebrows raised expectantly.

"Jane Turner," she said, and smiled.

"A great pleasure." He turned back to me. "I've an appointment and I'll be going out myself in another hour. But I'll leave the card for Frau Schroeder, with a note. Is there anything else I ought tell her?"

"You can tell her I'll be back here at one thirty."

"Yes," he said. "I'll do that."

THE ROMANISCHE CAFÉ was at the end of Kurfürstendamm, across from a big church with a soaring dark spire. We arrived at the restaurant at ten minutes to twelve, and Putzi showed up exactly ten minutes later, moving through the tables toward ours, bobbing his big head at people he knew.

It was a massive place, the café, and it probably held a thousand people. The main floor, where we sat, was filled with the buzz of chatter and the smell of coffee and cigar smoke. Nearly all the tables, large and small, were occupied. Poets and artists scratched away at notebooks. Young couples leaned toward each other and breathed from the same cubic foot of air. Old couples nibbled at tea cakes. Matrons eyed each other's finery. Waiters in white coats swooped around the room like swallows in a barn.

Before we ordered lunch, Putzi told me that he'd arranged a meeting this evening, at six, with General von Seeckt. I said I was looking forward to it.

Everyone in Berlin seemed to know Putzi, and a lot of them stopped by to say hello while we ate. A small, stylish count who was—Putzi told us, after the count left—a Red but "very classy." An intense young artist named Grosz who was—said Putzi—another Red but "as sharp as a tack." A sleek young Russian émigré who taught tennis and wrote short stories. He wasn't a Red, Putzi said. His father had been shot by the Reds last year, while the young man was studying at Cambridge.

When we weren't saying hello to Putzi's friends and acquaintances, we were deciding what to do next. I wanted to talk to Frau Schroeder, to see if she could lead us to Nancy Greene. Miss Turner wanted to talk to Dr. Hirschfeld at the sex institute, to see if he could lead us to Greta Nordstrum. It was broad daylight and I didn't think that anyone would be shooting at Miss Turner in a sex institute, so she got her way. We agreed to meet back at the Adlon by five thirty. If either of us got delayed, we would telephone the hotel and leave a message for the other at the front desk. I gave her the slip of paper Putzi had given me yesterday, with Nordstrum's description on it.

After we finished eating, we all walked out through the big revolving door into the rumble of traffic on the Kurfürstendamm. Miss Turner got into a taxi and set out for the institute. Putzi and I got into another.

"MY ENGLISH," SAID Frau Schroeder, "is not so good."

"My German," I told her, "doesn't exist. But Mr. Hanfstaengl will translate for us, if that's all right with you."

"*Ja,*" she said, nodding. "*Sehr gut.*"

We were sitting in her parlor. In the air, beyond the faint smell of cabbage, was the fainter smell of must. The fading purple fabric of the velvet chairs and the long velvet sofa was protected, along the arms and backs, with antimacassars of yellowing lace. Hanging along the pink floral wallpaper were small, framed paintings dark with age. There were two substantial mahogany bookcases, fronted with glass, that held portly, old-looking leather books. There was a mahogany display case, also fronted with glass, that held small porcelain figurines and delicately painted porcelain plates. On the floor was a Persian carpet, a bit threadbare in spots.

It was a room that someone had spent a lot of money on, but not recently. In the thin light that drifted between the lace curtains, it looked like a display in a museum, everything brightly polished, spotlessly clean, but all of it heavy and dated and stiff.

Putzi and I sat on the sofa, behind a long dark mahogany coffee table. Frau Schroeder sat in one of the chairs. Wearing a gray cotton dress, she was a short, heavyset woman in her late fifties or early sixties.

She seemed concerned. She said something and Putzi translated it—
"You said that you're an investigator, Mr. Beaumont. Miss Greene isn't in
any trouble, is she?"

"No, no," I told her. "But she may be able to help me with an investigation. Do you have any idea where she might be?"

"None at all. Are you sure I can't get you some tea? Or a beer? I have
some beer in the icebox. Sometimes, you know, before I go to sleep, I like
to have a little glass of beer while I read."

As Putzi translated this, his big bushy eyebrows were raised hopefully.

The eyebrows sank when I said, "No, thank you, Frau Schroeder.
How long has it been since you've seen Miss Greene?"

"Two days. Monday afternoon. She was going out to work. She's a performer, you know. A singer."

"She didn't come back that night?"

"She may have. I go to bed at ten o'clock, usually, and she doesn't
come home until quite late. But if she did come back that night, she must
have left early the next morning, before I got up. Tuesday morning, I
mean. I never saw her. And when she didn't come down for coffee at
lunchtime, I knew she wasn't here." She smiled. "Miss Greene doesn't
come down for breakfast, ever. She works so late, you see. But she always
comes down for coffee at lunchtime. She says I make the best coffee in
Berlin." She smiled again, pleased.

"She has her own key to the front door?"

"Yes, of course."

"Does she ever bring people here?"

She blinked and put her hand to her breast. "To her room, you mean?
Men?"

"Yes."

"Never! Miss Greene, she is adventurous, perhaps, but only because
she's so young and so full of energy. Life is always an adventure when
you're young, isn't it? But she's a very good girl. She would *never* bring a
man to her room. And she has brought only one of them to the house, for
me to meet."

"And who was that?"

"The young man from Munich. Herr Sontag."

"Gunnar Sontag?"

"Yes, that's right. A very nice young man. A gentleman."

"When was he here last?"

"Last week."

"Around the eighth?"

She thought again. "Yes, on the eighth exactly. On Tuesday. He came here Tuesday morning, and he and Miss Greene went out for the day."

"When did she get back?"

"Around six. And then she changed and went to work."

"Has anyone come to see her since?"

"No. No one."

"Has she received any telephone calls recently?"

"Herr Sontag telephoned."

"When?"

"This past Sunday. In the afternoon."

"Do you know what they talked about?"

Her face stiffened. "Mr. Beaumont, you understand that I never listen to my lodgers' telephone conversations."

"No, of course not. I thought that maybe Miss Greene had said something to you about it."

Mollified, but not by much, she shook her head. "No. She didn't."

"Did Mr. Sontag call her often?"

"Not often, no. Usually only when he was coming to Berlin. And then again, when he got back to Munich, to let her know he had arrived safely. He called last Thursday, to tell her he was back."

"But that call on Sunday was the only call she got this week?"

"Someone called yesterday, but Miss Greene wasn't here. He didn't leave his name."

That had been Putzi.

"Frau Schroeder," I said, "has Miss Greene ever disappeared like this before?"

She frowned, probably at the idea of Miss Greene disappearing.

"Once, but only for a day. For a night, I mean. She told me that she'd spent the night at a girlfriend's apartment."

"Do you think that's true?"

"I have no way of knowing, do I?" Maybe she heard the brittleness in her voice. She added more softly, "But really, Mr. Beaumont, she's a good girl. She's lively and independent, yes, but she's really very sweet."

"When was this? The night she didn't come back?"

"Two months ago. In March."

"Do you recall when in March?"

She frowned, trying to remember. "The middle of the month. The fifteenth? Yes. My husband's birthday, rest his soul, was on the fourteenth. And it was the next day."

"Did Gunnar Sontag telephone her around that time?"

"No." She shook her head. "She's not like that, Mr. Beaumont. She wouldn't have spent the night with him."

"Okay. Do you know the names of any of her friends?"

"Not really. But Mr. Norris might know. Another lodger of mine. You met him. The Englishman. He sometimes has tea with Miss Greene, at the Englisches Café." She smiled. "The English, they can't live without their tea, can they?"

When Miss Turner and I had spoken with him, Norris had told us that he scarcely knew the girl.

I said, "What was Miss Greene wearing when you saw her on Monday?"

"She always dresses very well, you know. She doesn't have much money, but she has wonderful taste."

"And on Monday?"

"Yes. Her black silk dress. And silk stockings. She always wore silk stockings when she went to work. And nice black shoes, very delicate. And a little black cape, also silk. And a hat, a cloche, small but very pretty. Very chic."

"Okay. Thank you. Frau Schroeder, would it be possible for me to take a look at Miss Greene's room?"

She blinked in surprise. "Oh no, I'm sorry, but I just couldn't allow that. Miss Greene is a very private person, you know. Very private. And I respect her privacy. She keeps her room locked and I never go inside when she's not there. Except once a week, on Friday nights, to change the sheets."

"All right," I said. "I understand. Do you know where I can find Mr. Norris?"

"He told me this morning that he had a business meeting this afternoon. But he should be here tonight. He's usually here for dinner. At seven."

"What business is he in, do you know?"

"He imports things. And exports them."

"Do you know what things?"

"No, not really. I do try not to pry into my lodgers' lives."

"Good for you." But not good for me. I stood up. "All right, Frau Schroeder. Thank you very much."

She was watching, in some awe, as Putzi raised himself to his full height.

"I'm staying at the Adlon hotel," I said. "When Miss Greene comes back, could you ask her to call me there? You can tell her that I'll make it worth her while."

"I'll tell her," she said.

As she was walking us to the front door, down a long dark hallway, she murmured something else to Putzi in German. He grunted.

"What did she say?" I asked him.

"Pardon? Oh, sorry. She says she hopes that the girl comes back soon. Some animal, probably a mouse, has died in Miss Greene's room and the smell is getting worse. She wants the girl to get rid of it. Mice give Frau Schroeder the willies."

I stopped walking. "Putzi," I said. "Tell her to go check Miss Greene's room. Right now. We'll wait here."

He frowned. "But—" His bushy eyebrows rose. He opened his mouth and then closed it. "No. You don't—"

"Just tell her, Putzi. Please."

He spoke to her in German. She answered, looking back and forth between Putzi and me, the confusion on her face slowly turning into alarm. Putzi was firm with her, and finally she reached into the pocket of her dress and pulled out a large ring of keys. They jingled as she turned and walked toward the stairway.

She looked back at us briefly, uncertain, her lower lip caught between her teeth, and then she started climbing the stairs. Her small feet made muffled thumping sounds on the stairway's runner of carpet.

"Phil," said Putzi. "You don't think—"

"I don't know. We'll find out in a minute."

He looked up, toward the ceiling. We waited.

The house was solid and well built. The thick walls blocked the sound of the traffic that moved along the street outside.

But the scream from upstairs, when it came, was unmistakable.

CHAPTER FOURTEEN

I RAN UP the stairs, taking them three at a time. Behind me, I could hear Putzi's big feet banging at the runner. At the top, I wheeled around the banister and sprinted down the landing. Five doors, two of them open. Opposite one of the open doors stood Frau Schroeder, her back slumped against the wall. She looked as if some force had hurled her through the air and slammed her there. Her head was lowered and her hands were covering her face.

I ran past her, into the room and the smell of death it held.

It was a large room. There was a red chenille sofa, a small writing desk and chair, a plush black armchair and ottoman. A wardrobe, painted pink. Heavy red curtains, opened, at the tall window.

The bed was set against the far wall. Nancy Greene was lying on it, above the covers.

She was wearing part of the outfit that Frau Schroeder had described. A sleeveless black silk dress and silk stockings. No shoes, no hat, no cape. Except for the faint bluish cast to her skin, she might have been sleeping. Her eyes were shut and her thin attractive face was slightly flattened, the flesh slack against the bone beneath. Her short brown hair was fanned back from her cheeks onto the bolster. Her hands were lying, one atop the other, between her small breasts. I noticed that her fingernails had been painted with emerald green polish. Her toenails, beneath the sheer silk, were the same color. There were some small bruises at her throat.

"My God!" It was Putzi. Ducking his head below the top of the door-jamb, he came into the room and stopped. "Is she—" He swallowed, and then he coughed.

"Very." I lifted her left wrist. It was limp—rigor mortis had come and gone. I dropped the wrist, but the chill of her skin lingered on my fingertips. "Probably since Monday night." I wiped my hand against my pants.

I hadn't known Nancy Greene, but when I looked down at the body on the bed, I felt a sense of loss, as oppressive and personal as if I had.

It was that silly nail polish of hers. The bright green fingernails—a young girl's choice, probably a playful pun on her last name—made her distinct, individual, a specific human being, gone forever now.

"Phil," Putzi said. "We should leave. We should scram before the police come."

I turned to him. "Forget it, Putzi. Frau Schroeder knows who I am. She knows where I'm staying."

He glanced back at the door, as though he were thinking of running into the hallway and rubbing out Frau Schroeder. He turned back to me, his big shoulders sagging hopelessly.

"We telephone Biberkopf," I said.

SERGEANT BIBERKOPF WASN'T smiling now. "You have this girl's name," he said, "when you talk to me this morning, *ja*? And you don't give it to me."

I said, "She's been dead since Monday night or Tuesday morning. Even if I'd given you the name this morning, she'd still be dead."

Putzi and I were sitting on the sofa again. Biberkopf, wearing his suit coat now, was sitting in the chair that Frau Schroeder had used. Frau Schroeder herself, her eyes red, her cheeks shiny with tears, had gone to lie down in her bedroom, at the back of the house.

Biberkopf said to me, "Tell me again how you get this girl's name."

"I already told you once."

He nodded. "So now you tell me two times."

"One of the names on that list," I said, "the list of people who knew that Hitler would be in the Tiergarten, was Gunnar Sontag."

"*Ja, ja.* I talk to him, after the shooting in the Tiergarten. The young man."

"Mr. Hanfstaengl found out that Miss Greene was a friend of his."

"Sontag," said Biberkopf, "he never tells me about no Miss Greene."

"Maybe it slipped his mind."

"He sees her when he's in Berlin?"

"That Tuesday," I said, "according to Frau Schroeder."

He looked at Putzi. "He tells me he's with Maurice, the chauffeur. Maurice says the same."

Putzi shrugged. He started to speak in German, but Biberkopf held up his hand. "English, please. We are international here, *ja?*"

"I had no idea where he'd been," Putzi said. "I was with Herr Hitler all day."

"And who gives you the name of the girl?"

"Rudolf Hess. In Munich."

"Herr Hess is the private secretary to Herr Hitler?"

"Yes."

"This girl. This Nancy Greene. She is in the party?"

"No," said Putzi. "She was just someone Gunnar knew. A friend."

"A girlfriend, hah? A sweetheart?"

"Yes."

"He lives in Munich and he has a sweetheart in Berlin?"

"He met her in Munich, I understand," said Putzi. "When she moved to Berlin, they kept in touch. He saw her whenever he came here."

"So he sees her when he's here with Herr Hitler. A week ago?"

"Yes."

"And this week? Today? He is where?"

"He's in Munich."

"*Ja?* You're right now in Berlin, and you know who's in Munich?"

"When I spoke to Herr Hess yesterday, he mentioned that Gunnar was there, in Munich."

"And Herr Hess, he always tells the truth?"

"Why would he lie?"

Biberkopf shrugged his big shoulders. "Who knows?" He turned back to me. "And so. Mr. Pinkerton. You have time to look around this Nancy Greene's room. To investigate, *ja?*"

"I took a quick look," I admitted.

"And you put your fingerprints everywhere?"

"I was careful not to."

He nodded. "And you think *what* happens in there, on Monday night?"

"There's an indentation on the back of her head. And bruises on her neck."

He turned to Putzi. "Indentation. *Vertiefung?*"

Putzi nodded.

I said, "I think he knocked her out first, and then he strangled her."

He nodded, his pink face sour. "An indentation on her head. You take a quick look only. *Ja,* I see."

"It wasn't something I enjoyed."

"Ja." He nodded. *"Ja.* So tell me. Why is he knocking her out first?"

"Maybe he didn't want her to fight while he strangled her. Or maybe he didn't want her to know she was dying."

"Ja, he's totally full of respect for the girl."

"He arranged the body on that bed. He put her hands together on her chest."

"So maybe he wants me to think he's full of respect."

"Maybe. But I think they knew each other. I think she brought him here."

"Ja? Why?"

"Her shoes were under the bed. Her cape was hanging in the wardrobe. Whoever killed her, I doubt that he bothered to put away her things."

"Frau Schroeder, she says the door is locked."

"Yeah. And Miss Greene's key is on the nightstand, by the bed. So whoever killed her has another key."

"If he got a key, he don't need to come in with her."

"Maybe not. But if he came in after she did, she knew he was coming. There are no signs of a struggle in the room."

"He comes in *before* she comes, he waits for her. When she comes, he hits her. Then he strangles her, like you say."

"Maybe. But why? What's his motive?"

"Maybe he's crazy. Maybe he don't need no motive."

"Okay, but why her? And how would he know when it would be safe to come into the house and sneak up the stairs? And why would he bother to take her cape off afterward and hang it up? And there was money in her purse, and jewelry in her dresser. None of it was taken."

"Maybe he wants to fool the stupid police."

"Why go to the trouble? She's dead. All he really needs to do is get out of there."

"Frau Schroeder thinks she don't bring no men to her room."

"Frau Schroeder thought that the smell in there was a dead mouse."

"*Ja?* So?"

"Frau Schroeder doesn't seem very worldly to me, Sergeant. Miss Greene could have had men in the room before, twenty or thirty times, and Frau Schroeder would probably never have known."

He nodded. He sat back in the chair. "*Ja.* Maybe." He looked down at the floor for a moment, then looked back at me. "So why he kills her?"

"I don't know."

"*Ja.* Me too. I don't know."

"Is that it?" I asked him. "Can we go now?" Miss Turner was out there somewhere, looking for Greta Nordstrum. From what Putzi had said, Nordstrum was the only other person in Berlin who might know about Hitler's meeting in the Tiergarten. If someone was coming after Nordstrum the way someone had come after Nancy Greene, I didn't want Miss Turner standing in his way.

He looked up at me. "I want any other names you got. People like Miss Greene, people in Berlin who know people on that list."

"I only have one other name. Greta Nordstrum."

He nodded. "A Frederich Nordstrum is on the famous list."

"His sister."

He turned to Putzi. "When we talk, you and I, after the Tiergarten, I hear nothing about a sister."

"I didn't even know she existed," said Putzi, "until yesterday."

"And she is where?"

"I don't know," Putzi said. "She's a prostitute."

"A registered prostitute?"

"I don't know. I would doubt it."

I said, "We were told that she sometimes works for a Dr. Hirschfeld. At a sex institute on—"

"*Ja, ja,* Beethoven Strasse. He is famous, this Hirschfeld."

"My associate, Miss Turner, went there earlier this afternoon, to see if she could find the woman."

He nodded. "And maybe when she finds her, this Greta Nordstrum, she's dead already, like this one."

"I hope not."

"*Ja,* it's good you hope. If she gets killed today, after you don't give me her name this morning, then we have a long talk, you and me."

"I understand. But can we go now, Sergeant?"

"First you go to Alexanderplatz. I want your fingerprints. Both of you. I make a telephone call, I tell them you're coming." For the first time since he'd arrived at Frau Schroeder's house, he smiled. "This way," he said, "they don't beat you up too bad."

CHAPTER FIFTEEN

IN THE TAXICAB, heading for the Alexanderplatz police station, Putzi was sulking.

"I wish, Phil," Putzi said, "that you hadn't given the sergeant that information about Greta Nordstrum."

He glanced ahead, at the driver and the uniformed policeman that Biberkopf had sent along with us, as "a guide, so you don't get lost." This taxi had no sheet of glass between the front seat and the back.

"Putzi," I said, "people are dying. If Nordstrum's in danger, I can't keep her name from the cops. And Miss Turner is wandering around Berlin, trying to find her. What if the guy who killed Nancy Greene wants to kill Nordstrum? And what if Miss Turner's there when it happens?"

"Yes, of course, Phil, I understand. I get that. But it's possible that the death of Nancy Greene has nothing to do with your investigation."

"She was involved with one of the men on your list. He saw her the day of the sniping in the Tiergarten. He telephoned her the day before she was killed."

"Gunnar's good boy, Phil, and he was absolutely nuts about the girl. And besides, he's in Munich. He couldn't have done this."

"Maybe not. But her death came awfully soon after the sniping. The odds are, it's connected somehow."

He glanced at the cabdriver and the cop. "How is it connected?"

"I don't know. We need to find out. And listen, Putzi, why do you care whether the cops have Nordstrum's name?"

"Herr Hit—" He took another look at the driver and the cop. "The gentleman in Munich," he said, "is a politician, Phil. It's extremely important that there be absolutely no scandals associated with his name, or with the name of the, ah, group he leads."

"It's not his fault that the Nordstrum woman's a prostitute."

"No, certainly not. It's not Frederich's fault, either. But even the possibility of a scandal could be damaging. You remember Caesar's wife?"

"No," I said. "We never met."

WE HAD OUR fingerprints taken at the station. None of the cops beat us up.

Afterward, we took one taxi down König Strasse to the Central Post Office and switched to a second taxi there. No one seemed to be following us.

The Institute of Sexology, three buildings of polished pale gray brick, sat at the edge of the Tiergarten, shaded by tall oak trees. The central building held Dr. Hirschfeld's office. Putzi learned from the receptionist that the doctor was upstairs, in the museum. We went up the marble steps.

We stopped at the counter and paid a couple of thousand marks' worth of admission fees. We learned from the woman behind the cash register that Hirschfeld was at the back of the building.

The museum was doing a brisk business. Well-dressed men and women wandered along the aisles, looking studious and intent, as though they were gazing at reconstructed skeletons of dinosaurs. What they were actually gazing at were platoons of wooden paddles and regiments of upright dildos in a wide variety of shapes and sizes and colors. There were photographs of naked people who had to be double-jointed to be doing the things they were doing to each other. One counter held an extensive selection of merkins, thatches of artificial pubic hair—yellow, black, red, and one that was a bright turquoise blue. Carefully brushed and fluffed, they looked like disembodied beards.

It was bizarre, all of it, but it did a fine job of keeping my mind off Nancy Greene.

Beside me, Putzi sniffed. "Disgusting."

"The museum? Or the idea that people use these things?"

"Both. But, yes—mostly, I suppose, the idea that people would actually require all this . . . paraphernalia."

I smiled. "I doubt that any one person actually requires all of it."

"No, of course not. But a real man has no need for such things, does he, Phil?"

"Probably not, Putzi."

Certainly, I couldn't think of many situations that required a bright blue merkin.

As we'd been told we would, we found Dr. Hirschfeld at the far end of the museum, leafing through an album of photographs.

"Dr. Hirschfeld?" I said.

"Yes." He held out his hand. "Dr. Magnus Hirschfeld, at your service."

He was a short, boxy man with thick graying hair, a broad weathered face, an imposing nose, and a big floppy walrus mustache. He wore a long black frock coat and an elaborate black cravat. His eyes, behind a large pair of pince-nez, were brown.

I shook the hand. "Phil Beaumont. This is Ernst Hanfstaengl. Doctor, I think you spoke today with a colleague of mine. A Miss Jane Turner?"

He smiled. "Yes, of course. A charming woman."

"Do you know where she might be now?"

His eyebrows rose. "This is remarkable. First, your Miss Turner arrives. She is looking for Greta Manheim, she says. And then, after she leaves, two policemen arrive, *also* looking for Greta. And now *you* arrive, looking for Miss Turner. My day is becoming a Restoration comedy!" He lowered his eyebrows and leaned toward me, smiling. "What game, may I ask, is afoot?"

"I'm not sure, Doctor. Greta Manheim's real name is Nordstrum?"

"Ah," he said, smiling as he leaned back and clasped his hands behind him again. "What is 'real,' precisely, Mr. Beaumont? I believe that at bottom we all have a right to decide upon our own identity, rather than have it imposed upon us by society."

"Right. Did Greta Manheim ever go by the name Nordstrum?"

He smiled. "Indeed she did."

"How is she connected to your institute, Doctor?"

"You know that she is a prostitute?"

"Yeah."

"She hands my Psycho-Biological questionnaire out to her friends and then collects them for me. She's been very helpful. With her assistance, I have acquired much valuable information."

"And what did you tell Miss Turner? About where Miss Manheim might be?"

"The same thing I told the policemen. That Greta is very likely at the Toppkeller bar, on Schwerin Strasse. She often goes there in the afternoon."

"Thank you, Doctor."

"And you," he said. "You're a Pinkerton detective as well, are you?"

"Yeah."

"Would you be interested in answering the questionnaire? It would be extremely useful for me to have answers from a Pinkerton detective, male or female. I asked Miss Turner, but she was in a something of a hurry."

"Sorry, Doctor, but so are we. Maybe some other time."

"I'VE HEARD OF this Toppkeller bar," said Putzi.

"Yeah?"

We were in another cab, heading south through the Tiergarten on Hofjäger-Allee.

"Yes. It's a lesbian hangout." He sounded glum. "It's filled with them."

"Putzi," I said, "we're investigating a crime. We can't pick and choose where we ask our questions."

"First that greasy little man, that Hirschfeld, with his disgusting sexual gadgets." He sighed. "And now lesbians."

"You can wait outside if you want. But I need to find Miss Turner."

"No, no, Phil," he said quickly. "I wouldn't dream of letting you go in there alone."

I smiled. "Thanks, Putzi."

IT WAS FOUR thirty by the time we reached number 13 Schwerin Strasse. We went down the steps and through the wide wooden doors. Inside, the

Toppkeller was a big room with ornately carved wooden walls that sported, here and there along their length, big hand-painted murals of forest and jungle scenes. Hanging from the high wooden ceiling were maybe a hundred paper herons, each of them three feet long, with delicate wings extended to float over the billows and streamers of cigarette smoke. The cocktail hour had apparently begun.

Women sat at the long cloth-covered trestle tables and at the smaller tables nestled against the wall, around a parquet dance floor. No orchestra was playing now, but two couples, all women, were dancing anyway, slowly, cheek to cheek. Some other couples, men and women, probably tourists, were gazing around the room with the same studious faces of the people at the Museum of Sexology. A few single men were scattered around, some of them looking eager and prosperous and some of them looking only eager.

Putzi and I walked over to the long zinc-topped bar. Two stools were free, between a tall woman on the right and a burly man on the left with a broad back inside a tight brown cloth jacket. Putzi lowered himself onto the stool next to the man, a bit like a circus bear climbing onto a unicycle. I took the other stool.

The tall woman turned to me and looked me up and down, her brown eyes distant beneath a fringe of short brown hair. Her eyebrows were heavily penciled into twin arches and her lipstick was the color of arterial blood. Handsome, slender, she wore a long brown leather coat over a white wool sweater. She said something in German.

"Sorry," I said. "I don't speak German."

Putzi said, "You see, Phil? This is what happens in these places. She's a boot girl. A prostitute. She asked if you wanted to taste her whip."

I smiled at her. "Thanks," I said. "But I was thinking more along the lines of a beer."

Putzi translated.

She turned away, elaborately bored, and sipped at her drink, something pale green and translucent, probably absinthe.

"So we get some beers?" said Putzi. Getting some beers was an idea he liked.

"Yeah. And we talk to the barmaid."

The barmaid was an attractive heavyset blonde woman wearing a white apron over a black silk blouse and a black cotton skirt. Her lipstick was white, her eyelids were outlined in thick black mascara. Putzi gave her our order and I took out my wallet and slid an American twenty-dollar bill from inside it. When the woman brought the beers and set them on the bartop, I lay the bill down between the glasses. She looked at me. Twenty American dollars was a lot of money in Berlin, probably as much as she made in a couple of weeks.

I said to Putzi. "Ask her about Miss Turner."

When he got to the name "Greta Manheim," I saw the barmaid's glance flicker for an instant toward the burly man on Putzi's left.

"Nein," she said, then added something.

"She says," Putzi told me, "that she hasn't seen Greta Manheim. But she's been busy all afternoon, working the bar. Maybe the Manheim woman sat at one of the tables, she says, and maybe Miss Turner talked to her there."

"Does she know where Manheim lives?" I said.

Putzi asked her.

"Nein," she said.

I told him, "Ask her if she'd ask the waitresses."

He did.

She nodded and reached for the twenty. I stabbed my finger at it and held the finger there. I smiled at her. "When we get Greta Manheim's address," I said.

Putzi translated that. She shrugged and sauntered toward the end of the bar, where a waitress was waiting.

Putzi lifted his glass and held it out. *"Prosit."*

I raised my glass and tapped it against his. "Your health, Putzi."

We drank.

Behind Putzi, the burly man stood up from his barstool. If he moved away, I was going after him. I wanted to know why the barmaid had given him that look when Putzi mentioned Greta Manheim's name.

He didn't move away. He came around Putzi, toward me. I saw that I'd been right about the *burly* but wrong about the *man*. It was a woman. She had broad shoulders and round muscular breasts that swelled out against her blue denim shirt. She was wearing baggy black trousers, the too-long legs of these piled up at the ankles of her heavy leather work boots. Her short, limp, unwashed blonde hair was parted on the left. She wore no makeup. Above a thin, pinched mouth, her nose was small and upturned. At the corner of the mouth a lighted cigarette dangled, and her small gray eyes were narrowed against the drifting smoke.

I turned on the stool to face her. Putzi hadn't noticed her yet. He was savoring his beer, staring happily down into the glass, which was now nearly empty.

She stopped a few feet away, put her hands into the pockets of her jacket, and said something.

Putzi swung around, surprised.

She repeated what she'd said. Her right hand moved inside the pocket as though she were fondling some favorite toy in there.

Putzi turned to me. "You see, Phil?"

Without taking my eyes off the woman's face, I said, "What did she say?"

"She wants to know what we're doing here."

"Tell her. We're looking for Miss Turner and Greta Manheim."

He told her.

The woman spoke. Her glance didn't waver from mine.

"You're a nuisance," Putzi translated. "Get the hell out."

"I can't do that," I told her.

She said, "When I whistle, ten of my friends will run over here and stomp you into a bloody pulp. Both of you." Inside her right pocket, the hand moved again.

CHAPTER SIXTEEN

AFTER HIS TRANSLATION, Putzi added, "Well, you know, Phil, maybe we should just amscray."

I hadn't looked away from the woman and she hadn't looked away from me.

"Tell her," I said, "that we're looking for Fräulein Manheim and Miss Turner because they're in danger. One woman has already been killed. If our friend here is a friend of Manheim's, she'll tell us where she is. And where Miss Turner is."

The woman looked from me to Putzi, looked back at me. "Who are you?" Putzi translated for her.

"My name is Beaumount. I'm a Pinkerton detective. Miss Turner is my colleague."

She jerked her head toward Putzi. "And who's he?"

"A friend."

She stared at me for a moment longer, probably balancing her injured pride against her concern for Fräulein Manheim. Then she said, "I'll take you. But not him. Just one of you."

Putzi glanced unhappily around the room at all the women, as though he were pretty sure that as soon as I left, they were going to run over and stomp him into a bloody pulp. "It's okay, Phil," he said. "I'll wait here. But remember, we've got to see the general at six."

"Why don't you wait outside, Putzi. I'll be back as soon as I can."

"Fine," he said, and grinned. "Fine, Phil. I'll wait outside."

. . .

GRETA NORDSTRUM-MANHEIM LIVED a few blocks away in a small, two-story wooden building behind a big brick apartment house. A stairway on the side led up to the second floor, and the two of us climbed it, her in the lead. She knocked at the door. We waited. No one answered the door. She said something in German and turned to go back down the stairs.

"No," I said. After Nancy Greene, I wasn't too happy about unopened doors. "Do you have a key?" I put out my hand, my bent thumb and curled forefinger pressed together, and I mimed unlocking a lock.

Her eyes narrowed. She didn't trust me.

I didn't much care. I wasn't leaving until I knew that Miss Turner wasn't in that apartment.

She must have realized that. She reached into her pants pocket and pulled out a key. With a sour look at me, she unlocked the door. She turned, held up her hand, said something, and went inside the apartment. I waited.

She came back, shaking her head, and started to close the door again.

I put my right hand on it. "No." I pointed my finger of my left hand at my eye, pointed it into the apartment. "I'll look for myself."

Her face colored again. But there weren't ten friends around at the moment, and I think she knew that going for the knife would be a bad idea.

Reluctantly, she moved aside. I stepped into the apartment.

There was no one in the living room and no one in the kitchen. In the sink were two saucers and two empty coffee cups, rinsed out but not washed. I touched them. Cool.

There were two doors at the end of the apartment, beyond the bathroom and the toilet. One door was opened and led into a simple, uncluttered bedroom. No one there. The other door was locked.

When I turned to the woman, she was already shaking her head. She said something in angry German.

There's no point in carrying around a pistol if you can't take it out occasionally and show it to people. I reached into my pocket, pulled out the Colt, and showed it to her.

She spat some more German at me, but she got another key from another pocket, unlocked the door, and threw it open. It banged against the wall.

There was no Miss Turner inside, and no Greta Manheim. It was a room smaller than the bedroom. Now it was filled with groceries—bulging sacks of flour and rice and sugar and salt and coffee, barrels packed with potatoes and beets and carrots, cases of whiskey and gin and wine and beer. Hanging from hooks set in the ceiling were whole dried hams and fat salamis and loops of plump sausages.

I didn't know what their personal relationship was, but it looked as if Fräulein Manheim and this woman were selling food on the black market.

"Okay," I said. I put the pistol back in my pocket and I nodded back toward the living room.

She slammed the door shut and locked it, twisting the key so hard I thought she might snap it.

There was a bulky black Bakelite telephone on the end table beside the couch. I pointed at it. "Can I use the phone?"

Her small mouth grim, she held out her right hand and rubbed her thumb back and forth across her fingertips. Money.

I took out my wallet, tugged loose a twenty. I could have bought a new telephone with that, and probably a large percentage of the apartment's furniture, but I'd been pushing her around all day.

Her face empty, she snapped it from my fingers.

I called the Adlon and asked if Miss Turner had returned. The clerk told me that she'd picked up her key an hour ago and had gone up to her room. He asked me if I wanted to speak with her, and I said that would be very nice.

"Hello?"

"Miss Turner," I said.

"Mr. Beaumont. Are you in the hotel?"

"No, I'm with Putzi. I just wanted to check in with you. You sound a little out of breath—are you all right?"

"I'm fine. I was across the room."

"You talked with the woman? Nordstrum?"

"Yes. She gave me a name. The man has gone to Munich. But should we discuss this over the telephone?"

"No. Are you meeting von Dinesen for dinner?"

"He's supposed to ring me up. Did you find Miss Greene?"

"Yeah. I'll tell you about it later. Putzi and I are off to see General von Seeckt. And there's another errand I need to run. I probably won't be back there until after eight."

"I may be gone by then. But I shan't be late getting back. Tennish?"

"Okay. I'll see you then. I'll wait for you in the bar. But be careful."

"Yes."

"And bring the Colt."

"Of course," she said.

I hung up. I took out my watch. Five thirty. I didn't want to keep the general waiting.

The woman and I left the apartment. As we walked back to the bar, she didn't say a word and she didn't look at me. She kept her head lowered sullenly and her hands deep in her pants pockets. When we arrived back at the Toppkeller, Putzi was pacing back and forth along the sidewalk. The woman headed for the stairs without even a backward glance, but I called out, "Wait!"

She turned, glowering at me.

"Putzi," I said, "tell her that I don't care about the stuff in the closet."

"What stuff?" he asked me.

"Never mind. Just tell her. Tell her it's none of my business."

He spoke to her. She said something back, angrily, her small eyes squeezed into slits, and then she wheeled around and went stomping down the stairs.

"What was in the closet?" he asked me.

"Food. What did she say?"

"She said you were absolutely right."

I smiled. "Did she say *absolutely*?"

"No. Sorry. She said—"

"That's okay. I got the gist."

"What about Miss Turner?"

"She's fine. She's back at the hotel. Let's go see the general."

Hotel Adlon
Berlin
Wednesday evening
May 16th

Dear Evangeline,

In my letter of this morning, I mentioned my naïveté in such a way as to suggest that after the revelations of last night I had somehow been cured of it, as one might be cured of measles. This suggestion was misleading.

After the further revelations of today, I begin to believe that my naïveté may be less an affliction (like measles, or virginity) than a fundamental state of being.

Today, after ricocheting all over Berlin with Mr. Beaumont from the Hotel Adlon to the Alexanderplatz to Charlottenburg, I came briefly to rest at a Museum of Sexology in the Tiergarten. I was seeking out its *Direktor*, a psychoanalyst named Dr Magnus Hirschfeld, a man who might possess information about a woman we wished to question, a prostitute named Greta Nordstrum. Dr Hirschfeld, I was informed at the reception area, was in the museum, and I climbed up the stairs to ferret him out.

The room, or series of rooms, in which I found myself was really quite extraordinary. I should have spent most of my time blushing, had I not been so busy clenching my teeth to prevent my jaw from dropping.

Among the exhibits were photographs of couples, male couples and female couples and a mixture of both, who were performing sexual acts of a complexity that quite took my breath away. I was speechless, Evy. Not so much from shock as from resentment. It seemed (and seems) hardly fair that certain people in this world could have advanced to so flamboyantly acrobatic a level of sexual activity while certain others, who shall remain nameless, have not much advanced beyond a devilish little trick taught by one inmate to another at Miss Applewhite's boarding school, all those long years ago.

I did ultimately find the good doctor, who was tidying up an artful display of chains and whips, like a fussy *Hausfrau* arranging the pots and pans, and from him I learned that Frl. Nordstrum, who was now calling herself Frl. Manheim, could probably be found at the Toppkeller bar on Schwerin Strasse.

And so it was that in the middle of the afternoon I was ambling through a lively *Bierkeller* in Berlin West, nearly all the occupants of which were women.

The bar was bright and cheerful, and it had an air of easy female camaraderie, or so it seemed to me—but possibly this was, once again, naïveté. There were a few mannish types, wearing boots and dungarees, like bricklayers; but everyone else, Evy, was dressed brilliantly. It was as though they had all gathered there before departing, en masse, for some wonderful nearby festival—a *Karneval,* say. Some of them were swathed in long, swashbuckling leather coats above boots of vividly coloured leather, red and green and sienna. Some were gamins, outfitted like Parisian children in dark, short trousers and brightly striped jumpers. Some wore gorgeous little French dresses of silk or tulle or chiffon. Two or three women, strikingly attractive, wore slim dinner jackets and trousers, a costume that seemed on them not so much masculine as wickedly, stylishly feminine.

A waitress told me that Frl. M. was standing at the end of the bar. When I approached it, I saw two women there, one of them a bricklayer, the other a tall woman in a long, black, shiny leather coat that fell below the tops of her knee-high black patent leather boots. Beneath the coat she wore a black roll-neck jumper of silk. You'll have guessed by now (as I had) which of the women was Frl. Manheim.

'Excuse me,' I said.

They turned to me.

'I'm looking for Fräulein Greta Manheim,' I said.

The tall woman smiled. 'You've found her.' Her cool glance moved up and down my gray cotton suit. 'What can I do for you?'

GOODNESS. IT'S SO strange to be in a hotel room that has a telephone. When it rang just now, I leaped up from the chair like a kangaroo, my heart pounding; I thought that the fire alarm had gone off.

It was Mr Beaumont. He and Mr Hanfstaengl are on their way to interview a German general. That will be great fun, I'm sure.

WE RETURN TO Frl. Manheim. She was an inch or so taller than I, nearly six feet in height. Her short black hair, slick and shiny, was combed straight back along her scalp and behind her small pointed ears. He features were feline: evocative hollows beneath her cheekbones, almond-shaped green eyes, and dark black eyelashes, long and dense. Like the lashes, her eyebrows were dark black. Her nose was strong, almost aquiline, and her bright red lips were wide.

She was a dazzling creature, Evy, one of those women whose sleek animal beauty makes one feel ungainly and dim. Their presence is almost palpable; it invites admiration, and then resentment, and then a kind of hopeless surrender.

'I wonder,' I said, 'if I might speak with you alone.'

Beside her, the other woman frowned. She was, unfortunately, not so dazzling. Almost aggressively slovenly, she reminded me of Mr Ripley, the greengrocer in Torquay. She had the same small embittered mouth, the same suspicious gray eyes trapped in the same wide fleshy face.

Frl. Manheim said, 'About what?'

'Herr Hitler,' I said.

One of her eyebrows arched. 'And who are you?'

'My name is Jane Turner. I work for the Pinkerton Detective Agency.'

'Oh yes?' She smiled. 'The Pinkerton detectives have an office in Berlin now?'

'I'm from London. Could we talk, fräulein? It's really quite important.'

She looked me over once again, then turned to her companion. 'We'll be at the flat.' With the tip of her finger, lightly, she tapped the woman's lips. Her fingernails were long and red. 'I'll see you at midnight.'

The woman nodded, glanced at me without much fondness, and turned aside.

Frl. Manheim told me, 'Come along.'

I followed her across the room. At the door, two lovely young women were coming in, both in their early twenties. They knew Frl. Manheim and the three of them exchanged embraces. The two newcomers eyed the stranger thoughtfully, but Frl. Manheim made no introductions.

'Actresses,' she explained as we climbed the steps up to Schwerin Strasse. 'The first one, a Swede, is named Greta, too. The other, these days, is called Marlene. But I knew her back when she was little Maria.'

Frl. Manheim lives not far from the Toppkeller, on the second floor of a small white house at the rear of a courtyard, behind a large brick block of flats. The sun was shining today, amazingly, and the linden trees in the courtyard, three or four of them, were filled with birds, all twittering in amazement at the end of the rains.

I marched up the exterior stairs behind her. She pulled a set of keys from her pocket, unlocked the door, opened it, and passed inside. I followed her. As she closed the door behind me, I walked through the foyer into the flat.

I don't know what I expected, really. Something rather like an opium den, I expect. But the room was an ordinary middle-class parlor, very cosy, with quite ordinary middle-class furniture. At one end of the room, in the corner, was a small black coal stove.

Frl. Manheim turned to me. 'Sit,' she said. I lowered myself to the sofa and put my handbag on my lap.

She took off her leather coat and hung it in the wooden wardrobe. I saw that the roll-neck jumper had no sleeves. Her long languid arms were bare. Her tight black leather skirt came to just above her knees, leaving only an inch or two of flesh visible between the skirt and the lace-up boots. It was a striking outfit, although not, I suspect, the sort of thing that one might wear to Harrods.

'I made coffee a few hours ago,' she said. 'I can warm it up.'

'Yes, please. That would be very nice.' You will observe that being alone with a lesbian prostitute in her Berlin flat had in no way diminished my conversational skills.

'Cream?' she asked me. 'Sugar?'

'Both, please.'

When she left to prepare the coffee, I looked around. As ordinary as the room seemed, I felt that something was missing from it. After a moment, I realized what it was. Books. There were no books anywhere, not a one.

A living space without books always seems somehow barren to me. Books humanize a room, don't you think? And collectively, for a professional nosey parker such as I, they provide a convenient road map of the personalities who own them.

I was thinking about my father's study, the row upon row of books on the shelves, when she returned, carrying a wooden tray. She set it on the coffee table, handed me a cup and saucer.

'Thank you,' I said.

She smiled, took the other cup and saucer, and moved over to the chair opposite. She sat down, balancing the saucer on her lap, and crossed her long legs. 'I've never met this Hitler fellow,' she said. 'I wouldn't know him if I walked past him on the street.'

'But you know who he is.'

'A politician. In Munich.' She moved her slender shoulders in a shrug. 'I don't pay any attention to the politicians here in Berlin. Why should I pay attention to the politicians in Munich?'

I tasted the coffee. Several hours ago, it had probably been very good. 'You do know that your brother is a member of his party?'

'It was Freddy who gave you my name?' She sipped at her coffee.

'Indirectly. Did you know that Herr Hitler was here in Berlin a week ago last Tuesday?'

'No.'

'Someone tried to shoot him in the Tiergarten.'

'They must have missed, or it would have been in the papers.'

'They missed, yes.'

She smiled. 'Even so, poor Freddy probably had a heart attack. He idolizes his Führer. Freddy was too young for the War, but he still wants to fight it.'

'When was the last time you spoke with him?'

'Years ago. In 1921. After my mother died.'

'You didn't know that Herr Hitler was coming to Berlin that day?'

'And wouldn't have cared, if I had.' She sipped at her coffee. 'My turn to ask a question.'

'Yes?'

She smiled. 'I'm going to ask the same question that the idiots are always asking me. How did you get into this work?'

I smiled. 'Chance, really. I was involved in an investigation in England. The Pinkerton detective who conducted the investigation believed that I might enjoy the work.'

She drank some more coffee. 'And do you?'

'Yes, I do.' I was about to say something more, but I hesitated.

She saw the hesitation and she smiled. 'I won't think you're an idiot,' she said. 'How did I become a whore?'

'If you don't mind my asking.'

'One hand washes the other,' she said. 'I needed the money. After the War, here in Berlin, times were hard. There wasn't much else

I could do. I knew a woman who was a domina—you know the word?'

'Yes.' Erik had told me.

She smiled. 'Well, she believed that I might enjoy the work.'

I laughed. 'And do you?'

'Sometimes. In a way, you know, it's like being a doctor. I have some steady clients—patients, let's say—and they come to me for help, for a particular kind of treatment. Each one of them needs something a little different. And I know exactly what they need, and I give it to them. And afterward, everyone is happy.'

She sipped once more at her coffee. 'Some of them are important people. Intelligent people. Interesting people.' She smiled. 'They're not all interesting, naturally. A while ago I had some little yokel who wanted a golden shower—you understand?'

'Yes, I think so.'

'For fifteen minutes he jabbers about the sanctity of women, their purity, and then finally he admits what he wants. So I do it, it's not a problem. But then he starts calling me his Rhine Maiden, over and over, Rhine Maiden, Rhine Maiden, and then he's shouting it, like a maniac. I had to kick him to shut him up.' She smiled. 'This was in one of the big hotels, an expensive place, and they don't like noise.'

I smiled, a bit wanly, I expect.

She nodded. 'I've shocked you.'

'No. Saddened me, perhaps, a little.'

She shook her head. 'Nothing to be sad about. Who knows where they come from, the fantasies they have? Something creates them, something in their past, and these people can't be happy until they live them out. And what's wrong with that? Everyone lives with one kind of fantasy or another. Socialism. Democracy. The Happy Ending. For Freddy, it's Blood and Soil.' She smiled. 'What's your fantasy, Fräulein Turner?'

'I'm not sure. The Happy Ending, perhaps.'

She laughed. 'It's a popular fantasy. I hope you find it.'

I smiled. 'Thank you. Now, Fräulein Manheim—'

'No, no. Call me Greta.'

'Greta, yes. And you must call me Jane.'

'Jane. What were you about to say?'

'You said that you're not interested in politicians. But Greta, do you know of anyone, anyone specific, who might want to kill Herr Hitler?'

'Yes,' she said. 'Maybe I do.'

I felt a Pinkertonian flicker of excitement. 'Who might that be?'

'I've been trying to think of his name. He's an Englishman.'

EVY, I MUST go. Erik has just rung me up. He's downstairs! I'll post this now and write more later.

All my love,
Jane

CHAPTER SEVENTEEN

G ENERAL," I SAID, "I appreciate your taking the time to talk to us."

"You can best show your appreciation," he said in English, "by taking as little of it as possible."

As German generals went, General Hans von Seeckt was pretty much perfect. A tall, trim man in his sixties, he wore a spotless military uniform spangled with medals and ribbons. At his neck was a Knight's Cross, and he had a shiny monocle screwed into his right eye.

He held himself so stiffly upright behind his broad wooden desk that his spine could have been welded to the back of his chair. Below thinning white hair, where a parting on the left showed a line of pink as fine and straight as a saber scar, his face was narrow and ascetic. He had shrewd gray eyes, a pointed nose, a white mustache, and a thin, unsentimental mouth.

"I'll try to get this over with quickly, sir," I told him. I haven't hob-nobbed with a lot of generals, but I was fairly certain that most of them liked to hear that "sir." Liking it was one of the reasons they became generals.

"You do know," he said, "that I've already spoken to the police about this matter." He kept his hands together on his desktop, his slender fingers interlocked. His nails were manicured.

"Yes, sir. But I'm conducting an independent investigation."

"What is there to investigate? Some lunatic fires a shot and he misses. I should think that a Pinkerton detective would have better ways to occupy his time."

"Yes, sir. Probably. But this is the way I'm occupying it right now. May I ask my questions?"

He unclasped his hands, lifted his right hand lightly from the desk, and lightly flipped his fingers. Proceed.

"Is it true," I said, "that Mr. Hitler was here in Berlin to ask your permission to stage a putsch against the government?"

Putzi was sitting off to my left. I heard him let out his breath in a kind of surprised cough.

The general smiled a thin smile. "You come straight to the point, I see, Mr. Beaumont."

"Yes, sir. It usually saves time."

He nodded. "I agree. I tell you, first, that certain of my junior officers possess an admiration for Herr Hitler that I do not share. At their urging, however, I agreed to meet with you, and to be as candid as circumstances would permit."

He narrowed his eyes slightly. "But what I say to you now is privileged information. If I discover that you've disclosed it to anyone, I will see to it that you are imprisoned. If you are no longer in this country, I will see to it that no Pinkerton ever operates in Germany again. You understand me?"

"Perfectly, General."

He looked down at his clasped hands for a moment, then looked back up. "I'm an officer. My loyalty is to the army, and to the German state. But when the German state has been taken over by rabble, by Socialists and opportunists, then all loyal Germans are under a moral obligation to consider what their alternatives might be."

"Yes, sir. And did you consider Mr. Hitler's alternative?"

"I did not."

"You knew, before you met with him, what he wanted to ask you?"

"I suspected."

"And you thought it wouldn't work. The putsch."

"No."

"But you met with him anyway?" I said.

"Yes."

"Why?"

"To register my displeasure."

"At what?"

"A week before, his filthy little broadsheet in Munich—I can hardly call it a newspaper—the *Munich Observer*, published a vicious article by the editor, a swine named Rosenberg. It was a personal attack on my wife."

"Your wife? Why?"

"My wife is Jewish. Rosenberg is an anti-Semite. A vicious anti-Semite. He claimed that my wife, as a Jewess, was poisoning my mind and, through me, was poisoning the German army."

"Hitler knew about the article?"

"According to my sources in Munich, nothing goes into that filthy rag without Hitler's approval."

"But Hitler didn't know that *you* knew about the article."

"No." A small, cold gleam of satisfaction flickered in his eyes. "He was rather surprised when I mentioned it." He smiled another thin smile.

I nodded. The general had let Hitler drive all the way from Munich to Berlin, something like three hundred miles, in the hope that the German army might get behind his putsch. And then the general, deliberately, and with a certain amount of pleasure, had yanked the rug out from under his feet.

The general was not a man I would want unhappy with me.

"What did Hitler say?" I asked him.

"He denied everything. He said that Rosenberg had published the article on his own. He, Hitler, had nothing against the Jews. He was lying, of course. I've read accounts of his speeches. The worst sort of anti-Semitic drivel, pandering to the lowest elements of the masses."

"But, General," said Putzi, "forgive me, but sometimes it's necessary to mobilize the masses. Sometimes—"

The general had turned to him. "Not by attacking my wife."

"General," I said. "What happened next? After Hitler denied knowing about the article?"

"Some idiot fired that shot at him. Hitler ran and hid behind a tree. I tried to determine the direction from which the shot had been fired."

"And did you?"

"It seemed to have come from the south, from the grounds of the Zoological Garden. I started walking in that direction, but Colonel von Hippel prevailed upon me to stop. We left the Tiergarten together. I spoke with the police later."

"Did you consider the possibility that the shot was meant for you, and not for Hitler?"

For a moment he looked at me as though I had suddenly started speaking some unknown language. Then he smiled. "I can say without arrogance, Mr. Beaumont, that if someone had shot me, the entire army would have taken up arms. They would have torn the country apart, looking for the individual responsible."

I nodded. It must be nice to be liked by an entire army. "Before the meeting took place," I said, "did you tell anyone about it?"

"I had given my word that I would not."

"What about your aide, Colonel von Hippel?"

"What about him?"

"May I talk to him?"

"No, you may not. He, too, gave his word. His word is good enough for me, and it will be good enough for you."

"Do you have any idea who fired that shot?"

"None." He stood up. "And that, gentlemen, is that. I'm afraid that I have duties to attend to."

AFTER WE GOT into the taxi, I said to Putzi, "Did you know about this article?"

"No. Not before the meeting, I mean. Herr—" He glanced at the taxi driver, who was safely ensconced behind a sheet of glass. But Putzi didn't trust glass. "The gentleman in Munich told me about it afterward. He was furious with Rosenberg. He was as mad as a wet hen."

"The general says he approves whatever goes into the newspaper."

"Not true, Phil. He's too busy to check every issue. He leaves all that to Rosenberg. Would it make sense for him to permit an attack on the general's wife when he was planning to ask the general"—another glance at the taxi driver—"what he did ask him?"

"Not a lot of sense."

"And listen, Phil, it's not true what the general said, that, um, the gentleman hid behind a tree. He was only using the tree to cover himself while he took out his Luger and prepared to defend himself and the general."

"He carries a Luger?"

"His life is constantly in danger, Phil."

"But he never fired it in the Tiergarten?"

"No target presented itself."

"Okay. One more question."

"What?"

"What is it about the Jews?"

"What do you mean?"

"Why is this Rosenberg so down on them? Why is the gentleman in Munich?"

"No, no, Phil, it's not all the Jews. There are some wonderful Jews around. Hundreds of them, maybe thousands. There's a professor at the university here, Albert Einstein, a really great fella. He's famous—you've heard of him?"

"Yeah."

"I had dinner with him, in town, and it was great fun. We argued about which is better, Munich beer or Berlin beer." He grinned. "You know what he said?"

"What's that?"

"He said it's all relative." He laughed his deep, booming laugh. "You get it?"

"Yeah. So what is it about the Jews?"

"Not all of them, Phil. The profiteers, Phil. The Jewish capitalists, the Jewish bankers. They're sucking the life out of Germany. They're lining their pockets with German gold while good German citizens are suffering. You've seen the beggars, Phil. You've seen the prostitutes."

"All the bankers are Jewish? All the capitalists?"

"No, no, of course not."

"Doesn't sound like this Rosenberg was making any kind of distinction. I'd be surprised if the general's wife was a banker."

"Well, yes, of course, there are people in the party who are anti-Semites. Rosenberg is one of them. But most of us are reasonable people." He waved a big hand in the air. "And, Phil, this isn't the important thing. The important thing is to find out who tried to hurt the gentleman in Munich. What's our next step? What do we do now?"

"We grab another taxi and we head back to Nancy Greene's boardinghouse."

"But we've already talked to Frau Schroeder. She doesn't know anything."

"It's not Frau Schroeder I want to see."

"THAT SERGEANT," SAID Frau Schroeder, Putzi translating for her. "Sergeant Biberkopf. He said I shouldn't talk to anyone but him."

She was standing at the door to her house, keeping the door opened only three or four secure inches. Her tears had dried, but in the pale light of the overhead lamp she looked worn and desolate.

"I understand, Frau Schroeder," I said. "It's Mr. Norris I'd like to talk to."

"But he's not here."

"You said he was always here for dinner."

"Yes, when he's in town. But he's gone off on business, you see. He left almost two hours ago."

"Do you know where?"

"Munich."

"He told you Munich?"

"No, I—" She hesitated, and her cheeks reddened. "I heard him on the telephone, calling for a taxi." So sometimes she did listen to her lodgers' telephone conversations. "He said he had to be at the station at five, in time to catch the Munich train."

"Did you know he'd be leaving today?"

"Oh no. It was a complete surprise. Usually, when he takes a business trip, he tells me about it a day or two before. But something important had come up, he said, and he had to leave."

"Frau Schroeder," I said, "did you mention to him that I'd asked about him? About when he'd be here tonight?"

"Yes, of course. Just before he told me that he had to leave."

Hotel Adlon
Berlin
Wednesday night
May 16th

Dearest Evy,

Only a few words. Something quite horrible has happened here. Not to me, nor to Mr Beaumont. To a Miss Greene, whom we believed might become an informant. We leave for Munich early in the morning. I must pack. I'll write more on the train.

All my love, as always,
Jane

P.S. Erik told me the most incredible story tonight.

Jane

INTERLUDE: BAYREUTH

CHAPTER EIGHTEEN

I T WAS A day train, the 9 a.m. express from Berlin, and there were no sleeper cars. Putzi, Miss Turner, and I shared a small first-class compartment, a row of three comfortable seats at each end of the small cubicle, the two rows facing each other. Putzi felt the same way about fellow passengers that he did about taxi drivers, and he had booked all six seats. There was one empty seat between me and Putzi, and two empty seats next to Miss Turner, who sat beside the window, opposite me.

We would be stopping at Hof, south of Leipzig, and from there we would be taking a different train to Bayreuth.

Before we left the Adlon, I had checked at the desk. There hadn't been any message from Cooper. I sent one to him, telling him that we were off to Munich.

I had also telephoned Sergeant Biberkopf and told him that Mr. Norris was heading for Munich, and that we were about to do the same. He said he would look into Mr. Norris, and he gave me a name and a telephone number in Munich—a copper I could trust, he told me. I asked him how he knew. The man was his cousin, he said. I asked him if his cousin spoke English. He said yes, but not so good as him.

South of Berlin, beneath a broad blue sky where a few fat white clouds slowly drifted, the countryside was as flat and empty as Kansas. It was mostly fields, some of them freshly planted, long precise rows of pale green plants shimmering in the breeze. Closer in, they were bullied to the ground by the slipstream from the train, thin strands of green hair furiously flattened against rows of black, bald dirt. Some of the fields lay fallow, their gray stubble looking bleak and blasted in the thin May sunlight.

Occasionally there was a thick stand of woodland, as dark and dreary as the forests in the Brothers Grimm. Witches might be lurking in there, and trolls, and werewolves.

Beside me, Putzi was snoring softly, his big head slumped against the compartment's wall, his big arms folded across the chest of his chalk stripe suit coat.

I glanced across at Miss Turner. Today she wore a white silk blouse with a ruffled front, a black wool blazer, a black cotton skirt, black leather high-heeled shoes. Her legs were crossed at the knees, and they were still good legs.

She was busy with another chapter of her epic. The nib of her pen darted across the sheet of letter paper, supported by a magazine on her lap. Her hair was curtained forward, against her cheeks, and her face was tight with concentration, like a young girl's, her eyes screwed nearly shut, the corner of her lower lip caught lightly between her teeth. Last night, when I'd met with her in the bar at the Adlon, her face had been relaxed and slightly flushed. With wine, maybe, or with excitement. Maybe with both.

I HAD BEEN sitting at one of the marble-topped tables for half an hour, drinking bourbon on the rocks.

For a weekday night, the bar had been doing a brisk business. There were the boot girls, and the sailor boys, and the plump shiny businessmen, and the glittering young couples in expensive new clothes. The chatter and the murmur rose and fell around me, punctuated now and then by the sudden rattle of laughter.

A little after ten thirty, Miss Turner showed up.

She dropped into the leather chair, slapped her purse onto her lap, and let out a small quick whoosh of air. "I'm sorry I'm late. The traffic was wretched."

Under her topcoat, she was wearing a dress she'd bought in Frankfurt, black silk, Empire-waisted, with a matching jacket. If I paid attention to things like that, I would have said that she looked a good deal less businesslike than she had in the daytime.

"That's okay," I told her. "You want something to drink? A glass of wine?"

"Goodness, no. Perhaps a coffee?"

I signaled the waiter.

"Where did you eat?" I asked her.

"Kempinski's, on Leipziger Strasse. It's an enormous place, really quite marvelous." She leaned forward, her hands on her purse, her eyebrows raised above the rim of her spectacles. "But tell me. What happened with Nancy Greene?"

The waiter arrived then.

After he had taken our orders and gone off to get the drinks, I told her what had happened with Nancy Greene.

"Dead?" she said. She sat back and seemed to grow smaller within the black silk dress.

"She was murdered," I told her. "Strangled."

"But why? By whom?"

"I don't know."

"Where did it happen?"

"In her room at the boardinghouse. Where you and I went this morning. I found her there this afternoon."

She stared at me for a moment. "When did it happen?"

"Late Monday night or early on Tuesday morning."

She parted her lips and then closed them. "She was there, in that room, while we were at the front door?"

"Yeah."

"She'd been in there for two days? No one had asked after her?"

"The landlady assumed she was out."

Slowly, she shook her head. "But that's so . . . terribly sad."

"Yeah."

She looked at me. "Did she know something? Might that be the reason she was killed?"

"Maybe. She and Greta Nordstrum were the only people in Berlin with connections to the people who knew about Hitler and the Tiergarten."

"But what could she have known?"

"No idea."

"It's so sad," she said. "If only we'd been able to reach her sooner."

"When it happened," I said, "we were still on the train from Frankfurt. At that point, we didn't even know she existed."

The waiter arrived. He set down the coffee cup and saucer, the pitcher of cream, the bowl of sugar, the glass of bourbon.

After he left, I said, "Tell me about Greta Nordstrum."

"She calls herself Greta Manheim now." She raised her cup and saucer, lifted the cup, and sipped at her coffee.

"I know," I said. "I tried to track you down after I found Nancy Greene. I talked to Hirschfeld, at the sex institute. What did she give you?"

"Well, to begin with—" She frowned. "You tried to track me down?"

"Someone had killed Greene. Maybe someone was after Nordstrum. I wanted to make sure you weren't in the wrong place at the wrong time."

"Oh." Her eyelashes fluttered, and she looked down, then quickly back up. She was blushing. "Oh, well, I thank you."

I smiled. "All part of the service." I swallowed some bourbon.

She nodded, looking at me, and then she took another sip of coffee. "Well, yes. Of course. But I do thank you."

"What about Nordstrum?"

"Manheim. She hadn't known that Herr Hitler would be coming to Berlin. She hasn't spoken to her brother in years."

I nodded. "You said on the telephone that she gave you a name?"

"Yes. A Colonel Household. He's English, a retired officer. She doesn't know his first name. She overheard him talking in the hotel bar at the Kaiserhof. He was saying that the only way to deal with people like Hitler, demagogues, was to nip them in the bud. Kill them now, before they become too powerful."

She smiled. "I realize that this doesn't really make Colonel Household a legitimate suspect. From the way Greta described it, it could very well be the sort of mindless comment a retired military man might make in a bar. Especially if he were in his cups."

'Greta'? The two of you got along, sounds like."

"We did, actually. She's a bright young woman. I liked her."

"She speaks English? That's how she understood Household?" I drank some bourbon.

"No. Household was speaking in German."

"When was this?"

"Two weeks ago. The weekend before the Tiergarten."

"So the timing is right. Who was he talking to?"

"Just some local people, she said. Businessmen. No one important. None of them had ever heard of Hitler. You realize that he's not that well-known here in the north?"

"Don't tell Putzi that," I said.

She smiled. "And Colonel Household couldn't have known, of course, that Mr. Hitler was coming to Berlin the next weekend. Honestly, Mr. Beaumont, I very much doubt that he's the man we're looking for."

"How did Household know who Hitler was?"

"Household lives in Munich."

"Was he here the following week, the week of the sniping?"

"Greta doesn't know. But she thinks that he'd gone back to Munich. She hasn't seen him since."

I nodded. "So Household's probably in Munich. Along with everyone else."

"Everyone else?"

"Mr. Norris. You remember him? The Englishman we talked to at the boardinghouse. He's in Munich now, according to the landlady."

"But how does that concern us?"

"He told us he hardly knew Greene. But the landlady says that the two of them, Greene and Norris, were buddies. They had tea together all the time."

"Perhaps he simply didn't wish to speak with us, for whatever reason of his own. Something perfectly innocent."

"Maybe. But at that point, theoretically, he didn't know that Greene was dead. And if she'd still been alive, she would've been able to contradict him."

"You're saying that he *knew* she was dead?"

"I'm saying it's possible."

"But he seemed like such a pleasant, harmless sort of person."

"If everyone was what he seemed, we'd be out of a job."

"Do you think he killed her?"

"I don't know. But as soon as he heard from the landlady that I'd be coming back there to see him, he told her he had to leave town. He went to Munich. And that's what we're going to do."

"Pardon me?"

"We're going to Munich."

She had raised her coffee cup again. She blinked. "When?" She sipped at the coffee.

"Tomorrow morning. I had Putzi make the reservations."

"But isn't this awfully sudden?"

"We've done everything we can here. Biberkopf will be investigating Nancy Greene's death, and he won't want us interfering. The only leads we've got are in Munich. Mr. Norris. This Colonel Household of yours. And the people on that list."

"But Colonel Household probably isn't the man who fired that shot. And as for Mr. Norris, how on earth will we find him?"

"The Munich police will have a registry of hotel guests. Biberkopf gave me the name of a contact on the force."

"And what about Erik von Dinesen?"

"What about him?"

"I thought you wanted me to determine how he learned about us."

"Did you determine anything tonight?"

"Well, no. He told me about his war service, but not much else, I'm afraid."

I nodded. "Like you said, he's not going to come out and admit he's a fraud." She opened her mouth to speak and I held up a hand. "If that's what he is."

"But you asked me—"

"I know. And if we were sticking around here for a while longer, I'd say keep at it. But we should get to Munich. And I want to talk to those people in Bayreuth. The Wagner people. Where Hitler and the others stayed, on their way up here."

"He asked me out to dinner tomorrow night. Von Dinesen. I was hoping that I might be able to learn more."

"I'm sorry, Miss Turner. We should get to Munich."

"Yes. Yes, of course." She smiled. Like the laughter around us, the smile seemed forced. "Well, I'll just ring him up in the morning, then, and tell him we're leaving, shall I?"

"Fine."

She said brightly, "And what about that general you went to see?"

"Nothing there. But I have a feeling that if the general's wife hadn't been Jewish, Hitler probably could've gone ahead with his putsch."

"What do you mean?"

I told her about General von Seeckt.

NOW, AS THE German countryside trundled past the window, field after field, sometimes a distant old stone farmhouse crouched amid a few bright green trees, she sat across from me and scribbled away. From time to time, with the back of her right hand, she brushed her swaying brown hair away from her cheek. She wasn't wearing her spectacles. She didn't need them, apparently, for close-up work.

She must have sensed my watching her, because she looked up and smiled quizzically. Without the glasses, her blue eyes were a darker blue, and they seemed to be set deeper in her oval face. "What is it?"

"Nothing," I said. "I'm sorry. I didn't mean to stare. I was just wondering who you were writing to."

"An old friend of mine. We went to school together, a million years ago."

To my left, across the empty seat, Putzi yawned and unfolded his long arms and stretched them horizontally out into the compartment, balling his big hands into fists and slowly turning them in the air. "Ah," he sighed. "What a lovely little nap."

He looked around the compartment, smiled at Miss Turner, glanced out the window at the countryside rushing by, reached into his pants pocket, and pulled out his watch.

He looked at me. "Twelve o'clock," he said. "Time for a beer, eh, Phil?"

Train to Hof
Thursday
May 17th

Dear Evangeline,

Drat, drat, drat.

Mr B. and the Hanfstaengl and I are on a train, dashing head-long through dismal German fields and forests, racing irrevocably away from Berlin and Erik von Dinesen.

I—

Listen to me. What a monster I am. What a mindless self-centred cow. A young girl was killed in Berlin, murdered, and here I sit whingeing about Erik von Dinesen.

I didn't know her. The young girl. Miss Greene.

I spoke about her with the man who employed her, a cabaret manager. He complained about her elaborately and at length: her tardiness, her flightiness, her carelessness with men. But he was smiling all the while, and shaking his head in cheerful amazement.

The image that I formed, after speaking with him, was that of a vibrant, vital, often extravagant, sometimes foolish, young Englishwoman living in a foreign country on her own terms. She was probably as often infuriating as she was endearing; but I suspect that, had I met her, I should have envied her. And now she's gone. Strangled. By whom, we don't know.

I should clarify a remark that I made in my last letter. In my haste to finish that saga, I made it seem that Greta Manheim, the dazzling domina, had provided me the name of an Englishman who wanted to kill Herr Hitler. Well, the man is indeed an Englishman, and he indeed may wish to kill Herr Hitler, but I very much doubt that he ever attempted to do so. If he's guilty of anything, I suspect that he's guilty only of a bit of boring barroom bluster.

Erik, I might add, seems admirably immune to this malady.

Mr Beaumont insisted that I learn—he effectively *ordered* me to learn—as much about Erik as I could. Obediently, then, ever the compliant junior operative, I accompanied him to Kempinski's Café last night, and it was there, over the trout and the arugula salad, that I began my interrogation, artfully disguised as innocent conversation.

'When did you first learn of your gift?' I asked him.

He smiled. He has a smile that might melt the heart of someone less hardened and less superbly trained than I. There's something of sadness in it, or of pain; usually he smiles with only the right side of his mouth, as though his soul were oppressed by some physical weight. The smile seldom reaches his eyes: the eyes soften, but they do not sparkle.

'In the War,' he said.

'How did it happen?'

He raised one black eyebrow. 'Jane, you can't really want to hear about the War.'

'I'm curious.' I smiled a guileless smile. (I've been practicing.) 'But if you don't wish to discuss it, then of course I shan't press you.'

He sat back. He was wearing, once again, a black dinner jacket, beautifully tailored. At his throat, perfectly knotted, was a white bow tie. For a moment, staring at the table, he toyed with his champagne glass, moving it an inch to the left, then an inch to the right. Then he looked up at me, his face serious. 'I was in a *Sturmbataillon*. You know that during the War, the line at the Western Front was often static? That it sometimes didn't move for months?'

'Yes.'

'The *Sturmbataillon* was to be the solution. Shock troops. We would be specially trained and specially outfitted. Hand grenades, pistols. Moving as a single unit, we would smash across the lines and race through the enemy trenches. In this way, we might force a break in the front, for the regular infantry.'

'Was it successful?'

'Sometimes, yes.' He smiled his half-smile. 'And sometimes not. In one such attack, I was wounded. Here.' Lightly, he touched the side of his head. 'I remember nothing of it. I remember only our charge across the wires, the clatter of the guns, and then nothing.'

He sipped at his champagne.

'My comrades carried me to the rear. When I came to consciousness, I was lying on a cot, in a small room with walls of stone and a single square window. Beside me was a woman dressed in white. A slender woman with golden hair, very beautiful, perhaps thirty-five years old.'

He looked off, as though remembering.

I prompted him: 'A nurse?'

He looked at me. 'So I thought. But then she reached out and felt my forehead. As soon as her fingers touched my skin—even today I can recall how cool they were, her fingers—as soon as she touched me, images flooded into my mind. But they were images, Jane, not of my life, but of hers. I knew, all within a single instant, that her husband had died early in the War and that she was the owner of this château. I saw scenes, hundreds of them, from throughout her life. I saw her as a little girl, playing alone beneath an apple tree swollen with pink blossoms. I saw her in a crowd, dancing a waltz in a long, candlelit hall where the walls were hung with brilliant tapestries.'

He sipped again at his champagne. 'As I say, I saw all of this within only a moment. And I knew her name. Marie. As she stroked my forehead, I said it aloud. *Marie.* She was startled, of course. She was a woman of remarkable courage—I knew that, knew it as well as I knew her name. But of course she was startled. This wounded German soldier knew her name.'

'She was French?'

'Yes. Our army had commandeered her château. We were using parts of it as a field hospital.' He lifted the bottle of champagne, poured some into my glass and some into his own, set down the bottle. 'I lost consciousness again. When I next awoke, she was gone.'

'But surely you saw her again?'

'Later that day. She came with the doctor, bringing food. He examined my bandages. After he left us, she fed me. I was still very weak. Neither of us spoke until I finished eating. Then she set aside the bowl and spoon and she asked me how I knew her name. "From your touch," I told her. We spoke in French. "I know everything," I told her. "When you were ten, you had a dog named Pierre. When you were fifteen, you were in love with a boy named Jean. Your husband's name was Emile. He died in 1915."

'She simply stared at me. Finally, she said, "This is impossible."

'I said, "No, madame. I do not understand it myself. But it is real."'

Erik smiled at me, reached into his pocket, pulled out a watch, glanced down at it. (No man in Europe can survive, apparently, without a pocket watch, and without admiring it regularly.) 'Shall I continue?' he said.

'Yes, of course!'

'Very well, but not here. There's a place I'd like you to see.'

And so we left Kempinski's and I found myself at the Red Mill, a stunningly seedy cabaret that was chockablock with pickpockets and safecrackers and cat burglars and brigands and desperadoes of every conceivable stripe. (I loved it, *natürlich*.) In one musty corner, a pair of musicians, a drummer, and an accordionist battled heroically with snippets of American jazz music, but consistently lost.

Over another bottle of Dom Pérignon, in his silky baritone, Erik told me the rest of the story.

Marie visited him every day. Inevitably, he said, one thing led to another, and the two of them fell in love.

(In my own life, I frequently find this inevitability business to be rather less than reliable. Often, in my experience, one thing leads to utterly nothing. Witness my presence on this train.)

As his strength returned, Erik said, he began to realize that his 'gift' extended beyond Marie. Whenever anyone touched him—anyone at all, the doctor, the orderly—he would receive a flood of images, scenes from the life of that individual. And soon he discovered that by simply focusing on a person—attuning his mind, as he puts it, to the mind of the other—he was able to receive these images without making any physical contact. He kept this ability a secret from everyone but Marie.

Finally he was well enough for the doctors to send him back to Germany. He and Marie vowed to see each other as soon as the War was over. They corresponded every week, she from the castle, he from the hospital in Hamburg. The armistice was declared. They made plans to meet in Munich. Eagerly, each set out.

Already, Evy, as I did, you begin to suspect the outcome.

On his way there, by train, sitting in a crowded second-class compartment, he was abruptly overcome by a crushing wall of blackness, of paralysing grief, and he knew with absolute conviction that Marie had died.

'But how had she died?' I asked him.

'Murdered. By the Communists, during the uprising. When I reached Munich, I found her body and I arranged for it to be sent back to France.'

'I'm so sorry.'

He smiled that wounded smile of his. 'Thank you, Jane. But it was a long time ago.'

'Surely you must think of her, even now.'

'Yes, of course.' He leaned forward, reached out his hand, and gently placed it on mine. 'But remember, I knew her. Knew her as well as any human being can know another. And I know how brave she was. I know that she would have wished me to be brave as well. That she would have wished me to continue with my life.' He gave my hand a small squeeze and then he sat back again, his fingers trailing along my skin for a moment as he drew away.

What had he seen? I wondered. Had he read my mind?

'Is it because of Marie,' I said, 'that you sympathize with Herr

Hitler and his party?' The skin of my hand was still tingling. And so, curiously, was the small of my back, as though Erik's hand had stroked me there as well.

'No,' he said. 'If Marie had never existed, I should still oppose the Bolsheviks. They are against everything I hold dear.'

'Against what, for example?'

'Germany. The land itself and the people who live in it. Do you know of the *Wandervogel?*'

'No.'

'A youth movement, before the war. It may still exist, for all I know. I sincerely hope that it does. Back then, many of us belonged. It was grand, Jane. Being part of a group of boys, idealistic boys from all over the country, camping in the forests together. Telling tales beneath the stars, tales of Charlemagne, of Barbarossa, of the Teutonic Knights. Developing a sense of history, of German history, and a sense of oneness with it. With the land, with the spirit that moves it, with the people. The Communists and their so-called internationalism—which really only means obedience to Moscow—in an instant, they would destroy all that.'

Camping in the forest, particularly while listening to tales of Charlemagne, will never hover high on my list of Favourite Moments. But men, even otherwise sensible men, do love these alfresco distractions, and Erik spoke with obvious fervour.

Suddenly he smiled. Not that constrained, wounded smile of his, but a bright, open smile, very merry. 'I wonder,' he said, 'whether Sergeant Biberkopf was ever in the *Wandervogel.*'

'You've spoken with Sergeant Biberkopf?'

This sergeant is the officer in the Berlin Police Department who's investigating the attempted assassination of Herr Hitler.

'On the telephone,' he said. 'Tomorrow I'll be going to the police station, to examine that rifle the police found in the Tiergarten. You must remember to thank your friend Beaumont for me. According to the sergeant, it was on Beaumont's suggestion that the rifle was made available to me.'

.   .   .

EVY, WE'RE COMING into the train station at Hof and I see a post-box. I'm going to run out and drop this in while we change trains. I'll write more later and explain about the rifle, and why Erik must be very prudent when he discusses it with Sergeant Biberkopf.

All my love,
Jane

CHAPTER NINETEEN

W E ARRIVED IN Bayreuth at a little after three in the afternoon. Putzi had spoken to the Wagners in the morning, from Berlin, and the three of us had been invited for dinner, at six. After we got rooms in the train station hotel, Putzi decided to take another nap. Miss Turner asked me if I wanted to play tourist with her, and I said that sounded like a fine idea, and the two of us wandered around the town for a while.

It wasn't much of a town and it didn't take us long to see most of it. At twenty minutes to six we picked up Putzi. Ten minutes later we were walking up the driveway of Wahnfried, the Wagner house. In the center of the drive, surrounded by a low-lying circular hedge, was a large bronze bust on a flat, broad stone cylinder. According to Putzi, this was King Ludwig the Second. Ludwig and Richard Wagner had been pals.

The house itself was a sedate three-story building of yellow stone, with a wooden door at its center, tall and wide, bracketed by fluted pillars. I pulled the bellpull.

When it opened, about two feet wide, I thought for a moment that no one was there. But then I heard a thin female voice—"Papa says I *must* speak English tonight."

I looked down and saw a small blonde girl in a summery white dress, maybe six years old, staring up at me.

"He says you people don't speak German," she said.

"Some of us do," I told her.

She eyed me doubtfully. And then, as though to test me, she rattled off some rapid German.

Beside me, Miss Turner rattled some German back. The girl burst out laughing, her fine blonde hair flapping as she tossed back her head.

"Friedelind?" A male voice, slightly petulant. "Friedelind? Are you annoying our guests?"

The door opened wider and a man stood there, a glass of white wine in his hand. In his fifties, short, he wore delicate white patent leather shoes, a long pair of gray stockings over the leggings of his white jodhpurs, a white suit coat, a white shirt, and a crisp little red bow tie. He was clean-shaven and his face was pink. At the top of his egg-shaped head there were two small stiff wings of white hair, as though a butterfly had settled there and then been by blasted by a blizzard.

"I am Siegfried Wagner," he announced. "The Master's son." His breath smelled of wine. "Good afternoon, Herr Hanfstaengl. You will do the introductions, please."

Putzi explained who everyone was. Everyone was delighted to meet everyone else, and said so. Then Siegfried Wagner led us through the house. We crossed a broad entrance hallway, whose floor was parquet and whose ceiling was three stories high, and came into a huge salon. At the far end of the room, a sweeping rotunda looked out onto a bright green garden. The girl, Friedelind, was tagging beside Miss Turner, chatting happily up at her in German.

"No, no, no," Wagner told the girl. He wagged a finger at her. "No German tonight. You speak English."

"But Papa, *she* speaks German."

"But not everyone does, my child. Tonight you speak English."

She made a face, which he missed because he was busy swallowing some wine. He looked over at me and Putzi and Miss Turner. "Come, come," he said. "Everyone is outside. It is too nice a day to be indoors."

On the grass, around a circular fountain, someone had set out wicker chairs, a few small white wooden side tables, and a trestle table that held wine bottles, glasses, and steins, everything sparkling in the slanted early-evening sunlight. People were sitting about and standing about. Two maids were marching here and there with bottles of wine and pitchers of beer. Three children, two young boys and a girl of about three, were playing off to the left with a woman who was probably a governess. Friedelind ran over to them and began to tell them, waving excited hands, what she'd just scouted out.

Wagner took us around and introduced us. First, sitting in the shade beneath a tree, was his mother, Mrs. Cosima Wagner, a short, thin, white-haired woman in her eighties. She wore an old-fashioned black dress, yards and yards of draped silk. Her face was narrow, her cheeks gullied on either side of her prominent nose, and she seemed frail, almost ethereal. Her voice was faint, the English heavily accented, but when she insisted upon shaking my hand, I could feel the wiry strength in her fingers.

Then there was Siegfried's wife, an Englishwoman named Winifred, short and sturdy, in a white dress with lace at its collar. Her hair was dark, folded into a thick chignon across the back of her neck, and her face was strong, the cheekbones broad, the jaw heavy. She was in her midthirties, about twenty years younger than her husband. She smoked a cigarette as though she'd read somewhere that smoke was better for you than oxygen.

Then there was his brother-in-law, his sister's husband, a burly, myopic Englishman in his tweedy sixties named Houston Stewart Chamberlain. After he shook my hand, he peered at me from beneath bristling white eyebrows and said, "American, eh? But from the name, French originally, eh?"

"A long time ago."

He nodded. "But blood will tell, old boy. Blood will tell."

He was very gallant with Miss Turner, bowing over her hand and smiling widely. "Turner. Any relation to the painter?"

"None, I'm afraid."

Putzi said, "But her mother was German, you know."

"Ah," said Chamberlain, and beamed at her. "Smashing! Good Teuton stock, then."

Watching this without much enthusiasm, like a kid left out of the tree house, was Siegfried's sister, Eva, another short woman with dark hair. We met her next. She wore a gray dress that seemed a bit drab to me, and deliberately conventional, but she still looked maybe ten years younger than her husband, Chamberlain.

We also met the governess, a Frau Schnappauf, a tall woman with a pinched, bitter mouth. And we met the other three children, Wolfgang, Wieland, and Verena. Friedelind, standing off to one side, said, "See, he really *doesn't* speak German."

"Enough," Wagner told her. He wagged his finger again. "Or bed without dinner."

Theatrically, her eyes wide, Friedelind clapped her hand over her mouth. Then she bent forward, her shoulders shaking, delighted with herself. Her brothers ignored her. Her sister giggled. Frau Schnappauf glowered.

Siegfried turned back to us. His wineglass had magically been refilled. "Come," he said. "I shall introduce you to the Master."

Putzi, Miss Turner, and I followed him around the fountain and across the lawn to a thick slab of dark granite lying flat along the grass. There was no inscription in the stone. "Here," he said, and nodded toward the slab, "lies the grave of the greatest artist and thinker in the history of the world."

I was tempted to ask him why he'd planted his father in the backyard, but that was probably none of my business. Maybe the local cemetery was filled. Or maybe you just didn't stick the world's greatest artist and thinker into a village cemetery packed with riffraff.

A small voice said, down at my side, "Momma says you came here to ask about Uncle Wolf."

I looked down. Friedelind.

"Who's Uncle Wolf?" I asked her.

She said, "They make me call him that. His real name is Adolf. I don't like him. He wears lederhosen."

"Enough," said Siegfried.

"But you said I *had* to talk in English."

"Not when you interrupt the adults. Get along now. Go play with your brothers and sister."

"I never get to do *anything,*" she said, and pouted.

"Go," he said, and waved her away.

She turned and walked off, slowly, tragically, her head bent, her feet dragging along the grass.

Siegfried turned back to us and sighed elaborately. "Children. Sometimes a blessing, sometimes a curse." He swallowed an ounce or two of wine. "But now we get you some drinks, yes?"

"Would it be all right," I said, "if I asked a couple of questions?"

"At dinner, please." Smiling, he reached out, squeezed my arm, and blew some wine fumes my way. "Now we relax."

I knew how Friedelind felt.

CHAPTER TWENTY

W E ATE DINNER in a large formal dining room just off the entrance hall. The walls were papered in red velvet. The black silk curtains, pulled shut, were brocaded with gilt. There were candles on the rectangular table, in golden candlesticks, and there were bright electric chandeliers hanging from the ceiling. The white damask tablecloth glistened like a ski run.

Siegfried Wagner sat at the head of the table. The older Mrs. Wagner, Cosima, sat to his right. I sat to his left. To my left was Eva Chamberlain, then Putzi, then Miss Turner, then Chamberlain at the foot of the table, then Winifred Wagner, then an empty space between her and Cosima.

None of the children were around. Maybe Frau Schnappauf had taken them down to the basement and strangled them.

We were served by the same two maids who'd been working the garden. The first course was a kind of bean soup. In a delicate china bowl, on the surface of a watery gray liquid, three or four injured white beans floated alongside a pale yellow shaving of carrot. I tasted the soup. It wasn't nearly as good as it looked.

"So, Mr. Beaumont," said Cosima Wagner. "You are investigating this terrible thing in Berlin. When someone tries to kill that lovely Mr. Hitler."

"That's right," I said. "Did Mr. Hitler mention, while he was here, just what he'd be doing in Berlin?"

"Chap told us," said Chamberlain, "that he was planning a chin-wag with General von Seeckt. About throwing out those bounders in Weimar."

"Silly idea, really," said Siegfried, and swallowed some wine.

"A wonderful idea," said his mother firmly. "The country is falling apart. No respect for tradition. No respect for culture. Nigger music in the nightclubs. Jews everywhere."

"Herr Wolf," said Winifred, from across the table, "wants to bring Germany back from the brink of destruction."

"Herr Wolf is Mr. Hitler?" I asked her.

Cosima said, "It is the name he uses when he travels, he told us."

"It's safer for him, Phil," said Putzi, "to travel under a *nom de route*."

"Understandable," said Chamberlain. "Bolshies hiding under every bed. Filthy rotters."

"But I think it suits him perfectly," said Winifred. She turned to Cosima. "He's very like a wolf, isn't he? Strong and silent. And yet wise, one feels, to the ways of the world."

"I thought," said Siegfried, "that he was rather common." Holding his spoon with his pinkie extended, he dipped his mouth down, daintily, into some soup.

"But that's exactly his strength," said Winifred. "He's of the people, of the *Volk*. He draws his strength from them."

Siegfried was about to say something, but his mother cut him off.

"Exactly," she said. "I thought he was wonderful."

Siegfried put down his spoon, picked up his glass, and swallowed some wine. He looked over at me and smiled. The smile was a bit blurry.

"Did any of you," I said, looking around the table, "mention Mr. Hitler's plans to anyone else?"

"Absolutely not," said Chamberlain. "Chap swore us to secrecy, didn't he, Mother?"

Cosima nodded. "We would not be telling you now, Mr. Beaumont, if Mr. Hitler had not telephoned yesterday and asked us to cooperate with you. We are to answer any questions you have."

"I spoke with him myself," said Winifred proudly.

Miss Turner asked Winifred, "Have you known him long?"

"Oh no," said Winifred. "That was the first time. He was motoring to Berlin, and some friends of ours in Munich suggested we invite him. We'd heard of him, of course, and we were all anxious to meet him. And we all thought he was wonderful." She turned to Cosima. "He seemed to be the answer to our prayers, didn't he, Mother?"

"Indeed he did," said Cosima.

"Which prayers?" Miss Turner asked her.

At that point, Cosima looked over and nodded at the maids, who were standing, hands clasped in front of them, against the wall. They began clearing away the soup bowls.

"For a reborn Germany," said Chamberlain. "Been damned discouraged, all of us, with the way things have gone lately. The war, Versailles, international Jewry, those bounders in Weimar—"

"Mr. Beaumont," said Cosima. "Are you all right? You eat nothing, it seems."

"My stomach's a bit upset. Probably the food I ate on the train."

"Meat of some kind," said Cosima. "I am right?"

"Yeah."

"It will kill you, you know. In the long run it is lethal." She smiled sweetly. "But I assure you that no animal products were used in this meal."

"Great," I said. "By the way, were the maids serving dinner when Mr. Hitler was here?"

"No," said Winifred. "Herr Wolf had asked for us to dine in private. Mother gave the maids the night off."

The maids in question were placing plates in front of people. On each plate, floating in a yellow puddle, was a small round mound of what looked like yellow porridge.

"Thanks," I told Winifred. I turned to Chamberlain. "Sorry to interrupt."

"Not at all, old man." He swiveled his white head toward Miss Turner. "Those bounders in Weimar. The Bolshies. This terrible inflation. The Teutonic race has taken a terrible trouncing. Things were looking pretty damn bleak, I don't mind saying. And then this chap Hitler shows up."

I tasted the porridge. It was probably pureed turnip, but I wouldn't have bet on it.

"Seems like a miracle, in a way," said Chamberlain. He looked to his left. "Well, as you said, Winifred, the answer to our prayers, eh?"

As I swallowed the first mouthful of porridge, I felt something tap gently against my right foot. I looked over at Siegfried, the only person who could have been responsible. He was picking up his glass of wine.

An accident. I moved my foot a bit to the left.

Winifred asked Miss Turner, "Have you read Houston's book?"

"No," said Miss Turner. "I'm afraid I haven't. Which book is that?"

"*The Foundations of the Nineteenth Century*," said Eva, beside me. This was the first thing she'd said all evening. "It's simply superb." She smiled dreamily at her husband.

Something tapped at my right foot again, harder.

I glanced at Siegfried. He seemed to be sitting an inch or so lower in his seat, but he was still working his way through the porridge. I crossed my right leg over my left, moving it farther away from the end of the table, and from Siegfried. I glanced across the table at Winifred and wondered whether she knew that her husband had a roving eye, and a foot to match.

She was saying to Miss Turner, "It's all in there. The entire history of mankind."

I drank some more wine. So, I noticed, did Siegfried. One of the maids refilled his glass.

"A remarkable book," said Cosima. "The Master would have loved it. I think it a great shame that he never lived to see it."

Chamberlain was flushed with pleasure. "Couldn't have done it, though, you know," he told Miss Turner, "without those who went before. Like Newton, I stand on the shoulders of giants. Including the Master." He smiled at Miss Turner. "You've read *The Jews in Music,* have you?"

"I can't say that I have."

"Oh, you must. A smashing piece, really, simply smashing. One of the Master's best. Explains why every human being has an instinctive physical aversion to the Jew."

"But I shouldn't think," said Miss Turner, "that every human being actually does."

"Not every adult, it may be," said Chamberlain. "Instincts get eroded by education—which these days is infested with Jews, of course. But science has proven that if you take a small child, especially a small young girl, some little Teuton girl who hasn't the faintest clue as to what a Jew is, and you show her a Jew, an utter stranger, she'll burst directly into tears. An amazing fact, but there it is. I'll wager that if we had little Verena in here, and we trotted in some grubby Jew from the streets—"

"Please, Houston," said Cosima archly, "trot no grubby Jews into my dining room."

The group laughed merrily. Most of them did, anyway. Miss Turner looked over at me and blinked behind her spectacles. Putzi studied his porridge, prodding it with his spoon.

Chamberlain said to Miss Turner, "What my book does, in its own small way, is demonstrate that the Teutonic race has been responsible for every creative achievement in mankind's history. And that the most creative, the most forceful, branch of the Teutonic race has always been the German."

Something scraped at the inner ankle of my left foot, insistently.

"Siegfried," said Cosima, "do sit up. You will hurt your back, slumping like that."

Siegfried had nearly disappeared beneath the table. Smiling at his mother, he pulled himself more fully upright, dabbed at his mouth with his napkin, then went back to work on his porridge.

"Your Jew," said Chamberlain, "on the other hand, has never created anything. His brain simply isn't constructed that way. He's a mongrel, you know. Part Hittite. Your Jewish nose, for example, that's an example of the Hittite legacy."

Miss Turner was staring at him, her mouth slightly open.

"But for years now," Chamberlain went on, "they've been stealing their way into banks, our schools, our universities. Trying to pollute us with their mongrel philosophies. Socialism. Marxism. Well, if this Hitler chap has his way, their days are numbered, I can promise you." He turned to Cosima. "You know, Mother, I see him as the distillation of everything the Master ever said about Germany."

"Yes," said Cosima. "He is, in a way, the fulfillment of all the Master's hopes."

Winifred said, "He's so dynamic, isn't he? And yet so self-effacing." She looked at her mother-in-law, as though checking to see that she'd gotten it right.

"Yes," said Cosima. "He is almost bashful, really. I found him quite charming."

Siegfried drained off what was left of his wine, pushed himself back from the table, and stood. His face was a deeper shade of pink now, a color that nearly matched the red of his crisp little bow tie, and shiny beads of sweat were clustered on his forehead. He ran a hand over the two white tufts of hair at the top of his head. They jumped right back up, like coil springs. "Excuse me," he said. "I am indisposed." He turned, took one step, and fell forward and crashed against the floor. On the table, plates and glasses rattled.

"Oh dear," said Cosima. "His allergies again."

CHAPTER TWENTY-ONE

I SPRANG UP and rushed around the table to Siegfried. When I gently rolled him over, he was snoring quietly. No broken bones. No bruises, or at least none that showed.

"He will be all right," Cosima told me. She was standing opposite me, on the far side of Siegfried. Chamberlain stood next to her, his arm around her thin shoulders. "This happens once or twice every spring," she said. "He merely needs some rest, the poor dear."

"It's that damned pollen," said Chamberlain.

I didn't know whether the two of them actually believed what they were saying, or whether they believed that I might believe it.

"You want me to carry him somewhere?" I asked Cosima.

"I have sent for the gardener. He will be here—ah, Fritz."

The gardener must have been waiting in the wings. He was a burly young man wearing a rough gray woolen sweater and rumpled gray woolen pants. Cosima said something to him in German. He nodded, walked over to Siegfried, bent over, pulled him upright, and slung him over his thick shoulder, like a sack of fertilizer. Siegfried's arms dangled limply. I noticed he was wearing French cuffs with gold cuff links shaped like a kind of broken cross.

The gardener turned to us all, tugged at his forelock, smiled, muttered some cheerful German, then turned back and carted Siegfried off.

"We must not let this interrupt our meal," said Cosima. "Come, Mr. Beaumont. Please be seated. You must try to enjoy your food."

The next course was cabbage stuffed with tomatoes, or tomatoes stuffed with cabbage—it had been cooked for so long I couldn't tell which one had originally been outside. While I tried to enjoy this, Chamberlain talked at length about the Jews to Miss Turner, who was looking more and more pale.

Finally, over dessert, when Chamberlain started repeating himself, Miss Turner said, "But what about Christianity? Surely it was a Jew who created that?"

Chamberlain chuckled like a fond uncle. Cosima and Winifred smiled small, sympathetic smiles. I glanced at Eva, to my left. She was smiling the same smile. All of them had heard this before.

"That's a common misconception," said Chamberlain. "But the Bible tells us that he was a Galilean, and science has shown that Galilee at the time was swarming with non-Jewish elements. It is an indisputable fact that Jesus was not a Jew."

"But what, then, was he?"

"Impossible to say, at this juncture. Greek, possibly. But a Teuton for certain. Only a Teuton could have produced so sublime a philosophy. I see the crucifixion as the ultimate negation of Will. Nothing could be more Teutonic."

Miss Turner did some more staring.

WE SEPARATED A bit later, the men and the women. Chamberlain led Putzi and me up the stairs to the library, where brandy and cigars were waiting.

Before Chamberlain could get started on the Jews again, I asked him if he had any idea who might have wanted to kill Adolf Hitler.

"The Bolshies," he said. "Filthy swine. They know that if the chap comes to power, then they're in for it, all of 'em."

"But how did the Communists find out that Hitler would be in the Tiergarten that afternoon?"

It was the same question that Miss Turner and I had been asking since we arrived in Germany.

"Well," he said, "they certainly didn't learn it from any of us, old boy. As I said, we were sworn to secrecy."

And so were the people on the list that Putzi had given me. But someone had learned that Hitler would be in the Tiergarten that day, and someone had shot at him.

AFTER I FINISHED up my brandy, and while Chamberlain was holding forth on Famous Teutons in History, like Socrates and St. Paul, I excused myself to use the WC. It was down in the basement. As I passed by the opened door to the dining room, I could hear the women chattering away in German. I wondered how Miss Turner was doing.

They were still chattering when I came back. I climbed up the stairs to the library. As I walked into the room, Putzi was saying, "So there's this big fat Yid who—"

He stopped when he saw me, his eyes blinking, his hand frozen in the air. The hand held a cigar and, from its white ash, smoke spiraled slowly upward.

We stared at each other for a moment.

"Putzi," I said, suddenly deciding, "I think Miss Turner and I should be getting back to the hotel."

He set down his brandy snifter and stood up. "I'm ready whenever you are, Phil." He said this quickly, his eagerness driven by guilt, or by the need to mask it.

"That's okay," I told him. "There are some things that Miss Turner and I should talk about. We'll see you in the morning."

Chamberlain said, "Shall I ring up a taxi for you?"

"Don't bother. It's not that far to the hotel, and it's a nice night."

Putzi was still standing there, looking as though he didn't know what to do with his long arms. "Are you sure, Phil?" He raised his bushy eyebrows hopefully. "It's really not a problem for me, leaving now."

"You finish up your brandy. Like I said, we'll see you tomorrow, at breakfast."

"Yes. Well. All right, Phil. Whatever you say." He sat back down slowly, awkwardly.

"Good night," I said to Chamberlain.

"Good night, old boy." He hadn't noticed anything wrong. "Have a lovely trip to Munich tomorrow. Bon voyage, eh?" That was probably for the benefit of my French blood.

"Thanks," I said.

When I showed up in the dining room, Miss Turner had no objections to leaving. She asked about Mr. Hanfstaengl. I said that he was staying for a while. We said good-bye to all the Wagner women.

Outside, when we were eight or nine feet away from the house, Miss Turner leaned toward me and said, in a quick sharp whisper, "*Thank* you. I was getting ready to scream. Those people are poisonous."

"Yeah."

"I've never in my life heard such low, mean, *beastly* nonsense."

"Yeah."

"I'd thought that Mr. Chamberlain was bad. But those women—you should have heard them. They were *vile*. How on earth can Mr. Hanfstaengl stand to be around any member of that family?"

"Mr. Hanfstaengl is up in the library, telling Jew jokes to Chamberlain."

For a moment she said nothing. I could feel the weight of her stare along the side of my face. She said, "You liked him, didn't you? Mr. Hanfstaengl."

"Yeah."

"You didn't know that he was like that."

"No."

"I'm sorry."

"Me too."

We walked in silence for a while.

The streetlamps were dim, and the streets were mostly empty until we reached the center of town, where a few cars grumbled along the cobblestones. Some of the cafés were still open, and there were people on the sidewalks. The lights were brighter here, and we could see our reflection in the windows of the darkened shops.

We were about a hundred yards from the hotel when Miss Turner said quietly, "Mr. Beaumont?"

"Yeah?"

"I may be wrong, but I believe we're being followed."

"You're not wrong," I said.

There were two of them, keeping their distance, about two blocks back. They wore peacoats and watch caps, like the men who'd come after Putzi and me outside the Mikado.

CHAPTER TWENTY-TWO

T HE MEN KEPT their distance all the way to the hotel. When we got inside, I went to the front desk and arranged to use the lobby telephone. I called the Wagner home and one of the maids answered. I gave her Putzi's name and I added *"Bitte,"* which pretty much exhausted my German. When Putzi came on the line, I told him not to walk back to the hotel. Telephone for a taxicab, I told him.

"And why is that, Phil?" he asked.

"Remember the men at the Mikado?"

"Yes, of course."

"Some friends of theirs are in town. Miss Turner and I were followed back to the hotel."

He was silent for a moment, and then he said, "But you are okay, you and Miss Turner?"

"We're fine. But I don't want you walking back here alone."

Another silence. "Yes. Yes, Phil. Thank you. Thank you very much." Gratitude had tightened his voice.

There was nothing personal in my warning him. He had been useful in the past, and he would be less useful in the future if he was dead. But I didn't see any reason, just then, to share that point of view with him.

"I'll see you in the morning," I told him.

"Yes, Phil. Absolutely. Thank you. Ten thirty in the café at the hotel."

We were scheduled to take the eleven-fifteen train to Munich.

After I hung up, Miss Turner and I went into the café and we talked about the two men and what we should do about them.

. . .

THE NEXT MORNING, Miss Turner and I were out on the street by nine o'clock. We saw no men in peacoats, or anyone who seemed even slightly interested in us. We did some quick shopping, returned to the hotel, and packed our bags. I went to Putzi's room to tell him what was going on. Before I got started, he thanked me again for my warning him last night. I told him to forget about it.

"But you see, Phil," he said, "I thought you were angry with me."

"Why would I be angry with you, Putzi?"

"Well, perhaps . . . I thought because of that little joke. The one I was telling Houston Chamberlain. It was a completely innocent joke, Phil, really. As I told you, I have nothing against the Jews."

"Don't worry about it. You get packed up and we'll see you in the café at ten thirty."

There had been a time when I hadn't paid much attention to jokes like Putzi's. I hadn't liked them much, but they hadn't bothered me. That had been before the War, and before I walked into a bullet, and before a corporal named David Rosenblum had picked me up and carried me a couple of hundred yards to the rear. Later that day, he was wounded himself. By the time someone picked him up and carried him to the rear, he was dead.

But this was something else I saw no reason to share with Putzi.

AT ELEVEN O'CLOCK, when the three of us arrived at the train station, the men were already there. Two of them were wearing peacoats. They were standing under the wooden canopy at the near end of the track, their hands in their pockets, chatting quietly and doing a fine job of ignoring us.

I looked around to see if I could spot any others. There were some couples, a few parents with children, some plump businessmen in sleek suits reading newspapers.

Halfway down the platform, there was a big man who wore a slouch hat and a long black trench coat. The sun was shining; the morning air was warm. Unless he was naked underneath it, he didn't really need that trench coat. But its deep pockets would be a good place to park a big pistol, like a Luger or a Mauser.

When the train came puffing into the station, we walked down to the end of the platform, to the first-class car. We passed the man in the overcoat, who was staring at his pocket watch as though he were watching the hands move. We climbed aboard the train. Our compartment was the first one in the car. Putzi and I slid our luggage in the overhead racks, and I helped Miss Turner with hers.

The man in the trench coat walked past the compartment door. He didn't glance in.

We sat down. A few moments later, the conductor popped his head into the doorway to say hello. Putzi asked him where we could find the dining car. The conductor said something and jerked his thumb back toward the front of the train.

"The next car," Putzi told me.

"Okay," I said.

The three of us stood up and we stepped out into the corridor.

The man in the trench coat was standing about six feet away, toward the rear of the car. From there, he could keep an eye on us and our luggage. At the moment, he was still ignoring us. He had opened a window and lighted a cigarette, and he was staring out the window like someone who had never seen a train station before.

With Putzi leading, me at the rear, the three of us walked out the door, through the vestibule, out the exit door of the car, across the metal panel that covered the train's coupling, and into the dining car. Some of the businessmen were sitting at the tables, reading their newspapers. The train suddenly lumbered forward and we quickened our pace. I glanced back. The man in the trench coat wasn't following.

We went through the door at the other end of the car, and this time we turned right at the vestibule. Putzi tugged open the entrance door, and then, one by one, we stepped briskly down off the slowly moving train and walked across the platform toward the station.

I looked back at the train. No one else had gotten off.

Inside the station, Putzi found a porter, handed him some money, and sent him to the hotel to fetch the new bags that Miss Turner and I had bought this morning, the bags that the three of us had packed with our things.

If the men in peacoats, or the man in the trench coat, opened the bags in our compartment's luggage compartment, they might be disappointed with the sacks of flour that we'd used to give the bags some heft. But maybe not. In Germany these days, flour was pricey stuff.

We went into the station café and found a table. A waiter arrived. Once again, I ordered coffee, Miss Turner ordered tea, and Putzi ordered beer.

"I still don't get it, Phil," said Putzi. "If those men were following us—"

"There's no *if*, Putzi," I said. "They were following us."

"Okay, yes, they were following us. But all they need to do now is wait at the Munich station until we show up."

I said, "Maybe. But I don't like them being on that train. They probably already know where Miss Turner and I will be staying in Munich. They could've waited and picked us up there. Why were they sticking so close to us?"

He looked puzzled. "Hold on, Phil. How would they know where you'll be staying in Munich?"

"The same way they knew we'd be taking the eleven-fifteen train today."

"They could've have *known* that. They've probably been at the station all morning, waiting for us."

"Putzi," I said, "we didn't have to take the train today. Theoretically, we could've stayed in Bayreuth for another month. But when Miss Turner and I went out this morning, no one was looking for us. They *knew* we'd be in the station at eleven fifteen."

"And," said Miss Turner, "more to the point, Mr. Hanfstaengl, they knew that we were in Bayreuth. How did they know that?"

Putzi jerked back his big head, surprised by what probably seemed like an attack. He glanced back and forth between Miss Turner and me, as though we were suddenly ganging up on him. In a way, I suppose, we were.

He turned back to me, his face open, his bushy eyebrows arched, trying to persuade me to shift from opponent to referee. "Phil, how could I know? They must have followed us from Berlin."

"No," I said. "There were no peacoats in the Berlin station. And none at Hof. Those men got here after we did."

"Or," said Miss Turner to Putzi, "*before* we did."

This was something she had suggested last night.

He looked at her. "Bushwa," he said. "That's impossible."

The waiter delivered our orders. Putzi paid him a couple of hundred thousand marks.

As the waiter left, I asked Putzi, "Who knew that we'd be going to Bayreuth yesterday?"

"Hess. Only Hess, in Munich. He was the only one I told."

"And you told him that we'd be taking the eleven-fifteen train today?"

"Yes, of course. But you can't think that *Hess* would send those men here? Why would he do such a thing?"

"I'm not saying it's Hess. But look, Putzi, take it in chronological order. We leave Frankfurt for Berlin on Monday night. On the same night, in Berlin, Nancy Greene is murdered. On Tuesday night, those goons show up outside the Mikado."

"But Phil, Hess never knew about the Mikado. We didn't know ourselves—not until we got the message in the restaurant, from Captain Roehm."

"Then unless von Dinesen told someone, the goons must have followed us from the Adlon. How'd they know we were there?"

Putzi frowned. "What are you saying, Phil?"

"What I said before, Putzi. Someone is talking."

"Someone on that list, you mean."

"Maybe. You've booked us into a hotel in Munich, right?"

"The Vier Jahreszeiten. The Four Seasons. One of the best in the city."

"Right. We're not staying there. What else is there?"

"What sort of hotel would you prefer?"

"Something large. A big staff, a lot of entrances."

"There's the Bayerischer Hof. It's quite good."

"Fine."

"But if the goons are waiting for us at the station in Munich . . ."

"Yeah. Miss Turner was looking at the Baedeker last night. The train stops at a small town just before Munich." I turned to her. "What's it called?"

"Dachau," she said.

I turned back to Putzi. "We'll get off there and grab a taxi. We'll drive to Munich."

"But that will cost a fortune."

"I've got a fortune. American dollars, remember?"

"Yes, but Phil, what about Hess?"

"What about him?"

"Should I tell him which hotel you'll be using?"

"When we get to Dachau, you call him and ask him to meet us there tonight. At the hotel. Is there some way you can do that without actually mentioning the name of the hotel?"

He frowned. "Why?"

"Maybe Hess's phone line is being intercepted."

He thought for a moment. "Yes. He and I had a drink there once. On his birthday. I can mention that."

"Okay. But tell him not to tell anyone else where we are. Anyone at all, Putzi."

"Except for Herr Hitler, of course."

"Except for no one."

WE GOT ON the twelve-fifteen train, carrying our new luggage. We arrived in Dachau at six o'clock. Putzi called Hess, and Hess agreed to meet Miss Turner and me at the Bayerischer Hof Hotel at ten that night, at the bar. And then Putzi found a cabdriver who was delighted to get twenty American dollars to drive us to Munich. For the same money, he would have driven us to Moscow.

Putzi lived in Uffing, ten or fifteen miles southwest of the city. We drove south from Dachau and dropped him off at the train station in Pasing, a few miles to the west of Munich, so he could take the train back home.

Miss Turner and I arrived at the hotel at seven thirty. We checked in, and I talked with the desk clerk for a while and gave him an American twenty-dollar bill. I sent another telegram to Cooper in England, telling him where we were. Afterward, we talked for a while to the concierge, Herr Braun, and I gave him a twenty too. Then we went to our rooms and washed up. At nine, we met downstairs in the restaurant. We ate dinner and then, at ten o'clock, we went to the bar. Rudolf Hess was there, waiting for us.

MUNICH

Train to Munich
Friday
May 18th

Dear Evangeline,

Last night was one of the most disagreeable evenings of my life. Mr Beaumont, the Hanfstaengl, and I had dinner at Wahnfried, the home of Richard Wagner, who fortunately for us spent the evening beneath a granite cenotaph in the garden; and his wife, Cosima, who unfortunately did not.

She is, one thinks at first, a charming old woman. And then she opens her pale, prim purse of a mouth, and the vilest, foulest, most sickening sentiments come scrambling out of it, like ogres tumbling from a gutter.

Her daughter, Eva, and her daughter-in-law, Winifred (who by the way is British, born in Hastings), are worse.

Did you know, Evy, that the Jews have taken over the world? An international conspiracy of Jewish bankers and stockbrokers has insinuated itself into governments everywhere and is secretly manipulating all of our benighted little lives. Do you remember Mr Susskind, who owned the dry goods store next to the greengrocer's? Well, despite his innocent appearance, like all Jews he was a member of the conspiracy. While you and I were dawdling over the penny sweets, he was polishing up his report on the Gentile resistance in Torquay.

Also present for dinner, and also British, was Eva's husband, a demented old man named Houston Stewart Chamberlain.

Did you know, Evy, that Jesus was a German? His real name was Hans, and he came from Essen. And it wasn't bread and fish he multiplied, it was pretzels and bratwurst. And—

Never mind. I don't want to talk about these people. They were vile.

Where had I left off, in that last letter?

Yes. Erik and the rifle.

In brief, the Berlin police are aware that a certain rifle, deliberately left near the site from which someone attempted to assassinate Herr Hitler, was not in fact the rifle used in the attack. I don't think I've mentioned this, but Erik, in addition to being a psychic, is also a 'psychometrist'. When he holds in his hands some item taken from an unknown individual and 'attunes' himself to it, he can tell you reams and reams of useful things about that person. It has something to do with vibrations and harmonics, as I understand it, which (obviously) I don't, really.

In any event, Erik has been after the police to let him handle the rifle, so he could help them identify the person who used it.

I asked Sergeant Biberkopf, when Mr Beaumont and I spoke with him, what would happen if Erik were to say that the rifle hadn't been used. He effectively said that Erik might then become a suspect himself. The sergeant is not a believer in psychic phenomena.

So today, while Mr Beaumont and the Hanfstaengl and I were playing hide-and-seek, dashing from one Munich train or another—it's a long story, Evy—Erik was possibly putting himself in jeopardy with Sergeant Biberkopf.

I'm likely being very foolish. Even if Sergeant Biberkopf does suspect Erik, I'm sure that Erik has a perfectly good alibi for the time of the attack. And since the odds are excellent that I'll never see Erik again, I should simply forget about all this. Dismiss it from my mind. Ruthlessly.

But I don't like not knowing. (This is, I would argue, a useful characteristic in a Pinkerton.) And I believe that I'll ring Erik up tonight. Just to make sure that he's all right.

We'll be getting into Munich soon. I'll post this when we arrive.

All my love,
Jane

CHAPTER TWENTY-THREE

H ESS WORE A gray suit. He was in his late twenties, tall and lean, with black wavy hair that was beginning to retreat at the sides, away from his widow's peak and toward his temples. He had square shoulders and a square face that stopped just a shade short of handsome. What stopped it was his chin, which receded slightly, and his dark brown eyes. The eyes were set a bit too deeply in their sockets and they made his forehead, with its thick eyebrows, seem heavy and angular. But despite their depth, they had a kind of shining, liquid intensity. They were the eyes of a sincere young priest, or a sincere young door-to-door salesman.

He had been sitting at a table in the corner. He stood up when we arrived and he pumped my hand, grinning furiously, as though he liked nothing better than shaking hands, especially mine. He took Miss Turner's hand and bowed over it. And then he said, "Sit, sit, please. Can I get you some refreshment, Miss Turner?" He leaned toward her eagerly, like a waiter toward a dowager with a solid line of credit.

"A glass of wine?" she asked him. "Red wine?"

"Of course. And you, Mr. Beaumont?"

"A cognac would be nice."

"One minute," he said, and scuttled over to the bar. In only a little over a minute he was back with the brandy, the wine, and a stein of beer for himself, holding the drinks within the circle of his slender, spatulate fingers. He set the glasses down carefully and took his seat. He grabbed the stein and raised it. "To your stay in Munich. Much success."

We all clinked glasses. I tasted the cognac. Miss Turner sipped at her wine. Hess slugged back half of his beer, his big Adam's apple twitching.

He set down the stein, sighing, and turned to Miss Turner. "The wine is acceptable?"

"It's fine, thank you."

"The bartender said it was the very best he had."

"It's fine. Really."

"Good. And your cognac, Mr. Beaumont?"

"Fine."

"Good, excellent." He looked back and forth between us. "So," he said happily, "Pinkertons. I have read about Pinkertons many times, in the books and the magazines, but I have never met one before. You are my very first." He turned to Miss Turner. "My two very first."

Miss Turner smiled politely.

"And you, Miss Turner," he said, "you are from England?"

"That's right, yes."

"I have always very much wanted to visit England. 'This scepter'd isle, this earth of majesty, this seat of Mars.' It must be very lovely, yes?"

"Very lovely," she said, and added diplomatically, "but then so is Germany."

"Yes, of course. They are in many ways much the same, I believe. In terms of geography, the scenic landscapes and such. And of course they are both inhabited by Teutonic races. My father lived for a time in England, actually. Before I was born."

"You haven't been there yourself?"

"No, no, I was raised in Egypt. We came to Germany when I was fourteen. But I am looking very much forward to visiting England at some time in the future."

He turned to me. "And how are you enjoying our country, Mr. Beaumont?"

"It's fine. But there are a few things we need to talk about."

"Yes, of course." His face went serious and he sat forward and folded his hands together on the table. He nodded once, briskly. "I am at your disposal completely."

"First thing," I said. "Did Mr. Hanfstaengl ask you about Captain Roehm? About pulling him off his investigation of the sniping?"

"Yes, he did. And the Führer—Herr Hitler—he agrees with you entirely. He knows that you must be permitted to conduct your own inquiry, without hindrance or impediment. He has spoken with Captain Roehm, and the captain will desist."

"Fine."

"By the way," he said, "the Führer wishes me to tell you that he deeply regrets that he cannot meet with you himself at the present time. He very much wants to converse with you, with both of you. But unfortunately just now he has many vital political matters that require his attention. He hopes that you understand this."

"Sure. Second—"

"He wishes me, however, to invite you to his speech on Sunday. He will be at the Bürgerbräukeller at six thirty in the evening. He would like you both to come as his special guests, at six o'clock, and to join him afterward, for a dinner."

"That'll be fine," I said. "We look forward to it. He understands that we'll need to talk to him about Berlin?"

"Yes, of course."

"Next thing," I said. "Putzi asked you not to tell anyone that we're staying here? At this hotel?"

"Yes. Not even the Führer, he said. He was most insistent. He said that you would explicate the matter." He raised his thick eyebrows, waiting for me to explicate.

I said, "Did Putzi tell you about the men who tried to jump us after we talked to Captain Roehm?"

"Yes. And I spoke with Captain Roehm about it. They were Communists, of course. The Communists are violently opposed to the party, and to the Führer. I have no doubt but that you and Miss Turner will discover that they were responsible for the cowardly attack in the Tiergarten."

"Yeah. But the important thing is that, whoever they were, they probably followed us from the Hotel Adlon. They knew how to find us, right from the beginning. And yesterday there were more of them in Bayreuth."

"They followed you from Berlin?" He looked from me to Miss Turner and back to me again.

"No," I said. "They knew that we'd be there. They tried to get on the same train today."

"But you eluded them, yes?"

"Yeah," I said. "We eluded them."

"Good. Excellent." He frowned. "But you are suggesting that there has been a breach of security. I take this very seriously."

I said, "I know you've been in contact with Mr. Hanfstaengl. Have you talked to anyone else about us?"

"Only with the Führer. He has naturally been following your progress with great interest."

"No one else?"

"No one, I can assure you."

"What about the meeting in the Tiergarten. Before it happened, did you tell anyone about that?"

"No. Absolutely no one."

"You keep notes, records?"

"Yes, but I leave them in a safebox in my office."

"Who has the key?"

"There is only one. It is on my person at all times."

"What about your telephone line?" I said. "Could someone be intercepting it?"

He frowned again. "Intercepting it?"

"It's possible to cut into a phone line and listen to the conversation."

"Yes, yes. The British did this to our battlefield lines, during the War. But it requires that someone monitor the line at all times."

"No," I said. "It's possible to hook up the intercepting line to a wire recorder that'll operate only while a conversation is going on."

"Fiendish." He shook his head. "Diabolical. And you believe that the Reds have established such an interception?"

"I believe it's possible that someone has."

"Diabolical. And what do you recommend?"

"I recommend that you have someone check the line."

He nodded. "I will arrange for this in the morning. The very first thing."

"And I recommend that from now on you don't talk about this case over the telephone. To anyone. Even if the line seems all right."

"But how will we communicate, you and I?"

"I won't be communicating with Mr. Hanfstaengl?"

"Now that you are here, I think it best if we communicate directly with each other. Herr Hanfstaengl will of course be available to you, should you require any assistance from him. Translations and such." He turned to Miss Turner and smiled. "But I understand that you speak fluent German, Miss Turner."

"Hardly fluent," she said, and smiled.

"I am sure you are being modest, in the typical English fashion." He turned back to me. "Do you have suggestions as to how we might communicate?"

"Is there somewhere we can meet? A bar, a restaurant? Somewhere busy, with a lot of traffic."

"The Hofbräuhaus. You have heard of it?"

"No."

"It is always busy. It would be capital for this purpose."

"All right. If I need to talk, I'll call you and ask for a meeting. We'll meet there."

"Excellent. But for this you will require my telephone number, yes?"

"It might come in handy."

"Yes, of course." Hess was probably good at a lot of things, but irony wasn't one of them.

He slipped a pen and a notebook from his inside suit-coat pocket, tore off a sheet of paper, uncapped the pen. He scribbled across the paper. "My office telephone number. And the number at my home." He gave me the sheet.

"Thanks." I took my wallet from my pants pocket, slid the sheet inside, and took out the list of names that Putzi had given me in Berlin, at the Adlon. "Okay." I handed the list to Hess. "When can I talk to these people?"

He looked down at the list, then back up at me. "You understand that all of these men are dedicated party members."

"Yeah. I still need to talk to them. They were the people who knew that Mr. Hitler would be in the Tiergarten."

"None of them would ever betray the Führer."

"I still need to talk to them. It's my job."

"Yes. Very well." He looked down again at the list. "You have already spoken to Captain Roehm. And to Herr Hanfstaengl, of course. I can arrange for you to interview Herr Rosenberg and Emil Maurice tomorrow. And Frederich Nordstrum. And also Gunnar Sontag, my assistant."

"What about Captain Goering?"

"I will be seeing him in the morning. If he cannot come to my office at a later time, can you meet with him tomorrow at the Hofbräuhaus?"

"Yeah."

"Excellent. If you will telephone me in the morning, at ten o'clock, I will inform you of the time. Is there anything else?"

I swallowed some cognac. "Yeah. Maybe you can tell me why everyone is so sure that the Reds are responsible for all this."

"As I said, Mr. Beaumont, the Reds are violently opposed to the Führer."

"And why is that?"

"Because of what he is offering to the German people."

"And what's that?"

"Put simply, it is a future without selfishness, without class distinctions, without the bitter disharmony between capitalist and worker." His eyes were beginning to glitter. "Every German will work with every other German, as brother and sister. All political parties will disappear, and all Germans will be united as one *Volk,* one people. This will be a difficult journey, of course. It will require sacrifices from all of us." Now the glistening eyes were staring off, into the heroic future. He couldn't wait to start making those sacrifices. "It will require struggle. Blood and toil. It will not happen overnight."

"No," I said, "probably not."

He looked at me. "But I believe sincerely, Mr. Beaumont, that in the end it *will* happen. All of us in the party believe this. And we believe that the Führer, Herr Hitler, with his deep understanding of the German people, will bring it about."

"Uh-huh."

"Surely you can understand how such a program, such a future, would threaten the Communists, with their archaic, self-centered insistence upon the class struggle."

"Yeah. Sure."

He turned to Miss Turner. "You do see that, Miss Turner?"

"Oh yes," she said. "Quite clearly."

He sat back. "Good. Excellent." He turned back to me. "Is there any other assistance I can provide you?"

"No. Thanks. I'll give you a call in the morning, Mr. Hess."

"Please. You must call me Rudy."

"Fine. Thank you, Rudy." I held out my hand and he took it. I noticed that he blushed.

He stood up. His arms stiff at his sides, he gave a quick little bow to Miss Turner. *"Enchanté."* He turned back to me. "I will look forward to hearing from you."

"I'll call at ten."

"Excellent."

He left the table and walked away.

For a moment Miss Turner and I looked at each other.

I said. *"Führer.* What does it mean?"

"Leader. Guide."

I nodded. "What do you think of Rudy?"

"I think he's very earnest. What do you think?"

"I think we're on the wrong side."

She nodded. "Yes. Is there something we can do about it?"

"Like head back to London?"

"Yes."

"If we don't find this guy, then probably they're going to find him. And they won't be telling Sergeant Biberkopf about it."

She nodded. "Yes, of course. We soldier on, then."

I smiled. "We soldier on."

Hotel Bayerischer Hof
Munich
Saturday morning
May 19th

Dear Evangeline,

I tried ringing Erik from the lobby telephone, here at the hotel, before I met Mr Beaumont for dinner. The operator rang back and told me that there was no answer. This was at a quarter to nine, over three hours ago.

I tried again just now, with the same results. There is no telephone in my room here, an insufferable omission, and I was forced to dress again and trot downstairs to the lobby.

I do hope that Erik is all right.

It's Friday night, and perhaps he's out somewhere.

Evy, all of this is beginning to wear me down. I don't mean Erik. I mean everything else. The beggars, the prostitutes. The despair. The indifference to the despair. The Wagner family and their nonchalantly toxic hatred.

Tonight, after dinner, Mr Beaumont and I discussed the case with Herr Hitler's private secretary, Rudolf Hess, a paragon of gravitas. Well, to be truthful once again, Mr Beaumont and the Paragon discussed the case. As I am for the Hanfstaengl, for the Paragon I was merely a sort of accessory of Mr Beaumont's, an adornment, like a watch fob.

I don't like these people, Evy. The people who belong to this party. The Hanfstaengl, the Paragon.

I don't like Germany. There is a darkness here, and in the darkness a sickness is spreading.

I want to go home.

Yours,
Jane

CHAPTER TWENTY-FOUR

THE HOFBRÄUHAUS WAS huge and the main food hall was nearly full when Miss Turner and I arrived there at twelve thirty. All the people were eating and drinking and shouting happily at each other. Burly waitresses in billowing brown dresses and billowing white blouses sailed between the tables, ferrying huge trays laden with fat ceramic steins of beer.

Captain Goering was waiting for us where Hess had said he would be, at the far end of the enormous room. He stood up as we approached, so we wouldn't miss him.

Missing him would have been difficult. He was wearing a costume that could have come out of an operetta. The shirt and the jacket were brown, and there was a wide shiny black belt and a shiny black shoulder strap. Chunky loops of gold braid dangled from the epaulets. Across the chest, the jacket was studded with medals I didn't recognize, and with the Pour le Mérite, which I did. At his neck he wore an Iron Cross, First Class. Wrapped around his upper left arm was a red armband with a white circle on it. In the center of the circle was a kind of black crooked cross, the same symbol that Siegfried Wagner had been wearing as gold cuff links in Bayreuth.

He was handsome in a fleshy way, with dark blond hair, sculpted sensual lips, and deep blue eyes. The skin of his face was smooth, almost feminine, and his cheeks were rosy with health. Or with wine from the bottle that stood beside him on the table.

He held out his hand and I took it. He crushed my fingers enthusiastically and said something in German.

"He welcomes you to Munich," said Miss Turner.

"Thank him for me," I said.

Miss Turner did, and Goering hooked his thumbs over the belt and bowed toward her. I think he clicked his heels, but I couldn't tell—the din of happy diners was too loud.

He gestured for us to sit down, and we did. As he sat down himself and poured what was left of the wine into his glass, he said something to Miss Turner.

"He said," she translated, "that he wouldn't have picked this place to meet. The food is tolerable, but the wine selection is very poor."

She turned back to him and for a moment the two of them chatted in German.

"He recommends the soup with the liver dumpling," she told me. "Or the pork knuckle with potato dumpling and cabbage salad."

"I'm trying to avoid pork knuckle this week," I said. "Liver dumpling too."

Just then the waitress arrived. She and Miss Turner talked for a while, with Goering tossing in a sentence now and then. Miss Turner asked me, "Would you like the roast pork?"

"That'll be fine."

"I'll try that, as well. And Captain Goering says that the 1921 Chavignon, a Sancerre, is the only drinkable wine on the menu."

"Fine."

She turned to the waitress, gave her our order. As the waitress sailed away, Miss Turner turned back to me. "The captain speaks no English at all. Shall I translate word for word?"

"Please."

"He asked if you served in the American army."

"Yeah," I said to the captain.

"*Ja,*" Miss Turner told him.

Through Miss Turner, he asked me, "The infantry?"

"Yeah. And you?"

"At first the infantry. I earned my Iron Cross there. Later I joined the Air Service and earned my Pour le Mérite. I was an ace. I made twenty-two kills. You have heard of von Richthofen's Flying Circus?"

"Of course."

He nodded. "After von Richthofen, I was the most accomplished pilot in the Air Service. Following his death, I became the commander of the Circus. I flew one of the first Fokker D-Sevens. This was a biplane with a Mercedes liquid-cooled, six-cylinder in-line engine, one that produced one hundred and sixty horsepower. I am an utterly crashing bore."

"Miss Turner," I said.

She turned toward me, her face innocent, her eyebrows raised behind the spectacles. "Yes?"

"Word for word, please. No editorials."

"Yes. Quite right."

I turned to Goering. "That sounds like an impressive airplane."

Goering said, "It was a wonderful airplane, truly. I deeply miss those days. The excitement, the valor, the camaraderie."

"Too bad the War had to end."

"Shall I translate that?" said Miss Turner.

"No. Ask him how long he's been a member of the party."

She did.

"Since last year," said Goering. "From the first moment I heard him speak, I knew that Adolf Hitler would become the savior of Germany."

"Putzi Hanfstaengl said that you're the head of the party's athletic department?"

"Yes. The *Sturmabteilung,* the Storm Division. Herr Hitler wanted a competent military man to lead it. We do training in calisthenics and weight lifting."

I tried to picture Goering lifting a weight other than himself. I failed.

"Boxing," he said, "running, et cetera. Good healthy exercise for the virile young men of the party. And, of course, when the Communist gangs try to interrupt our meetings, as they often do, our men are prepared to deal with them."

I said, "All the athletes in the Division wear uniforms?"

Goering nodded. "The uniforms provide discipline and order. And esprit de corps. This is very important."

"Right."

The waitress returned then with another bottle of wine and two glasses. She set them on the table and Goering poured the wine. He raised his glass. "To good health," he said.

We clicked glasses with him. We all drank.

"Captain," I said, "do you have any idea who tried to kill Mr. Hitler in the Tiergarten?"

"Obviously," he said, "it was the Communists."

"How did they know he'd be there?"

"They have spies everywhere."

I took out my list. "According to Mr. Hess, these were the only people who knew that Mr. Hitler would be meeting General von Seeckt that afternoon. Tell me about Frederich Nordstrum."

"He is my aide. He is absolutely loyal to me and to Herr Hitler."

"Okay. Emil Maurice."

"Hitler's chauffeur." He smiled. "And it was he who first founded the Storm Division, before I accepted its command. He is quite the ladies' man, if you know what I mean. But again, his loyalty is in no doubt."

"Gunnar Sontag?"

"Hess's assistant. The same."

"Alfred Rosenberg."

"The same. He was raised in Russia, and he came here after the Bolsheviks took over. He is rather common, but he is totally loyal to the party." He smiled again. "Another ladies' man." He leaned toward us. "He has a Jew girlfriend."

"I thought he didn't like the Jews."

Goering chuckled. "He makes an exception for this one."

"What's her name?"

"Cohen. Sarah Cohen. Not bad looking, if you like the type. Hair like a black mop." Grinning, he raised his right hand, fisted, and held his hooked index finger in front of his nose. "Typical Jew beak. Am I not a fat, repellent worm?"

"Miss Turner."

"Sorry."

I asked Goering, "Where does she live?"

"With her father, in Obermenzing, somewhere not far from my own house. Why?"

"I'll need to talk to her."

"Rosenberg would have told her nothing. She is a Jew."

"Right. But I still need to talk to her."

He shrugged. "I don't know the address. Rosenberg can tell you."

The waitress arrived again, carrying a tray full of food. Goering had ordered sausage and sauerkraut.

For the rest of the meal, when he wasn't shoveling food into his face, Goering entertained us with stories of his adventures during the War. Maybe *entertained* is too strong a word. He told us, at length, what a wonderful pilot and a wonderful human being he was. Miss Turner did a lot of editorializing: "Am I not a thing of splendor?" "Have you ever seen my like before?" "Look on my works, ye mighty, and despair."

This was a bit distracting at first, but after a while I just let her go with it. Without her comments, Goering's monumental self-absorption would have put me into a coma.

Before we left, on our way to see Hess and the others, I asked the captain about the symbol on his armband.

"It is the swastika," he said. "An ancient Aryan symbol. It represents the purity of the blood."

"Very classy," I said.

Miss Turner looked at me. "How would you like me to translate that?"

"I don't care. Tell him I think it's swell."

She said something and Goering grinned, obviously pleased, before he answered her.

"He says that it was Herr Hitler's idea to use the swastika. It's on their party flag, as well."

"Great."

CHAPTER TWENTY-FIVE

MISS TURNER SAID, "All of them. They all hate the Jews."

We were in a taxicab, crossing the River Isar and heading for the East Train Station. The sun was out again today, and sunlight skipped along the slick brown surface of the water.

"Maybe because they lost the War," I said. "They need to blame someone."

"It goes deeper than that. And it affects even the children. Even little Friedelind, the Wagner girl. She talked about the Jews as though they were a different order of being."

We discussed the Wagner family for a while, and what peachy folks they were.

At the train station, we left the taxi, snaked our way through the crowd for a while, then grabbed another cab and took that back across the river. So far as we could tell, no one was following us. The time was ten minutes before two. I'd told Hess we would meet with him at two.

The Nazi Party headquarters was on Reichenbach Strasse, a couple of blocks from the river. Our taxi let us out behind a long, low, black Mercedes limousine. As we passed the car, heading for the front door of the brick building, I saw an intricate coat of arms on its rear door.

Inside the building flags were hanging everywhere, all of them red, all of them flaunting the white circle with the black swastika inside it. Young men strode importantly down the corridors, wearing brown uniforms and deadly serious expressions.

Just as we reached Hess's office, the door opened and a delicate little middle-aged man came out, walking in short, mincing steps. He wasn't wearing a brown uniform. Over a black suit and a clerical collar, he was wearing a long purple silk robe with a caped collar. On his head was a purple skullcap. Hess was holding the door for him.

"Ah, Mr. Beaumont," said Hess. "Permit me to introduce Archbishop Pacelli, the papal nuncio."

I wasn't sure of the proper etiquette in the circumstances, but I held out my hand and said, "Archbishop."

Peering at me from behind the thin, black rims of his spectacles, the archbishop smiled sweetly. He gave me his own hand, which was as small and fine-boned as a young boy's, and said, "Pleesta meetcha."

Then he tried out his French. Miss Turner answered him in the same language. He smiled sweetly at her, said something else, nodded to me, nodded to Hess, and then minced down the corridor, his purple robe fluttering behind him.

Hess looked at me. "The archbishop follows the politics in Germany with great interest."

"I'll bet."

"Come. Everyone is waiting for you. They all understand that the Führer wishes them to cooperate with you in your investigation."

As we walked down the hallway, Hess said to me, "This morning I instructed a technician from the telephone company to inspect our lines. He has reported to me that no one is intercepting them."

"Not right now, maybe. But someone could've intercepted them yesterday, and someone could do it tomorrow. You probably shouldn't use the telephone for anything you want to keep private."

"Yes. I spoke of this with the Führer last night. In person, of course. And he agrees with you entirely."

We came to another door and Hess pulled it open.

It was a conference room. Bright electric lighting overhead, pale green walls, brown wooden venetian blinds at the two windows, the slats closed. In the center of the room was a large, empty, rectangular wooden table. Around the table were ten or twelve wooden chairs. Four of these were occupied.

I said to Hess, "Miss Turner and I need to talk to them individually. Is there an empty office we can use?"

"I have anticipated you." Hess smiled, pleased with himself. "The office across the hall has been cleared for your use."

"Great. Thanks."

Hess turned to the four men and rattled off some German. I heard "Pinkerton" and my name, and Miss Turner's. Hess turned back to me. "You wish first to speak with whom?"

"Gunnar Sontag," I said.

GUNNAR SONTAG WAS young, around twenty-four years old, and physically he was everyone's idea of a perfect German. He was tall and handsome and blond, his thick hair darkened slightly by the brilliantine that slicked it back from his high forehead. His eyes were blue and his features were even. He wore a trim gray three-piece suit, a white shirt, a black foulard tie, and heavy black brogues.

Hess had arranged the seating in such a way that Miss Turner and I sat behind the big battered wooden desk, facing a single uncomfortable-looking wooden chair. Sontag sat on this, his arms crossed over his chest, his right leg crossed over his left, at the knee. He was turned slightly away from us. All in all, it was a defensive posture, and it probably meant that he wouldn't be very forthcoming.

"Tell me about Nancy Greene," I said. Miss Turner began to translate.

He interrupted her. "I speak English," he told me.

"Fine," I said. "Speak it."

"What would you like me to say?"

"Where did you meet her?"

"Here in Munich. At the English Garden."

"When was this?"

"Last year."

"When last year?"

"In July."

"What was she doing in Munich?"

"An aunt of hers died. She came here to deal with the estate. She was the inheritor."

"A big estate?"

"No property. But there was some currency. In a lockbox, at the bank."

"German marks?"

"British pounds."

"How many British pounds?"

"Four hundred."

Last year, that had been a fair amount of money. This year it was enough to buy a country club or two.

"Why did she go to Berlin?"

"She was a performer, a singer. There was not much work for her in Munich."

"If she had four hundred pounds, why did she need to work?"

"She wanted to work. It was what she loved, she said. She insisted on going to Berlin."

"You didn't want her to go."

He frowned. Annoyed with himself, I think. He'd said more than he wanted to.

He shrugged dismissively. "It was her decision."

"When did she leave Munich?"

"October."

"She still had the money then?"

"Yes."

"You kept in touch with her?"

"On the telephone, yes."

"And you saw her."

"Sometimes. When I was in Berlin."

"How many times was that?"

"Six or seven times."

"Why go to Berlin so often?"

"Party business." He shifted his position, uncrossed his right leg, crossed his left leg over it. "I cannot discuss this. You must ask Herr Hess."

"Fine. When was the last time you saw her?"

"A week ago. On Tuesday."

"When you were in Berlin with Hitler."

"Yes."

"You told Biberkopf, the police sergeant in Berlin, that you'd been with Emil Maurice all day."

His eyes didn't shift. He'd been ready for that—someone had told him that Miss Turner and I had talked to Biberkopf. "Yes. I did not want to involve Miss Greene with the police. She is a foreigner, an Englishwoman. They could cause her much trouble."

I nodded. It was the longest statement he'd made. It might even have been true. "Before that Tuesday, when was the last time you saw her?"

"In March."

"When in March?"

"The fifteenth."

That had been the night that Miss Greene hadn't returned to her boardinghouse. The night, she told Frau Schroeder, that she'd spent with a girlfriend.

I said, "You didn't call her ahead of time to let her know you were coming."

He frowned. He was wondering how I knew. "No. I went to see her at work. At the Black Cat. It was a surprise."

"And the two of you spent the night in a hotel."

He lifted his chin slightly, defiant. "Yes."

"Okay," I said. "At that point, how much of the British money was left?"

"Most of it, she told me."

"And as of last Tuesday? How much was left then?"

"I do not know."

"You didn't ask her?"

"It was not my business."

"But it was something that the two of you had already discussed."

"She volunteered that information. I never asked her."

"In Germany right now," I said, "that's a lot of money to spend in a couple of months."

"Yes."

"Did she use drugs?"

"No."

"If she didn't spend it, where did she keep it? It wasn't in her room." I hadn't found it when I'd searched.

He said, "Perhaps she kept it in a lockbox, as her aunt did."

I nodded. "You called Miss Greene last Sunday."

"Yes."

"Her landlady, Frau Schroeder, said that you only called Miss Greene when you were about to go to Berlin."

He blinked. "Frau Schroeder is mistaken. I sometimes called Miss Greene simply to exchange greetings."

"Why'd you call her on Sunday?"

"For this reason. To exchange greetings."

"Where were you last Monday?"

"Here, in Munich."

"Can you prove that?"

"Anyone can tell you. I worked with Herr Hess. I had lunch with Herr Rosenberg."

"Where?"

"At the Tambosi, in Odeonsplatz."

"What did you eat?"

"The fish. Salmon."

"What did Mr. Rosenberg eat?"

"The pasta."

Not many people can remember, that quickly, what their lunch companion ate five days ago.

"Did Miss Greene ever give you a key to her room?"

"No. Never."

"All right. Who do you think fired that shot at Mr. Hitler?"

"The Communists. There are gangs of them everywhere. They want to destroy us."

"Right." I turned to Miss Turner. "Do you have any questions?"

Adjusting her spectacles, she looked at Sontag. "Did you love her?"

He frowned. "Pardon me?"

"Miss Greene. Did you love her?"

He stared at Miss Turner for a moment. He swallowed, then cleared his throat. "She was a good girl. She was . . . fun. I liked her." He looked away, blinking, then turned back to us, lifting his chin once again.

"All right, Mr. Sontag," I said. "Thank you. Could you ask Mr. Nordstrum to come in here?"

He stood, looked from me to Miss Turner, then walked to the door, opened it, and stepped out.

"He denies having a key," said Miss Turner.

"If he killed her, he'd have to deny it. Whoever killed her used the key to lock the door when he left."

"Those pound notes," said Miss Turner. "Could they have been a motive for her murder?"

"There was money in her purse and jewelry in her dresser. A thief wouldn't leave either of those."

"But where are the pounds, then?"

"Like he said, maybe in a safe-deposit box at the bank. Or maybe she spent it. I'll telephone Biberkopf later today. What did you think of Gunnar?"

"I thought he was rather quick with that restaurant menu."

"Yeah."

"I think," she said, "that he killed her."

CHAPTER TWENTY-SIX

⬦

FREDERICH NORDSTRUM CAME in.

Short and thin and younger than Sontag, about twenty years old, he was wearing the brown shirt, brown tie, and brown pants of Goering's "Storm Division."

He seemed eager to help us. But it didn't take us long to find out that he couldn't. Like Sontag, like everyone we'd talked to since we'd arrived in Germany, he believed, or said he did, that the Communists were responsible for the assassination attempt against Hitler. Like everyone else, he had no idea how they could've known that Hitler would be in the Tiergarten on the eighth of the month.

He told us that he hadn't seen or spoken to his sister, Greta, since the funeral of their mother in 1921. He had never met Nancy Greene. Yes, Gunnar Sontag had been here in Munich last Monday. Yes, he had actually seen him here.

We thanked him and asked him to send in Emil Maurice.

As he closed the door behind him, I turned to Miss Turner. "What makes you think that Sontag killed Greene?"

"I think he loved her."

"And that's why he killed her?"

"No. That's why he feels bad about killing her."

"But *why* did he kill her?"

"I don't know. Perhaps she knew something she wasn't supposed to know."

"Like what?"

"I've no idea. But you said that he rang her up when he returned to

Munich, on Thursday. Perhaps he let something slip. And he rang her up *again* on Sunday, the day before she was killed. Frau Schroeder told you that he telephoned only when he was about to come see her."

"He denies that."

"Why should Frau Schroeder lie?"

"Everyone—"

The door opened and Emil Maurice came in.

In his midtwenties, he was tall and thin and he looked more Spanish than German. With his dark, lean, handsome face and his easy, feline poise, he might have been a Cuban bandleader. He wore a gray pin-striped suit, and he wore it well. I could believe what Goering had told us, that he was a ladies' man.

He lifted the chair, swiveled it gracefully around, then straddled it backward, resting his arms across the top of the chair's back. He looked out at us from over the arms, smiling amiably, his head cocked.

He might have been amiable, but he was no more help than Nord-strum had been. The Communists had tried to kill Hitler. No, he had no proof. No, he didn't know how they'd learned of the meeting in the Tier-garten. And, yes, Gunnar Sontag had been in Munich on Monday.

I pointed out to him that he'd lied about Sontag's whereabouts to Sergeant Biberkopf in Berlin.

He smiled. "Yes," Miss Turner translated for him, "but that was a matter of honor. Gunnar didn't want to drag Miss Greene's name into a police investigation."

"How do we know you're not lying now?"

He raised his eyebrows, his face elaborately innocent. "Why should I lie? Ask anyone. Gunnar was here on Monday."

"All right, Mr. Maurice. Thank you. Could you ask Mr. Rosenberg to step in?"

When he closed the door, Miss Turner said, "They're all lying."

"Probably. But I still don't understand why you think Sontag did it."

She frowned. "I'm not sure, really. That phone call on Sunday suggests that he was planning to see her on Monday. And he denies having loved her, when he clearly did. Why deny it?"

"Why do *you* think he's denying it?"

"To make it easier, perhaps, for him to accept the fact that he killed her."

The door opened and Alfred Rosenberg stepped in.

Rosenberg was something special. He was wearing a blue suit, a brown vest, a purple shirt, and a red tie. He looked like an explosion in the men's department.

Physically, he could have been Gunnar Sontag's older, shorter, less attractive brother. His hair was the same dark blond, and it was slicked back the same way, but his head was a bit boxy, and his features—his nose, his forehead, his jaw—were coarse, as though his flesh had somehow thickened over the years.

He nodded to me, smiled at Miss Turner. He turned the chair back around, facing us, and sat down in it, crossing his arms across his chest, as Sontag had done. He put his right ankle atop his left knee. He was wearing brown shoes and white socks.

For a while he answered my questions, Miss Turner translating for us both, in pretty much the same way that the other men had. It was the Communists. The filthy swine had spies everywhere, probably even within the party. Yes, of course Gunnar Sontag had been in Munich on Monday. He and Rosenberg had eaten lunch together, at the Tambosi on the Odeonsplatz.

The other men, when they'd answered my questions, had all focused on me, basically ignoring Miss Turner. Rosenberg basically ignored me and focused on Miss Turner. From time to time as he spoke, he smiled a sly smile at her, as though he knew something about her that maybe she didn't know herself.

"What did you eat?" I asked him.

"The pasta," he told Miss Turner.

"And what did Sontag eat."

"The fish. The salmon."

Once again, no hesitation. That fish was beginning to smell.

But maybe not. Even if Rosenberg and Sontag had, in fact, sat down together and made sure they had their stories straight, the stories could still be true.

Things got interesting when I asked Rosenberg for Sarah Cohen's address. For the first time he looked at me directly. His eyes were a watery gray.

"How did you know about Cohen?" he asked me.

"That doesn't really matter, does it. The address, Mr. Rosenberg?"

"Why do you want it?"

"So I can talk to her."

"She knows nothing."

"I still need to talk to her. Did Hess mention that Hitler wanted you to cooperate with us?"

He smiled a quick smile, allowing me the point, then recited an address. I wrote it down.

"Does she have a telephone?" I asked him.

He gave me the number.

I said, "Tell me something, Mr. Rosenberg."

"What?"

"You don't like Jews."

"They are vermin. They are a bacteria within the body of the German state."

"And yet you're involved with one."

He smiled the sly smile at Miss Turner. "Sometimes I like the way that vermin . . . make love."

I asked Miss Turner, "Is that what he said?"

"No." Her voice was flat. "He said *fuck*." She was looking directly at Rosenberg.

Rosenberg was looking directly at her. He smiled again. "They are like minks, hot and eager. And I like their bodies. The thick black hair. The fat breasts. And the nipples. They have thick nipples, you know." He held up his right hand, the fingers closed except for the index finger. He pressed his thumb between the first and second knuckle of that finger. "Like the tips of a finger. The man is vile."

"Okay," I told Miss Turner. "Mr. Rosenberg. Just before Mr. Hitler's meeting, you published an article that attacked General von Seeckt and his wife."

He stopped smiling at Miss Turner and turned to me. "His wife is a Jew."

"But why publish the article just before Mr. Hitler meets with the husband?"

"It was an essay, not an article, and it had been written the week before."

"You didn't have time to remove it?"

"I never believed that von Seeckt would see it. And this is, of course, none of your concern."

I nodded. "All right, Mr. Rosenberg. Thank you."

He stood up slowly. He adjusted his tie. He tugged down the bottom of his brown vest. Smiling again, he walked toward the desk. To Miss Turner he said, in fluent English, "Vile, is it? You know, fräulein, not all Englishwomen feel that way about German men."

Her face was red as she looked up at him. I couldn't tell whether she was angry or only embarrassed at being found out. "Possibly not," she said, her voice constricted. "But this one does."

He nodded. He turned to me. "I told Herr Hitler that bringing in you people was a mistake."

"You're welcome," I said, "to tell him again."

"I intend to do so."

"Fine. In the meantime, you can go."

He turned again to Miss Turner. I stood up. I was a good five inches taller and I outweighed him by twenty or thirty pounds.

I said, "Good-bye, Mr. Rosenberg."

He smiled and let his glance slide up and down my length, so he could show me that he was tough, even though he was smaller and leaving the room. He nodded to me and then he nodded to Miss Turner. "Good-bye, fräulein."

He turned and walked to the door, opened it and stepped out, pulling it shut behind him.

Miss Turner turned to me. "I apologize," she said stiffly. "That was completely unprofessional of me."

"Which?" I said. "Calling him vile or telling him, afterward, that you really meant it?"

She smiled wanly. "Both, actually. I'm terribly sorry."

"Don't worry about it. He *is* vile. Let's get out of here."

IT WAS ABOUT four thirty when we reached the hotel. As we came in the lobby door, the concierge waved to me. Miss Turner and I approached him.

Herr Braun was a tall, burly man about fifty in a gray suit. In heavily accented English he said, "Herr Beaumont. You tell me to speak with you if someone is asking for you or Miss Turner. The desk clerk says—ah, here is the gentleman now."

I turned.

Looking tall and polished in a three-piece suit of lightweight black wool, Erik von Dinesen held out his hand and said, "Mr. Beaumont, so good to see you again. And, Jane, what a pleasure this is."

Hotel Bayerischer Hof
Saturday evening
May 19th

Dear Evangeline,

Erik has *not* been arrested! He is here, in Munich!

And not only in Munich, but he's actually *downstairs* at the moment!

He's waiting for me in the hotel bar. He and I are going out to dinner.

I'll write more later, and I'll tell you all about it.

And I must tell you, too, about a serious mistake I may have made. I learned something while we were at the Wagner house, something I thought trivial at the time. It may in fact be trivial, but it's something I really ought to have mentioned to Mr Beaumont.

More later.

All my love,
Jane

CHAPTER TWENTY-SEVEN

I SMILED AT von Dinesen. "Quite a coincidence," I said, "running into you here."

"Oh no," he said. "Not a coincidence at all." He smiled at Miss Turner. "After I spoke with you yesterday, Jane, and you told me that you were going to Munich, it occurred to me that I hadn't performed here for over a year."

He turned back to me. "As you know, I am between engagements at the moment. It was a good time, I thought, to come down and talk to some of the theater managers. To learn what they might be willing to part with." He smiled. "Usually, alas, they do not pay as well as the managers in Berlin."

He turned back to Miss Turner. "But why not, I thought, mix pleasure with business? I knew it would be wonderful to see you again. When I arrived at the train station, I called all the hotels. The people at the Vier Jahreszeiten told me you had canceled your reservations there. When I called here, the clerk told me you were not registered." He turned to me and smiled. "But he was a very bad liar."

After we arrived last night, I had paid the night manager twenty dollars and asked him the same thing I had asked the concierge: to tell anyone who inquired about us—anyone but the cops—that we weren't staying in the hotel. And I'd asked him to let me know if anyone did inquire. This morning, before we left for the Hofbräuhaus, I had done the same thing with the day manager.

Apparently, my plan hadn't worked too well.

Or maybe von Dinesen was psychic.

Or maybe someone had told him where we were.

Von Dinesen was smiling at me. "So I dashed right over," he said. He turned to Miss Turner. "I'll be staying here myself."

"What a nice surprise," said Miss Turner.

I was a bit less pleased.

I had known that, even with my precautions, it wouldn't take long for the Opposition, whoever they were, to find us. I hadn't known that they'd be sending von Dinesen.

But maybe they hadn't. Maybe he'd come to Munich, as he said, only to talk with theater managers and to spend time with Miss Turner. I didn't know much about theater managers, but I couldn't blame him for wanting to spend time with Miss Turner.

But someone had told him about our backgrounds before we met him. About my brother, my army experience. About Miss Turner's childhood headmistress.

And von Dinesen, for whatever reason, had used the information to demonstrate his psychic talents. I hadn't trusted him much back in Berlin, and I didn't trust him much now.

"May I buy the two of you a drink?" von Dinesen asked me. "I understand that the bar here is rather good."

"Sure," I said. "But I need to do something first. Why don't you take Miss Turner, and I'll be there in a few minutes."

"It will be my pleasure," he said, and turned to her and smiled.

I HAD BEEN planning to call Biberkopf from the hotel, but I didn't like the idea that von Dinesen, and anyone with access to a telephone, knew exactly where we were at the moment. And thoughts of a telephone put me in mind of interceptions and wire recorders.

I walked over to Herr Braun and told him that I wanted to make a phone call but didn't want to use the hotel's telephone. He'd been a concierge for a while. He never blinked. He told me there was another, smaller hotel around the corner and a few blocks up the street.

I found the hotel. The telephone was in a small, plush-lined booth to the side of the front desk. I slipped some money to the desk clerk, gave him Biberkopf's name and phone number, and I waited by the booth. After a couple of minutes, the telephone rang.

I stepped into the booth and picked it up. "Sergeant Biberkopf?"

"Ah, *ja*." His voice sounded distant and thin, as though it were being strained through gravel. "The famous Pinkerton. How is going your investigation?"

"Gunnar Sontag says he wasn't in Berlin on Monday. Four witnesses agree with him."

"And you believe them?"

"I'm keeping my mind open."

"This is a smart thing you do, I think. You got anything else for me?"

"Did Miss Greene have a safe-deposit box at any of the banks?"

"Why you are asking?"

"Miss Greene inherited four hundred British pounds last year. According to Sontag, she still had most of it in March."

"And you believe Sontag?"

"Did she have a box?"

"Yes," he said. "We find it."

"You got a warrant?"

"A warrant? Oh, *ja*." He chuckled. "No, we don't need no warrant. We are the police, Mr. Beaumont. We find it, we open it."

"And?"

"Inside, there is two hundred and eighty British pounds."

"So the money had nothing to do with her death."

"No."

"Has Mr. Norris turned up? The Englishman from Miss Greene's boardinghouse?"

"No. But we know he takes the train to Munich on Wednesday."

"Have you talked to the Munich police about him?"

"To my cousin, Hans. He is the only Munich police I trust. Hans looks for the name in the hotel registry files. But it takes some days for all the records to reach the police headquarters."

"I've got another name for you. An Englishman named Household.

A retired colonel, or so he says. A few days before the Tiergarten, he was talking about assassinating Hitler. He lives here in Munich."

"Ah, *ja*. This prostitute, this Greta Manheim, she tells me about him."

"You found her."

Another chuckle. "We are the police, Mr. Beaumont."

"You talked to your cousin about Household?"

"*Ja*. Hans, he talks to him. Household is in Munich when Hitler is in the Tiergarten."

"Witnesses?"

"*Ja.*"

"I'll have to talk to Hans."

"He is off duty today. He is home now, perhaps."

"Okay, thanks," I told him. "You find anything else, besides the safe-deposit box?"

"No."

I wondered whether that was true.

"And you, hah?" he asked me. "You got anything else?"

"Nope," I told him. We said good-bye and I went back to the desk clerk and gave him the telephone number I'd gotten from Rosenberg.

When the phone rang, I stepped into the booth and picked it up. "Hello?"

An older man's voice said, "*Ja?*"

"Do you speak English?"

"Ah." His tone was amused. "Well, that would depend, you see, on the person with whom I am speaking."

"Is it possible for me to talk to Sarah Cohen?"

"Possible, yes. If Sarah were here, you could certainly talk to her. But I rather doubt that she would talk back. Sarah speaks no English whatever, you see." He was still amused. I was too, but probably not as much.

"Will Miss Cohen be there tomorrow?"

"And who, if I may ask, are you?"

"I'm an investigator, a Pinkerton detective. From London."

"A Pinkerton detective from London. Goodness. And you've come all that way to speak with Sarah?"

"No. I'm working on something. Miss Cohen isn't in any trouble. I just want to ask her a few questions."

"And your name?"

"Phil Beaumont."

"You do not sound very English, Mr. Beaumont."

"I'm an American."

"But a Pinkerton detective. From London."

"Yeah."

"Curious. Are there many of you, Mr. Beaumont?"

"No. I'm unique."

I heard a chuckle at the other end. "Perhaps so, yes. All right, yes, very well. Let us say that you come here tomorrow morning, at ten o'clock."

"Ten o'clock. Fine."

"You have the address?"

"Yes."

"Until then," he said, and hung up.

I made one more call, to Biberkopf's cousin. He was home. I asked if I could see him. In an hour, he said, and he told me how to get there.

BACK AT THE bar at the Bayerischer Hof, I found Miss Turner and von Dinesen sitting at a small table in the corner of the crowded bar. It was after five o'clock and twenty or thirty red-faced businessmen were nursing themselves with beer steins the size of oil drums.

Miss Turner and von Dinesen were leaning toward each other. As I approached, von Dinesen spotted me, smiled, and rose from his chair with smooth athletic grace. Miss Turner turned toward me, blinking behind her spectacles. She smiled a bit vaguely.

"Please," said von Dinesen. "You must join us in some champagne."

I sat down, followed by von Dinesen. There was a bottle of Dom Pérignon on the table, and three flute glasses. The glasses in front of Miss Turner and von Dinesen were half-filled. The third was empty. Von Dinesen filled it up, poured more champagne into the other two glasses, set down the bottle, handed me the glass.

He held up his own glass. "To my favorite Pinkerton agents."

Miss Turner and I raised our glasses. I tasted the champagne.

"I have taken the liberty," said von Dinesen, "of inviting Miss Turner to dinner. You are, of course, welcome to join us."

I glanced at Miss Turner. She was looking down as she sipped at her champagne. She didn't encourage me to join them, and she didn't discourage me.

"Thanks," I told him. "But I've got some errands to run."

Miss Turner looked up. "Do you need any help?" She didn't sound eager, but she didn't sound resentful.

"No thanks," I said. "I'll be fine. You go out and have a good time. But tomorrow's another big day." I pulled out my watch. Time for me to leave.

"I shan't be late," she said.

"Good. Thanks."

"Did you know," von Dinesen said to me, "that Herr Hitler will be giving a speech tomorrow night, at the Bürgerbräukeller?"

"Yeah. We'll be meeting him there."

"Splendid. I shall be there as well."

"Great." I took another sip from my glass and then put it on the table. To von Dinesen I said, "I've got to run. Thanks for the champagne."

He didn't insist that I finish what was left in my glass. He only nodded, smiling.

To Miss Turner I said, "If you're back in time, meet me here at ten thirty."

Miss Turner didn't insist either. "I'll be here," she said.

Von Dinesen smiled at me. "Once again, I assure you that Miss Turner will come on time."

And, once again, I wondered whether von Dinesen was toying with me, using language that had two meanings. But his smile still had no hint of a smirk in it.

Which might mean only that he was amusing himself and didn't want me to know it.

I stood up, smiled at von Dinesen, at Miss Turner, then turned around and waded back through the red faces of the businessmen.

I wasn't happy with the situation. The men in peacoats might still be looking for us. And I didn't trust von Dinesen.

But von Dinesen probably wouldn't hurt Miss Turner, not when he knew that I knew he was with her. And with him attached to her, the men in peacoats would probably stay away.

And I'd told Miss Turner, back in Munich, that I wanted her to learn whatever she could from him. And she was an adult, and a trained operative. And she had a pistol.

I said all those things to myself, but I still wasn't happy with the situation.

I wondered if I was unhappy because I didn't trust von Dinesen, or because Miss Turner did.

But she was an adult, and a trained operative . . .

Let it go, I told myself, and I headed for the front door of the hotel.

CHAPTER TWENTY-EIGHT

Hans Mueller lived on the first floor of a narrow apartment building in Schwabing, north of the city center. It took me longer to get there than I thought it would, but that was probably because the taxi driver circled the city a couple of times before he dropped me off. I didn't tip him, but that wasn't much of a victory.

The front door of the building was unlocked. I walked into a narrow hallway crowded with the smell of cabbage. There was one bare light bulb over the entryway and two more beyond the landing, dangling from the low ceiling on thin twists of black wire. On the floor, scuffed yellow linoleum was peeling away from the edge of the wooden wall, curling upward like the edges of a huge dying leaf.

I found Mueller's door and knocked on it.

After a moment, he opened it. There was some resemblance to Sergeant Biberkopf, but not much. He was pink and blond, but he was younger than his cousin, in his midtwenties. He was also thinner and shorter, and his hair wasn't cut quite so close to his scalp. He was wearing heavy black boots, a plaid wool shirt, and gray overalls splotched with grease. He was wiping his hands on a towel.

"Herr Beaumont?"

"Yeah. Officer Mueller?"

Grinning, he held out his right hand to me. I shook it.

"I am more clean than I look," he said. And his English was better than Biberkopf had said it was. "I am working on my motorcycle before. But I wash my hands." He held them up, to prove it.

"What kind of motorcycle?" I asked him.

"A Megola. You know this marque?"

"No."

"It is manufactured here in Munich. You wish to see it?"

He obviously wanted me to see it. From his eagerness, he probably wanted everyone to see it.

"Sure," I said.

Another grin, this one very pleased. "Come, I show you."

He pulled shut the door and led me back out through the entryway. We went out the front and down the steps and around the side, to a small alley.

"Do you know about motorcycles?" he asked me.

"A little. I haven't ridden one for a while."

"What did you have?"

"A Cyclone."

He turned to me. "Yes? Truly? The V-twin? From the Joerns Motor Manufacturing Company?"

"Yeah."

"A beautiful machine. Totally beautiful. Forty-five horsepower, they say, yes? It must be very, very fast."

I wondered if he'd learned his English from motorcycle magazines. "Too fast, sometimes," I said. "I don't think I'd ride it now."

We had come to a wooden shed at the rear of the alley. The door, slightly wider than a normal door, was padlocked shut. Mueller reached into his pocket.

"You do not have it still?" he asked me.

"No. I sold it before the War."

"Ah. The War. Yes." He nodded sadly. And then he smiled. "But after this Cyclone of yours, you will find my moto not very interesting, I think."

He didn't really believe that. I could hear it in his voice and I could see it in his quick, confident movements as he unlocked the padlock. He slipped the lock off the hook, flipped out the hasp, pulled open the door. Reaching upward into the darkness, he stepped inside.

Another bare dangling bulb suddenly flared alight. The gleaming black motorcycle stood upright beneath, on a spotless cement floor. Even standing still, it looked as though it were racing.

It was the strangest and probably the most beautiful motorcycle I'd ever seen, long and low and streamlined. Where the engine should be, there was only the downward swooping line of the narrow body, a body that, beyond the foot pegs, swept up beneath the sprung leather seat and the passenger pillion and became a sleek, flat-sided, black fender enclosing all but the lower half of the rear wheel.

In the center of the front wheel was the engine, five small cylinders in a star shape around the hub. It looked like the engine on an airplane propeller.

"What size is the engine?" I asked him.

"Six hundred and forty cubic centimeters. One hundred and twenty-eight per cylinder. It produces only fourteen horsepower. Nothing like the engine on your Cyclone. But the machine is very light, yes? And with the engine in the front, it handles very well. Even in the sand, a child could ride it."

"It's a beauty," I said, and I meant it.

"I have made some modifications. The passenger seat, the bolts for the panniers. These are not standard. But the seat is good for the gals, you know?"

"The gals?"

"Yes. The gals love to go riding."

I smiled. "How fast will it go?"

"A hundred and fifteen kilometers an hour. Because, you see, the machine is so light."

Over seventy miles an hour.

"It is not so fast as your Cyclone, of course," he said, and smiled. He didn't really care how fast my Cyclone had been. He knew that he owned one of the most beautiful motorcycles in the world.

"No," I said, "but fast enough."

"Yes," he said happily.

We talked some more about the bike, and he showed me, enthusiastically, and at some length, how it operated. And then we went back to his apartment.

· · ·

HIS LIVING ROOM was small and sparsely furnished, but scrupulously clean. There were a couple of upholstered chairs and an upholstered sofa. In one corner was a simple wooden stand that held the telephone. The wooden floor had no carpets. Probably he spent most of his money on that motorcycle, and on keeping it running. And maybe some of it on those gals who rode as passengers.

He offered me an Asbach Uralt, a German brandy, and I accepted. He gave me the drink in a tooth glass and then sat down in one of the chairs, holding a glass of his own. I sat at the end of the sofa.

I said, "Sergeant Biberkopf tells me that you talked to Colonel Household."

"He is no colonel. In the War, he was a sergeant in the British army. He worked in supplies—this is how you say it, yes?"

"Supplies, yeah."

"He made much money doing this. Working on the black market, you understand?"

"Yeah."

"He does the same now. You know that there is much money being made in the black market?"

"Yeah. How does he work it?"

"He buys food goods and he sells them, but only for gold or jewelry. When that prostitute sees him, in the bar, he is in Berlin to fill a truck with smoked hams. These he sells, some in Berlin, some in München."

"He admitted all this?"

He grinned. "I am very scarifying, yes? I am in my uniform when we talk, and he is a small man. I tell him I care nothing about what he does. I want only to learn if he is in the Tiergarten on that day. If he cooperates, I leave him alone. So he cooperates."

"Biberkopf told me he wasn't in Berlin that day."

"No. He has witnesses, receipts, every kind of evidence."

"People on the black market keep receipts?"

"Some of his business is legitimate. He is in München on the eighth. He buys some wooden cases on that day. Boxes, you know? Crates."

"If he really wanted to kill Hitler, he could have prepared an alibi."

"I talk to the people who sell him the crates. He is there on the ninth. You must understand about this Household. He is a small man, but with a big mouth. He says big things."

"Like killing Hitler."

"A good idea, perhaps, but he would never do this thing. He is not the sort, I believe, who kills. Not in the War, and not now."

"If you think it's a good idea, killing Hitler, why are you helping me?"

He took a sip of his brandy. He lowered the glass, looked down into it, looked up at me. "My cousin Franz, he says you promise him something. He says if you learn who shoots at Hitler, you will tell Franz before you tell the Nazis."

"Yeah."

"The Nazis, they will kill him if they find him."

"Probably."

"Not probably. For sure. That is how they are."

"Yeah."

"So I help you for this reason. I am a policeman. A copper, you say?"

"A cop."

"A cop. So, because I am a cop, I do not like it if people believe they can kill other people. This is not the way that things are designed to be. You understand?"

"Yeah."

"And I think that this person who wants to kill Hitler, he is not so bad, perhaps. Hitler is a man who deserves to be killed, perhaps. So I help you, to stop the Nazis from killing this man. Okay?"

"Okay. Thank you."

He shrugged. "For nothing. I do only my job."

I nodded. "The Nazis think it was the Communists who tried to kill Hitler."

"No. If it was the Communists, I would know."

"Because you're a cop?"

"Because I am a Communist." He grinned. "You are scarified now?"

"Very much."

He laughed. "It was not the Communists, I promise you."

"You know what all the Communists in Germany are doing?"

"No. But about this, I would know."

"Okay. Then maybe you'd know about something else. Some people were following my partner and me. In Berlin, and later in Bayreuth."

"They are Communists, you think?"

"I don't know. I know that one of them was Russian."

"How do you know this?"

In my jacket pocket was the seaman's card that Roehm had pulled from the body behind the Mikado. I was tempted to give it to him. But if the body had been identified, back in Berlin, I would have a hard time explaining how I'd gotten the card. "I can't say. Not without putting someone in jeopardy." Me.

He nodded. He knew about jeopardy. As a Communist in the Munich police department, he probably knew a lot about it.

"Not all Russians are Communists," he said.

"I know. These men were wearing watch caps and peacoats, like sailors."

He shook his head. "I know nothing about them."

"That doesn't mean they're not Communists."

"No. But I do not believe that any Communist is trying to kill Hitler. It could have been one of his own people. One of the Nazis."

"If it was, I'll find him."

He took another sip of his brandy and leaned forward. "Listen to me. You must be very careful with these Nazis. They are not good people, and they are everywhere. Not just in the Munich police. They are in the state police as well, and the army. Here in München, they are very powerful."

"I know."

"If I can help you, I will. But I must be careful, also."

"I appreciate your help."

He nodded. "I do what I can."

I sipped at the brandy. "Your cousin said that you haven't been able to locate the man from Munich. Mr. Norris."

"No. The hotels are required to hand in registration forms for all their guests, but sometimes they are slow. If he is in a hotel, I will find him. But if he is staying with a friend . . ." He shrugged.

"Yeah. If you do find him, I'll need to talk to him."

"Of course."

"You can leave a message for me at the Hofbräuhaus. In a sealed envelope. Or you can telephone and leave one. Tell me to call Mr. Smith. I'll call you, at your home number, as soon as I can. Okay?"

"Okay."

"And I'll need to talk to Household. You have his address?"

"But I tell you—"

"I know. And I believe you. But my superiors will want a report. From me."

He knew about superiors. "Yes. Of course. One moment."

He stood up, left the room, returned in a few moments with a scrap of paper. He handed it to me and sat down.

"Thanks. There are a couple of other things."

"Yes?"

"There's a member of the party named Gunnar Sontag. I think he might have been in Berlin last Monday, but he's got friends who say he wasn't. One of them said he had lunch with him on Monday, at the Tambosi."

He nodded. "That I can learn, perhaps. I know a waiter there. Did he say what food he ate?"

"The salmon."

Mueller smiled. "Maybe we are lucky, yes? Maybe there was no salmon at the Tambosi on Monday. This has to do with the death of the Englishwoman, Miss Greene?"

"Yeah. But be careful when you're asking around. I don't want you getting into trouble."

He smiled. "Nor me. Do you have an address for this Sontag?"

"No."

"No matter. I will find it."

I asked him about a few other things, and he was helpful. After another five minutes I stood up. "I'm grateful for your help," I told him.

He rose from his chair. "Franz says he trusts you."

Biberkopf had never mentioned that to me.

Mueller smiled. "Up to a point," he added.

HE TOLD ME how to get to the nearest main street—Belgrade Strasse—where I could find a taxi. I got there, found one, and went to the address he'd given me for Household.

Household was a nervous little man who probably should've been in another line of work. Mueller had been right about him—he was an opportunist, and maybe a parasite, but he had never killed anyone and never tried to. And by this time, after a visit from Officer Mueller, and one from me, he probably regretted his barroom talk in Berlin more than he had ever regretted anything in his life. I thanked him for his time, left his apartment building, found another taxi, and took it to the back to the Bayerischer Hof.

It was nine o'clock when I returned. I checked at the desk. Still nothing from Cooper.

I went into the restaurant, ate a meal of fish and salad, then went into the bar. I sat down at a table, ordered a drink from the waiter, and waited for Miss Turner.

The Hotel Bayerischer Hof
Saturday night
May 19th

Dear Evangeline,

I'm rather giddy. IT may happen tonight.

You remember IT? We talked about IT at Miss Applewhite's. You defined IT, clever girl, as 'The absolute, irreversible, and devoutly to be wished disserveration of a female human being from her rag dolls.'

Erik is staying here in the hotel. Did I mention that? No matter. Here's the crux: in the lobby, before he escorted me to the hotel bar tonight, where Mr Beaumont awaited me, he suggested that I join him in his suite later, for a drink.

Oh, I neglected to say that in the taxi, on our way back from the restaurant, he kissed me. And I kissed him.

I shall begin at the beginning.

Yes. Well, this afternoon Mr Beaumont and I met with some of the members of the dreadful Nazi Party for whom, alas, we are working.

When we arrived back at the hotel, and we were walking through the lobby, Erik suddenly appeared, as suave and as elegant as ever. He has, truly, an astounding presence. One gets the sense that an ethereal spotlight keeps him in focus at all times. Everything and everyone else seems to fade into the background.

For a moment, when I first saw him, I was stunned. Happily stunned, but stunned.

Mr Beaumont ran off on some errand, so I had an opportunity to quiz Erik as to what happened with Sergeant Biberkopf.

You remember the rifle? The one discovered in the Tiergarten by the police? Well, Erik told the sergeant that, from the 'emanations' of the rifle, he knew that it had never been fired at Herr Hitler.

Naturally, as a devout nonbeliever in the occult, the sergeant was suspicious. He queried Erik as to his whereabouts on the day the rifle had been fired. Erik was able to satisfy the sergeant that he had been with a group of people at the time in question.

Now. As to tonight.

We had dinner in the Fränkischer Hof, where the food approached, without at any moment ever actually becoming, genuine French.

While we were eating, I mentioned to Erik something that had begun very much to bother me.

'So many of these people,' I said, 'in the party, they're rather violently anti-Semitic.'

He nodded. 'Many of them are. They're looking for someone to blame for Germany's collapse. And as it happens, there were many Jewish bankers who took advantage of the War to increase their own wealth.'

'But surely not all the profiteers were Jewish?'

'Of course not. But many of them were. And, naturally, they are resented for this.'

'But it seems to me,' I said, 'this hatred, to be something more fundamental than that. It's as though these people, these people in the party, as though they actually hate the Jews, all the Jews. For no other reason, really, than the fact that they *are* Jews.'

'In some cases, unfortunately, that's true. You must understand, Jane, that in a sense the Jews have been too smart for their own good. Because their tradition is steeped in a kind of legalism, in argumentation and debate, they put a premium on education.'

'And what's wrong with that?'

'Nothing at all, inherently. But as a result, they've become disproportionately represented in the professional fields. The percentage of Jewish doctors, lawyers, publishers, educators—it's a percentage much higher than their percentage of the population.'

'And what, exactly, is wrong with that?'

He smiled his wounded smile. 'In the best of worlds, Jane, nothing. But no world, these days, is the best of worlds. And this world, the Germany of today, is very far from it. By their very success, the Jews have made themselves the targets of envy and resentment.'

'But why the Jews as a group?'

'Because most Germans, I expect, see the Jews as perceiving themselves as Jews first, and as Germans second.'

'Even if that were true, why should it be such a bad thing? Isn't it possible to be a Jew *and* a German?'

'Of course it is. And it goes without saying that there are many Jews who are loyal Germans. But Germany is tottering on the brink of catastrophe, Jane. Most Germans feel that we must stand together, without hesitation, without dividing our loyalties in any way, to prevent our falling over that brink.'

'So you believe that the Jews should do . . . what, exactly? Abjure their religion?'

'No, of course not. But I believe that it's important for them to make clear, to other Germans, that they're willing to participate, as Germans and as Jews, in the security and the future of the country.'

'And that's all that would be required? You really believe that if they did that, made that clear, then these people would stop hating them?'

Another smile. 'No. Not these people. Old habits die hard. But I believe that if the Jews help bring about the rebirth of Germany, then the next generation of Germans will see them as brothers, and as fellow Germans.'

I thought then of the Wagners, their poisonous, reflexive animus. An animus that was already a part of their children's inheritance.

'But enough of this,' he said. 'Let's talk about you. How is your investigation progressing?'

'I'm sorry, Erik, but I—'

Smiling, he held up a hand. This was an easy smile, relaxed and charming. 'Forgive me. Of course not. But then you must tell me how you've found Germany. So. Which do you prefer, Berlin or Munich?'

And so we talked for a while about Germany, and then we ate, and as we ate we talked some more, and we lingered over our cognac and coffee, and then Erik paid the bill, and then we went outside, where a taxi was waiting.

And we come now to the kiss.

We were sitting there on the seat of the taxi, the passing street-lamps along the boulevards creating within the vehicle an endlessly changing chiaroscuro, shadows sliding into light, light sliding into shadow, matter dissolving into darkness and then starkly re-creating itself. Erik turned his body toward me, put his left forearm on the back of the seat, behind my neck, and looked into my eyes.

'Jane,' he said, 'there is one thing I must tell you.'

His face flickered briefly into shadow, then returned. His eyes were very dark. One could lose oneself in eyes like those. Perhaps one has already done so.

'Yes?' I said.

'Whatever happens,' he said, his deep voice rumbling along my spine, 'I want you to know that the few moments we've spent together, you and I, have been perhaps the most special moments I've ever spent.'

'I—'

'No, you needn't say anything. I only wanted you to know. It was important for me to say it.'

'I . . . Well. Thank you, Erik.'

He smiled, and in the flat white shifting light I saw it was that wounded smile of his, the smile that never quite reaches his eyes.

He bent toward me, and gently he placed his right hand along my cheek. His palm was warm but dry, and it seemed to me that every molecule of my flesh, along that membrane of suddenly shared skin, could feel and celebrate every molecule of his. My heart, abruptly, was beating like the drummer in some demented jazz band.

He moved still closer, his lips parted slightly, and I raised my chin. His mouth met mine, and a new membrane was invented, tingling and trembling. My heart was pounding so loudly now—in my ears, my forehead, at the base of my stomach—that I thought for sure Erik must hear it. I thought for sure the driver must hear it, and the pedestrians outside, as they stood marveling by the roadside.

And then I felt his left hand at the back of my head, and his right hand drifted slowly down from my cheek, down along the arched skin where my blood hammered at my throat, smoothly down over the whispering silk fabric of my dress—

Enough.

It has just gone twelve thirty in the morning. I am dressed. What I shall do now is leave my room and post this letter. Here in Bayerischer Hof, as in the Adlon, a mail chute runs alongside the door to the lift. After I post the letter, and only then, I shall decide whether to take the lift up to Erik's room, on the top floor.

There are good arguments in favour of my taking the lift—the desire that drones through my heavy head and weakens my knees, for one.

And there are good arguments against it. I'm certain, at any rate, that there must be.

Wish me well, Evy.

We who are about to die salute you.

All my love,
Jane

CHAPTER TWENTY-NINE

WHEN MISS TURNER joined me for breakfast on Sunday morning, she looked as though she hadn't had much sleep. She was wearing a white dress, circled at the waist by a white leather belt, and over it a lightweight white cotton blazer, everything summery and cheerful. But floating above all that white, her face seemed slightly gray.

"Good morning," she said. She held her hand delicately to her mouth and gently cleared her throat.

"Good morning. Are you okay?"

"Why?" She touched her hair. This morning it was pulled back into a bun. "Is something wrong?"

"No. You just look a little tired."

With her left hand she took off her spectacles. With her right hand, using forefinger and thumb, she massaged the bridge of her nose. "Yes," she said. She put on the spectacles again and then quickly, briefly, she shook her head, as though clearing it. She looked at me and smiled brightly. "Yes, silly, isn't it? For some reason I didn't sleep well."

LAST NIGHT, WHEN she appeared in the crowded bar, she had looked a lot different. Once again, as in Munich, after her last evening with von Dinesen, her face had been flushed and her eyes had been shiny. I didn't ask whether she'd had a good time, because it was none of my business, and because it was obvious that she'd had a good time. But I did ask her if she'd learned anything more about von Dinesen.

"Yes." She had leaned toward me. "You remember the rifle?"

"The Tiergarten rifle."

"Yes. Sergeant Biberkopf let Erik examine it."

"Yeah?"

"And Erik told him that it hadn't been used against Hitler."

I smiled. "That must've made Biberkopf happy."

"Erik had an alibi."

"Good for him."

She sat back and canted her head slightly to the side. "You still don't like him, do you?"

"It's not a matter of liking him. But I admit that if he's anything like the rest of these Nazis—"

"He isn't. He's nothing at all like them. And he *knew,* don't you see, that the rifle hadn't been used against Hitler."

"Right."

"You don't sound terribly impressed."

"I don't know how secure the Berlin Police Department is. Maybe that piece of information trickled out."

She smiled. "You're really just a hopeless cynic, aren't you?"

"A hopeful cynic."

"What does that mean?"

"It means I like to believe that people are exactly who and what they say they are. But unfortunately, and fairly soon, they almost always start turning into something else."

Another smile. "It must be very tiresome for you."

"Very."

"And what about your errand of last night?" she asked me. "Did you talk to the sergeant's cousin?" Changing the subject, but that didn't bother me.

I told her what I'd learned from Hans Mueller. That Household hadn't been in Berlin when the Tiergarten shot was fired. That the Communists, according to Mueller, weren't responsible for the shot.

"How can he be so sure?" she asked me.

For just a moment I hesitated. Mueller probably wouldn't want it getting around that he was a Communist. And Miss Turner kept demonstrating a fondness for someone I didn't trust very much.

But she was my partner, and if I didn't trust her, I might as well pack up and go back to London.

"He's a Communist," I said. "He says that if the Communists had tried to kill Hitler, he would've known about it."

"He told you he was a Communist?"

"Yeah."

"Why did he tell you?"

"We got along. We talked motorcycles."

"Motorcycles," she repeated.

"Yeah."

She nodded. "Motorcycle fanciers belong to some secret masculine brotherhood, you mean. Like the Freemasons."

"Exactly."

THE NEXT MORNING, after our breakfast, we took a taxi to Obermenzing, in the northwest of Munich. It was a wealthy area, the streets lined with tall sedate trees. Sitting back on large plots of grassy land, the serene old stone houses looked as impregnable as bank vaults.

The Cohen house hid behind a dense barricade of trees, thick-trunked oaks and elms that had been there for a while. The taxi let us off in the paved driveway, beside the sunny flagstone walk that led up across the grass to the front door. I gave the driver some money and Miss Turner asked him to wait.

On the door was a large brass knocker. I lifted it, let it fall.

In a few moments, the door opened.

The man who opened it looked like a garden gnome in a business suit. He was short and bald except for a woolly fringe along the sides of his shiny pink scalp. His trim mustache and his beard, a small tuft of wool on his chin, were the same color. He had a small cheerful mouth, a strong nose, and a pair of small ironic brown eyes.

"Mr. Beaumont, is it?" he said, and held out his hand.

"Mr. Cohen," I said. "This is my associate, Miss Turner."

"A pleasure," he said, and made a little bow to Miss Turner. He turned back to me and smiled wryly. "Two of you it takes? To talk to one little girl?"

"Miss Turner speaks German," I told him.

"Good. Very good." He admired her for a moment, smiling, then turned back to me. "And you've got there a very nice associate. *My* associates, they're all old men with hair in their ears." He smiled at Miss Turner. "But come in, come in."

He stood aside and then shut the door behind us. "First," he said, "let me ask you this. No insult intended, but you have some identification, yes?"

"Of course," I said. I got out my wallet, showed him the card with my photograph on it. Miss Turner opened her purse, found her card, and showed it to him.

"Good," he said. "Thank you. This way, please. Sarah is in back."

The house was filled with books. Tall bookcases lined the wide hallway, climbing from floor to ceiling, some of the cases fronted with glass, some of them not. The books inside seemed to be arranged in no particular order. Some were novels, some were textbooks, some I couldn't identify. They were in German, in English, in French, and in a few languages I didn't recognize. As we passed the arched entrance to the living room, I saw that on the far side of the thick white carpet, flanking the windows, more bookcases climbed toward the ceiling.

Mr. Cohen led us out onto a kind of enclosed stone porch. No bookcases. Between heavy red silk curtains, windows looked out onto an informal garden where gravel pathways wandered through the shrubbery.

Here inside, elegant chairs were scattered about, upholstered in a cream-colored, nubby fabric. A Persian carpet lay on the parquet floor. A small, dark-wood coffee table held an elegant silver coffee service and some white china cups and saucers. Beyond the table was an elegant cream-colored sofa, and at one end of it sat an elegant young woman.

Wearing a white blouse and a gray skirt, she was maybe twenty-two years old and she was beautiful. Her hair was thick and black and it fell in a tumble of glistening curls to her shoulders. Her eyes were large and brown. Her forehead was high, her cheekbones were curved, her nose was straight. Her mouth was wide and sensual, a handsome mouth, but it seemed a bit petulant—its corners were turned down as though her mood were somewhere between boredom and annoyance. At the moment, she seemed to be hovering closer to annoyance.

Mr. Cohen spoke to her in German. She nodded curtly to me and to Miss Turner.

"Sit, sit," said Mr. Cohen. We sat. "Some coffee?" he asked us.

"Please," I said.

"Yes, please," said Miss Turner.

He poured it for us, handed us saucers and cups. We thanked him.

He walked around the coffee table and sat down on the sofa, at the end opposite his daughter. "So," he said. "You have questions. Ask them."

"Miss Cohen," I said. "I understand that you know a man named Alfred Rosenberg."

"I knew it." said Mr. Cohen. He held up his right finger. "I knew it was him."

I said, "Mr. Cohen—"

The single finger was joined by the other four, and he waved them back and forth, as though wiping clean an invisible blackboard. "Sorry. No more." He put the hand on his thigh.

Miss Cohen had turned to eye her father. She was still annoyed.

"Miss Turner," I said, "could you translate what I said?"

She did.

Miss Cohen looked from her to me. *"Ja."* A single weary word, sighed slowly out. She had shifted down from annoyance to boredom.

"Did Mr. Rosenberg," I said, "tell you that the leader of the party, Mr. Hitler, would be in Berlin on the eighth of this month?"

Miss Turner translated that, and then the woman's answer—"Alfred and I never discuss politics."

"What do you discuss?" I asked.

Sighing again, she shook her head slightly, in distaste. This was all so tedious. "Literature. The arts."

"He never mentioned Mr. Hitler's meeting in the Tiergarten? Before the eighth?"

"Not before the eighth, and not after it. May I go now?"

"You're sure? You didn't know about the meeting?"

Boredom shifted back up into annoyance. "I've said so, haven't I? Three times."

"Have you talked to Mr. Rosenberg recently?"

Another sigh. Back to boredom. "Yes."

"When?"

"Last night."

"You saw him last night?"

"We spoke on the telephone."

"Did he tell you that we might be talking to you?"

"Yes."

"What else did he say?"

For the first time, the corners of her lips moved upward, faintly. "He found you amusing." She had enjoyed saying that.

I said, "Did he tell you to deny knowing anything about the Tiergarten?"

Back to annoyance. "No."

I said, "Do you know anyone who might want to kill Mr. Hitler?"

Again the corners of her mouth moved upward. "Only my father."

Mr. Cohen's head jerked back, as though she'd slapped him. He turned toward her, held out his hands, palms up, and he said something in aggrieved German. She looked away, bored once more, and he turned to me.

"Never," he told me. "This Hitler, all right, yes, I admit it, I don't care for the man. I don't care for his politics. But kill him? Take a life? Never."

His daughter was watching him, and again she was faintly smiling.

I said, "Miss Cohen—"

Miss Turner said to me, "May I ask her something?"

I nodded. "Go ahead."

She rattled off some German.

Miss Cohen glanced at her father and then looked to Miss Turner. She raised her jaw in defiance, or something like it, and she gave her answer.

Over at his corner of the sofa, Mr. Cohen slowly shook his head like someone who'd had a lot of practice doing it.

I said to Miss Turner, "What did you ask her?"

"I asked her what she liked about Mr. Rosenberg. She said that he was a real man. The first real man she's ever met."

Miss Cohen said something else.

Miss Turner told me, "She wants to know if she can go now."

"Yeah," I said. "Thank you, Miss Cohen."

After Miss Turner translated that, the young woman stood up. Without another look at any of us, she walked around the coffee table, walked between me and Miss Turner, and disappeared into the house.

"It's my fault," said Mr. Cohen. "Her mother died when she was only ten. I raised her on my own. Difficult, she's always been. Headstrong, she's always been. But this I never thought. Never this. A man like Rosenberg."

"How long has she known him?" I asked him.

"Months now. I told her, I said, this man, he is only using you. Read what he writes about the Jews in that disgusting gutter sheet, I said. He doesn't care what's in your head. He doesn't care what's in your heart. But does she listen? No. She's become one of them. A bully boy, like the rest." He snorted with amusement, an amusement uncomfortable to watch because it had so much pain in it. "A bully girl."

As though catching himself, he glanced quickly between me and Miss Turner. He sat back. "I talk too much." He looked down at the floor. "I'm an old man."

"Mr. Cohen," said Miss Turner.

He studied the pattern in the Persian carpet.

"Mr. Cohen?" she repeated.

He looked up.

"I don't want to alarm you," she said. "But I believe that these people, these Nazis, are really terribly dangerous. If you can do anything at all to get your daughter away from Rosenberg, you should do it."

Once again, he held out his hands. "Do what? What can I do? Chain her to her bed? Lock the door? She's a grown woman."

"Mr. Cohen—"

He put his right hand into the air, palm forward. "Listen, miss, I know you mean well. You're a kind person, I can see that." He lowered the hand and leaned slightly toward her. "But about these people, you can tell me nothing. Nothing. I know them. All my life, I know them. The boy groups, the *Wandervogel,* the schools, the army. Dreams of blood and glory. They think that they are the Teutonic Knights. They think that on their finger they wear the Ring of the Nibelungen. They are all romantics." He sat back, his lecture finished, and he smiled wryly. "And there is nothing in the world more ruthless than a romantic."

He was calmer now, as though by talking about the Nazis, by explaining them, he had somehow regained his emotional balance, and the detachment with which, I suspect, he normally looked at the world.

His shoulders moved in a small, resigned shrug. "She will be hurt. My daughter. The swine will break her heart. But then we will move on, she and I. We will continue with our life."

"But what if things get worse?" said Miss Turner. "Mr. Cohen, these people *hate* the Jews. They—"

"What will they do? Arrest us all? Listen, miss, always it has been like this. Not just in Germany. Everywhere. And always it will be like this. I worry only for my daughter. For her heart."

No one said anything for a moment. Then he turned to me, a small, hopeful smile forming on his lips. His eyes narrowed shrewdly. "Someone tried to kill this Hitler? That's the truth?"

"Yeah," I said. "But no one's supposed to know about it, Mr. Cohen. If you spread it around, you might get into trouble."

He held up his hand again. "Not a word from me. You're trying to find the person? Why?"

"We'd like to find him before anyone else does."

"Before the Nazis, you mean?"

"Yeah."

"If I could help you, believe me, I would. But she tells me nothing. Sarah. She tells me nothing at all." He smiled, and the smile almost came off as ironic. But not quite. "Children," he said.

. . .

AS SOON AS we were back inside the taxi, Miss Turner said to me, "Do you believe her?"

"No way of knowing whether she's telling the truth. But even if she knew about the Tiergarten, I doubt she told anyone else."

"She wouldn't do anything, you mean, that might jeopardize her relationship with Rosenberg."

"Yeah."

I was sitting on the left of the rear seat as the taxi pulled out of the driveway. Glancing out the window, I saw that a black Mercedes was parked against the curb, fifty or sixty feet down the road. Two men were sitting in the front seat.

As the taxi swung around and began to head back toward the center of the city, I turned and looked out the back window. The Mercedes had left the curb and it was following us.

I said to Miss Turner, "Tell the driver to pull over and stop."

She did, and he slowed down and pulled over to the right. Behind us, the Mercedes did the same, still about fifty feet away.

"What is it?" Miss Turner asked me.

I knew that the Colt was in my jacket pocket. I'd been putting it there every morning since that night outside the Mikado. But I tapped the pocket, just to make sure.

"I'll be right back," I told her.

CHAPTER THIRTY

✧

I SLAMMED THE car door and walked back along the street, toward the Mercedes.

It was another fine day. A warm breeze blew, carrying the sharp sweet scent of freshly cut grass. Above me the heavy limbs of an oak tree slowly swayed. Leaves whispered and chittered up there.

The two men in the front seat watched me coming. The driver turned and said something to his partner. The partner laughed.

When I was even with the front door and standing a few feet from it, the driver rolled down his window. He was wearing a flat leather cap. In not very good English he said, "Herr Rosenberg, he says—"

I held up a hand. "Wait. Before you tell me what Rosenberg says, let me tell you what I say."

I reached into my pocket and pulled out the Colt. The driver's eyes widened.

The .32 Colt has a grip safety, a swelling at the back of the grip that has to be compressed for the gun to fire. It compresses when you hold the pistol. There's also a slide safety. I thumbed this down and then I shot at the front tire, once. A .32-caliber slug isn't the most potent projectile in the world, but it will do a pretty good job on a tire. There was a satisfying pop, then a quick, satisfying hiss as the car began to settle down onto its left front fender.

I bent down and leaned into the window, my left forearm resting on the door, the pistol pointed directly between the driver's eyes and about five inches away. The eyes crossed as they stared at the muzzle. Wisps of smoke were still drifting from it.

He was a big man who needed a shave. The passenger was smaller and a little better at personal hygiene. He looked alarmed.

"What I say," I told him, "is this. If I ever see you again, either of you, it won't be the tire I shoot. Do you understand?"

He swallowed, and he tried to bring some hardness into his face. It's not an easy thing to do when you're staring into a gun barrel.

His partner said something in German, softly. A warning, I think.

"Yes or no?" I said. "One word."

"Yes." It came out fast and angry, as sibilant as the hiss of the tire.

"Fine," I said.

I stood back, flicked on the safety, and slipped the pistol back into my pocket.

As I walked away, my back felt exposed, and about the size of a movie theater screen.

But I didn't think that these two would do anything without permission from Rosenberg, and I didn't think that Rosenberg had given them permission to kill off a Pinkerton hired by Hitler. As I moved closer to the taxi, I told myself several times that I didn't think those things.

When I opened the car door, I saw that Miss Turner was arguing with the driver.

"What is it?" I said, sitting down.

"He wants us to leave. He thinks we're gangsters."

I looked at him. He was twisted around in the seat, staring at me with horror, as though I'd just shot at a classroom filled with children.

I smiled at him and patted the air in front of me, reassuringly. He wasn't reassured, because he flinched when I reached around behind me. I patted the air again and I pulled out my wallet. I opened it, took out a twenty, and handed it to Miss Turner. "Give him it to him," I said. "Tell him that the men in the Mercedes were the gangsters. Tell him they're white slavers. Tell him they were trying to kidnap you."

"He's not going to believe that."

"He will if he wants the twenty."

She held out the money and said something in German. He looked from her to me, dubious, and then at the money in her hand, then past me, out the rear window. I looked back. The two men were out of the car now and were both staring down at the flattened front tire as though it were some puzzling phenomenon of nature.

"*Ja,*" said the driver, and snatched the twenty from Miss Turner's fingers. He turned around and slipped it into his shirt pocket. He put the car into gear and we rolled forward.

Miss Turner sat back and looked over at me. "Who were they?"

"Muscle. Rosenberg sent them."

She nodded. "The girl. Sarah. She talked to him last night. She must have told him what time we'd be arriving."

"Yeah."

"What did they want?"

"We didn't get that far."

She looked at me for a moment and then she laughed. "You're quite mad, you know."

"Not mad. Angry. I'm tired of people following us."

She laughed again. "But firing a pistol in broad daylight! Out here, in a neighborhood like this!"

"Only once. Even if the neighbors heard it, they probably thought it was a car backfiring."

She smiled. "And what if you'd missed the first time?"

"The tire was only four feet away. And it wasn't shooting back."

"Rosenberg won't be happy," she said.

"Good."

WHEN WE GOT back to the hotel, we stopped to say hello to Herr Braun. He told us that there was a message for me at the front desk.

We went to the front desk and I talked to the clerk. He spun around, professionally, and put his hands behind his back and carefully studied the cubbyholes assigned to the hotel rooms. He found mine, plucked an envelope from it, and spun around again and handed it to me with a flourish. He was a man who took his job seriously. I thanked him.

Miss Turner and I moved away from the desk and I opened the envelope.

Inside it was a single small sheet of paper, identical to one I'd seen last night.

On it was written: "Mr. Schmidt. Hotel Becker. 16 Impler Strasse."

"What is it?" Miss Turner asked me.

I handed her the paper. "Officer Mueller has found Mr. Norris for us. Want to go see him?"

IMPLER STRASSE WAS in Sendling, toward the southwest edge of the city, not far from the South Train Station. The Hotel Becker was a narrow five-story building wedged between a tailor shop and a restaurant that was closed, and possibly condemned. Like the restaurant, the hotel looked as though it had seen better days, but not recently.

Miss Turner handled the desk clerk. We were lucky. Mr. Norris, said the desk clerk, was in.

There was no elevator, so we climbed up four flights of stairs to the top floor. Even in the dim electric light, I could see that the carpet runner was frayed and that the dark paint on the wooden banister had been worn away in spots, where hundreds of hands had grasped it over the years. The stairwell smelled like too many stairwells I'd been in over the years, of cigar smoke and sweat and exhausted dreams.

Mueller's room was number 505. I knocked on the door.

No answer for a moment.

I knocked again.

A voice came, calling out in German.

As I'd asked her to do, Miss Turner called back and said she was the maid.

The voice came once more, querulous now.

Miss Turner said something.

I heard a chain being unlatched and then the door swung open about four inches, showing a wedge of Mr. Norris's surprised face. I slid the toe of my shoe against the base of the door and I smiled at the wedge. "Hi," I said. "Got a minute?"

I thought that he might try to slam the door. Instead he lowered his head, resigned, and stood back away from it. We went in.

Like the driver of the car this morning, Mr. Norris hadn't shaved. His cheeks were pale with white stubble. He was wearing rumpled black trousers and a rumpled white shirt without a collar, its first three buttons undone. His feet were bare. On his head was his handsome gray wig, but he'd put it on too quickly and it wasn't seated properly.

"Remember us?" I said. "Phil Beaumont. Jane Turner."

He had raised his head, and he had gone from resignation to a kind of desperate cheerfulness. "Yes, yes, of course, dear boy. Forgive the room. I wasn't expecting guests, you see."

The room would be hard to forgive. In the thin light that filtered through the dirty window, it was cramped and drab and smelled of unwashed clothes and unwashed flesh. The walls were pale green, the color of thin pea soup. The bed had been made, sort of, by throwing the sheet and the threadbare blanket back over the mattress. Afterward, someone had clearly lain down on them. There was a deep long furrow in the blanket, and a gray dent in the pillow at the top. Beside the furrow was a book, opened facedown. The door to the cheap wardrobe hung open, and in it I could see some suit coats on hangers, and some clothing lying in a pile at the bottom. On the nightstand beside the bed was a bottle of brandy and a glass, half-filled.

Norris glanced at Miss Turner, then fumbled at his shirt buttons. "Well," he said to me, buttoning the shirt, "this is quite a surprise." He looked around the room, as though he'd just noticed that it was there, and that he was in it. He smiled at me apologetically. "I'd offer you a seat, but there appears to be only one."

"You sit there," I said, and pointed to the bed. "Miss Turner?" I offered her the single wooden chair.

"Thank you," she said. If she was uncomfortable about being in a man's hotel room, she didn't show it.

Mr. Norris had sat down on the edge of the bed and he was looking up at me attentively. "What can I do for you, dear boy?"

Miss Turner sat. I moved over to the low wooden dresser and perched my right hip on it.

"It was funny," I said. "You leaving Berlin so quickly like that."

"Something important came up. You know how it is." He smiled hopefully.

I took a long deliberate look around the sad cramped room. "Yeah," I said. "It must have been very important."

He glanced over at Miss Turner, then back at me. He decided to take the offensive. Puffing up his chest, he said, "Now see here. You've no right to come in here—"

"Mr. Norris," I said. "Stop."

He stopped. His shoulders sagged and his chest deflated. He looked down, looked off to the side, then looked back up at me. "What is it you want?" His voice was surly and defeated.

"I don't think you killed her," I said. "Here's what I think happened."

CHAPTER THIRTY-ONE

I SAID, "I think you saw something, or someone, on Monday night. I think it didn't mean anything to you until Wednesday, when you learned that Miss Greene was dead. And I think you realized then that what you'd seen was something dangerous, dangerous to you. So you decided to take off."

I was giving him a story to work with. By my reading of Mr. Norris, if he denied it, then probably it was the truth, or something close to it. If he accepted it, then probably it wasn't.

"That's ridiculous," he said. "I had business to attend to, here in Munich."

"What business?"

"Importing."

"Importing what?"

"Agricultural goods, if you must know. A shipment of flour from Czechoslovakia. I'm acting, you see, as the middleman between the buyer and the seller."

I nodded. "Do you know who hired us, Mr. Norris?"

"No." He remembered then who he was, or was supposed to be. "I can't see why that should be of the slightest interest to me."

"The Nazi Party. Maybe you've heard of them. Former *Freikorps* people, a lot of them. They're fairly powerful here in Munich."

"I've heard of them. They're hooligans. And outside of Bavaria, they're utterly insignificant."

"Right now you're inside Bavaria. And the Nazi Party has an active interest in anyone who knows anything about Miss Greene and her death."

"Ridiculous. Why should they?"

"I think that one of them killed her."

He stared up at me.

"What if I gave them your name?" I said. "Told them I was pretty sure you knew something."

"But I know *nothing* about it. I told you, I scarcely knew the woman."

"According to Frau Schroeder, you had tea with her on a regular basis."

"Frau Schroeder is an idiot."

"What did you see, Mr. Norris?"

"Nothing, I tell you. Nothing at all."

"Okay. Suit yourself. Come on, Miss Turner."

Miss Turner stood. She looked down at Mr. Norris. She said, "Honestly, Mr. Norris, you're making a dreadful mistake. We can help you. If the people in the party find you, they'll get the answers they want, but by then it'll be too late. For you, I mean."

She delivered the lines well, and they were good lines.

But Mr. Norris wasn't buying. "I don't *know* anything."

She nodded sadly. "I'm terribly sorry you feel that way."

She moved toward the door. I pushed myself up off the dresser and I followed her.

She was reaching for the doorknob when Norris said, "Wait."

We both stopped and turned to him.

"What does she mean?" he said. "How can you help?"

I said, "We can get you a ticket back to Berlin. We can arrange for police protection there."

"You said you were working for the Nazis."

"I'm also working with the police in Berlin."

He looked at Miss Turner. He looked back at me. He looked off to the right, toward the window. He sighed.

I said, "What was it, Mr. Norris? What did you see?"

"I saw her return to the house," he told the window. He looked at me. "It was quite late, after three in the morning. I was returning myself, from a small party on the Kurfürstendamm."

"Was she alone?" I asked him.

"No," he said. "She was with a man."

AFTER THAT, IT was fairly easy. Norris described the man. Blond, tall, good-looking. It could have been Sontag.

I asked him, "Had you ever seen him before?"

He was still on the bed. Miss Turner had returned to the chair. I was back at my perch on the dresser.

"No," he said. "I assumed it was someone she'd met at the cabaret."

"Did Miss Greene ever mention a man named Sontag?"

"Yes. Gunnar. A boyfriend. From here in Munich. I never met him."

"Did she mention that he was a Nazi?"

He looked up at me. "He's a member of the party?"

"If it was Sontag you were running from, Mr. Norris, you picked just about the worst place in Germany to hide."

"I had no idea who it was. As I said, I'd never seen him before. And whoever he was, I wasn't running from him."

It wasn't that hot in the room, but a drop of sweat had beaded at the front of his wig, and now it began to roll down his forehead. He wiped it away with the back of his hand.

"Why run?" I asked him.

"I didn't want to become involved. Some of the business I undertake is, ah, well, it skirts along the edges of the law, you might say."

"Black market."

"Gray, let us say. I didn't wish to suffer any scrutiny from the police. When I learned that Miss Greene had been killed, I thought it might be a good time to leave Berlin for a few days."

"Why come to Munich?"

"I know the city. Better than I know Frankfurt or Stuttgart. I had no idea that the man I saw was Gunnar Sontag. Or that he was one of them. The Nazis." He glanced toward the window uneasily, as though he expected to discover Gunnar Sontag floating outside it, peering in.

"Did they see you?" I asked him. "Miss Greene or the man?"

"No. They were at the door. I could see them in the overhead light. I was just at the hedges, on the side of the lawn. I hid."

"Why?"

"I didn't want to embarrass Miss Greene. She was looking in her handbag—for a key, I thought. And then the man pulled a key from his pocket and he opened the door. They went inside."

"What did you do?"

"I waited for a few minutes and then I went in myself. Quietly." He looked from me to Miss Turner and back to me. "If I'd known that he was going to . . . hurt her—if I'd known that, I should have done something. To prevent it, I mean to say. That's the truth. I quite liked Miss Greene."

"If it was Sontag you saw on Monday," I said, "the Nazis aren't going to be happy you saw him."

"But what interest have the Nazis in Miss Greene? Why should they want her dead?"

"I don't know yet. But in the meantime, you're not safe here in Munich."

"Yes. Yes, I understand. In light of that, of course, I'm more than willing to cooperate with the authorities in Berlin. It's the only thing that makes sense, really, isn't it? For me, I mean to say."

"Yeah." I pulled out my watch. One o'clock. "Okay. Get packed."

WHEN WE GOT to the main station, at a quarter to two, we learned that a train was leaving for Berlin in twenty-five minutes. I bought a ticket for Mr. Norris, then Miss Turner and I sat down with him in the waiting room, Norris on my right, Miss Turner on my left.

"Listen," I told him. "I'm going to call Sergeant Biberkopf as soon as you leave. If you're not on the train when it arrives in Berlin, he'll let me know. And I'll give your name to the Nazis."

He glanced around the big room and then leaned toward me. He was wearing a collar and tie now, but the tie was crooked. His voice low, he said, "You keep saying that, dear boy." I was "dear boy" again. Putting on the tie had restored some of his confidence. "I do wish you'd stop."

"They'll find you, Mr. Norris, wherever you are."

"Please. It's in my own best interest to speak with Biberkopf. I understand that."

"I hope so."

We walked him to the train. As he disappeared into the passenger car, Miss Turner asked me, "Do you think it was Sontag he saw?"

"The description fits. And he had a key. It was someone she knew."

"Why didn't we keep Mr. Norris here for a while and let him identify Sontag?"

"I don't want to expose Norris. Right now, no one knows about him. Seems to me, the best thing to do is to send him out of town, somewhere safe. Biberkopf will get the description from him. Maybe he can have an artist do a picture."

"Do you think that he'll be able to arrange for Sontag's arrest, here in Munich?"

"I don't know. Maybe not. But maybe he can have him picked up, next time he goes to Berlin."

"And what about Mr. Norris?" she said. "Do you think that he'll actually go to Berlin?"

"He'd be crazy not to."

She canted her head slightly to the right. "You wouldn't really give the Nazis his name, would you? If he didn't?"

"No. But that doesn't mean they can't get if from someone else."

"From whom?"

"Maybe from someone in Berlin. In the police department."

"Not from Biberkopf, surely."

"No. But I don't know the Berlin Police Department. And except for Biberkopf and his cousin, there aren't a lot of people in Germany I trust right now."

The Hotel Bayerischer Hof
Sunday evening
May 20th

Dear Evangeline,

No. No IT.

I did take the lift up to the seventh floor, where Erik is staying, and I did walk down the long corridor to his room. The corridor's inordinate length afforded me several thousand opportunities to change my mind, back and forth, pro and con, as I floated past all those closed, silent, bluntly unhelpful doors.

When I reached his suite, I did raise my hand to knock.

And then I lowered my hand and I turned and walked back down the corridor to the lift, returned to my own floor, and my own room.

I'm not entirely sure why, really.

It has something to do with Mr Beaumont.

Don't ask me to explain it, Evy, because I cannot. It's obviously none of Mr Beaumont's concern what I do or don't do. If I *had* gone into Erik's suite last night, Mr Beaumont should never have known about it; and had he known, I'm sure he shouldn't have cared.

But the clandestine nature of it, the secrecy, just seemed . . .

I don't know, Evy. It seemed rather sordid, somehow.

Mr Beaumont is in many respects irksome. He is forever complaining about the food. He can be so laconic on occasion that an observer might be forgiven for believing that, at some recent point in time, he had passed away.

But he *is* my partner. And he *is* rather good at certain things. Today, for instance, when he discovered that we were being followed—

Well, no. Perhaps I'd best tell you about that when I see you again.

It could be, of course, that I'm deceiving myself about last night, and that my return to my room was a simple failure of nerve. Simple cowardice. Perhaps I've been trapped in virginity for so many years that my body has become terrified at the prospect of escaping it, like some long-caged lunatic who shudders at the thought of liberty.

Ah well. Tonight we'll be meeting Herr Hitler. We'll be attending a speech he's giving. And I'll be wearing my Vamp-in-Training dress.

I wonder what Erik will think of it.

All my love,
Jane

CHAPTER THIRTY-TWO

⬧

THE BÜRGERBRÄUKELLER WAS on Rosenheimer Strasse, on the far side of the Isar. When we arrived in our taxi at six o'clock that evening, a small crowd was mulling around the beer garden outside the entrance.

I paid the taxi driver, got out of the cab, then helped Miss Turner out. She didn't look much like a Pinkerton tonight. Her brown hair was loose and full, and she was wearing a black silk shawl over a glossy, low-cut, black silk dress that she'd bought in Frankfurt.

We crossed the street. Off to the west, the sun was beginning to slide down the sky.

In the beer garden, the tables were all filled and a quite a few people were standing. A platoon of large, pink-faced, blonde waitresses were carrying trays and shouting at everyone, and a few small, unobtrusive women were standing or sitting quietly at the sides of their husbands or boyfriends, looking as though they had never shouted at anyone in their lives.

But most of the customers were men, and a good many of them wore the brown uniform and red swastika armband of Goering's athletic Storm Division. Some of the athletes were extremely athletic, with broad shoulders and bulging chests beneath their uniform jackets. Some of the bulges, the ones on their left sides, weren't muscle.

Everyone was extremely jolly. Cigars and cigarettes were being smoked. Beer was being drunk. Laughter was being laughed, loudly.

As we moved through all of this toward the entrance, I heard someone call out, "Hey, Phil! Phil Beaumont!"

I turned and saw Putzi Hanfstaengl towering over the others as he came barreling through the crowd. He banged into the shoulder of a waitress, who managed to prevent a disaster by hurling her arm around the glasses on her tray, like a mother protecting her children, and by continuing the dizzy spin of her body in the direction she'd been slammed. She finished the spin and landed flat-footed, her pink face now a bright red, and she hollered something unpleasant at Putzi's back. German is good language for unpleasantness, but Putzi didn't hear her.

He grabbed my hand. "Great to see you again, Phil! And you also, Miss Turner."

He nodded to her, almost distractedly, and then he noticed the dress. His glance slid down her body, then up. When it met hers, he blushed. He said, "You look most . . . captivating tonight."

She smiled. Politely, which was pretty much the way she usually smiled at Putzi. "Thank you," she said.

Putzi was wearing another gray chalk-striped suit and, like the athletes, a red band around his left upper arm, emblazoned with the white circle and the black swastika. I noticed that his tie was the same shade of red as the armband.

I had decided, back at the Wagners' house, that I hadn't liked Putzi. But I discovered now that I was glad to see him. Maybe it was the silly tie, exactly matching that band around his arm. It made him seem like a big overgrown child, inept and innocent, eager to please. After people like Hess and Goering and the rest, he was a relief.

"Come," he said, his voice excited. "Herr Hitler wants to meet you. I promised him I'd bring you as soon as you turned up."

Four more athletes were at the front door, guarding the gates, but they nodded at Putzi and raised their right hands in a kind of stiff-armed salute. Putzi gave them a couple of big jovial nods. He liked being saluted.

Inside, we walked across a stone entryway, into the smell of damp and a wall of noise—music and laughter and chatter and shouting and shuffling and whistling and stomping, everything piling on top of everything else to create an almost seamless, thunderous din. We came out into a hall the size of an aircraft hangar. It was crammed with long wooden tables and wooden chairs, all of them tightly packed together, all the chairs occupied. In the blue fog of cigarette smoke, waitresses struggled down narrow aisles between the tables to deliver their beer.

The music was coming from a small band—some trumpets, a tuba, a drummer—at the front of the room, to the left of the stage. It was loud and boisterous and probably patriotic.

I looked around the room. Once again, men were in the majority. They were dressed like farmers, peasants, clerks, students, workers, shopkeepers, pensioners. Young and old, they all seemed delighted to be here, delighted to be drinking lots of beer and making lots of noise.

Along the walls on either side of the room, at intervals, hung four or five red flags so long they reached nearly to the floor. Spotlights had been set up along the ceiling, and they cast bright blue funnels of glow through the swirling smoke and lit up the flags' stark black swastikas, making them stand sharply out against the pure white circular background. Lurking between the flags were more of the athletes in their crisp brown uniforms. They held truncheons. As they studied the boisterous crowd, left and right, right and left, they bounced the truncheons idly against their opened palms.

I remembered the man outside the Mikado, the man that Roehm had killed. He had bounced his truncheon in pretty much the same way.

Truncheons were a bit like guns—when you had one, you wanted people to know about it.

Putzi turned back to me and shouted into my ear, "Come." I could barely hear him.

He led us down the center aisle, toward the stage, which was draped along its edge with a black cloth that reached to the floor. Two more swastika flags stood on tall poles at the back of the platform, on either side of it. On the side opposite the band, the right side, two athletes stood rigidly with their hands behind their backs, flanking a narrow wooden door. These two didn't need truncheons. On their hips, in shiny black holsters, they wore pistols.

They gave Putzi the same stiff salute he'd gotten outside, and one of them turned with swift military precision, opened the door, then snapped back away from it. We followed Putzi into a dimly lit, narrow hallway. When the door shut behind us, the noise abruptly dropped to a dull muffled rumble.

We walked down the hallway, passing two doors on the left and stopping at a third. Putzi knocked. He looked back at me, excited, expectant, as though the door would open onto a sultan's secret treasure trove.

The door opened, instead, onto Gunnar Sontag, still tall and handsome and blond, and still wearing the same gray suit, or another just like it. He glanced at Putzi, nodded, glanced at Miss Turner and me with no expression at all, and then stood away from the door to let us in.

A group of men stood, their backs to us, huddled around something at the opposite end of the small room. There was a mirror beyond them, but their heads were lowered, hiding their faces, and I didn't recognize anyone. Putzi called out, "Herr Hitler?" and at once all the men turned around and I saw who they were.

It was the whole cavalcade, all the Nazi Party members we'd met since we arrived in Germany. Captain Roehm. Captain Goering. Frederich Nordstrum. Rudolf Hess. Emil Maurice. Alfred Rosenberg.

They all backed away from the seated figure around whom they'd been gathered, and I saw that it was Adolf Hitler.

He stood up, smiling happily, and he came toward us, his hand extended.

As Putzi had said, back in Berlin, he looked like nothing special. He was wearing a white shirt, a black tie, and a brown suit that could have used some ironing. A flop of limp brown hair bounced against his pale forehead. His chin was weak. His nose was a bit bulbous. Between the smiling lips, his teeth were gray. The terse brown mustache above them seemed almost comical, as though some prankster had snipped off the ends of it while its owner was asleep.

But his eyes were impressive. They were a pale blue, with large and very black pupils in the centers, and they looked into mine with such warmth and candor that, despite everything I'd heard about him, and everything I'd guessed, I found myself shaking his damp hand with real enthusiasm, and barely hearing Putzi's introduction.

He released me and turned to Miss Turner, and I saw those blue eyes of his dip downward as they took in the dress she wore. They swung quickly back up and looked into hers, and he blinked, and then he smiled, apparently delighted. Holding his hands at his side, he made a stiff little gallant bow. Still smiling, he said something in soft, appreciative German, and she responded, politely smiling once more.

Putzi leaned toward me. "He says," he told me proudly, "that I have understated her beauty."

Hitler turned to the men behind him, called out something, raised his right hand and briskly waved it in a small tight circle.

The men glanced at each other and then—reluctantly, it seemed—they began to leave, shuffling past us toward the door. Rosenberg and Maurice openly ogled Miss Turner. But the rest of them glared over at me from beneath lowered eyelids, sulky, surly, like a pack of suitors who've been dismissed to make room for the New Boy in Town.

When all of them but Putzi had gone, Hitler turned to me, grinning, and said something.

Putzi said, "He heard how you handled those two men that Rosenberg sent to you. You did well, he says. He told Rosenberg that it was wrong to send them, to interfere with you."

Grinning still, Hitler clapped me on the shoulder and said something more.

"But you did well," Putzi translated. "Direct, forceful. Exactly the proper attitude with lackeys like those."

"I'm glad he's happy," I said.

Putzi translated this.

Hitler laughed, the skin around his blue eyes crinkling, and he said, "Ja, ja."

He turned to Putzi, asked him something. The two of them spoke for a while. In the midst of the conversation, Hitler glanced again at Miss Turner and flashed her a quick, dazzling smile. It would have been more dazzling if his teeth had been better.

Putzi turned to me. "Herr Hitler asks me to escort you to your seats. He looks forward to seeing you at dinner."

I said, "He knows we've got to talk to him about what happened in Berlin?"

"Oh yes, of course. He looks forward to that, also."

CHAPTER THIRTY-THREE

I SHOUTED AT Putzi, "Who are all the people in the front? The people in uniform?" Officers, mostly, each of them wearing enough medals and ribbons to ballast a battleship.

We were in the middle of all the noise, at a table in the seventh row from the stage, along the right side of the center aisle. One of Goering's athletes, a big one, had been saving the chairs for us. After we arrived, and Putzi spoke with him, the man had lumbered off toward the rear of the hall. Miss Turner sat on the aisle, I sat beside her, and Putzi sat to my right.

He shouted, "You don't recognize General Ludendorff? In the War, he was the leader of the German army!"

"Back then," I hollered, "I didn't see a lot of him."

"Next to him is Major General von Epp. He commanded the King's bodyguard. The King of Bavaria, that is. And he saved Munich from the Reds. And on the general's other side is Captain Ehrhardt. A *Freikorps* captain."

"Him, I've heard of."

"A great patriot," Putzi shouted. "He gave the Reds in Berlin the old twenty-three skiddoo, I can tell you. Also up there, with the rest, is—"

To my left, someone was bowing down beside Miss Turner, his head hovering beside hers. I turned and saw that it was Erik von Dinesen, wearing a dinner jacket and carrying a long camel-hair coat over his left arm. With all the noise around me, and Putzi's bellowing, I couldn't hear what he was saying. Von Dinesen looked over at me, smiled cordially, and nodded toward Putzi. Putzi waved at him but never stopped reeling off his list of names.

Dinesen said something else to Miss Turner and then stood upright and walked away, toward the front of the room. He sat down at a table only one row from the front.

Putzi kept up his recital. Gustav von Kahr, the prefect of Upper Bavaria. Dietrich Eckart, a writer and one of the founders of the party. Gregor Strasser, another party leader.

Putzi was still going strong when one of the waitresses arrived at the table and started setting out fat steins of beer in front of us. That shut him up, and he reached into his pocket for his wallet. The waitress held up her hand and shouted something in German.

Putzi swayed toward me. "She says that Erik has paid the bill. We must remember to thank him."

"Yeah," I said.

"Have you tried the beer of Munich?"

"Not yet."

"But Phil, you must. It makes the beer of Berlin taste like soapsuds."

I tried the beer of Munich. It was beer.

Putzi was leaning toward me still, an expectant look on his face.

I nodded and held up the stein. "Swell," I shouted.

"Absolutely," he shouted back, nodding happily, and he raised his glass to his mouth.

I leaned over toward Miss Turner. "What did von Dinesen want?" I shouted to her.

She turned to me and began to answer, but at that moment the audience burst into applause, wildly clapping and shouting, stomping their feet and whistling. It felt, from where we sat, as though we were trapped somewhere between the racing pistons of a gigantic internal combustion engine.

It was Hess, walking up the steps to the stage. He reached the center of the platform and walked toward the front and stood there, grinning as he held his arms in front of him, parallel to the stage, and moved his hands up and down, signaling silence.

It took a while, but the audience finally quieted, and Hess went into his introduction.

I couldn't understand a word of it, but from its rhythms and pauses it seemed like the same kind of thing that one American politician said whenever he introduced another: *"I give you a man who . . . [applause], and a man who . . . [applause], and finally a man who . . ."*

After a while, Hess was getting energized, his eyes growing larger and his voice more shrill. Then, dramatically, he threw out his left arm toward the narrow door, the same door through which Miss Turner and I had passed not long ago. The two athletes were still standing there. One of them briskly opened the door and then jerked back to attention.

From the darkness of the doorway, Adolf Hitler emerged.

The crowd went wild again.

As they erupted, Hitler walked to the stage. He didn't look out at the audience as he climbed the steps. He crossed over to Hess, who stood waiting for him with his hand outstretched and a huge proud smile on his face. Hitler shook Hess's hand and clapped him on the shoulder. Then he released Hess and turned toward the hall and moved to the front of the stage. Hess trotted across the platform, down the steps, and off to the right.

As the tumult of applause swept through the hall, and more whistles shrieked, and more feet stomped, Hitler stood there stiffly, his hands clasped together below his waist. He looked to the left, nodded to someone. He looked to the right, nodded to someone else.

Gradually, the applause staggered, slowed, and then finally it stopped.

Hitler looked slowly around the room, covering it all, then looked slowly back. After a moment, he began to mumble.

There was no microphone, and he was speaking so softly that no one, probably not even the people in the first row of tables, could make out what he was saying. I heard the creak of chairs, the whisper of clothing, as three or four thousand people, all of them holding their breath, leaned forward.

Gradually his voice rose, then it dipped. It rose again, dipped again.

I glanced at Putzi. He was staring, mesmerized, at the stage. I glanced at Miss Turner. She was doing the same.

I drank some beer.

The beer didn't last long. Miss Turner hadn't touched hers. I lifted her glass, held it out to her. She glanced at me blankly, saw the beer, shook her head impatiently, and turned back to the stage.

For a while I sipped at Miss Turner's beer. Occasionally, I took a look around at the audience. Every member of it, apparently, was as hypnotized as Miss Turner and Putzi. So far as I could see, I was the only person whose attention wasn't focused like a spotlight on the stage.

The audience loved him. Now and then he must've cracked a joke, because from time to time everyone in the hall burst out laughing. I took another look at Miss Turner and saw that she was smiling.

About forty-five minutes into the speech, when Hitler's voice had risen to nearly a shout and he was beginning to wave his hands and clutch at the air above him, I noticed a movement off to my right. Toward the end of the row in front of ours, a man at one of the tables had stood up, and now he shouted something. Instantly, three of Goering's athletes were on him, one of them swinging his truncheon in a single swift downward stroke while the other two grabbed at the man's shoulders and hauled him from his seat.

While this was happening, the people in the row behind him merely leaned to the side, left or right, trying to peer around the interruption.

I glanced at Miss Turner. She hadn't noticed.

I looked back again at the athletes. The three of them were marching the man up the aisles, past one of the swastika flags. The man's head was lolling limply forward and his legs weren't moving. No one in the audience, except me, was paying any attention.

I took a deep breath and then I took another sip of beer.

Ten or fifteen minutes later, it looked as if Hitler was going into his finale. His hands were balled into fists and he was shrieking as he stomped his foot. He seemed to be in some sort of ecstasy, or rage, or frenzy. I glanced at Putzi. Tears were rolling down his cheeks.

I was little bit afraid to look at Miss Turner, but I did it anyway. She was staring up at Hitler, her eyes narrowed, her lips compressed.

Hitler wrapped it up with a few more screeches, a few more stomps of his feet, and then a sudden rapturous shout as he hurled his right fist triumphantly into the air, his index finger pointing toward the heavens.

The band started playing and the audience erupted. The four Germans in front of us leaped to their feet and howled, frantically smacking their hands together. All around us, people were jumping up, shrieking with pleasure and pounding their fists passionately against the wooden tables.

Hitler saluted the crowd, first on the left side of the room, then the right, and then he turned and strode off the stage, down the steps, and across the floor to the door, and through it. The crowd roared.

Putzi was standing, his big flat hands pounding at each other. I felt a tug at my left arm. Miss Turner. She was leaning in my direction, her hand cupped around her mouth. I cocked my head toward her, but even only an inch away I barely heard her shout, "We had better stand, I think."

She was right. If we stayed in our chairs, didn't show the proper respect, someone in the next row might try making a field goal with our heads.

We stood. She wrapped her hands around my upper arm and pulled me toward her. Into my ear she shouted, "I hate that man."

CHAPTER THIRTY-FOUR

PUTZI LEAD US from the beer hall, his bulk driving a wake through the excited crowd. We bobbed in it, trailing behind him like flotsam behind an ocean liner. All around us, most of the people were wide-eyed and jabbering at each other, but a few of them stood there with their eyes empty and their mouths loose, as though they'd just been poleaxed.

Outside, the sun had moved farther to the west. The air was still warm, but it was cooling now and the light was growing thin and dusky, blurring everything into a soft pointillistic haze.

When we got past the clamor of the beer garden, Putzi slapped me on the back. "What did you think, Phil?"

"He knows how to give a speech," I said.

He laughed. "And you, Miss Turner?"

"It was"—she searched for a word, found it—"overwhelming."

He laughed again and turned to me. "I told you. Herr Hitler is the real McCoy."

"Yeah," I said. "What's the plan now, Putzi?"

"A taxi to the restaurant. We will meet Herr Hitler and the others there."

WHEN WE GOT to the restaurant, in Odeonsplatz, Putzi told us that it was the Tambosi Café, where King Ludwig the First had entertained Lola Montez. I was more interested in the place because it was here, according to them, that Gunnar Sontag and Alfred Rosenberg had entertained each other at lunch last Monday. I hoped that Hans Mueller wasn't in there at the moment, checking out their story with his waiter friend.

Inside, we were sent upstairs to a kind of mezzanine. At the back of this, in an alcove lined with flocked wallpaper, a long table had been set up—plates and glasses and menus neatly organized along the bright white damask. We sat down, and, when the waiter arrived, Putzi gave him our order. A whiskey for me, a glass of white wine for Miss Turner, a beer for Putzi.

The others showed up about twenty minutes later. It was the entire cavalcade again, all of them jostling around Hitler like chorus girls around a Broadway producer. The speech and its success had left them all looking a bit feverish. Everyone's movements were a little more jerky than normal, everyone's eyes a little brighter. Hitler himself was visibly pleased—with himself, with the company, with everything. His face was flushed and he was grinning gaily and his gestures were quick and expansive.

Erik von Dinesen had come to the restaurant with the others, his camel-hair coat draped over his shoulders like a cape, and he was the only one who wasn't restless with excitement. Maybe that was because he was a stage performer himself. Whatever his reasons, he moved on a quiet trajectory of his own, a part of the group and yet apart from it, tall and elegant and isolate. When he arrived at the table, he shook my hand, shook Putzi's, and held Miss Turner's while he bowed over it and kissed it.

Standing at the head of the table, Hitler took control of the seating arrangements, assigning positions like a cheerful general disposing his troops. With another gallant bow to Miss Turner, he pointed to the seat to his right. He said something to me, and Putzi told me that he wanted me on his left. Putzi sat beside me. Goering was placed to Miss Turner's right, and Hess to Putzi's left. The rest of them—Sontag, Nordstrum, Rosenberg, Maurice—were sprinkled around the table, with von Dinesen sitting at the other end of it, opposite Hitler.

When the waiter returned, Hitler conferred over the menu with Miss Turner. She decided on the veal. Hitler liked the pasta with cream sauce. With Putzi's help, I decided on the salmon. As I told Putzi what I wanted, I glanced at Gunnar Sontag. He was watching me. I smiled, and he looked away.

The food was all right, when it came, but the dinner itself wasn't the most interesting event I've ever attended. I'm not sure why Hitler had wanted me to sit so close to him. For most of the evening, he seemed to forget that I was there. He spent nearly all his time huddling with Miss Turner. He nodded thoughtfully at whatever she said and gave long and elaborate answers to the questions she asked him, and probably to some she hadn't.

Under his breath, Putzi translated a few of these for me:

"Yes, exactly," with another thoughtful nod. "The state must make it possible for every capable and industrious German to obtain a higher education. We must destroy the old bonds of the class system, the discrimination, the prejudice—we must eradicate them completely. Talented children of poor parents, whatever their station or occupation, must be educated at state expense and permitted to rise as high as their initiative will take them. . . .

"Apart from the Bible, *Don Quixote* and *Robinson Crusoe* are the two books most often read in the world. Cervantes's book is the world's most brilliant parody of a society in the process of becoming extinct. Defoe's book gathers in one man the history of all mankind. Two more of these universal books are *Gulliver's Travels* and *Uncle Tom's Cabin*. Each of these works contains a great basic idea. . . .

"Roads, Miss Turner, not canals or waterways but roads, these are the most important routes throughout the modern state. I envision in the future a vast network of modern, well-maintained roadways connecting every geographical area of the German nation with every other. And I envision an inexpensive but efficient automobile that will permit every German, no matter his economic status, to travel those roads and to refresh himself with the beauty of the German countryside."

Miss Turner asked him something, and once again he nodded thoughtfully. Once again, Putzi translated:

"Ah," he said, "the Jews." He smiled sadly. "What are we to do with them? With their war profiteering, their capitalism, they have hopelessly antagonized the German people. Perhaps at some time in the future it will be possible to assist them in setting up a Jewish homeland—in Palestine, perhaps. That would be best for all concerned, I believe."

Hitler listened carefully to the next thing Miss Turner asked him, then nodded thoughtfully once more. "Yes," he said, "I confess that I do appeal to this antagonism, as I appeal to anything, any emotion, that will help me unite the German people, help them to focus upon the difficult and painful duty ahead of us all—to bring Germany back from defeat and destruction, from the horrors of war and economic collapse, to a position of security and stability in the world."

I waited until we were all eating dessert to bring up the attack in the Tiergarten. Putzi translated for me.

Hitler looked up at me from a cake piled high with whipped cream, and he smiled. With his left hand he patted my forearm gently. His blue eyes crinkled merrily and he said something in amiable German.

Putzi translated, "It would be a pity to concern ourselves with such grim matters now. But perhaps, with your permission, your partner could join me tomorrow morning for breakfast. It would be delightful for me to spend a few more moments with someone so charming. And at that time, I would be happy to answer any questions she might have."

I looked at Miss Turner.

"I've no objection," she said.

I said to Hitler, "Neither do I."

And that was settled.

A HALF AN hour later, as we were being driven away from the restaurant in another taxicab, Miss Turner turned to me and said, "He was lying."

"When?"

"When he said that he was merely using anti-Semitism as a tool to unite the Germans. His speech was vile. It was filthy. Anti-Semitism is no tool for him—it's a part of his wretched little personality. He's a pig. He's worse than the others."

"Probably. But we've still got a job to do."

She looked out the window. "I doubt that he's ever even opened up a copy of *Don Quixote*."

"That doesn't really matter, does it?"

Still staring out the window, she said glumly, "I wish that I'd worn a raincoat over this ridiculous dress."

I smiled. "I'd say the dress made a good impression."

"He kept *gaping* at me."

I said nothing.

She looked at me. "We're supposed to learn about him whatever we can, isn't that right?"

"According to Caudwell, that's what Cooper wants."

"And exactly how far, in that regard, am I supposed to go?"

"As far as you feel comfortable with," I said. "And not an inch farther."

She nodded, then looked out the window again.

"What did von Dinesen want?" I asked her. He had approached her again after dinner, as I was shaking hands with Hitler.

"Pardon?" She turned to me. "Oh. He wanted to know if I wanted to join him for a drink, later tonight. I declined. All I want to do now is take a bath. A long, hot bath."

The Hotel Bayerischer Hof
Sunday night
May 20th

Dear Evangeline,

What a perfectly ghastly evening.

First there was Herr Hitler's speech.

He delivered it in another of those oppressive Patagonian food barns that the Bavarians so relish. The place was seething with his rabid followers, everyone wailing and howling with a kind of delirium. The awful noise and the press of heated, beer-soaked bodies were nearly overwhelming.

Mr Beaumont and I had met with him, briefly, before his performance. He is not at all as I had expected him to be. Physically, he is for the most part unprepossessing. He is perhaps five feet, six inches tall. His skin is sallow, his teeth are bad. His face is undistinguished, except for his eyes, which are really quite extraordinary. A penetrating pale blue, they are surprisingly beautiful, in an almost feminine way.

And the man himself was not without charm. Indeed he had vast amounts of it. He was ever so polite, ever so *gallant* and complimentary. (And he was ever so taken by my Vamp-in-Training dress. So much taken by it that at times I was afraid he might rip it from my shoulders.)

But the speech.

Yes, well, Mr B. and I returned to the auditorium (we had been in a sort of dressing room, backstage), and shortly afterward, Herr H. appeared and ascended the platform. Thunderous applause. After it had finally died away, he began the speech very softly. In almost a murmur he said, 'When we ask ourselves today what is happening in the world, we are obliged to cast our minds back to those happy years before the Great War.'

Because his voice was so muted, everyone in the room strained forward to hear it. This, I have no doubt, was his intention.

'I remember,' he continued, 'watching my mother prepare the family dinner in our little kitchen. I can see her now as she browns the pieces of rabbit in the hot oil, and I can see the sweet-smelling smoke rise from the pot and circle round her small gray head . . . '

He went on with this for a while, painting an infinitely homey portrait of a poor but proud matron in her poor but proudly kept kitchen, crafting in her careful, determined, loving way a German meal of surpassing nutrition and succulence. (Had Mr Beaumont understood German, he would have been most dubious about all this.)

'But now,' he said, 'the mothers and wives of Germany can no longer afford something as cheap as rabbit. They cannot afford even the oil to cook it. Even a simple loaf of home-baked bread is beyond their means, for they cannot afford the flour with which to make it. Flour! Our German women can no longer afford flour!'

And now he lowered his voice again, and he asked reasonably, 'How did we come to this pass?'

He proceeded to answer the question. First he attacked the right, the rapacious Jewish capitalists and the unscrupulous Jewish speculators who had encouraged the Kaiser to make the War; and who had hoped, with it, to line their own stinking pockets. Then he attacked the left, the Socialists and Communists (also Jewish, by the way) who had betrayed Germany at the armistice; and who had hoped to bring the great race of Germans into slavery, dominated by the ruthless, cunning Yids of Moscow.

He is really quite extraordinarily clever in the manner by which he manipulates the audience. He gets first one side of it, and then the other, to agree with him; and by so doing, *allez-oop,* to agree with each other; and then he presents them both with his solution to their mutual problems.

And what is that?

It's quite simple, really.

'First, we Germans must erect dams against the flood of filth that is polluting us. We must remove from our midst everything that defiles us, everything that endangers our pure, sacred German way of life. That would be the Jews, of course. Then we must come together as Germans, not as capitalist and worker, but as brothers and sisters, as fellow members of the greatest *Volk* on the face of the earth.'

As he neared the end of the speech, he seemed transported. His voice rose higher and his scarlet face streamed with perspiration. It was as though some spirit or demon had entered into him, possessed him.

'Soon,' he shouted, his hands grabbing spasmodically at the air, his head raised and the cords of his neck taut with tension, 'when we have gained power, we shall take these creatures of *ruin,* these *traitors,* and we shall hang them on the *gallows* to which they belong! Only by facing our future bravely, *together,* as *Germans,* do we develop the will to rise again! *Our* will! Our *indomitable* will! Two million German *dead* remained on the field of battle. Millions more were *crippled,* and *orphaned,* and *widowed.* We owe it to those *millions,* and we owe it to *ourselves,* to build a new and vibrant *Germany!*'

The crowd went bonkers. Had I been a Socialist or a Jew, I should have sunk to my hands and knees and slithered along the floor toward the exit, hoping that no one spied me.

The dreadful thing is that tomorrow, early in the morning, I shall be seeing the man again. I must interview him about the assassination attempt.

All my love,
Jane

CHAPTER THIRTY-FIVE

THE NEXT MORNING, at eight thirty, before Miss Turner went off to her interview with Hitler, she and I were sitting across from each other at a table in the hotel's café.

"Where's this supposed to happen?" I asked her.

"At the Four Seasons Hotel. On Maximilian Strasse." She sipped at her tea. "The party has a flat there."

Today she was wearing a crisp gray suit that revealed, between the prim lapels of her jacket, only a narrow, businesslike triangle of buttoned white blouse. Her hair was pulled back and bound tightly into a bun at the base of her neck. Unless you looked carefully, you would find it difficult to believe that this woman and the woman who wore last night's low-cut black dress were the same person. I was looking carefully, as usual, and I still found it difficult to believe.

"You don't have to go through with it," I told her.

"What do you mean?"

"We can call the hotel. Say that you're not feeling well."

"Why on earth should we do that?"

"Miss Turner, you obviously don't like the man."

"I despise him. But, as you said, we've a job to do, and this seems the most efficient way to accomplish it."

"You're sure?"

"Quite." I heard brusqueness in her voice, and maybe she did too, because she softened it by smiling and adding, "But I do appreciate your concern."

"Okay," I said. "Fine."

She raised her cup, took another sip of tea. "And what will you be doing today?" Still trying to soften that brusqueness, I think.

"See if I can reach Cooper. He knows where we are. We should have heard from him by now."

"You still believe that Mr. Caudwell provided information to Erik von Dinesen?"

"I think it's possible."

"He isn't like the others, you know. Erik, I mean. I'm quite certain of that."

"Good for him."

She smiled again. "I wish there were some way to persuade you."

"Maybe Cooper can persuade me."

She nodded, looked around the room, looked back at me. "What time is it?"

I pulled out my watch. "Twenty to nine."

She pulled herself upright, took a deep breath. Bracing herself. "I'd best be going."

"It's not too late to change your mind."

She shook her head quickly, firmly. "No. I'll be quite all right."

It would have been a good thing for her, a good thing for both of us, if she had in fact changed her mind. If she hadn't gone to meet Hitler that morning.

But neither of us would know that until later in the day.

AFTER I ATE breakfast, I walked a few blocks to the hotel that I'd used to telephone Hans Mueller on Saturday. The same clerk was working the desk, and he remembered me. I handed him a lot of money, even by American standards, and asked him to put through an international call for me, to England. I gave him Cooper's number in London and then I sat in a club chair in the lobby and waited while the people at the telephone exchange performed their miracles.

Forty-five minutes later, the clerk signaled to me that my call was ready. I walked into the cozy little booth and picked up the earpiece. "Hello?"

"Beaumont?" Cooper, the strong familiar voice riding over the static on the line.

"Yeah. Good morning."

"Good morning to you. Your connection clear, is it?" He meant safe.

"Seems to be," I said, "but there's no guarantee it'll stay that way."

"Got your telegram," he said. "Had some people look into the matter. Sorry to say this, but it looks as though you may be right."

"About Coburn?" I said, just to be sure. Coburn was the code name I'd used for Caudwell.

"That's right, yes. We're grateful to you, of course, for bringing it to our attention."

I had a feeling that Miss Turner wouldn't be grateful.

"Haven't got back to you," he said, "because first we'd like to know what organization he's working for."

"It's not Leeds?" Leeds was code for the client, in this case the Nazis.

"No, no, we're quite sure it's a local firm." Someone in London.

"Why would a local firm help Leeds?"

"There's an interest in your subject here, it seems."

"What interest?"

"That's what we're looking into, old man. Any progress on your end?"

"Everyone here thinks it was the Manchester group." The Communists.

"You don't sound persuaded."

"I'm not."

"Not at all like you, Beaumont. You're usually so trusting."

"I'm having a bad day."

"And how's your associate doing?"

"Fine."

"Need anything?" He pronounced *anything* the British way, *en-nething.* "A set of schematics?" False documents—passports, visas.

"Yeah," I said. "What we have, we got from Coburn. He knows what's in them." I doubted that we'd need a new set of false passports, but having them handy was probably a good idea.

"Yes," he said. "That won't do, will it. Have a new set delivered to you, shall we, there at the hotel?"

"Yeah."

"It'll take us take two or three days to get someone there."

"That's okay."

As things turned out, I was wrong about that. It wasn't okay at all.

AFTER I FINISHED with Cooper, I went back to the desk and arranged for a call to Berlin. In five minutes I was talking to Biberkopf.

"Mr. Beaumont, so good to hear your voice again."

"Yeah. Yours too. Did you get the package I sent?"

"Ah. You cannot talk?"

"I'd rather not."

"Yes. Yes, the, um, package arrived safely. It took us some time to open it, hah?" He chuckled. "But I believe it contains everything we need. And you? You are close to, um, a resolution?"

"I don't think so. I'm beginning to think we won't find it in Munich."

Biberkopf and I talked about a few more things, and then we said good-bye.

I WENT BACK to the Bayerischer Hof and up to my room. I took off my coat, hung it on the chair by the desk, and lay down on the bed. For a while I flipped through Mr. Baedeker's book. According to him, there were a lot of swell places to visit in Munich. Among them were the Nymphenburg Palace and the adjoining park. I wondered if Miss Turner would like to visit the park this afternoon.

By one o'clock, I was wondering if Miss Turner was ever going to get back to the hotel. She should have finished up the interview with Hitler long before this.

At ten minutes after one, someone knocked on the door to my room, and I thought it was she. I put the book down on the bedspread, rolled off the bed, walked to the door, and opened it.

Gunnar Sontag was out there, pointing a gun at me.

The Hotel Bayerischer Hof
Munich
Monday
May 21st

Dear Evangeline,

Where to begin?

My hand is still trembling. My heart is still pounding.

I've just come from confronting Erik. He is despicable. He is a liar and a swine.

And Herr Hitler, that insufferable little troll, is a madman. He made—he makes—my skin crawl. My meeting with him today was a catastrophe.

I'm scribbling away in one of the small lounges that adjoin the lobby of the hotel. This one is empty at the moment, containing only me and some spindly reproductions of Louis Quatorze furniture. The solitude suits me perfectly.

Sooner or later, however, I must speak with Mr. Beaumont and tell him what happened during my meeting with Hitler. I must let the catastrophe out of the bag.

Oh dear. I am deranged.

I will collect myself.

I will begin at the beginning.

To conduct my interview with Herr Hitler, I arrived at the Vier Jahreszeiten hotel at a little before nine o'clock in the morning. The clerk at the front desk told me that I was expected, and that I should take the lift up to the sixth floor. Herr Hitler, he said, was in room 607.

And indeed Herr Hitler was. He opened the door wearing a longish silk dressing gown, one patterned in red fleurs-de-lis against a black background, *sehr modisch*. Beneath this were a white shirt, a black tie, black trousers, black stockings, and black shoes.

He was as gracious as he had been the night before, but today I felt that there was something forced about it. The graciousness seemed a facade, one designed to conceal some underlying nervousness. It was as though a timourous servant were trying to impersonate his urbane master.

I wondered why this should be so. Last night he had seemed filled with confidence. I told myself that perhaps he was simply unused to being alone with a strange woman.

As we shall see, it was not, in fact, the woman who was strange.

Smiling, bobbing his head, he ushered me into the parlour, where a table had been prepared for breakfast. To one side stood a burly, white-coated waiter, who sprang forward as I entered the room and smoothly slid a chair out from under the table for me. Hitler sat down opposite.

The meal was quite a production, an elephantine version of the 'typical' British breakfast. There was enough food for a ravenous family of twelve, and all their ravenous chums.

After the waiter had served us both, Hitler dismissed him. As soon as we were alone, he leaned forward, placed his elbows on the table, wrapped the fingers of his right hand around his left fist, and rested his chin on this perch. His strange blue eyes peered into mine. 'It is remarkable,' he said. 'The resemblance is really quite striking, you know.'

'The resemblance?' I said. I took a small bite of egg.

'To the Stuck painting. *The Sin.* Hanfstaengl mentioned it, but until I met you last night, I believed that he was exaggerating. I must tell you that I admire this painting very much.' He smiled, but the smile was edged (like everything about him this morning) with a kind of electric tension. He looked down at his plate, his eyelashes fluttering, and then looked back up to me.

I told you about the painting, Evy, the one at the Städel Art Institute in Frankfurt. I've since learned (from that swine Erik) that

Stuck had, in effect, mass-produced the thing, churning out perhaps a hundred versions of it. Herr Hitler is also familiar with the painting: it is, according to the Hanfstaengl, one of his favourites.

I said, 'Mr Hanfstaengl showed me a reproduction. To be honest, I didn't really see the resemblance.' In the history of language, how many craven lies have sadly limped behind *to be honest*?

'Ah well,' he said. 'If you insist, Miss Turner. But here, please.' He picked up the pitcher and poured more orange juice into my glass. 'It is very important to keep the body properly hydrated.'

'Thank you.'

'And you must eat.' He raised his eyebrows anxiously. 'Is the food not to your liking?'

'No, no, I'm sure it's all wonderful. But you yourself aren't eating much, Herr Hitler.'

'Adolf, please,' he said. 'This is only because I am so very delighted to be in your company.' He smiled his nervous smile and then he added, blinking shyly, 'But if you insist upon it, then of course I shall eat.'

I returned his smile. 'I'm scarcely in any position to insist upon anything.'

'Oh, but of course you are. By your beauty, your poise, you may rightly place yourself in any position you choose. So then . . .' Smiling again, he lowered his head slightly and looked out at me from beneath his eyelashes. Almost coyly, he said, 'Do you insist, Miss Turner?'

This coyness was rather embarrassing. And, coming as it did from the potent demagogue I had witnessed last night, it seemed so peculiar that I felt a small frisson of . . . what was it, exactly? Disquiet. Unease.

But I humoured him. 'Very well,' I said, and smiled. 'I insist, then, Herr Hitler, that you eat something.' As though to show him how this might be accomplished, I took another bite of egg.

'Adolf, please,' he said.

I swallowed. 'Adolf.'

'Your wish,' he said, 'is my command.' He plucked a roll from
the salver. He has long, delicate, almost feminine fingers, and with
them, carefully, he tore the roll in half. He picked up his knife, swept
a plump yellow dollop of butter from its plate, daintily spread this
across one half of the roll, then scooped a large portion of peach jam
from the ceramic crock. He daubed this over the butter, taking great
pains with it, smoothing it, stroking it, soothing it into shape.

'You see?' he said, looking across the table to me. 'I am following your instructions to the letter.'

'Yes. I see.' I took a sip of my water.

He leaned forward, rising from his seat, and reached for the
bottle of mineral water. 'May I replenish your water?'

The level in my glass had retreated by no more than a quarter of
an inch, but once again I acquiesced. 'Yes, please.'

He poured from the bottle of mineral water, and I saw that his
hand was trembling slightly. He sat back. He hadn't yet eaten any
of the roll, which was still in his left hand, apparently forgotten.
He said, 'Water is, I believe, truly the elixir of life. It purges the system of all the accumulated poisons. It flushes them away. We can
never drink too much water. And, naturally, this is especially true of
women. Their constitutions are more sensitive and more refined.'

'Yes,' I said. 'Herr Hitler—'

His face looked wounded. 'Please. You must call me Adolf. I
beg it of you.'

'Yes, very well, Adolf then. Could you tell me about the Tiergarten?'

'Must we discuss that depressing incident?' Like a small child,
triumphantly, he held up the roll. 'You see? I haven't eaten my roll.
Ought I not finish it first?'

This was becoming tiresome. 'Yes, of course,' I said. 'Please. Do
by all means finish your roll.'

He offered me, once again, that curiously coy look: his chin
tucked in, his eyes peering up at me from his lowered head. 'Do
you *insist* that I finish it?'

At that point I felt like snatching the bloody thing from his hand and hurling it out the window. But once again I played my part. 'Very well. Yes. I insist that you finish it.'

'Adolf,' he said.

'Excuse me?'

'Please, Miss Turner, say it. "Eat your roll, Adolf." '

At this, as you might imagine, my sense of unease began to grow. I said, 'But . . . Herr Hit—Adolf, I—'

'Please, Miss Turner?' he implored me. 'I promise you that I'll answer all your questions. I swear it.'

He seemed so desperate, Evy, so pathetic. And, short of bolting from the table and racing from the room, I saw no way around this. We *did* need information from him. But the request made me feel somehow . . . unclean. I hated him at that moment, for having made it, and for having put me in such an absurd position. I actually snapped it at him: *'Eat your roll, Adolf.'*

Savagely, he jerked it to his mouth and, with bared teeth, he ripped away a chunk. As he lowered his hand, I saw that it was shaking heavily now. His blue eyes stared at me unblinking as he chewed, his chin and his curt little mustache making small ragged circular motions. Beads of perspiration had sprouted on his forehead.

They had sprouted on mine as well. The room was stifling—or so it abruptly seemed—and I was hugely uncomfortable, both physically and psychologically.

I took my napkin from my lap and placed it on the table. 'Would you excuse me for a moment?'

He swallowed, dropped the roll to his plate, then sprang to his feet so quickly he knocked over his chair. He ignored it. 'How may I assist you?'

'Where might I find the *toilette*?'

With his hands clenched into fists at his sides, he performed a stiff little bow. 'Come. I will show you.'

He led me from the room, his shoulders hunched beneath the dressing gown. I followed him down a narrow hallway to a closed door. He opened the door, reached in, and pressed an electric light switch.

When he turned back to me, his face, normally a sallow yellow, was now a bright shiny red. Those blue eyes of his were blinking.

'Please,' he said. 'May I ask? Will you be purging your system?'

'I—what?'

Suddenly he collapsed before me. In one swift movement, as though in a swoon, he slumped down onto his knees. He threw back his head, his eyes wild, his mouth gaping, and he reached out for me, his hands grasping at the air. I jumped away, but I was trapped against the wall, and he hobbled forward, jerkily, frantically, and wrapped his arms around my legs. He lowered his head, crushing his shoulder against my knees. I was so startled that I froze. He twisted his neck to look up at me.

His voice quavering, he said, 'You must let me assist you, my Rhine Maiden. My Rhine Maiden, you must let me help you with this. Please, my Rhine Maiden, I beg you.'

In a flash, I remembered my conversation with Greta Manheim in Berlin. Her account of the 'patient' who had said exactly the same thing.

'My God,' I said. 'That was *you* with Greta Manheim. The domina. In Berlin.'

And then I did something foolish. I laughed.

It was partly, I think, the result of hysteria. His rugby grip around my knees, his ridiculous pleas; the entire situation, Evy—it was all so preposterous, so impossible, that for a moment I feared I was losing my mind.

But then I looked at his face. It had drained of colour. His mouth was set in a thin white line. The blue eyes glared out at me from between narrow angry slits.

He pushed himself away from me and jerked himself to his feet. Still glaring at me, he brushed off his knees and then ran a hand quickly through his dishevelled hair. Then he rammed his hands into the pockets of his dressing gown and straightened his back.

For a moment we both stood there, staring silently at each other. And then he spoke. He said one word. *'Bitch.'* He spat it out at me.

I said, 'I think we'd best—'

'Filthy *bitch.*'

I began to babble. 'I do thank you for breakfast, it was—'

'You think you're such a *princess?* You think you're something *special?*'

Slowly, I began to back away, toward the parlor and the front door of the flat. 'Not at all,' I said. 'No, actually, I think—'

He had stalked slowly after me, his feet shuffling along the carpet, his arms swinging stiffly at his sides. His hands were balled into fists again. 'I know all about you and von Dinesen. Kissing him, *fondling* him. In a taxicab! In the *backseat,* like some foul cheap *trollop!*'

I was still backing away, but in a daze I said, 'Erik? How did—'

He laughed, a bitter, nasty laugh. 'You didn't know? My little princess didn't know? My sneaking, *back*stabbing princess didn't know? Hah! Dinesen *works* for me. He *reports* to me!'

'But—'

I had reached the end of the hallway, and now I began backing across the parlor toward the door. Hitler, still only four or five feet away, shambled toward me.

'Did he tell you,' he said, 'that he was a Jew boy? Did he tell you, *whore?*'

Something must have passed across my face.

He laughed again, the same gloating, rancorous laugh. 'He *didn't,* did he? He gave you his fairy tale about the French countess. *Didn't* he, slut? Brave little wounded Erik, recovering in the French château. Lies! He was a *deserter,* you rotten strumpet bitch. He spent half the War in *prison.*'

I was at the door and fumbling for the knob. The knob turned, but the door held fast. It had been locked, probably by the waiter as he left.

He stopped moving toward me and held out his arm, his finger pointing directly at me. His face once again was bright red. 'Go!' he said. 'Get out! You sicken me! You are filth. You stink in my nostrils like *shit!*'

His face contorted with fury, he glanced quickly around the room, looking for something. He strode over to the armoire and from it he ripped a large red vase. He raised it over his head and hurled it with all his strength to the floor. It shattered spectacularly, shards spinning out across the carpet.

I spun around, found the lock, twisted it, ripped the door open.

I glanced back at him. His head lowered, his body humped, he used both arms to sweep the top of the desk and send everything sitting on it—books and photographs and crystal knickknacks— flying through the air.

I slipped through the door and ran toward the lift. But I was afraid that he might follow, so I ran past the lift and tore through the door that led to the stairway. I dashed down these to the first floor, then raced through the lobby and out into the street.

And now we come to Erik.

As soon as I returned here, to the hotel, I—

OR PERHAPS WE won't come to Erik. Something curious has just happened.

Herr Braun, the concierge, has just found me, here in the lounge. He said that a young man with blond hair has asked at the front desk about me and Herr Beaumont and has gone up to Mr Beaumont's room. The man asked that I join the two of them when I return to the hotel. (Only Herr Braun knew that I had, in fact, already returned; I forgot to return the key to the desk when I came storming in, looking for Erik.)

But this ought not have happened. The desk clerk had instructions from Mr Beaumont to deny that either of us was staying in the hotel. Herr Braun knows this.

I must go see. I'll post this and write more later.

Love,
Jane

✢

CHAPTER THIRTY-SIX

✢

SONTAG'S PISTOL WAS a Broomhandle Mauser. It was a big piece of armament, nearly three pounds of precision tooling. It was cocked. If the magazine, in front of the trigger, was fully loaded, it would be holding ten rounds of nine-millimeter Parabellum cartridges.

My own pistol was in the pocket of my jacket, which was hanging on the chair, about seven feet from where I stood. Seven very long feet.

I backed away from the door.

Sontag closed the door behind him. He was still tall and handsome and blond, but today his suit was black rather than gray. Maybe he had decided that, in the circumstances, black was more appropriate.

In his left hand he was carrying a black leather briefcase. That was probably where he'd been transporting the gun. There's a leather holster built for the Mauser, and one made of wood that turns into a shoulder stock, so you can fire it as a carbine. But they're both bulky, and either of them will spoil the drape of your suit coat.

"Where is Turner?" he said.

"Why?"

"I ask the questions. Back up. Sit on the bed. No, farther back. Now bring up your legs and cross your ankles. Good. Now your hands. Put them behind your neck."

It was a position from which I couldn't do much, not without giving him plenty of warning.

Holding the pistol steady on me, Sontag walked to the desk, tossed the briefcase onto the dark green blotter, pulled out the chair, and turned it around. He sat down on it and crossed his legs, right knee over left knee.

He put his right hand, the hand with the pistol, on his thigh, and rested it there.

Now he and the big Mauser were directly between me and the little Colt automatic. Not that, at this point, it made much difference.

"Where is she?" he said.

"I don't know."

He glanced at the door, looked back at me. "No matter. I left a message at the front desk. She will come here."

"And then what?"

"You will learn."

"What happened?"

He shook his head. "I told you. I ask the questions."

"Everything was going fine. Miss Turner and I were getting along with everyone. Peaches and cream. And then someone sends you here with a gun."

"Quiet."

I played the only card I had. "You were seen, you know. In Berlin. Before you killed Nancy Greene."

His head snapped back as though I'd slapped him. "I never—" He stopped. Maybe he realized that denials wouldn't make any difference now. He glanced at the door again, then turned back to me.

"You are lying," he said.

"On Monday night," I said, "the two of you went back to her boardinghouse. It was late, a little after three. She couldn't find her key at the front door. You used yours."

His eyes narrowed.

"When you got her into her room, you hit her with something. Maybe that." I nodded to the Mauser.

His glance darted down to the pistol. He looked back at me and raised the barrel slightly.

"While she was unconscious," I said, "you strangled her. Then you put her on the bed. You took off her shoes. You arranged her hands. Very thoughtful. Miss Turner thinks you loved her."

"She was *nothing*!" he snapped. His eyes widened. I think that the anger in his voice had startled him. He shook his head, as though clearing it. He looked at me. "A brainless English girl," he said dismissively. "A nonentity. But this story of yours, it is *nonsense*. You have no proof of anything."

"The police in Berlin have a witness. And you know what, Gunnar? I think your friends here in Munich know that. The people who sent you here." I doubted this, but a little smoke never hurt. "I think you're expendable right now. You say you asked about Miss Turner? That desk clerk is going to remember you."

"It will make no difference. The two of you will be found together." He smiled. "You killed her, you see, and then you killed yourself. No one will worry about some guest you had before the"—another smile—"tragedy."

"Why did I kill her, exactly?"

"You discovered her affair with Erik von Dinesen."

"And naturally von Dinesen will back that up."

"Naturally."

"Well, Gunnar, I think that's a fine plan. Look, do you mind if I put down my hands for a minute?"

"Back! Behind your head!"

"Okay, okay. But listen, just answer one question for me. Just one."

"Ask it."

"Why did you kill Nancy Greene?"

He said nothing, didn't respond at all. He just sat there, watching me.

"Was it something you said to her?" I asked him. "Something you shouldn't have said?"

He sneered. "Do you really believe I would tell Nancy Greene anything? That I would reveal anything of importance to a foolish little girl like that?"

"So what was it?"

He narrowed his eyes. "You truly have no idea, do you?"

"Not a one."

He looked toward the door, turned back to me. "She saw something she should not have seen. Something I had with me, when we were together on Tuesday."

"What was that?"

"Identification papers."

"Why kill her because of identification papers?"

"They were blank seamen's cards. In Russian."

And one of them, made out in the name of Pyotr Semnovitch, was still lying at the bottom of the inside pocket of my coat.

I felt like an idiot. If I'd given the card to Biberkopf, then sooner or later he would have learned that it was a phony.

"It was all a setup," I said. "Those men outside the Mikado. They were Roehm's."

He shook his head. He smiled—pleased that, once again, I was wrong. "Captain Goering's. From the SA. The Storm Division."

"But you saw Greene before someone shot at Hitler. You had the cards then, before the Tiergarten?"

"I obtained them on Tuesday morning, before I saw her." He smiled. "They were intended for other purposes."

He was fairly chatty now, probably because we were talking about what a nitwit I'd been.

"What other purposes?" I asked him.

"To infiltrate Red organizations. And to assist us when we eliminate a threat to the Movement. A card is placed on the body, and other identification removed. With a Russian, a Red, the authorities do not concern themselves overmuch."

I nodded. "Nice."

"We had the cards. It was decided to use them with you. To persuade you that the Communists had been responsible for the attack on Herr Hitler."

"Who decided that?"

"Captain Roehm."

"Did Hitler know?"

"The Führer knows everything."

"Who *did* shoot at him in the Tiergarten? Was that a setup too?"

"It was the Communists."

"Right. None of you know any more about it than I do."

He smiled grimly. "What you know is no longer of any concern to us."

"Those men at the Mikado. Roehm shot one of them. Killed him."

He nodded once, curtly. "Wolfgang Lessing. He had been instructed to make his escape when Captain Roehm appeared. Instead, he attempted to make the attack more realistic. He ran toward Captain Roehm. The captain had no choice."

"Is that what they told you?"

He frowned. "What are you saying?"

"Come on, Gunnar. The only way for that swell plan to work would be for me to see the seaman's card. Otherwise, what's the point of using it? And the only way for me to see the card would be for someone to die."

"It was an accident."

"Wrong. Roehm deliberately killed one of Goering's people."

He shrugged, as though that were no big deal. "Wolfgang would gladly have given his life for the Movement. For the Führer. We would all do so."

"How did Nancy Greene see the cards?"

"They fell from my briefcase. I told her they were a joke."

"And then Roehm decided to use them on me. And he told you. And you had to let him know that you'd made a mistake. That Greene had seen them. And so they sent you up to Berlin, to take care of the mistake before Miss Turner and I arrived. If I talked to Greene and found out about the cards, your plan was shot."

He raised his head. "It was my carelessness. It was my responsibility."

"Why did Hess give Putzi the woman's name, back at the beginning? If I'd never heard of her, I'd never have talked to her."

"Hess knew nothing about the plan."

"I thought that Hess was important."

"Not so important as he thinks."

"But he *did* know about Miss Greene. And you suspected, or Roehm suspected, that he'd tell me about her."

Sontag nodded.

"But Hess said that you were here last Monday. You weren't. You were in Berlin."

"Hess was finally told everything. By the Führer. On Thursday, the day before you arrived in Munich."

"Here's the thing I don't understand. Why did Roehm want me to think the Communists were after me?"

"When your investigation concluded that the Communists were responsible for the assassination attempt, Herr Hitler would go with that information to General von Seeckt. Von Seeckt would then give permission for a march on the Weimar government."

"Von Seeckt already thinks it was the Communists. And he doesn't much like your friend Hitler."

"Captain Roehm has prepared evidence that points directly to an important member of the Weimar government."

"And when was I going to find this evidence?"

"Soon."

I smiled. "You don't know, do you, Gunnar? They're not keeping you up-to-date, are they?"

He waved the gun barrel an inch or two, impatiently. "This is foolish. You want me to doubt my friends, my comrades. You will not succeed."

"Which member of the Weimar government is it?"

"That is not important."

"You don't know that, either."

"It is not my concern."

"No. Not when Roehm and the others are setting you up. You're a patsy, Gunnar. They know you're already going down for one murder. Nancy Greene. They figure they might as well use you for a couple more before they toss you to the wolves."

"You are being absurd."

"What happened today? Why'd they send you here?"

He smiled at me. "You can ask Miss Turner when she arrives. She knows."

And just then, as though Sontag had just delivered a cue, someone knocked at the door.

CHAPTER THIRTY-SEVEN

BEFORE I COULD do anything, Sontag switched the Mauser from his right hand to his left. Keeping the pistol trained on me, he stood up. He moved well, his body limber and loose. "Not a word," he said between clenched teeth. "If you speak, I will shoot through the door first, and then I will kill you." He jerked his head down toward the pistol. "I am very good with this. Using either hand."

I got myself ready. At some point, even if only for a second or two, he would have to deal with the person on the other side of that door. He would have to look away from me.

I would need to spring forward into a roll, off the bed and across the floor in a rush, hoping that I could reach him before he brought the gun to bear. It wasn't much of a chance. But the gun was in his left hand now. No matter what he said, no one was as good a shot with his weak hand as he was with his strong hand. If Sontag gave me a single opportunity, I would take it.

But he wasn't giving me any opportunities. He walked to the door backward, without once looking away from me. He turned his head slightly to the side. "Who is it?" he called out over his shoulder.

I heard her voice, muffled by the door. "Jane Turner."

Still without looking away from me, and without moving the barrel of the gun at all, he reached out his right hand for the doorknob. He fumbled a bit, then found it. "Please come in, Miss Turner." Still pointing the big Mauser at my center, he opened the door and said, "I am aiming a weapon directly at—"

Miss Turner shot him in the back, twice.

Sontag was so surprised that he forgot to shoot me. I was off the bed and across the room just as he was turning to Miss Turner and beginning to sag toward the floor. I ripped the Mauser away with my left hand, wrapped my right arm around his chest, and tugged him farther into the room, away from Miss Turner.

"Shut the door," I told her.

As she handled that, I handled Sontag, who had become dead weight. I needed to use both hands, one still holding the pistol, to lay him down.

I was on my knees as I set his head on the carpet. He opened his eyes.

His eyes focused on mine. "You will never get away," he rasped. "The train stations, the roads, we will be waiting."

I couldn't see any exit wounds in his chest—the .32 isn't a powerful cartridge. But he was bleeding badly in the back. The front of my shirt, where he had been slumped against me, was soaked with it.

"You will die," he whispered. He face suddenly tightened with pain. It takes a few seconds, after a bullet hits you, for your body to realize that it's been hurt.

"Maybe," I said. "But not right now."

"*Heil Hitler,*" he said.

"Sure."

His breathing stopped. His blue eyes stared upward, at nothing. I checked his throat for a pulse. Nothing.

I rose and looked over at Miss Turner. She was standing against the door, her face pale, her arms limp at her sides. In her left hand was a small leather purse. In her right was the little Colt automatic. She was staring down at Sontag.

She didn't look at me when she said, "Is he dead?"

"Yeah. Are you—"

"They told me that someone was here." She still hadn't looked away from the body. "Downstairs. I came up. I heard him through the door. I took out . . ." She raised the gun, looked at it. She frowned. She opened the purse, shoved the pistol inside it, held the purse to her chest as she looked down again at Sontag.

"He said you knew why this was happening," I said. "Why he came here."

"Yes." She turned to me. "I think so. Hitler. He—"

"Okay, you can tell me later. You have a bigger purse than that one?"

She looked at me blankly. "What?"

"A bigger purse. Something that'll hold more than that does. But something that doesn't look like a suitcase."

"Yes." She was staring down at Sontag again. "A leather handbag. I bought it in Frankfurt. You remember, we were—"

"Okay. Go to your room. Pack it. Whatever you'll need for a day or two. And then wait for me. I'll be there in a few minutes."

She looked at me. "But someone will have heard the shots."

I shook my head. "Middle of the afternoon. The maids are finished and the guests are out. You go ahead. I'll be right there."

She was staring at the front of my shirt. Something passed across her face. She said, "You're covered with him."

"I'll wash. Please, Miss Turner. Your room."

She looked up, into my eyes. She nodded. She turned, opened the door, and slipped away, pulling the door shut.

I stripped off my clothes, tossed them into a pile. I went into the bathroom and washed up. Afterward, quickly, I dressed in clean clothes. I took a look into Sontag's briefcase. Empty. I stuffed into it whatever I thought I might need—clean socks, underwear, some shirts, my razor, the Baedeker guide. I also slipped in both of my passports, the real one and the counterfeit.

There was still some room in the briefcase, so I shoved in the Mauser. You never know when a cannon might come in handy.

I snapped the case shut and grabbed my overcoat. It was another warm and sunny day, but I had a feeling that I'd need the coat before this was over.

I pulled out my watch. Ten minutes to two.

WHEN I KNOCKED on her door, it opened almost immediately.

"Ready?" I asked her.

"Yes." She was wearing another suit, black, and under the jacket a thin gray sweater over a white blouse. She had the handbag strapped over her right shoulder and she was carrying her overcoat in her left hand. She was doing fine.

"I'm sorry about this," she said. "It's all my fault."

"I doubt that, but you can tell me about it later. You understand that we're not coming back here?"

"Yes."

"You have everything you need?"

"Yes."

"Both passports?"

"Yes."

"Okay. Let's go."

We walked to the elevator, took it down to the main floor, and went through the lobby like two people strolling out for a late lunch. We nodded to Herr Braun as we passed him. He wanted to say something, but I waved at him and we hurried on. I flagged down a taxi, and Miss Turner asked the driver to take us to the main train station.

I looked back, through the rear window. No one was following

I looked at the driver. He was behind a wall of glass. I turned to Miss Turner. "Okay. What happened?"

She told me.

Basically, Hitler had made a pass at her, and not a very smart pass. And in asking it, he had revealed that he was one of the clients of Greta Manheim, the prostitute that Miss Turner had talked to in Berlin.

"It's such a ridiculous coincidence," said Miss Turner. "His meeting her. Of all the prostitutes in Berlin, thousands of them, he had to pick Greta Manheim."

"Not that ridiculous," I said. "He was staying in one of the ritzy hotels. There are only two or three of them, and she probably works them all. And she was a specialist. Not every prostitute would provide the services he wanted."

"But when did it happen? When did he meet her?"

"Probably that first night in Berlin. Monday. Putzi said that all of them went to bed after dinner. Maybe Hitler didn't."

She shook her head. "I thought he'd gone mad. This morning. His face—it was horrible."

I said, "Putzi said something in Berlin—it was important that there were no scandals attached to Hitler's name. I'm guessing that the incident with Manheim would qualify as a scandal."

"Greta," she said. "We must warn her. I gave him her name. If he's sending someone after us, then he'll be sending someone after her."

"We'll take care of it."

"There's something else."

"What?"

"Erik. You were right about him. Hitler told me. Erik's been reporting to him. All along. So you were likely right, too, about his getting information from someone."

"From Caudwell, directly or indirectly. I talked to Cooper this morning. He confirmed it."

"But why would Caudwell do that?"

"Cooper says that someone in London is interested in Hitler. He doesn't know who."

"But if that's true, then the passports that Caudwell gave us, the false passports, they're useless. He could have given the Nazis the names."

"Maybe. But we might have to use them anyway. If the Nazis put our names out, our real passports are definitely useless."

She shook her head. "I feel like such an ass. All along I've been thinking—"

"Look," I said. "You've done well. If you hadn't handled Sontag the way you did, he'd have killed us both."

She shook her head. "I hated doing that. They told me, in training, never to point a pistol at someone unless I intended to use it. And I was afraid that if I tried talking to him, tried to reason with him, I was terribly afraid that he'd simply shoot you. So I . . . did what I did." She closed her eyes for a moment, then opened them. "But I hated doing it."

"You're supposed to hate it," I said. "But you saved my life."

She turned and looked out the window at the buildings passing by.

When she spoke, her voice was strained, as though her throat was tight. "But what do we do now?"

The taxicab was pulling up in front of the main station.

"Right now," I said, "I call Biberkopf."

We had a couple of hours, I figured, before someone came looking for Sontag. The train stations were probably still safe, but not the trains themselves. We couldn't climb onto a train for Berlin and expect to arrive there. As soon as the body was found, a report would go out. If Sontag had been telling the truth, and if both the police and the army could be mobilized, then anyone who wanted us could make a telephone call to someone farther along the line, and people would be waiting for us down there.

I was inclined to believe that Sontag had been telling the truth. I remembered what Hans Mueller had told me—

You must be very careful with these Nazis. They are not good people, and they are everywhere. Not just in the Munich police. They are in the state police as well, and the army. Here in München, they are very powerful.

Inside the train station, I found the telephone booths and I arranged for a call to be put through to Berlin. When I got Biberkopf, I told him what had happened. He wasn't happy. I told him what I was planning to do. He wasn't happy about that, either, but he made some suggestions and gave me a telephone number. I wrote it down. I told him about Greta Manheim. He said he would do what he could.

Afterward, Miss Turner and I went out to the front of the station and got another taxi. We drove to Schwabing, to see Hans Mueller. It was a quarter to three.

WHEN WE TRIED it, the front door of Mueller's apartment house was unlocked, as it had been when I arrived here the last time. We went into the hallway. The same bare lightbulbs hung from the same black, twisted wires. The same scuffed yellow linoleum was peeling back from the floor. I knocked on Mueller's door. According to Biberkopf, his cousin wouldn't be working until this evening.

No one answered.

I tried the knob. It turned, and the door opened.

I didn't like that.

I entered the apartment, followed by Miss Turner.

We found him in the bedroom. Wearing pajama bottoms but no top, he was lying on his back on the floor. The covers on the bed were thrown to the side. He had gotten out of bed, it looked like, when they came for him.

CHAPTER THIRTY-EIGHT

HE HAD BEEN shot once in the chest, just over the heart. His still body, pale and angular, had that diminished, abandoned look I had seen too many times before.

There wasn't much blood, but the entry wound was large. Probably a nine-millimeter slug. Maybe a slug fired from the pistol I had in the brief-case. Sontag's briefcase. Sontag's pistol.

I moved down into a squat and touched his cheek.

Cold. He had been dead for a while. Since last night, maybe early this morning.

Beside me, Miss Turner said, "How? Why?"

I stood up. "He was checking out Sontag. The Nazis must've found out."

"But who killed him?"

"I don't know. Maybe Sontag."

I looked down at Hans Mueller.

The face was no longer pink. It was pallid now, and waxy.

I had liked him. His enthusiasm. His honesty. His concern.

They are not good people, and they are everywhere. . . . Here in München, they are very powerful.

And they had used that power. Mueller had tried to help me, and one of them had killed him.

"What now?" Miss Turner said.

"Now," I said, "we rob the dead."

His keys were on a small table by the wardrobe. I took them, slipped them into my pocket.

I looked around the floor for the cartridge case, but someone had already found it.

We searched quickly through the apartment, but we didn't find anything that told us who had killed him. Whoever had done it hadn't left a calling card.

But that could be fixed.

You never know when a cannon might come in handy.

In the living room, I opened the briefcase, took out the Mauser, used my handkerchief to wipe away my fingerprints. Careful not to leave any fresh prints, I laid the pistol on the coffee table, stuck the handkerchief back into my coat pocket.

Miss Turner was staring at me. "Why?"

"The police might find fingerprints."

"But you've just cleaned them off."

"The cartridges," I said. "Inside the magazine. Maybe Sontag left his prints on those."

"But what if Sontag didn't kill him? What if it's not the same gun?"

"Then everyone is going to be very confused. And right now, that's a good thing."

I looked over at the telephone. I asked Miss Turner if she could get through to Biberkopf in Berlin. She said she could try.

After a few minutes, she did reach him. She handed me the mouthpiece and the receiver. "I didn't tell him," she whispered.

"Sergeant?"

"*Ja?* Beaumont again? People will start to talk about us, hah?" He chuckled.

"Listen, Sergeant, I'm sorry. But I've got bad news."

For a moment he said nothing. Then he said flatly, "Hans." It wasn't a question. When I spoke with him from the train station, I had told him we were coming here.

"Yes," I said. "He's dead."

I glanced at Miss Turner. She was looking toward the hallway that led to the bedroom.

After a moment, Biberkopf said, "He is killed how?"

"A pistol, I think. Probably this morning. I don't know how they got in here."

"A master key. The police everywhere, they have them. In Munich, here, everywhere. And the police in Munich, they are swine. They are . . ."

He didn't finish. The silence began to grow.

I said, "I'm sorry, Sergeant. I liked him."

"*Ja.* You know who does this thing?"

"Maybe Sontag."

"I call Munich now. I get someone over there."

"If you do that, Miss Turner and I will never be able to leave town."

Another silence. Then another sigh. "Yes. Very well. You keep to the same plan?"

"Yeah."

"Yes, then go now. Tomorrow I talk to you."

"Okay. And thanks again, Sergeant."

"Yes. Go."

I hung the earpiece on its hook, put the telephone back on its stand. I turned to Miss Turner. "Okay." I reached into my pocket, pulled out Mueller's keys, handed them to her. "Outside, to the left, there's an alley."

"I saw it, yes."

"At the end of it, there's a shed. The door has a padlock on it. One of those keys will open it. You get it opened and go inside. There's an electric light. Close the door and wait for me."

"What will you be doing?"

"Waiting until you're in there. We've probably already been seen by the neighbors, but I don't want them to see any more of us than they have to. And especially not together."

"Yes. I understand."

I looked into her face. It had been a rough day for her. The nonsense with Hitler, the scene with Sontag. She had shot a man and then watched him die. And now she had walked in on another dead man. But she was still holding up. She was an impressive woman.

"Look," I said. "I know this is hard for you. But you're doing fine."

She blinked, and I saw that her eyes were shiny.

"It'll work out," I told her.

She blinked some more and lifted her chin. "Yes," she said. "I'm sure it will."

Her handbag was on the coffee table, beside the Mauser. I walked to the table, picked up the bag, walked back, and handed it to her. "Okay," I said. "Go ahead."

She swallowed, and then she nodded.

After she went out the door, handbag in one hand, overcoat in the other, I stalked around the apartment, wiping our prints from everything we might have touched. Five minutes later, I followed her, carrying along the briefcase and my own overcoat.

When I got inside the shed and pulled the door shut behind me, Miss Turner said, "We're not going to take the motorbike?"

"Yeah," I said. "We are."

The bike was resting on its center stand, looking sleek and swift even when it stood absolutely still.

"Do you know how to drive one?" she asked me.

"Yeah. You see any panniers around?"

"Panniers?"

"Metal boxes. Luggage. They attach to the back. Mueller told me he had some."

We found them underneath a tarpaulin at the rear of the shed. I slapped the dust from them, slipped them onto the bolts at the rear of the motorcycle, then tightened the wing nuts. Miss Turner stood off to the side, watching.

I opened the left-hand pannier and slid Miss Turner's handbag inside. It fit, with some room to spare. I took the Baedeker out of my briefcase—Sontag's briefcase—and shoved the case into the right-hand pannier. I put the Baedeker on the driver's seat and opened it.

"Here's the plan," I said to Miss Turner. She moved closer.

I unfolded the map in the front of the book, a map of southern Germany.

"Once we get out of Bavaria," I said, "we should be okay. Right now we're smack in the middle of it. Here. Munich. When the Nazis find

Sontag's body, they'll probably have their friends in the police department start setting up roadblocks. But I think they'll be expecting us to head north, for Berlin. This way. Or west, for France. Or south. They might figure we'd try to get into Italy by way of Austria."

"But where *are* we going?"

"East. A town called Passau. Right here, on the border with Austria."

"Why Passau?"

"Biberkopf has a friend there. Another cop. He can arrange visas for us. For Austria. We leave the motorcycle in Passau and we take the train to Linz."

She frowned. "It's rather the long way round, isn't it, if we're aiming for England?"

"Yeah. So maybe the Nazis won't be looking at it too closely. But from Linz we might be able to go north, through Czechoslovakia, and then come back into Germany. Somewhere here, above Bavaria."

"And if we can't?"

"Then we go to Vienna and head south from there. Down through all of this stuff. To Athens."

"But we'll be going even farther away from England."

"Yeah, and from Bavaria."

She looked at me. "Yes, of course."

"From Athens," I said, "we can get a boat to France."

She was staring down at the map, thoughtful. She looked up at me. "I speak no modern Greek, you know."

I smiled. People were trying to kill us and she felt badly about not speaking modern Greek. "That's okay," I told her. "I do."

She frowned. "Really? Wherever did you learn?"

"Long story. Are you ready?"

"Yes. And may I say something? I thank you, Mr. Beaumont. Sincerely. You've been very patient and very resourceful, and I've been a complete dunderhead. If I hadn't—"

"Miss Turner, it's not your fault. None of it. And listen, one way or the other, we'll get out of this."

CHAPTER THIRTY-NINE

⬧

THE MEGOLA HAS two gas tanks, a main tank hidden inside the sleek bodywork, and an auxiliary tank attached to the left side of the front wheel. You run on the auxiliary tank, and you use the main tank as a kind of reserve.

Mueller had shown me how to work the subsidiary tank's hand pump and transfer gas from the main tank. I did that now, filling the smaller tank. Afterward, the main tank was only half-filled. We looked all around the shed for spare gasoline, but we couldn't find any. Passau, according to the map, was about 160 kilometers away. About a hundred miles. I didn't know what kind of gas mileage the motorcycle was capable of, but I knew we'd need to refill the main tank before the end of the trip.

While we were looking for the gas, I found a pair of goggles and a pair of thin leather gloves. I tried the gloves. They were a bit tight, but they fit. I stuck them into my right-hand coat pocket, with the Colt. I stuck the goggles into the left-hand pocket.

The most difficult thing about getting out of the shed and onto the road was figuring out what to do with Miss Turner's skirt. There was no way for her to sit properly on the passenger pillion, put her legs on either side of the rear wheel, without cutting a slit in the skirt and her overcoat.

Mueller had told me that his "gals" rode sidesaddle. That didn't seem safe to me, especially when the machine was moving at speed. But Miss Turner was willing to try it, at least until we got out of Munich. "I've ridden sidesaddle on a horse," she said. "It's not my favorite way to ride, but I can do it." She smiled a tired smile. "And I do rather like this skirt."

"Okay," I told her. "The most important thing to remember is to move with the machine. When I turn left, I'll be leaning the bike to the left. Go with it. Don't counterbalance. Don't throw your weight in the opposite direction."

She nodded. "Move with the machine. Yes, I understand."

"It won't be hard. Just hang on to me."

"Yes. Yes, I shall."

I pulled out my watch. Four o'clock. The sun would be setting a little before nine o'clock. So we could probably reach Passau before dark—a good thing, because the Megola had no headlight.

We put on our overcoats and I tipped the bike off its stand. Miss Turner opened the door to the shed and I wheeled the machine out into the alley. As I climbed onto the bike, she shut the door and locked it. I took the goggles out of my coat pocket, slipped them over my head, pulled them down to my eyes. I took out the gloves and slid them over my hands. I buttoned up the overcoat. Bracing the bike with both feet against the ground, I told her to get on.

When she did, from my left side, the bike wallowed a bit, left and then right.

"Put your arm around my chest," I told her.

She did. The bike wallowed again.

I turned the key and flipped the ignition.

Nothing happened, but nothing was supposed to happen. The bike wouldn't start until I pushed it forward.

"Hang on," I said to Miss Turner, and I pushed. The engine coughed. I pushed again, and this time the engine caught and the bike began to move on its own. I felt Miss Turner's arm tighten.

The bike had only one gear—forward—and no neutral. To stop it, I would need to brake it and turn off the engine. To go forward again, I'd need go through the pushing process once more.

But to go forward now, all I had to do was give it some gas. I checked the traffic. Clear. We glided out of the alley and into the street.

"You okay?" I called back at Miss Turner.

"Yes," she said. "I'm fine."

"Here we go." I turned the throttle.

The bike shot forward. Once again, Miss Turner's arm tightened around me.

WE ZIGZAGGED THROUGH Munich for a while, and then we were on our way out of town, heading east. In another few miles, we were in the countryside, farmland and bright green, rolling pastures on either side of us, the smell of tilled earth and fresh manure in the air. Far off in the distance, to the south, I could see a range of mountains. The Alps.

There wasn't much traffic, maybe because the road was bad. It had only two lanes and the pavement was pocked with holes.

When we were about ten miles from the city, I slowed the bike, pulled it over to the narrow shoulder, and turned off the engine.

Miss Turner took her arm from my chest. "What's wrong?"

Bracing the bike, I turned to look at her. "Nothing. I just wanted to check on you. I need to see how fast this thing can go. Are you okay, sitting like that?"

"Yes, I'm quite all right. Thank you. To be honest, it's actually a relief to be out of Munich."

"Okay. Hang on tight. I'm going to top out the throttle for a while."

"Right." She smiled weakly. "Tallyho."

I smiled. An impressive woman . . .

I checked behind me for traffic. None. I turned on the ignition and pushed the bike forward. The engine caught. I rolled on the throttle and the machine leaped forward.

The bike kept accelerating, the sound of the engine climbing from a hum to a high-pitched roar. Finally I couldn't get any more out of it. The needle on the speedometer was tipping a hundred kilometers an hour. A little over sixty miles an hour. Mueller had told me that he'd gotten 115 kilometers, but he had probably been riding it solo, with no panniers attached.

The bike handled well, swooping left, swooping right. Miss Turner's arm was tight around my chest.

And then the engine sputtered. It caught again, sputtered again. I shut it off.

"What is it?" she said into my ear.

Braking the bike, I craned my head toward her. "Gas."

We had to find gasoline soon.

WE FOUND IT in a place called Mühldorf, a small town on the Inn River, about forty miles from Munich. Narrow streets, tiny stone houses, a marble fountain, a couple of stone churches with steeply gabled roofs. I located a garage and Miss Turner dealt with the owner, a jolly fat man.

Before we got back on the motorcycle, I asked Miss Turner if she was hungry.

"A bit, yes," she said, "but oughtn't we forge ahead, while the light is still good?"

"Yeah. We'll get food in Passau. Less than two hours now."

She smiled. "I can survive until then."

I checked my watch. Five o'clock.

The sun had moved down the sky since we began the trip, and the air against my face had grown colder. I was glad I was wearing the goggles and the gloves. I wished that I had a leather jacket. No matter how tightly I closed my overcoat, the wind knifed in, cold and biting, against my chest.

The farther east we went, the more hilly and heavily forested the countryside became. The road got even worse, and I had to slow the bike down. But around seven o'clock, when the shadows were growing longer and the blue of the sky was beginning to pale, we passed a sign that said PASSAU 10 KILOMETERS.

I didn't want to drive into town on the motorcycle. It was too distinctive a vehicle. And if someone had found Hans Mueller, then it had probably been reported as stolen.

About eight kilometers later, as we started shooting down a long hill, between dark deep walls of forest, I saw what looked like an abandoned barn up ahead on the right, in a patch of scraggly field. As we approached the barn, I saw that it was derelict, its roof collapsed. I slowed the bike and turned off the main road onto the dirt track that led up to the barn's gaping front door.

When I reached the door, I stopped the bike and shut off the engine. "Okay," I told Miss Turner, "you can get off."

"We're leaving the motorcycle here?" She slipped off the pillion.

"Yeah. Tomorrow, I'll tell Biberkopf where it is. If Mueller's family wants it, they can send someone to get it."

I rolled the bike into the barn. It was dark inside, the only light coming from the doorway and filtering down from a ragged gash in the roof, where the timbers had fallen. On the hard-packed dirt floor lay a big section of the wooden door. I wheeled the bike over to the wall, opened the panniers, took out the handbag and the briefcase, closed the panniers, carried the bags over to the doorway.

Miss Turner helped me lift the chunk of door. We hefted it over to the wall and placed it over the motorcycle. It wasn't perfect, but it would do.

Miss Turner used a compact mirror to arrange her hair. I ran a hand back through mine. It felt spiky and dirty.

We couldn't really get cleaned up until we walked into Passau and found a hotel.

FROM A TELEPHONE in the train station, Miss Turner called the number that Sergeant Biberkopf had given me. She spoke to someone for a while, then hung up.

She told me, "He said to go to the Ratskeller, down by the steamer pier. He'll join us there in an hour."

We walked through Passau. It was a attractive little town. Lots of trees, lots of narrow cobblestone streets climbing down the hill to the river Danube. Fairy-tale stone houses roofed with red tile.

The Ratskeller was on the Danube, and from our seat by the window we could see past the cheerful steamboats lined up at the pier, and out across the river to the steep, wooded cliffs on the far side, about 250 yards away.

It was hard to believe, surrounded by all that picture-postcard scenery, that there were people out there who wanted us dead.

But it had been a long day, and neither of us had eaten since breakfast, and we were both hungry. Miss Turner ordered beef with noodles and I ordered a steak and fried potatoes. We shared a bottle of wine.

Sergeant Stephan Heiden, Biberkopf's friend, arrived at a quarter to nine, just as the sun was setting. He was tall and thin, maybe thirty years old, and he was dressed in a gray civilian suit. He walked with a slight limp, favoring his right leg.

After he sat down and we all exchanged greetings, I asked him, "How do you know Sergeant Biberkopf?"

"From the War," he said in English. "We were in England together. Handforth. The prison camp."

I asked him, "Did Sergeant Biberkopf explain our situation?"

"Yes. He said you are in trouble with the Nazi swine in Munich. You wish to enter Austria. I can help. I have a friend in the Customs—if you will give me your papers, I will arrange tonight for a visa for you both. You can cross the border tomorrow. There is a train at noon."

I gave him the passports we'd gotten from Caudwell, for Joseph and Charlotte MacNeil.

He flipped through them, looked up at me, and smiled. "These are not your names."

"No."

"They are excellent forgeries." He sounded pleased, as though he genuinely admired the workmanship.

"There might be a problem with them," I told him. "It's possible that the Nazis have those names."

"There will be no problem. My friend will see to it. Have you found a hotel yet, for tonight?"

"No."

"I recommend the Passaner Wolf, near to the train station. I have spoken with the manager. There will be no difficulty with your registration."

"Thank you, Sergeant. We're very grateful for all your help."

He smiled. "The enemy of my enemy is my friend. The Nazis are the worst thing that ever happened to Bavaria. And they have become very powerful here in Passau. I am happy that I can do something that will displease them."

He stood up. "I will bring the visas to you at the hotel, at eight o'clock tomorrow." He smiled again. "I shall wait until then to say good-bye."

I stood and I shook his hand. "Thank you."

He nodded, made a crisp bow to Miss Turner, and walked away, limping slightly.

He had been with us less than twenty minutes, and in his curt, efficient way he had changed everything. Before he arrived, we had been fugitives. After he left, we were people who were going to be tourists.

We owed a large debt to Sergeant Heiden. And to Sergeant Biberkopf.

Miss Turner and I drank coffee and brandy while we made our plans. In the morning, once we had the visas, we would pick up some clothes and luggage, and tickets for the train to Linz.

We left the restaurant and walked back through the town to the Passaner Wolf Hotel. As Heiden had said, there was no trouble with our registration. We were given rooms on the same floor, three doors apart. A bellboy led us to them, and I said good night to Miss Turner and went into mine.

The Passaner Wolf wasn't the Adlon or the Bayerischer Hof, but it was clean and comfortable. I ran a bath, climbed out of my clothes and into the tub. A half an hour later I was lying in a warm, plump bed, under a clean sheet and a fluffy blanket. It took me almost two minutes to fall asleep.

They came for me early in the morning.

The Hotel Passaner Wolf
Passau, Germany
Monday night
May 21st

Dear Evangeline,

Mr Beaumont and I are in a bit of trouble.

I don't want you to worry. There is every likelihood that by tomorrow afternoon we will be safely on an Austrian train, rushing giddily toward Linz.

But, just in case something untoward does happen, I wanted to write to you.

I wonder if you remember a particular morning in Torquay, a very early morning before sunrise. It was in June, and the air was uncommonly warm, almost sultry. The full moon was in the west, and the sky to the east was beginning to lighten. The time was perhaps four thirty. We had crept, the two of us, from the window of Mrs. Applewhite's and padded along the pathway that wound through the beech trees to the promontory overlooking the Channel. We sat down on one of the damp wooden benches and stared out at the water. With the moon behind us, and no reflection on the water, the sea looked leaden and dull.

Clouds had piled up out in the east, above the horizon, and we were very concerned that the sunrise might not be as spectacular as we had hoped. But as we sat there, the distant clouds shifted, one melding into another; and then, just as the sun soared up from behind the rim of the world, they seemed to disperse, to dissipate, and a bright heart-piercing light came flooding out across the sea, red and orange and gold. And then briefly, lasting no longer than the wink of God's eye, amidst all those gaudy operatic hues, the corals and scarlets and vermillions, there was a sudden and quite startling flash of green.

I remember you snatching at my hand and saying, 'Did you *see* that? The *green?*'

'Yes!' I cried. My heart was pounding with excitement.

For several hungry moments we stared out at the sun, which was slowly losing its miraculous splendour and becoming merely its standard miraculous self, a bright round yellow wonder in the morning sky. We saw no more green.

I was disappointed. But I remember that, finally, you squeezed my hand.

With the utmost seriousness, you said, 'Having seen that, I feel that it should be perfectly acceptable if we were to die just now.'

For a moment I was shocked. We were how old then? Eleven? Twelve? Death simply wasn't something with which we concerned ourselves. Why, I wondered, had you even mentioned it?

But then I realized that of course you were right. We had been granted an extraordinary gift, one that had filled me with as much happiness and satisfaction as I had ever felt. If I were to die just then, at that very moment, I should be dying a happy and a satisfied human being. And who of us, really, at whatever age, could ask for more?

I have experienced, since then, only a few similar moments. But with each of them I was reminded of my first, the one I spent with you.

As I said, it is likely that tomorrow evening will find Mr Beaumont and me nibbling on linzer torte in some cosy riverside café. But, whatever happens, I wanted you to know that from the moment we saw it I have treasured this sunrise, and the sharing of it; and that after a lifetime of friendship I continue to offer you, as always,

All my love,
Jane

CHAPTER FORTY

✦

THE RAPPING WOKE me up. Someone knocking at the door.

The Colt was under the pillow. I slipped my right hand in there, found it, sat up, turned on the light. My watch was on the nightstand. Four o'clock.

I was wearing my shorts. I got out of bed and walked across to the door. Without opening it, I said, "Who is it?"

"The desk clerk. There is a problem."

Holding the pistol along my right thigh, I used my left hand to unlock the door. I left the chain latched. I opened the door and peered out.

I recognized the desk clerk, a short young man in a tightly fitting suit.

"What problem?" I asked him.

"With your friend. The woman."

"What's wrong?"

"She has been hurt."

"Hurt?"

"Yes, she came downstairs a while ago, and—"

"Hold on."

The moment I unlatched the chain, the door exploded open, slamming me in the forehead and smashing my right arm. Two big men in black over-coats spilled into the room and grabbed me. One of them kneed me in the crotch. As I bent over, gasping, something crashed against the back of my head. I saw the floor whirling up at me, and then I saw nothing.

I don't think I was out for long, maybe a couple of minutes, but when I came to, I was sitting on the floor, next to the dresser, my back against the wall. My head hurt and my stomach was weak and queasy.

Three men were in the room. Two were the men I had just met. In their thirties, they stood on either side of me, about a yard away, in front of the bed, and they both held Lugers. Between them I could see the third man, sitting on the bed. He too wore a black overcoat. He was a younger man, slender, with a pale, thin, earnest face, like a monk's.

I realized that I'd met him before too. He had been with Roehm, at the Mikado.

Kalter. Lieutenant Felix Kalter.

Kalter said, "Do not make a foolish mistake. We intend you no harm."

"I can see that," I said.

"The violence was necessary," he said. "There will be no more, if you cooperate."

I discovered a sharp pain in my side, along my rib cage. One of them had kicked me while I was out. Something else, probably, that was necessary.

"Where's Miss Turner?" I asked him.

"Downstairs. Waiting for you to join her."

"How'd you find us?" I asked him.

"You purchased petrol in Mühldorf. We have friends among the local police. One of them talked to the garage owner."

The jolly little man.

"So you guessed," I said, "that we were heading for Passau. For the border."

He shrugged. "It was a simple matter." He stood up. "Get into your clothes."

Standing up took a lot longer than it should have taken. I was stiff and sore. Shuffling like an old man, I walked around the bed and over to the chair, where I'd left my pants and shirt. The barrels of both Lugers followed me. Kalter stood watching with his hands in the pockets of his overcoat.

I tugged on the pants. The pockets had been stripped—my wallet, my comb, my penknife, all my loose change. I slipped into the shirt. I buttoned buttons. I sat down in the chair to put on my shoes and socks. As I was tying my shoelaces, I looked up at Kalter. "What happens now?"

"You come with us to Munich. Herr Hitler wishes to speak with you. He wishes to clear up this misunderstanding."

"Uh-huh," I said.

It would be a long trip to Munich. Lots of nice forest along the way. Plenty of places to hide a couple of bodies.

I stood up.

"Your coat," said Kalter.

The jacket and my overcoat were hanging in the opened wardrobe. I walked over, reached inside, took the jacket off its hanger. As soon as I held it, I knew that the Colt wasn't in the pocket.

I looked at Kalter.

He pulled his left hand from the pocket of his overcoat and showed me the little pistol.

I put on the jacket.

Smiling, Kalter slipped the Colt back into his pocket.

"Now the overcoat," he said.

I put on the overcoat.

From the right-hand pocket of his topcoat, Kalter pulled out a pair of handcuffs. He tossed them to me, over the bed. I caught them, looked down at them, looked at Kalter.

"It is merely a precaution," he told me. "If we wanted you dead, you would be dead already."

If they wanted me dead in the hotel, where the shots would disturb the other guests. And where they would have to worry about hauling my body away.

I tossed the handcuffs onto the bed. "I don't think so."

Kalter sighed. He shook his head. He said, "Klaus."

Klaus was the big man nearest me. He took two quick steps forward, raised the pistol, and feinted a swing. I was ready this time. I ignored the feint, slipped beneath the fast roundhouse left he sent my way, and I jabbed a left of my own into his stomach, just below the sternum. But I had been hurt, and I was sloppy and slow. He took the punch and he brought up the pistol and clubbed my forehead with it. The floor tilted and I was down again.

Klaus flipped me over, onto my back. He slipped the cuffs on me, *snap, snap,* then jerked me to my feet. I weigh two hundred pounds. I was impressed.

Across the room, Kalter was shaking his head. "This is all so unnecessary," he said. He said something in German to the other man, Not-Klaus, and the man snatched up my briefcase from the dresser, opened it, and plucked up my things from the night table—my notebook, my pen—and tossed them into the case.

He picked up my watch, hefted it experimentally, then glanced at me quickly, furtively, before he slipped it into the case. From the glance, I knew that he would be keeping the watch, and I knew that I had been right about Miss Turner and me never reaching Munich.

SHE WAS SITTING in the small lobby on a leather sofa, next to another man in yet another black overcoat.

She stood up when she saw the four of us parading from the elevator. So did the man next to her. He had been holding her handbag on his lap, and now he tucked it beneath his arm. Under her overcoat, she was wearing the same black suit she had been wearing before, but her hair was loose now, trailing down to her shoulders. On her wrists were a pair of handcuffs identical to mine.

I glanced at the front desk. The young man in the too-tight suit was back behind the counter. He looked away.

Miss Turner looked tired. Her face was drawn and her shoulders were slumped.

I asked her, "Did they hurt you?"

"Out," said Kalter, and nodded to the door.

Miss Turner shook her head. But I noticed a small bruise on her right cheek. I was suddenly very angry.

"Out!" said Kalter. "Out the door!"

The man with Miss Turner's handbag led the way, followed by Not-Klaus. Miss Turner and I walked side by side, followed by Klaus and Kalter.

The air outside was cool now, and damp from the river. The cobblestones beneath our feet were slick, coated with a film of mist.

Miss Turner said, "The night clerk. He—"

"Silence!" Kalter, from behind us.

Miss Turner looked at me. I shook my head.

We walked downhill, through a narrow alleyway between the stone buildings, and we came out along the riverside. Out on the black surface of the river I could see the tiny lights of a few boats, probably barges, moving slowly downstream. The street was empty.

We turned left and walked for maybe a hundred yards. The buildings we passed were shuttered and dark. There was no moon. The streetlamps were occasional, and from time to time we walked through patches of darkness. Out on the river, the firefly lights of the barges sailed slowly along the black mirror of the water.

I kept looking for an opportunity. There probably wouldn't be one, but that doesn't stop you from looking until they put a bullet into you.

We came to the wide, white wooden doors of what looked like a warehouse. The man carrying Miss Turner's handbag rapped his knuckles against the door. Nothing happened. He rapped again.

Kalter snapped something in German. The man grabbed the door, tugged at it. It swung slowly to the left, its bottom moving on small wooden wheels that rattled loudly against the pavement. When the man had pulled it all the way to the back, the opening was wide enough for two cars to drive through. The first few feet of oily cement floor were visible, lit by the soft glow of the streetlight. Beyond, there was darkness.

Kalter cried out, "Wilhelm!"

No one answered.

Klaus and Kalter moved forward. Klaus was standing just to my left. The man with Miss Turner's handbag stood farther to the left. Miss Turner was to my right. Kalter stood to her right, and Not-Klaus was to Kalter's right, and he was moving forward, into the darkness.

"*Wilhelm!*" Kalter called again.

A light went on. It was a kind of garage. Two shiny black automobiles were parked there, on the left. And standing off to the right, beyond an open space and next to the light switch, was Erik von Dinesen. He was wearing his camel-hair topcoat over a black dinner jacket, a white shirt, and a black bow tie. Draped around his neck was a dashing white silk scarf. In his hand was a dashing black Luger automatic pistol.

CHAPTER FORTY-ONE

MISS TURNER HAD done the right thing, back at the Bayerischer Hof. She had done what her instructors had taught her—when she had a pistol in her hand, she had used it. She had shot Sontag.

Now, standing inside the broad doorway, his pistol leveled at Kalter, von Dinesen did the wrong thing. He started talking. Maybe he did that because he was a stage performer, and talking was something he was good at.

He didn't get a chance to say much, because all the other men went for their weapons.

A lot of things happened quickly.

For me, it was an opportunity. As the first gunshots rang out, I interlocked my fingers and swung to my left, putting all my weight behind it, swiveling on my left foot, and I slammed my clenched fists at Klaus's throat. He was tugging his pistol from his pocket. He changed his mind about that and bent forward instead and started clutching at his neck. I ripped the Luger from his hand and smashed him over the head with it.

As he dropped toward the pavement, I brought up the Luger with both hands and put two rounds into the man with Miss Turner's handbag. He was busy firing toward von Dinesen, but he stopped doing that and he fell down.

I whipped around and saw that von Dinesen and Not-Klaus were both going down, and I was bringing the pistol to bear on Kalter, and he was bringing his pistol to bear on me, when Putzi Hanfstaengl came looming up behind him and hit him over the head with a big length of pipe.

Kalter collapsed to the ground. Putzi tossed the piece of pipe to the street. It clanged loudly, like a bell.

Miss Turner had run toward von Dinesen, who was sprawled on his back along the cement floor. She knelt down beside him.

Putzi grabbed my arm. He was wearing another gray suit and white shirt, but this was the first time I'd seen him without a tie. "Phil! We must go! The police will come!"

Yes, but probably not right away. We were in a commercial area, no houses nearby.

Before we left, there were things we had to do.

Still holding the Luger in both hands, I pointed it at the man with Miss Turner's bag. "Look in his pockets. Find the key to the handcuffs. And grab that handbag."

I scurried over to Not-Klaus and nabbed my briefcase. I turned to Kalter. I squatted down, set the Luger on the pavement, and checked his neck for a pulse. It was there, but faint.

I started going through his pockets. I got out the Colt, set it beside the Luger. I checked two other pockets before I found a handcuff key.

Kalter's arm moved a bit, a small twitch, and he moaned softly. I grabbed a handful of his hair, raised his head, then reintroduced it, quickly, to the pavement.

Two head injuries within a couple of minutes probably wouldn't do him any good. But I hadn't liked that bruise on Miss Turner's cheek. And I hadn't liked Kalter.

I opened the briefcase and took a quick look. Everything was there, including my wallet, my comb, and my penknife. I stuffed them all back into my pants pockets and shoved the Luger into the case. Standing up, I tucked the Colt into my coat pocket.

Putzi had moved over to Miss Turner. Holding her handbag, he stood there looking down at her. She was still kneeling beside von Dinesen, her head bowed.

I hurried over to them.

"He is dead," Putzi told me. His big face was slack.

I touched Miss Turner's shoulder. "We've got to leave."

She looked up at me. She was crying, softly. She nodded. "Yes, of course."

I offered her my hand. She took it and I pulled her upright. She swayed a bit, righted herself. "Yes," she said.

I unlocked her handcuffs. She barely noticed. She was staring down at von Dinesen.

"Putzi," I said. "The handbag."

He handed it to Miss Turner. "Check it," I told her. "Make sure everything's there."

"Yes." She took it, opened it, looked listlessly through it.

"Phil, we must go," said Putzi.

"Yeah," I said. I asked Miss Turner, "Ready?"

"Yes," she said.

"How did you know?" I asked Putzi.

"Erik telephoned me."

"How did *he* know?"

"Herr Hitler told him."

"Why?"

We were in the derelict barn to the west of Passau, where Miss Turner and I had left the motorcycle. The Megola was still there.

Outside, the sky was beginning to slide from black to a milky opalescent white.

Putzi and I were standing at the rear of an amazing vehicle. It was an ancient Daimler pickup truck, battered and dented. It was painted a dull black now, but the paint was chipped in spots and you could see that it had been painted several other colors over the years. Probably, during the War, it had been painted in camouflage.

Twenty minutes, maybe, had passed since we had left the garage.

I figured that we still had some time. It would take the police in Passau a while to work things out. If Kalter and Klaus were still alive, and I had serious doubts about Kalter, the two of them might tell the cops about us.

But, then again, they might not. Kalter and the others had been working on their own, without notifying the locals, and the locals might take that personally.

If Kalter was dead, then Klaus would probably clam up until he got orders from someone higher up on the Great Chain of Being.

But we didn't have an infinite amount of time, and we had to make some decisions.

We couldn't go back to Munich with Putzi in the truck. We couldn't get the visas and the counterfeit passports from Sergeant Heiden, not if it was possible that the rest of the Passau police department knew about us. Which meant that we couldn't cross over into Austria.

And we couldn't stay in that barn forever.

But I wanted to know how Putzi and von Dinesen had managed to arrive so conveniently. There hadn't been time to talk in the car, not with Putzi wheeling the bulky old truck through the streets of Passau as though it were a Bugatti.

"I'm not sure," said Putzi. "He told me that Herr Hitler wanted to rub his nose in it. Rub his nose, that's what he said. He wouldn't explain."

Miss Turner was standing four or five feet away, at the open doorway of the barn, leaning against the jamb with her arms folded beneath her breasts. She had been looking out at the whitening sky. Now, slowly, deliberately, she swung around to face us. "He was there," she said. "With Hitler. When Hitler rang up Lieutenant Kalter."

"He told you?" I asked her. "Just now?"

"Yes. He knew it would take some time for Kalter to organize his men. As soon as he could, he rang up Mr. Hanfstaengl."

"But why did Hitler let him know what was going on?"

"As Mr. Hanfstaengl said. To rub Erik's nose in it. In his relationship with me. Hitler is furious at me."

"He's not himself, Phil," said Putzi. "He's totally upset about Miss Turner. He's frightened. He knows that she knows about that prostitute in Berlin. About his striking her."

"Striking her?" I said.

"Erik told me about it," he said. This was evidently the story that Hitler had given von Dinesen. "But she was trying to steal his wallet, Phil. Hitting her was understandable, under the circumstances."

"Right," I said.

"But if it got out that Herr Hitler was seeing prostitutes, it would go badly for him. The scandal. His career would be seriously damaged."

I looked at Miss Turner. Her arms still folded beneath her breasts, she looked back at me. Neither of us bothered to correct Putzi. There didn't seem to be much point.

I turned back to him. "Don't you think," I said, "that his attitude is a little bit extreme, Putzi? He wants us dead."

"He's not thinking clearly, Phil. He's acting out of panic. I can talk to him. I can make him see reason."

"Right. Back to your story. Von Dinesen called you."

"Yes, and he told me that Hitler was sending some people from Passau to deal with you and Miss Turner."

"How was he going to get away with it? What would he tell the Pinkertons?"

"That you were killed by the Reds. Because you were getting too close, you see, to identifying them as the people in the Tiergarten."

"Right."

"So I dressed and went to my neighbor's house and woke him up. I have no car of my own. He couldn't give me his motorcar, he needed it today, but he was kind enough to lend me the truck. It's old, but he keeps it in tip-top shape. Then I drove to Munich to fetch Erik. When I got there, I told him it was hopeless, a wild-goose chase, but Erik insisted we had time. He said that Kalter needed to find someone who knew the city, knew Passau, and that this would take a while."

"But how'd you find us?"

When Putzi and von Dinesen had arrived outside Passau, Putzi told me, they had waited on the side of the road, hidden behind some trees. An hour later, when two cars passed by, going at top speed, they knew it was Kalter and his people. They followed them to the garage. Putzi had parked about fifty yards farther down the riverfront road.

They had seen Kalter and three men leave the garage. Von Dinesen had told Putzi to follow them. Von Dinesen would drive the truck two blocks south, away from the river, park it conspicuously, then go to the garage to deal with Kalter's two vehicles.

"Deal with them how?" I asked.

"I don't know," Putzi said. "Sabotage them, perhaps. And perhaps to see if there was someone else waiting there."

And of course there had been. Wilhelm. The man whose name Kalter had called out.

"Go ahead," I said.

The four men had gone into two other hotels before they entered the Passaner Wolf. When they didn't come back out, Putzi figured they'd found us. He waited, saw them escorting us out the door, and he followed the parade down to the garage. He watched as the man with Miss Turner's handbag opened the door.

"And then, of course," he said, "everything went nuts."

He had seen the flashes of the pistol, heard the gunshots, and grabbed the first thing he could find, that length of pipe, and rushed forward.

I said, "You did good, Putzi. Thanks."

"I had no choice, Phil."

"Yeah, but how are you going to explain it to Hitler?"

He shook his head. "I cannot. I will not. But I *will* speak with him, Phil. I'll get him to see reason. He's upset now, yes, but only because he's afraid that Miss Turner will talk. But I can assure him that you're Pinkertons, both of you, and that neither of you will reveal anything to anyone." He frowned. "That *is* true, isn't it?"

"More or less. But you're betting on the wrong horse, Putzi."

"I can reason with him, Phil. I know I can."

"I don't mean about this. I mean about Hitler in general."

"No, Phil. No. I know the man. He has greatness in him."

"Excuse me," said Miss Turner.

We turned to her.

She looked drained, as though she had no energy left. She said, "I don't mean to interrupt. But what do we do now?"

"I don't know," I told her.

Putzi said, "I can take you in the truck. I can drive you somewhere safe."

"There's nowhere safe," I said. "Not in Bavaria. And you've got to get back to Munich, and soon—you don't want Hitler to know you were here."

His furry eyebrows dipped. He looked over at the section of door that concealed the Megola. "The machine," he said. "It still operates?"

"Yeah. But we can't get very far with it. We'll need gasoline, and it's not safe for us to stop anywhere. That's how Kalter found us this time."

"There's a can of it in the back of the truck. Three liters. And Phil, I have an idea. An excellent idea."

CHAPTER FORTY-TWO

I TOOK MY Baedeker from the briefcase and opened the folding map at the front of the book. Southern Germany. I squatted down and spread the map out on the hard-packed earth.

Putzi got down on his knees. "Here," he said, taking out his pen. He uncapped it and tapped the nib at the map. "Just here, a few kilometers to the east of Passau, you will find the first path. It will go this way—"

"Wait a minute," I said. "We can't go through Passau. Not on the motorcycle. They know about it."

"We'll put the motorcycle in the truck. We'll drive across the river together, the Danube, and then continue east until we find the path. Approximately here."

I thought about it. In the truck, we would be safe enough. We had run away from the garage before anyone had spotted us. And so far as we knew, no one had spotted the Daimler.

I asked him, "And where does it go, this path?"

"There are paths all over the Bayerische Wald. It's a huge forest, part of the Oberwald, and the paths go everywhere. But it will be possible for you to go as far north as Weiden. Here. From there, you can take a good road to Bayreuth."

"Bayreuth."

"You will be safe in Bayreuth. It is still in Bavaria, yes, but no one there will know you."

"Except the Wagners."

"How likely is it that the Wagners will see you? You can take the train from there. If the police are looking for you, they'll be looking for two people, a man and a woman. All you need to is go to the station separately."

"And all the cops need to do is ask for our papers."

"I doubt this will happen. Bayreuth is too far north, too far from Munich. It is the boondocks, Phil. But if it looks dangerous, you can drive the motorcycle again and go north until you're out of Bavaria totally. This town. Plauen. Not far, you see? Fifty kilometers. And then from there you can take the train."

I got up from my squat. "How will we know which paths to take?"

With some difficulty, Putzi climbed back upright. He bent over and slapped dirt off his knees. "They are marked," he said, straightening himself. "The Forestry Commission attends to the signs. And you have the map."

"Putzi, from the map, that trip's got to be at least two hundred miles. More, probably. We're not going to have enough gas. Even with your three liters."

"But there are villages scattered all over the mountains. Woodworkers. Shepherds. You will find gasoline, Phil."

"How much gasoline do shepherds use?"

"Phil, I'm sure you will find it. *Someone* will have it."

I turned to Miss Turner. She was staring down at the map. "What do you think?" I asked her.

She looked up. Her face was drawn. "Have we any alternative?"

And so we filled both tanks of the Megola and took off the panniers. There was an old tarpaulin on the bed of the truck, bunched up against the cab, and we unfolded that and laid it down along the bed. Using the length of wooden door as a ramp, the three of us wrestled the bike up onto the tarpaulin and gently set it on its side. I flipped the bottom of the tarp over the bike, and then Putzi and I hauled up the door and maneuvered that over the tarp. We set the panniers on the truck bed, and then all of us got into the cab.

On the outskirts of Passau we stopped at the first garage that sold gasoline, and Putzi got out and had the can filled. When he returned to the truck, he told us that the big news in Passau that morning was the band of smugglers who had killed each other down by the river.

Smugglers in a border town. That would make sense to the cops.

"Any of them alive?" I asked him.

"One, but he is in the hospital, unconscious. That would be Lieutenant Kalter, don't you think?

Putzi didn't want to be responsible for Kalter's death.

"Yeah," I told him. "Probably."

At a small shop about two hundred yards down the road, Putzi bought a bag of groceries. And then we drove through Passau and across the Danube. There were no roadblocks, no police lines anywhere.

About five miles to the east, we found the path. A carefully painted wooden sign stood on a post at its entrance. Beneath a black arrow were the words RÖHRNBACH, GRAFENAU.

The path was wide enough for Putzi to drive the truck down its brown surface for forty or fifty feet, away from the traffic on the road. In a small clearing, we all got the bike back onto the ground.

It didn't look like the shiny, immaculate machine that had been standing so proudly in Hans Mueller's garage. It had been ridden hard and fast and it was dusty now. There were scratches in the once-glossy black paint.

I put the panniers back on and we filled them. Putzi's can of gasoline went into the left pannier, along with some of the food—hard sausages, bread, a bottle of beer. The briefcase and two bottles of mineral water went into the right pannier. Miss Turner and I put the rest—some candy, some cheese, some pretzels—in every available pocket we had.

Miss Turner arranged her handbag the way a mailman arranges his pouch, slipping the strap over her head and putting her right arm through it, so the strap ran down the front and back over her overcoat, and the bag hung under her right arm.

I told her she couldn't ride sidesaddle now, not when we'd be driving on a dirt track.

She nodded listlessly and began to unbutton her overcoat. "May I borrow your knife?"

I handed her the penknife and she stepped off to the side and went to work, cutting up along the seam.

As she did, I turned to Putzi and held out my hand. "Thanks, Putzi. I appreciate everything you've done."

My hand was buried inside his big paw.

"You are welcome, Phil." His face went sad. "I'm truly sorry about all this. It has been a catastrophe. All the trouble. What happened to Erik . . ."

He looked down for a moment. He had liked von Dinesen.

He raised his head. "But believe me, when I talk to Herr Hitler, I'll get everything straightened out. Everything will be copacetic."

"Sure."

He glanced at Miss Turner, saw that she was finished with her cutting, and made a small bow. "Miss Turner, I wish you a safe trip."

"Thank you." She came forward and solemnly offered him her hand. He took it.

He nodded to me again and then walked to the driver's door of the truck, a big man, bulky and slow, plodding along in a graceless shuffle. He opened the door and climbed in. He turned on the ignition and started backing the boxy vehicle down the track. I could see his big head through the windshield. Just before he disappeared behind the pine trees, he stuck his hand out the window and waved at us.

I waved back.

He was an anti-Semite. He was a Nazi.

But when someone called him in the middle of the night and told him that Miss Turner and I were in trouble, he had gotten dressed and driven a hundred miles in that unlikely truck.

And he had smacked Felix Kalter over the head with a pipe.

I looked at Miss Turner. She had adjusted her skirt so the slit was on the left side. She had made a similar cut along the side of her overcoat.

"Are you ready?" I asked her.

She smiled. It was a forced smile, almost a wince. She handed back the penknife. "Yes," she said.

I took out my watch. Eight o'clock.

. . .

THE TRACK WOUND down the mountainside, twisting between the pines. It was a good track, mostly free of rocks. But now and then we came to a small boulder that had tumbled down the slope and taken residence, or a branch that had toppled from one of the pines, and we had to stop the bike, get off it, and deal with the problem. Miss Turner was still moving slowly, deliberately, like a deep-sea diver. She didn't talk much. But she did her share of the work.

Despite the obstacles, we made pretty good time. By twelve o'clock we had gone maybe forty miles. We had passed two tiny villages, tight clusters of wooden houses amid the pine trees. But they had both seemed deserted. No one was standing around outside, cheering us on.

The sky was still overcast, and the gray was growing darker, but we hadn't run into any rain.

At around twelve thirty, we came to a clearing in the trees. Another brook, or maybe the same brook, looped lazily around it, through the trees. Wildflowers were growing along the bank, and tall green grasses. Brown pine needles covered the ground. A few feet from the stream, someone had created a sort of rough bench—a six-foot length of thick tree trunk lay on the ground, its top surface stripped of bark and smoothed flat. I braked the bike, turned off the engine, and we stopped beside the tree trunk.

"We should eat something," I told Miss Turner.

She slid off the pillion and stood there. I pulled the bike up onto its center stand and stepped off the seat. As I got the food out of the panniers, Miss Turner walked down to the brook. She stood looking at the water as it bumbled and splashed around the shiny round rocks.

When I had the food arranged in the center of the rough-hewn bench, atop my handkerchief—a sausage, the bread, some cheese, a bottle of mineral water—I called her.

She turned and walked slowly over to the bench. She sat down, on the opposite side of the handkerchief, and pulled her overcoat over her legs.

She didn't look at me or the food. Her head was lowered and she was staring down at the ground.

"Sausage?" I said. "Or cheese?"

She glanced at me. "I don't mind. Either."

I tore off a chunk of bread, used my penknife to cut a slice of cheese. I handed these to her.

She took the food and said, "Thank you." And then she sat there, staring at the ground, holding the bread and cheese in her hand.

I ripped another chunk from the small loaf, cut another slice of cheese. I took a bite. The bread tasted of the gasoline that had been lying next to it in the pannier, but I was hungry. We hadn't eaten since last night.

"How's your leg?" I asked her. Her left leg had been exposed while we rode. From time to time I had been conscious of it, her round knee against my hip, the skin covered only by a thin membrane of silk stocking.

"All right," she said.

I ate some more food.

Still not looking up, Miss Turner said, "I said terrible things to him yesterday."

She didn't have to use von Dinesen's name.

She said, "I called him a liar. A cheat. A mountebank." She looked at me. "I actually used that word. I called him a mountebank."

"He was all those things."

Her eyes narrowed. "He saved our lives. He *died* saving our lives."

"I know. We owe him."

"Then how can you say that?"

"Because it's true. He was a fraud. But it turns out that he was also brave. Most people are more than one thing."

Blinking, she looked away.

I ate some more bread and cheese. I took a sip of mineral water. I listened to the sound of the brook as it burbled and sloshed. I ate some more food.

She looked back at me. "Hitler said that Erik had told him that I'd . . . fondled him in a taxicab. I hadn't, of course, but—"

"It's none of my business what you did or didn't—"

"Please. Let me finish. Obviously it's not something I should wish . . . reported to someone else, regardless of whether I'd done it or not."

"No."

"And it was that, I think, which angered me the most. The thought that Erik would say that to Hitler."

"Sure."

"I was furious. I was actually screaming at him. But he denied it. He admitted that Hitler had asked him to keep an eye on us. He admitted that Hitler had given him our personnel files. He admitted to being a deserter during the War. He'd told me an elaborate story about his experience at the front. And it was lies, all of it, and he said so. He admitted it. But he denied ever having said anything like that to Hitler."

"Maybe he didn't. I don't think you can trust much of what Hitler says."

"No, of course not. That's precisely my point. Because if Erik didn't tell him, don't you see, then perhaps that was *why* he came to Passau. To convince me that he wasn't the sort of man who would do that. Who *could* do that."

I nodded. I didn't point out that even if he had been the sort of man who could do that, he might still have wanted to convince Miss Turner that he wasn't.

"And if that's true," she said, "then in a very real sense his death is my fault."

"Miss Turner, I don't know why he came to Passau. He was a complicated man, I think. But whatever his reasons were, they were his. He made a decision. It was a brave decision. Like you said, it saved our lives. And I think that by blaming yourself, you're taking something away from him. Away from the decision he made."

She looked at me for a moment. Then she said, "Yes. That's true, isn't it?"

"I think so. Listen. You should eat something."

She looked down at the food, raised her hand to her mouth. She gave me a quick, odd glance, almost puzzled, and then she took a bite.

CHAPTER FORTY-THREE

⟡

 I T TOOK US four days to reach Bayreuth.

The first night, Tuesday night, we stayed in a tiny village called Breitenberg, in a small house owned by an elderly couple named Schwartz. Miss Turner told them that we were spending our honeymoon exploring the Oberwald, and they thought that this was, as Miss Turner put it, terribly romantic.

Mrs. Schwartz clucked over Miss Turner's unconventional skirt and offered her a pair of Mr. Schwartz's old trousers. They were too big, and Miss Turner said that they made her itch, but they were better than a skirt with a slit cut up the side, and she wore them for the rest of the trip.

Putzi had been right. I was able to buy gasoline from a man in Breitenberg who owned a rattletrap Mercedes, probably twenty years old. I'm not exactly sure what he used it for, but we were only a few miles from the Czech border, and in the same shed with the Mercedes were empty beer crates stamped PILSEN, the name of a big beer-producing town in Czechoslovakia.

We got an early start that Wednesday, but the rain started and we had to slow down. Within only a few minutes we were both soaking wet, and Miss Turner was holding on tight as the bike slid and slipped along the muck. A couple of times I nearly went off the track, and once I nearly went over a cliff.

We made only about sixty miles before we stopped in another village.

The next day, Thursday, the sky was clear and we made about eighty miles. We made sixty miles on the day following, and by four o'clock in the afternoon, we'd found a farmhouse three or four miles east of

Bayreuth where the people were willing to put us up. And by then, Miss Turner was weak and feverish and I knew we couldn't go on until she felt better.

On Saturday, while she lay in bed, I walked into town and took a look around. I thought that the Megola was safe enough at the farm where we were staying, but I didn't want to drive it into town just then. At the train station, no one's papers were being examined.

Three days later, on Tuesday morning, we went to the station together. Miss Turner had composed a telegram for Sergeant Biberkopf, in German, and we sent it before we got onto the train. Early the next morning, we were in Berlin.

When we checked back into the Adlon hotel, I noticed that a number of the bellboys were a bit too bulky for their new-looking uniforms, and that some of them were wearing pistols under their jackets. Biberkopf's people.

Biberkopf himself showed up about an hour after we checked in. We talked for a while.

We had left the Megola just outside Bayreuth, hidden behind some trees. I hoped that whoever found it was someone who would appreciate what a fine machine it was. And as we walked away from it, toward the train station, I sent off a silent thanks to Hans Mueller.

WHILE MISS TURNER was out shopping, I called down to the desk from my room and asked the clerk to put through an international call. To Cooper, in London.

An hour later, the telephone rang.

I swung off the bed, walked to the desk, sat down, and lifted the earpiece off its hook. "Hello?"

"Beaumont. What the devil's going on? Where've you been?"

"Traveling," I said. "Things fell apart."

"So I gather. Is your connection clear?"

"Probably not. But it doesn't matter now." I would have enjoyed it, in fact, if someone had been listening in.

Cooper said, "You know that we've been dismissed from the case? As of last Tuesday?"

"I'm not surprised."

"What happened?"

I told him, all of it. Cooper didn't interrupt.

When I finished, he said, "Miss Turner is all right?"

"She's fine. Still a little weak."

"The two of you are in no danger?"

"Biberkopf has some people here. We'll be fine. What happened with Caudwell?"

"Ah. Caudwell. Well, as it happens, Caudwell's been transferred."

"Transferred? He gave out confidential information."

"Yes, but he gave it to the party people. And they were in fact our employers at the time. No real harm done there."

"He gave out confidential information," I repeated.

"Yes, and as I say, he's been transferred. He'll be closely watched in future."

Something was wrong. Caudwell should have been drawn and quartered for what he'd done, and Cooper knew it.

"What's going on?" I said.

"It's rather complicated, actually."

"Make it simple for me."

"It turns out the people for whom Caudwell was working, here in London, are quite highly placed."

"Highly placed where?"

"In the government."

"And who are they, exactly?"

"I'm not at liberty to say. We'll just leave it at that, shall we?"

"No," I said. "We won't. You're saying that someone in the British government wants to help the Nazi Party? Help Hitler?"

"I'm afraid so, yes."

"He's filth, Cooper. And he's dangerous. But we're in a position to do something about him. We could take Miss Turner's story and slip it into a German newspaper. We could destroy him."

"That's just it, you see. The people here in London don't *want* him destroyed. They feel he represents a valuable asset. A defense of sorts against a more dangerous enemy."

"The Bolsheviks."

"Exactly, yes."

"They're wrong."

"Perhaps so. But you won't be able to persuade them of that."

"But—"

"Listen to me, Beaumont. From everything you've told me, I'm sure you're right about him. But the fact remains—politics are politics. And just now some very important people want him to continue doing what he's doing. I've no more choice in the matter than you have."

"I don't like this."

"That's as may be. There's nothing either of us can do. Getting back to your investigation. I gather that it's been something of a washout. You've no idea who made that attempt on Hitler. Do I have that right?"

"Yeah."

"Just as well. The new line is that there never *was* an attempt. We've been instructed to destroy all our records."

"Instructed by whom?"

"The same people."

"Why?"

"Ours not to reason why. But I can give you a guess."

"Do that."

"An assassination attempt would suggest that there are people in Germany who don't much care for Herr Hitler."

"There are."

"But the people here in London don't wish for this to be suggested."

"We're a private firm. We don't work for the British government."

"We operate on sufferance, old man. They can bring to bear a huge amount of pressure. Look here, Beaumont, we'll discuss all this when you get back. You'll be returning in the next few days, I imagine?"

"No."

"Excuse me?"

"Miss Turner needs some rest. I wouldn't mind some myself."

"Out of the question, I'm afraid. I'd like both of you back in London as soon as possible."

"Miss Turner's had a rough time. People tried to kill her. And it's going to take me a while to convince her."

"Convince her? Convince her of what?"

"That she shouldn't talk to anyone about what happened. To the newspapers, for example."

For a moment, Cooper didn't speak. Then he said, "And just how long do you feel it might take you to convince her?"

"Four or five weeks."

"Four or five weeks."

"I thought we'd take a small trip."

"To where, might one ask?"

"To Athens. I hear Athens is nice this time of year. We can catch a train from here to Budapest, and then go south."

"And how did you plan to finance this little holiday?"

"We still have some dollars left." Nearly three hundred of them.

Another silence. "You know," he said finally, "you don't want to be *too* clever, Beaumont. It might come back at you."

Once again, I said nothing. I could've told him that I planned to have Miss Turner write an account of what happened. And that I planned to have Sergeant Biberkopf add a note or two. And that I planned to put everything in a safe place, where it would be opened if anything happened to me or to Miss Turner.

But Cooper knew me. He knew I wouldn't pull something like this without covering myself.

At last he said, "What about your Sergeant Biberkopf?"

"What about him?"

"Has he heard Miss Turner's story?"

"Of course he has. But he can't do anything with it if Miss Turner won't verify it."

Another silence. I listened to the crackle and hiss of the phone line.

"Four weeks," he said finally. "Not a day more."

"Fine."

"And when you reach Athens, get in touch with me. There may be a little something you can look into. For the Agency."

"In Athens?"

"In Athens, in Cairo. That general area."

"We're going on vacation."

"Yes, of course, and I wouldn't dream of interrupting it. But if something *does* turn up, and you happen to be nearby, I know you won't mind taking a quick peek at it for us."

"A quick peek," I said.

"That's the spirit. You give Miss Turner my regards."

He hung up.

I wasn't sure who had just conned whom.

The Hotel Adlon
Berlin
Wednesday
May 30th

Dear Evangeline,

This will be a difficult letter to write. So much has happened, and so much of it has been painful, that I don't really know where to begin. The fact that I have some good news seems, in the circumstances, quite insignificant.

The bad news first. Erik is dead.

Had he lived, Evy, I don't believe that I would ever have understood him. He was Jewish, something I didn't know until the end of my stay in Munich. How could a Jew involve himself with people who so violently despise the Jews? Had he a secret drive toward self-destruction? Or did he believe that if one were eloquent enough, suave enough, magician enough, one could persuade the Nazis to surrender their hatred?

I don't know. And I never will. He did and said things that were deceitful and possibly even wicked, and yet at the end he was recklessly brave. Mr Beaumont and I both owe him our lives.

Erik's has not been the only death. The Berlin domina, Greta Manheim, has been killed. Mr Beaumont tried to protect her by alerting Sergeant Biberkopf, but it was too late. The people who work for the party, in Berlin as in Munich, are ruthless. Her body was found in the Landwehr Canal. They are pigs, Evy. Worse than pigs. I hate them, all of them.

Greta Manheim, as you know, I admired. She was beautiful and intelligent and brave. She knew exactly who she was; and few of us, I believe, can say the same.

That is not, I realize, much of an epitaph. I wish that I had been able to spend more time with her. I wish that I were able to do so now.

If only it were possible for us to go back and erase the monumental blunders of our lives. If only there were second chances.

So many blunders over these past few weeks, so many losses, so many horrors.

I should tell you, however, that we did discover who attempted to assassinate the monster.

But you must never reveal this to anyone, Evy. Ever.

You recall that I mentioned, in an earlier letter, that I had learned something while we were at Wahnfried, the Wagner house in Bayreuth. It was something that at the time I believed was trivial. It was this:

While I was talking with young Friedelind, the daughter, she told me that her parents wanted to provide her a new English teacher, because the women who taught her at present, a Frau Grossman, was a Jew.

I didn't think much of this until I broached it to Mr Beaumont. We were in a taxicab, having just interviewed a pack of Nazis, all of them fervent anti-Semites, at the party headquarters in Munich. We were talking about how pervasive it was, the anti-Semitism, and I told him what Friedelind had said.

He frowned and said, 'I think we'd better talk to Frau Grossman.'

I realized, as soon as he said it, that he was right. It was possible that Friedelind had mentioned Hitler's Wahnfried visit to Frau Grossman, and possible also that she'd mentioned Hitler's upcoming Tiergarten meeting with General von Seeckt.

'I feel rather foolish,' I confessed to Mr Beaumont. 'I should have told you while we were still in Bayreuth.'

He was generous enough to smile. 'I wouldn't worry about it,' he said. 'The kids probably weren't allowed at the dinner table when Hitler was there. There probably wasn't any way for Friedelind to pick up the information.'

It seemed to me that Mr Beaumont was underestimating

Friedelind. Young girls, as you know, are most efficient at acquiring information, especially when it is information that they are not supposed to acquire.

But if I had in fact blundered by not mentioning Frau Grossman earlier, this was one blunder which could easily be erased, or so it seemed. We would merely stop in Bayreuth on our way back to Berlin, and talk to her then.

We did stop in Bayreuth on our way back, but we arrived there by a route very different from our intended one. I shan't go into details, except to say that we had a long and arduous journey. When we returned to the town, I was too ill to assist Mr Beaumont. I spent two days there in bed.

Fortunately, the town is small, and the people with whom we stayed knew of Frau Grossman and were able to provide Mr Beaumont her address. As I lay under the blankets, alternately freezing and sweltering, he set off to talk to her.

It was late in the afternoon when he returned. He had walked the entire distance, both ways, a total of perhaps twelve miles.

He knocked at the door and I called out for him to come in.

He closed the door, lifted a chair from its position against the bedroom wall, moved it near to the bed, and sat down.

'How are you feeling?' he asked me.

'Much better, thank you.' This was the truth. I had even managed to clean myself up a bit, so I wouldn't look quite so much the forlorn waif. 'You spoke with her?'

'Yeah,' he said. 'Friedelind told her.'

'Friedelind *did* know about the Tiergarten?'

'She heard her parents talking about it.'

'Frau Grossman admitted that?'

'Yeah.'

'Why?'

'I told her what had happened. To us, to von Dinesen. To the Nazis in Passau. She's a good woman. She had no idea, when she talked to him, that her brother would go after Hitler.'

'It was her brother?'

'Yeah. His name is Peter Friedman. He was living in Berlin. For the past year, he's been teaching at the university.'

'How did it happen?'

'Hitler was at Wahnfried on Sunday night. On Monday morning, Frau Grossman gave Friedelind her English lessons, at Wahnfried. That was when Friedelind told her—Hitler was meeting von Seeckt in the Tiergarten at five, to talk about a putsch. Monday's also the day that Frau Grossman calls Friedman, her brother. When she called him that evening, she told him everything she'd heard from Friedelind.'

'And the next day, Friedman tried to assassinate Hitler?'

'With help from a friend of his.'

'But why? I mean to say, just now, if someone offered me a rifle, I might actually attempt it myself. After all that's happened, I feel I have good reason. But why did Peter Friedman hate him so much?'

'He'd lived in Munich for three years after the War. He'd seen Hitler, heard him talk. He thought the man was too dangerous to live.'

'But why? Why did he believe that?'

'You saw Hitler. You heard him. I'm not a Jew, so I don't know what it feels like. To be hated that way. But it's got to be rough.'

'There are thousands of Jews in Germany, hundreds of thousands, and they aren't all running around with rifles, trying to assassinate people.'

'No. But this one was.'

I simply stared at him for a moment. 'What are we going to do?'

'Not much we *can* do. Friedman left the country. He and his friend.'

'Where did they go?'

'Frau Grossman doesn't know. She thinks Brazil. He telephoned on Wednesday and told her what he'd done. Told her he was leaving the next day. Almost three weeks ago.'

'But there are records. Passports. Visas. Sergeant Biberkopf— wouldn't he be able to find him?'

'Probably. But I don't think he'll want to.'

'Why not?'

'Friedman's not a career criminal. It's not like he'll be doing this again. And he didn't actually kill anyone.'

'You'll be telling Sergeant Biberkopf about him?'

'I told him I would, in the beginning.'

'But he's a policeman. He may not feel about Peter Friedman the way that you do.'

'I don't think Biberkopf wants to arrest a Jew for trying to assassinate the leader of the Nazi Party.'

'Oh my God. Of course not. The Nazis would exploit it terribly, wouldn't they?'

'I think,' he said, 'that Biberkopf will be happy to leave the case unsolved.'

And indeed, Evy, so he was.

Mr Beaumont has not told Mr Cooper, in London, about Peter Friedman. Apparently there are people in London, important people, who sympathize with the Nazis. (I didn't believe this, either, at first.) Mr Beaumont feels that if he revealed Herr Friedman's name, one of those people might obtain it and deliver it to the Nazis.

So. It is over.

I've been terribly indiscreet, not only in this letter, but in that earlier letter, in which I described my morning encounter with the little toad. I can do nothing about the earlier letter, except beg you to remain silent about it.

And you must remain silent about this one as well. My life may in fact depend upon your silence.

I won't be posting this letter until we arrive in Budapest. We'll be leaving tomorrow.

Yes, that is the first piece of good news. Mr Beaumont and I are going to Athens. The Agency has granted us a four-week holiday. Mr Beaumont has already purchased the tickets.

The second piece of good news concerns Mr Beaumont.

Well, no, actually. It concerns me.

We spent a full week as fugitives. Often we spent the night in impossibly close quarters. Throughout it all Mr Beaumont was in every way a gentleman. What happened was entirely my responsibility.

Yes. The rag dolls have been cast aside. Hurled aside, actually.

I love you, Evy. I'll write again, on the train.

Jane